The Stranger Who
Turned Her World Upside Down ...

"If you're not having a nice evening, we can always return to the inn," he said in a silky tone that made her back stiffen and her throat tighten.

She stared past him at the elegantly garbed people strolling through Vauxhall Gardens. She knew quite well what Jamie meant. He'd been the perfect gentleman and had teased her gallantly, but she was aware of the subdued sensuality in him, the hooded glances and soft caress, the slight touch of his hand on her cheek. He made her think of a patient tiger. He unnerved her. He terrified her. He intrigued her.

She swallowed and looked back at him. He was standing there with polite attention, but the leaping fire in his black eyes told her he was only biding his time, only waiting until they returned to the inn for his pleasure to begin....

He held out his hand, and when she put her fingers into his palm, she felt a small jolt race through her arm at the touch.

"Keep looking at me like that, lass," Jamie murmured in a rich purr that made her breath catch, "and I will forget about Vauxhall and kiss you until you swoon."

"I never swoon," she stated promptly.

"Shall we give it a try?" he said, taking a step closer....

Bantam Books by Virginia Lynn
Ask your bookseller for the title you have missed

RIVER'S DREAM
CUTTER'S WOMAN
SUMMER'S KNIGHT

Summer's Knight

VIRGINIA LYNN

BANTAM BOOKS
NEW YORK · TORONTO · LONDON · SYDNEY · AUCKLAND

SUMMER'S KNIGHT

A Bantam Fanfare Book / March 1992

FANFARE *and the portrayal of a boxed "ff" are trademarks of Bantam Books,
a division of Bantam Doubleday Dell Publishing Group, Inc.*

All rights reserved.
Copyright © 1992 by Virginia Brown Bianchi.
Cover art copyright © 1992 by Sharon Spiak.
*No part of this book may be reproduced or transmitted in any form or
by any means, electronic or mechanical, including photocopying,
recording, or by any information storage and retrieval system,
without permission in writing from the publisher.*
For information address: Bantam Books.

*If you purchased this book without a cover you should be aware that this book
is stolen property. It was reported as "unsold and destroyed" to the publisher
and neither the author nor the publisher has received any payment for this
"stripped book."*

ISBN 0-553-29549-7

Published simultaneously in the United States and Canada

*Bantam Books are published by Bantam Books, a division of Bantam Doubleday
Dell Publishing Group, Inc. Its trademark, consisting of the words "Bantam Books"
and the portrayal of a rooster, is Registered in U.S. Patent and Trademark Office
and in other countries. Marca Registrada. Bantam Books, 666 Fifth Avenue, New
York, New York 10103.*

PRINTED IN THE UNITED STATES OF AMERICA

RAD 0 9 8 7 6 5 4 3 2 1

To Virginia McKinney,
my traveling buddy,
my partner in crime . . .

Summer's Knight

Chapter 1

"Why, you can marry my niece if you want her so badly, Freeman," came the faintly amused drawl. "It will keep her fortune in our hands, eh?"

Summer St. Clair, walking unobserved on the second-floor landing, jerked to a halt at that languid comment. Her fingers dug into the smooth, lustrous wood of the bannister that curved gracefully up from the foyer below, and she couldn't move for a moment.

As the two men crossed the foyer to the parlor her uncle's voice drifted to her again, cool and slightly chagrined. "Something must be done soon, for Summer reaches her majority next year. I dare not risk losing control of her money. We need it to further our cause."

Summer leaned forward as they passed into the parlor, her heart pounding fiercely. Their voices were easily heard.

"And Talleyrand in France?" Tutwiler asked. "He will accept the money to—"

"Hush!" Barton Shriver's voice was sharp. "It is not to be discussed." There was a pause. "France is not at war with the United States, Freeman, but with England. There will be no repeat of the XYZ Affair since the settlement of 1800. But I do believe that *contributions* will be accepted and rewarded, and our fortunes will be made."

A rasping laugh greeted this statement. "Yes, and I expect Napoleon will be most grateful once he is in possession of New Orleans again."

Summer's teeth bit into her bottom lip. This was more than a marriage discussion—this was treason! Her fingernails scraped over the bannister as she edged closer to the bottom of the stairs, and she heard her uncle ask lightly, "What do you offer for my niece?"

"Anything! Everything! I just *want* her," Freeman rasped, sending a shudder along Summer's spine. "I crave the wench in my bed. . . ."

The fat, sweaty swine! She'd seen Tutwiler paw other young women not quick enough to elude him but had managed so far to avoid it herself. Other young ladies had family to protect them, and he had not been bold enough to pursue them openly. She had no protection. Her uncle was only too glad to sell her to the odious creature. The thought of Tutwiler having the *right* to touch her made Summer sway with nausea.

I crave the wench in my bed. . . .

Damn him, Summer thought, pushing impatiently at a tawny curl that dangled in front of her eyes. And damn Barton Shriver. He had greedily seized the St. Clair estate upon her family's death, when she had been merely fourteen years old. A year later, he had told her that she was of a marriageable age and had instructed her to smile at men he approved of and snub those he didn't. When she'd refused, he'd sent her to a convent. Though she had not been raised a Catholic, the nuns had agreed to take "a poor young lady unhinged by her parents' death and in need of rest and repose" in exchange for a generous donation to their order.

It had been to teach her a lesson in obedience, and it had taught her well. She'd been locked in a small cell. "For her own protection," "she might harm herself," "upon her physician's orders," had been several of the explanations given the good sisters.

Summer had languished for three months and had come out having learned an important lesson. She was a minor; therefore she had no voice. And being a female was another strike against her. Now she was twenty, but not yet of age. For the past five years Barton Shriver had used her as a pawn, hinting at marriages for her but never making a formal betrothal, always plotting to further his cause with the most advantageous alliance. Still, she'd had no idea that he would be so greedy or foolish as to stoop to treason.

A light shudder racked her slender frame again, and her sky-blue eyes darkened to the color of smoke as she stood indecisively on the landing. Shriver's and Tutwiler's voices were an indistinct murmur now, as they lingered in the front parlor, where she could visualize them drinking what was left of her father's fine brandy.

A faint sneer curled her lips. Jonathan St. Clair would have made short work of Shriver. That thought brought a knife-edged pain slicing along the still-tender memories of her dead parents and brother. There were times when the pain was so sharp that she felt as if someone had, indeed, plunged a knife into her heart. How could fate have been so cruel as to allow her loved ones to die from a fever and leave her alive and bereft?

With a sigh, Summer finally stirred herself enough to tread quietly down the stairs. The hem of her muslin gown frothed around neat, trim ankles as she slipped like a silent wraith past the parlor, with its half-closed doors.

She had to do something to stop her uncle from

whatever he planned against the American government—after all, her mother had been a loyal American, and her father half-American. And she had to save herself.

Instinct spurring her, she reached the front door. She knew where she would go. There was only one person who might be able to help her....

Her hand touched the coroneted latch of the door, and then Summer saw Chantal. She put a finger to her lips and quickly shook her head. The maid's smooth, coffee-colored face shuttered, and she gave a short nod of her brightly turbaned head. Chantal knew about Shriver and his rapacious clutches, but she was just as caught in his web as Summer was.

With Chantal's silent benediction, Summer eased out the front door. Sunlight struck her in hot, bright rays as she crossed the smooth tiled patio bordering St. Charles Avenue. The courtyard was tiny. A profusion of bougainvillea, begonias, and other bright, gay flowers flowed gracefully over stone urns and from terra-cotta pots. Wrought-iron balustrades laced the front of the two-story house that had just been painted a luscious shade of blue.

Summer passed through the tall gate and shut it with a click. She felt a mounting sense of urgency as she scurried down the banquettes that ran alongside the houses, which crouched close to the narrow streets. She had to reach Garth. He would know what to do.

Garth. Just his name made Summer's stomach flip and her heart do funny things in her chest. He was so handsome—a big blond Adonis. If only he would do more than chuck her under the chin and call her "little duckling." But Garth Kinnison didn't seem to know she existed except as the daughter of the man who'd helped him buy his first ship, a sleek, two-masted schooner that could outmaneuver pirates and still carry a full hold of cargo.

The St. Clair shipping lines had long boasted of plying routes to anywhere there was trade. But now that France and England were at war again after the short-lived Peace of Amiens treaty, it was much riskier. And it was said that Napoleon was about to become the French emperor. Did that mean he would try to wrest back the lands he'd just sold?

Her uncle obviously seemed to think so. And it looked as if he meant to help the Corsican. Shriver had expressed French loyalty to his Creole neighbors. Yet he had been instrumental in helping to arrange the Louisiana Purchase, using Summer's money to further his own private interests along the way. It had given him the power he sought so eagerly, and his known willingness to trade with both sides had given him a notoriety that frequently embarrassed Summer.

Many of the older aristocratic families were unwilling to snub Summer openly because of her father; but gradually, she had been left out of social events because of her uncle and his sordid business practices. Now Shriver's influence was far-reaching—and the St. Clair name was growing soiled. Even worse, he was skimming the profits from the shipping business to exploit his own shady schemes.

Summer hailed a carriage when she was far enough away from the house not to be seen. As it careened down the narrow streets, she stared blankly out the windows. It was traveling through a part of town that she didn't frequent, that indeed, she had never really seen. Such sights were not to be looked upon, Chantal had often scolded, not by a delicate young woman of quality such as Summer.

The St. Clair docks teemed with the bustle of enterprise and bawdy seamen, but Garth wasn't in the offices as he should have been. Anxiously, Summer asked where he could be found.

"I believe he's on his ship, Miss St. Clair," the harried clerk answered. He paused with an armload of papers, giving her a keen stare. "Is there some trouble?"

Everyone knew the daughter of the former owner and knew that she would one day own these lines. Summer had spent long, happy hours here as a child, sitting on her father's lap and doodling on scrap paper. Now Shriver ran the business with a heavy hand.

"No, I just need to discuss something with the captain. I'll find him, Perkins. Thank you."

As she walked down the crowded quays to find the *Sea Dancer*, Summer began to wish she had not so impulsively come to the docks alone. Men stared at her boldly, and her chin lifted faintly as she tried to ignore them. She should have brought Chantal along with her. No decent woman walked out without her maid or a chaperon.

When she found the vessel bobbing in the deep channel against a wooden quay, Summer heaved a sigh of relief. It was still being loaded. Yawning hatches stood open and ready to receive more goods. The wooden brow was down, slung from ship to quay. She lifted her skirts slightly to keep the hems from dragging over the filthy planks as she skimmed up to the main deck. The ship was empty, save for the watch, who nodded politely and said that Captain Kinnison was still ashore.

"He had a meeting with Mr. Tutwiler, I believe. Shall I tell him you were here, Miss St. Clair?" the sailor asked, and Summer paused.

She needed to see Garth now, but she certainly didn't need to allow Tutwiler or her uncle to see her here. "No, perhaps I'll see him later," she said, and the man nodded.

Summer started back down the brow, then decided to leave Garth a note. She didn't want to risk running into her uncle in the offices, and it was urgent that she get a message to Garth before Shriver was able to put his awful plan into action.

Turning, she went back up the gangplank, ducked into the hatch, and climbed down the narrow, musty companionway to the lower deck and the captain's cabin. She knew the way well. She'd frequently visited with her father.

When she'd written the note, Summer left Garth's cabin and started back up the narrow ladder to the main deck. Then she heard men's voices on the upper deck and recognized Freeman Tutwiler's raspy accents. Freezing in place, she realized she couldn't allow Tutwiler to see her on the ship and tell her uncle. She fled back down the steep ladder and into Garth's cabin.

She looked around wildly, then spied the tall cabinet built into the wall. It took only a moment to secrete herself in the cedar-redolent cabinet and shut the door. The air was stuffy, and she batted gently at the clothes hanging around her as she sat with her knees scrunched up and her chin resting on them. It was uncomfortable, but necessary.

She crouched and waited, her muscles cramping as she heard the men enter the cabin. Her neck began to ache from being bent into an awkward position, and she shifted to get more comfortable. Something pressed into her back, and she gave a start when she saw a faint glimmer of eyes in the shadows. Then she relaxed. It was only a gold-headed cane, with the face of a lion and two glowing topaz chips for eyes.

Her fingertips brushed against the chain she wore around her neck. A small, simple gold chain with her initials, entwined S's, dangling from the links, it had been a twelfth-birthday gift from her father, and her hand closed over it as if for luck. Briefly closing her eyes, she whispered a prayer that she would somehow manage to get away from her uncle and the hateful Freeman Tutwiler. Then her attention was diverted by recognizable voices.

Garth's deep baritone sent a shiver down her spine, and she smiled in the dark cabinet as she heard him discussing business details with Tutwiler in a faintly contemptuous tone. She didn't bother to listen to the words but only waited impatiently for them to finish so she could throw her woes on Garth's broad shoulders. He would rescue her, be her knight in shining armor.

Garth would help her. She'd *make* him help her. And then maybe he would take her in his arms and finally declare that he loved her and had only been waiting for her to grow up so he could marry her. Then he would kiss her, and her life would be good again.

And then, she thought grimly, Barton Shriver will have to leave New Orleans astride a rail—tarred and feathered!

The vessel rocked gently, bumping against the quay. It was too warm in the closet, and the men's voices droned on and on. Her eyelids grew heavy, and she yawned.

Summer never knew when sleep overcame her, or when the ship left the New Orleans port and sailed down to the Gulf.

Chapter 2

"Why won't you take me?" Summer stared up at Garth Kinnison with disbelieving eyes. "Why?"

The ship carrying Summer as an inadvertent stowaway had just anchored at the port of London. She'd been put into a jolly boat with Garth and carried to shore, but she still could not quite believe he would do this to her. Despite her confession of her infatuation for him, Garth Kinnison adamantly refused to allow her to remain on the *Sea Dancer*.

Garth helped her from the bobbing boat to the security of a long dock and then joined her. His first mate, Oliver Hart, stood close by. Summer didn't even notice the light rain as she looked up at Garth. Her rib cage hurt where her heart slammed painfully against it.

"Why?" she asked again, her voice a hoarse whisper.

"Summer, you're a pretty girl," Garth said gently, stroking her soft cheek and gazing down at her with an enigmatic expression, "but I cannot keep you with me."

Anger edged her voice as she spoke. "You've brought me this far, instead of putting me off in Santo Domingo—I insist that you keep me with you!"

His voice was impatient. "I told you, girl, that Santo Domingo was no place to leave you to wait for a ship back, even with a hired chaperon. They still have the yellow fever on occasion. Southampton is safer."

Summer's stare was disconcerting, and she knew it. "But you could have left me elsewhere, and you didn't," she persisted, her azure eyes slowly darkening to a slate gray. "I've been no trouble—I don't understand you."

Cupping her chin in his hard, callused palm, Garth said, "The West India docks are crowded, and I have a perishable cargo. London's legal quays leave cargo open to smuggling and plunder, and I can't afford that. I have a lot of work to do, and you'd only be left to your own devices. Besides, Shriver's too powerful a man to make my enemy."

"Is that why you won't take what I said seriously? I *heard* him say those things about money for Napoleon, and—" Her protest ended in a slight gasp when he grabbed her arm and snapped at her to be quiet before a zealous Englishman overheard them.

"It's nothing to worry about, Summer," he added in a kinder tone when she rubbed sullenly at her bruised flesh. "Now, be a good girl, and go back home."

Summer said in a small, fierce voice, "I will be sold to Tutwiler in a depraved marriage, and you don't even care, you fiend!"

She'd tried to make him care on the long voyage, but he had avoided her as if she carried a deadly plague. There was a bitter irony in that. Other men had leapt at the chance to court the heiress to the St. Clair Shipping company. Not Garth. He seemed to care little that wedding her would make him rich.

"I can't stop an arranged marriage, girl. Neither can you. 'Tis the way of the world for young ladies." He gave a shrug of his brawny shoulders. His pale eyes were hooded as he said softly, "Take a lover after you wed. It's done all the time."

Jerking her head up, Summer glared at him with stormy eyes. "Maybe I will! Are you available?" she shot at him, and saw with chagrin the amusement glittering in his eyes.

"Perhaps, when I return to New Orleans and you are a little older." A laugh threaded his voice, stiffening Summer's spine with humiliated fury. "Go with Oliver. He's found you a maid to chaperon your return, and I've provided you with a heavy purse."

His amusement stiffened her resolve as nothing else would have done. *So much for my fair knight!* she couldn't help thinking bitterly. Her chin lifted.

"Present your bill to my uncle, and he will see that you are repaid," she said in a taut voice. She would *not* cry. She had humiliated herself enough by pleading with him to keep her.

But when she was tucked into a hired post chaise—a bright yellow vehicle pulled by a pair and managed by a postboy—and given into the care of a hard-faced woman, Summer almost surrendered to tears. Garth did not want her. He would not rescue her from Freeman Tutwiler.

First mate Oliver Hart stuck his head inside the door of the coach and said softly, "Remember, miss, that your last name could invite trouble for you. Do not use it. The captain has arranged passage for you under the name of Miss Smith, and Mrs. Beasley will watch over you well."

"I'll remember," Summer said coldly. Even her name was a hindrance. It was French, and she was in a country at war with France. Besides which, if anyone connected her to the St. Clair shipping fortune, she might find herself in grave difficulties. Just the year before, a young heiress had been abducted, compromised, then ransomed back to her frantic parents for a huge amount of money. It was doubtful that Barton Shriver would bother to redeem his niece; he would consider it a blessing that she had been removed. Well, she'd dealt with the fortune hunters her uncle had teased with her inheritance and knew how to avoid them well enough. A villain was a villain.

"I'll remember," Summer repeated. The first mate shut the door with a good-bye nod.

The coach jerked forward, and she gave a last glance back at Garth as he stood with the wind ruffling his blond hair. When she'd first awakened in his cabinet and discovered that he'd sailed out of port with her aboard, she'd thought her prayers had been answered. She'd stayed hidden until she was sure they'd sailed too far to return her, then confronted him, certain he would take her with him, maybe marry her.

But he hadn't. He'd been first furious, then resigned, and had told her that she would have to go home. He'd kept to his word, it seemed.

Slicing a glance toward her uncommunicative chaperon, Summer settled back against the worn squabs of the coach in dull acceptance of her fate. Rain pelted the coach, and she could hear the coachman swearing softly on his high perch above. It was chilly. Huddling into the voluminous folds of her cloak and shifting the satchel of clothes Garth had bought for her, Summer stared out the windows at the dreary series of vast warehouses.

Cargoes of wine, sugar, timber, raw silk, ivory, coffee, tea, and aromatic woods such as cedar and mahogany were stacked as high as they possibly could be, and huge hoists lifted them from vessel to dock or to drays. Despite the drizzle, men worked to load and unload cargo, and the noise was tremendous. Hammers thudded, saws grated on wood, tackles groaned with shrill, unremitting whines, and bells clanked tinnily. Though a familiar sight, it was chaotic, fright-

ening. Men shouted, whips cracked, coaches rumbled
on the stones, and the penetrating odor of fouled water seemed to seep into her very bones.

Scrunching down in the seat, Summer slid another
glance toward her companion. Mrs. Beasley seemed
respectable enough, but something in her broad, stolid
face made Summer shift uneasily on the seat. Oh, well,
she would only have to suffer the woman's presence
for a short while.

Summer glanced out the window again and saw
her blurred reflection in the glass pane. She was
fiercely glad to see that her woebegone expression had
hardened into one of determination.

She was suddenly reminded of how one young man
had told her she had a face like a cat's. She'd laughed
at him then, but now she could see the faint resemblance. Her wide blue eyes slanted slightly at the outer
corners, and her face was oval, with a small chin and
mobile mouth that could stretch into a feline smile at
the slightest notice—or at least, had smiled often before her parents' death. The last few years had been
so unhappy, she rarely smiled anymore.

And there was certainly nothing to smile about
now, as the post chaise rocked wildly over curving
roads that led from London to Southampton. It gave
a shudder suddenly, then rocked violently to one side.
Thrown to the floor in a heap of skirts and cloak,
Summer heard the postboy damn a mail coach for
running them off the road.

Taking the accident in bad grace, Mrs. Beasley
shook a finger in the postboy's face when he wrenched
open the door.

"I've been 'ired to see this young miss safely to 'er
'ome, an' by all that's 'oly, that's w'at I'll do!"

The boy merely shrugged. "Pyrford's jus' ahead.
It's got a good inn with a common room. Wait there,
and I'll let ye know when we git th' coach outer th'
ditch. That's all that kin be done."

When Mrs. Beasley seemed inclined to argue, Summer said impatiently, "Oh, do come along! I'm tired of riding anyway and would like a hot meal." A light rain misting around her, she pulled up the hood to her cloak, picked up her satchel, and began walking down the road. Mrs. Beasley followed reluctantly.

The inn at Pyrford was on the banks of a slow-moving river. In spite of the slight drizzle that dampened her as she walked, Summer grudgingly admired the soft countryside with its deep woods and shady glades.

When she entered the common room of the inn, she was shown to a table looking out over the river. Summer wrinkled her nose at the acrid bite of smoke and faint scent of boiled vegetables.

"What kin I git fer ye, miss?" the innkeeper asked with a gap-toothed smile. She glanced distastefully at his food-spattered apron.

She ordered a pork pie and fruit; Mrs. Beasley asked for steak-and-kidney pie, a pudding, and several tarts.

"An' a bit of ale to wash it a' down wi'," the chaperon added happily as she sat down in a chair near Summer.

Eventually a steaming hot pork pie that was more crust than meat was set in front of Summer, along with a dish of small, unappetizing fruit covered in cinnamon and sauce. Summer was so hungry, she didn't care.

Mrs. Beasley ate noisily, literally licking the pewter plates clean, then heaved herself up from the chair and across the room. Glad to see her go, Summer ate slowly, leaving a few bites of the pork dish so she wouldn't seem a glutton. Her mother had always insisted upon such manners. Summer shut her eyes. *Maman.* She had looked so cold and still on her funeral bier, but her life had been warm and vivid.

Sighing, Summer opened her eyes and wiped her hands on a shabby square of napkin. Propping her chin in one palm, she gazed out the window at the rain-pocked river. She heard the innkeeper set down a tankard of ale on a table just behind her to one side and turned her head, slanting a glance from beneath her lashes. There were only three other people in the inn: two shabby-looking men in a corner, and one dark, dangerous-looking man sprawled indolently in a chair near the fire. Her gaze flicked toward him, and she saw that he was looking at her.

She looked away, but not before she had an impression of dark eyes, black hair, and a strong, masculine face. It was his eyes that startled her, riveting, staring at her, a faint smile curving his lips. He lifted his tankard of ale in a silent salute to her, and she flushed.

Who did he think he was? Or *she* was? She was no loose female to be impressed with idle admiration! Still, it was hard not to steal glances at him from time to time.

Shifting and crossing long, lean legs clad in the snug-fitting pantaloons and Hessian boots of a dandy, the man displayed an air of shabby gentility until she glanced at his face. It was a strong, hard face, with one black brow that slashed straight over his eyes, and high, rugged cheekbones that angled sharply down to a chiseled mouth that looked ready to smile. It was a most handsome face, a rogue's face. A face women would admire. How could they not?

Summer, however, was in no mood to admire a man, not when the sting of Garth Kinnison's rejection was so strong and achingly sharp in her mind and heart. She looked back at Mrs. Beasley, who had come from somewhere across the room to sit by her again. The woman's fleshy face looked grim, and Summer suppressed a twinge of annoyance at Garth for sticking her with such a gargoyle.

The sun began to set. Summer looked up as the innkeeper lit the lamps, grumbling about the cost of oil, and she saw the postboy come in the door.

She stood and put on her cloak, but her relief was short-lived. The postboy abruptly announced that the post chaise could not be fixed, that an axle was broken and they had sent to Surrey for another.

"It's almost dark. Ye'll 'ave ta stay th' night 'ere, I'm afraid," he added, shrugging at Summer's dismay. "There's no 'elp for it."

Mrs. Beasley rapped a heavy hand on the table. "There are rooms over th' pub 'ere. Shall I bespeak one from th' innkeeper fer ye, miss?"

"Yes, please," Summer murmured dispiritedly. She sank back into her chair. She didn't care suddenly if they ever got to Southampton. At least this chill, weeping weather fit her mood. Besides, why rush the inevitable interview with Barton Shriver? He would be furious at her truancy and would perhaps hasten the marriage to Tutwiler. *I crave the wench in my bed. . . .* A shudder tickled her spine.

When Mrs. Beasley returned, announcing that a room had been procured, Summer lifted the purse she had hanging beneath her cloak and stared hesitantly at the unfamiliar currency. Mrs. Beasley's eyes glittered slightly at the sight of the money, but she only helped Summer select the two shillings and three pence to pay for their meal from the jumble of strange coins.

Summer stood up and pushed back her chair. When she turned to go upstairs, her glance dragged across the figure still reclining lazily in front of the fire. The man looked directly at her, his jet eyes under one straight black brow raking her with interested curiosity. A bolt of alarm shot through her at the dark-browed man's intent scrutiny. Drawing her cloak more closely around her as if she could hide, she looked quickly away from his gaze.

Plague him. What did he want? She felt flustered under that heavy stare and stumbled over the hem of her cloak as she walked through the maze of scattered tables. Her cheeks flushed. She thought she saw him smile, a quick flash of white teeth in a dark face. *Plague take him!*

She could still feel his eyes on her as she reached the stairs to the second floor and could not resist a backward glance. To her dismay, the rogue stood up and swept her a mocking bow, his actions graceful and provoking. She set her teeth, and her face flamed.

He must think her interested, when she was only wary of a man who sat in a shabby inn with his booted feet propped on a table and a sword dangling from his side. He looked more like one of the highwaymen she'd heard roamed the high roads of England than any kind of a gentleman.

Swirling around, Summer stumbled over the bottom step of the sagging stairs and heard his soft laughter. She did not look back again but lifted her skirts in one hand and fled up the dingy staircase to the second floor.

Weary, heartsick, frightened, and more alone than she had ever been in her life, Summer St. Clair lay down fully clothed on the corn-husk mattress and fell asleep almost immediately.

She didn't know what woke her. Perhaps a faint scratch along the floor or a guarded whisper. But whatever it was, Summer awoke just in time to see something at her window, dark, wavering forms that were menacing and terrifying.

A loud scream burst from her throat as she sat bolt upright, and the figures at her window—there were two, she could see that—scrambled out the open shutter with muffled curses. She screamed again and heard pounding footsteps in the hallway outside her room. She was completely alone. Mrs. Beasley was not on her cot across the room.

Half sobbing, Summer stumbled to the door and saw that the bolt had already been drawn. She yanked open the door. The innkeeper stood there in his nightshirt, nightcap askew.

"What is it!" he demanded, and Summer pointed mutely to the window.

As the innkeeper dashed to the open window someone appeared in the hallway with a lantern, and light danced into the room in shifting sprays.

"Who was it? What happened?" the lantern holder asked, and the innkeeper turned with a disgruntled oath.

"Robbers, is my guess." He flicked a glance toward Summer. "Are ye missing ennything, miss?"

Suddenly Summer realized why someone had been in her room. She walked to the chair where she had placed her cloak and reticule and was not at all surprised to find only her cloak and small satchel of clothes still there. Nevertheless, she knelt and looked for the heavy purse under the chair.

The innkeeper grunted. "Ye won't find it, is my guess."

He was right. Summer straightened and looked at him. "Can't you catch them?"

"They're far and away by now, though I guess we can put the constables after 'em right enough," he said in a grudging tone. He eyed her narrowly. "Did they get it all? All your money?"

Summer nodded. "Yes," she muttered, "everything I had!"

"Ah," the innkeeper murmured, his manner deferential and sympathetic. "Then ye'll have to be sendin' a message to yer family, I suppose, so that ye can pay yer bill."

"I have no family," she burst out miserably, "no one to help me! Not here!" She looked around wildly. "And my maid is gone . . . Ah, *sacré bleu!*" she spat, using Chantal's favorite expression without thinking.

Staring at her suspiciously, the innkeeper growled, "Ye don't be French, d'ye? We be fightin' th' French."

Summer stared at him. "No, I'm American."

"Ye're American?" the innkeeper pursued, his bee-tling brow lowering as he began to see his payment fade away. His jaw thrust out, and he growled, "Then how d'ye expect to pay fer yer night's lodging, may I ask?"

It was then Summer realized her mistake. She stammered out a feeble plea for mercy, but it was only a few minutes before she found herself on the front stoop of the inn. Her cloak, the innkeeper said, and the pitifully few clothes she had in her cloth bag, would be applied to payment for the hours she had stayed there.

Numb, Summer could only stare at him. He closed the door in her face, and she stepped off the stone stoop into the squelching mud of the yard. At least it had stopped raining, she reflected as she looked around her. The clouds were gone, and a thin moon cast a dim light on the ground.

It finally occurred to her to wonder where Mrs. Beasley had gone; though in truth, she was glad to be rid of the old harridan. She had not liked the woman at all and gave her absence scant thought. The most pressing problem was to find a place to sleep that was reasonably warm.

She looked around. Her teeth began to chatter, and she wrapped her arms around herself and hunched her back against the wind. She'd have to find something before she turned blue. Certainly not the stable, not with the ostlers sleeping there. She'd be about as safe as a hen in a fox's den.

Summer spotted a low building that she assumed was a coop for the fowl she'd seen clucking and peck-ing around the side yard, and trudged toward it. But the innkeeper's geese took a hearty dislike to her pres-ence in the coop and drove her out amid a loud honk-ing and beating of wings, nipping at her with painful beaks. She tried to stand her ground, but one wily old gander arched his neck so menacingly and hissed so savagely at her that she finally retreated, but not be-

fore flinging a handful of mud toward the enraged
fowl.

She spent the remainder of the night propped
against a low stone wall that bordered the river. It was,
surprisingly enough, the driest spot she could find, as
a mulberry bush had kept the ground from becoming
too soaked. Huddled beneath the bush with a root for
a pillow and wet branches for a quilt, Summer fell
into a light sleep.

Soft sunlight pricked at her eyelids, and Summer
sat up suddenly, confused. There was no rocking of a
ship, nor was she in her familiar bed, and then she
remembered the horror of the night before. Her
stomach rumbled, and recalling the bits of pork pie
she had left on her plate, she wished she had not been
quite so fastidious.

Wiping her hands on her skirt, she emerged from
the spreading branches of the mulberry into the sunlight. It was one of those rare days that seem spawned
in paradise, with golden light filtering over the countryside and all of nature as in tune as a symphony.

"Fiddlesticks," Summer muttered resentfully at the
world in general.

She could see the front door of the inn from where
she stood. Horses milled about in the yard, steam
blowing from their nostrils and tails whisking in the
air, and people came out of the inn well-fed and content, ready to resume their journeys.

It was hard for a young woman who had been
gently bred and reared, existing in luxurious sur-
roundings all her life, to watch with an empty stomach
and dirty face as those fortunate enough to be well-
fed and clean went about their business. Summer
sighed and perched on the top of the wall ridging the
river below.

Swinging her feet, she banged the heels of her
fraying slippers against the stone wall, her hands folded

tightly in her lap. She had nowhere to go. She had no money. Her only hope was to return to the port of London and pray that the *Sea Dancer* had not yet sailed.

Ridiculous that passenger ships sailed from one port and cargo from another. Why weren't the ports closer together?

Straightening, Summer dragged her thoughts back to her present predicament. She was truly in dire need. All she could think to do was clean herself up as best she could, then approach a decent-looking person with her sad tale and a plea for help.

Summer gazed ruefully down at her clothes and soiled hands. "Well," she murmured, "it's the cold river for you, my girl!"

Cautiously edging her way along the stone wall furred with moss and lichen, she found a spot close enough to the water to allow her to lean over without falling in. Pulling herself to the top of the stones, she balanced precariously. Her skirts hung over the edge, and she drew them up; her white stockings were stained, her pumps muddy. If she could just dampen her feet the slightest bit, she could wash the mud from her shoes.

The stones scraped her palms, and she felt shaky as she drew her legs up under her and poised, trembling, on the wall. She poked one foot out toward the water.

"Hold, lass!" came a strong male voice, startling her. The stones were wet and slippery; to her dismay, she felt herself sliding from the wall toward the flowing river currents.

"Hold, lassie!" came the voice again, closer this time and commanding. "Don't jump!"

Summer could have replied that she had no intention of doing anything so foolish, but she was busily occupied with trying to keep her balance. A small, frightened shriek burst from her throat as she felt herself falling; she clenched her teeth together and braced for the cold splash that would greet her.

The splash didn't come.

Instead, hands gripped her by the skirt just before she teetered over the edge, holding her as she swung wildly. Glancing around, intending to grab at her rescuer, Summer instead found herself fighting him. It was the dark-haired, dangerous-looking man from the common room in the inn, the rogue who had stared at her for so long, had watched her purse....

"You!" she managed to gasp out, eluding his efforts to haul her back over the wall to safety. "Thief! Robber!"

Instead of appearing angry or worried that she'd recognized him, the man laughed. His dark eyes glittered, and he was grinning. He held her easily when she tried to avoid his reaching hands.

Panting with fear, Summer kicked out at him with one foot, but it put her too much off balance. She heard the rip of material and felt the gathering rush of a fall, then heard the man's rough curse as he tried to grab her.

It should have been easy for him to hold her, yet when he tried to adjust for the shift of balance, he lost his own. Summer pitched forward and felt her would-be rescuer go with her, over the stone wall and into the swift, cold waters of the rain-swollen river.

It wasn't very deep, but it was deep enough to thoroughly drench them both. Floundering about, trying to scream for help, Summer choked on the fast-moving water, her hands slapping helplessly against it. Oh, why hadn't she ever learned to swim? If she couldjustfindherfooting,shecouldmakeittotheside.... Summer's slick-soled slippers skidded from under her, and she plunged beneath the water's surface again, choking.

Dimly, she heard someone snapping at her to "Shut yer mouth before ye bloody well drown!" and felt a hand snag a fistful of her hair and lift her, still choking and sputtering, from the water. Then she was hauled unceremoniously onto the muddy bank, coughing.

She coughed until her rib cage ached; water seeped from her nose and dripped into her eyes. Flopping back miserably, she lay gasping for breath, her eyes closed.

"D'ye think ye're a bloody mermaid?" a voice growled at her from only a few inches away, and Summer opened her eyes to glare up at her rescuer.

His straight black brow was drawn down into a furious scowl, and his jet-black hair was plastered close to his skull; he looked even more dangerous. She shuddered and closed her eyes again.

"No," she choked weakly. "I can't swim."

"The de'il ye say. Then I guess ye were just thirsty. Wha' were ye about, lass, jumping in th' water if ye canna swim?" the irritated voice demanded. "Were ye after tryin' to drown yerself?"

Her eyes snapped open again, angrily this time. She was incensed that he would think she meant to kill herself in a shallow river. "If I were trying to drown myself, I believe I could do better than a ditch, with all of England surrounded by ocean!"

Sitting down and leaning back on his elbows, his clothes clinging to his body in wet, uncomfortable folds, James Cameron allowed her a grudging grunt of acknowledgment. He glanced at his wet clothes glumly. He should have known better. The next young woman he saw poised on the edge of a stone wall and bending over a river would go unrescued. There was no glory or gratitude in it, that was certain.

It was just that she'd looked so *desperate* from a distance. He had heard what had happened to her, of course, when he'd come down for his breakfast. Then he'd stepped outside to see the hapless female perched atop the stone wall.

It had occurred to him that she might do one of those inexplicable female things that were inherently

melodramatic and usually ineffective; gallant that he
was, he had hurried to her rescue and ended up in
the river with her.

There had been an expression of intense concen-
tration on her small, fierce face that had convinced
him of her grim determination at the time. Now she
just looked like a half-drowned kitten. An enraged
kitten, at that.

She sat in a puddle of wet clothes and pale stringy
hair that dripped ceaselessly into her eyes, and she
glowered at him as if it were his fault she was wet.

"How do you expect me to get any help now," she
demanded angrily, "when I look like a goose caught
in the rain? No one will want to come near me!"

"If you'd just keep your mouth shut, you might get
an offer from someone who's half-blind and addled
to boot," Cameron muttered as he rose to his feet. He
gazed down in disgust at his boots; when he moved
his toes, he could hear a loud squelching sound. His
shirt was ruined; his coat was beyond hope. Only his
pants were reasonably serviceable, but they clung to
the long muscles of his legs like a second skin, outlin-
ing every portion of his lower body to the discerning
eye. His gaze swung back to the girl.

She looked much the same as he; her muslin dress
was smoothed over her curves and almost transparent
from the water. He noted that the thin material hid
nothing from his view, and he didn't mind staring.
She was slender. Her ivory skin was prickly with
gooseflesh at the moment, but looked as if it would
be very soft to the touch. She had a small waist, gently
flaring hips, and her quivering legs were long and
well-formed. Not bad at all, he mused.

Jamie's gaze drifted again. He could see the faint
rosy nipples tipping her round breasts, puckered from
the chill water. His brow rose. What perfect little
breasts she had, small, firm, uptilted, and the tight
crests seemed to beg for the touch of his hand. Or
lips.

A happy smile slanted his mouth, and his dark eyes lifted to her wide blue ones. She was gazing at him with apprehension, and her tongue flicked out in a feminine gesture to moisten lips that were already wet.

There was a strange look in her eyes, as if she didn't know where to glance or what to say. Jamie felt a familiar tightening in his groin, and he knew it would be quickly evident in the tight, wet pants. Maybe it was better if she didn't know how easy it was to interest him. He knelt down, resting on his heels, his arms crossed casually and braced over his knees.

"The best thing to do under these circumstances," he said calmly, "is to get dry first. Then we can decide whose fault it was."

Her head tilted back, and her mouth quivered slightly as she said, "It was yours. There's no need to discuss it further."

"Fine," he said lightly. "It was my fault. Now come with me, and we'll put on dry things."

Summer hung back with a miserable face. "I . . . I can't. My money was stolen last night, and the inn-keeper. . . ."

"I know. Don't worry about it. I think that under the circumstances, he'll be most amiable. I'm certain he'll give you back your clothes, seeing as how you're in need."

She shook her head, and water droplets sprayed everywhere. "I don't think so. He was very annoyed when last I saw him."

"We're old friends," he assured her. "I'll explain."

Summer stared at him narrowly. "Are you certain it was not *you* in my room last night? I saw you watching me earlier."

"Lass, if it had been me in your room, I would not have been after your *purse*," he said with a wicked grin, "and I would not have left so quickly."

His black, liquid gaze swept her body from neck to ankle, flicking briefly over her breasts. She crossed her arms over her chest and lifted her chin. Her breath caught in her throat at the look in his eyes.

During the weeks at sea, she had enjoyed just watching Garth from afar. She had flushed the first time he'd stripped to the waist and climbed agilely up the rigging. A hot heat had suffused her face and neck with color and made her throat tighten, and Garth had noticed her owl-eyed stare and sent her below decks.

The next time, she had managed to school her reaction more carefully.

Admittedly, Summer had very little experience with men. She'd not been prepared for the funny, tight feeling in her chest when she looked at Garth or for the dreams that had come to her in the night as she lay in her chaste bed, feeling curious flushes in her body that she couldn't explain. It was odd, how her body frequently reacted in ways she'd never thought existed, as if it was rebelling against all she had been taught. Like now, when this dark-eyed stranger looked at her with knowing eyes, and her body felt flushed.

It was crudely evident from the tone of his voice and the flare in his eyes what he meant. She might be innocent, but she had listened enough to other young ladies to hear plenty of conjecture about what went on between men and women. She had thought about it and thought about it and finally come to the private conclusion that sex was something a man wanted that a woman merely endured, and that sometimes it took only a few minutes, and sometimes all night. Whichever, men never seemed to tire of doing it or talking about it, even in oblique ways, such as this man was now doing.

She swallowed the lump in her throat.

"Sir, I believe I find offense with that remark." Her gaze was steady, half-defiant, half-wary. "I am not what you may think. I am a decent woman who finds herself in a difficult position at the moment."

That one black devil's brow lifted slightly, and her

rescuer favored her with a nod. "My apologies if I have offended you, milady," he said, sweeping her a bow that was only half mocking. "My offer still stands, if you wish to take it." He offered her his bent arm as if they were at an elegant ball and waited.

Sighing, Summer slipped her small-boned hand into the crook of his arm, resting her fingers on the hard bulge of his muscle. She had little choice. And perhaps this arrogant, brash man could be persuaded to help her get back to the port of London.

Chapter 3

When Summer had changed into dry clothes, she came back downstairs and found her gallant rescuer waiting on her in the common room. She crossed to the table, and he stood up politely. Feeling odd and vaguely shy, she put a hand on the back of a chair and smiled at him.

He smiled back. "What are your plans, lass?"

Summer shook her head. Damp, stinging silk lashed her cheek, and she reached up awkwardly to push her hair into order. The tawny curls defied her efforts, winding around her fingertips as if alive, falling fetchingly over her brow. "I don't know."

"Have you no family nearby to help you?"

"No. My family is . . . dead." How easily the words slipped out now, when once she could not have said them without releasing scalding tears.

"Ah, I see." He paused. "Then you're alone?"

After a brief hesitation, she nodded. She couldn't quite meet his black eyes, and she felt the undercurrent in his voice and gaze that made her pulses race a little too fast and her breath catch in her throat.

"I'm quite alone."

"Maybe I can find someone to help you," he offered. "Would you like that, lass? Or would you prefer to stay with me?"

What I would like, she thought, is to be safely at home and not be presented with these dangerous choices. . . .

Summer twisted the satin ribbons of her last dry gown into a knot and considered him for a moment. Maybe she was overreacting. This tall rogue with the bold eyes and bolder tongue had not tried to force himself on her in any way. He had even insisted she use his room—privately—to change into the clothes he'd retrieved from the innkeeper for her. On the surface, he was gallantly polite. He'd even bought her breakfast, which he pushed toward her now. It was the speculative gleam in his eyes that bothered her, that made her shift uneasily and wonder what he had in mind.

She looked down at the coddled eggs swimming in butter and shrugged. "I don't know. Who would you ask to help me?"

His one dark eyebrow lifted slightly, and he raked her with a slow, lazy gaze that made her feel suddenly as if she were wearing only her shift. Her chin tilted at him; her eyes narrowed slightly.

"Me, of course."

She'd half-expected that reply but didn't quite know what to make of it. Somehow, she had the feeling he would expect something in return.

"I'll think about it," she said.

Laughing, he looked around the almost empty common room of the inn. "Do you have any other offers, lass?"

Her face flushed pink, and she shook her head because there was no point in pretending. "No."

His eyes danced as he leaned lazily against the paneled wall. To Summer, he looked much too cocky. His tall body radiated a raw masculine confidence that could be vaguely frightening, though the tingling it evoked deep inside her was disturbingly pleasant. He regarded her steadily. She tried not to notice how appealing that gaze could be, or the considering lights that sparkled in the depths of his eyes.

"So, you don't know what you are going to do, or where you can go," he said in a deep, rich voice that held a faint trace of a burr. He rolled his *R*'s slightly, giving his words an exotic twist.

"No," Summer repeated, "I don't. I have no money. All I have left is my clothes, and those only because you spoke to the innkeeper for me."

"Ah." He grinned, and slanted the glowering innkeeper a quick glance. "It took more than a few words to wrest your clothes from yon greedy innkeeper, lass." He shrugged. "A single glimpse of my dirk helped him recall his dereliction in providing safe sanction for his guests."

"Dirk?"

"My dagger. But don't look so shocked. I offered him a few paltry coins too."

Reeling from this information, all she could say was, "A few paltry coins?" Then, more strongly, "But didn't you recognize the value of my clothing? Are you unfamiliar with such things?"

"I dinna think they were worth much more than that, lass. Sorry."

She stared at him. It was obvious that this man had no idea of the value of good clothing. Perhaps his own was purchased secondhand; he must be nothing more than a poor adventurer, penniless and wandering. Summer sighed. Did it really matter, as long as he could get her to London? He was her only hope, it seemed.

She tried out her most beguiling smile, and it seemed to work. He met it with one of his own.

"Anyway," she said as she sat down, "thank you."

"You're quite welcome." He pulled out a chair and sat down across from her. Summer was much too aware of him so close to her and shifted uneasily.

She lowered her gaze and concentrated on her eggs. She could feel his gaze resting on her thoughtfully and hoped that he was considering what he could do to help her.

No options presented themselves to her as she ate, and she accepted the inevitable. This helpful stranger seemed to be her only mode of getting to London, if he didn't balk at the idea of going so far.

When she'd finished her eggs and milk, she wiped her mouth on a napkin that didn't look especially clean and sighed.

"Thank you for being so kind, sir. I don't know what I would have done if you hadn't helped me."

"Drowned, most likely."

Her mouth tightened slightly, "I *meant* about my clothes. Not the river. I would not have fallen in if you hadn't startled me."

His black brow tilted at one corner. "We could argue that for some time."

Smothering her growing irritation, Summer did her best to be agreeable. "True." She smiled again. "At any rate, I want you to know how very much I appreciate your chivalry."

"Oh, aye, lass. I'm a veritable Sir Galahad."

She doubted that, but she didn't challenge it as she said in a light tone, "Are you, by any chance, on your way to London, sir?"

He wasn't. He'd intended to avoid the city completely; but now, looking at this wide-eyed girl with the slightly tilted eyes and winsome smile, he hesitated in saying so.

It was the damndest thing, but whenever he met a young lady who took his fancy, common sense went right out the window. He didn't really want to listen to a tale of woe; what he wanted was to flirt with her, laugh with her, then take her to a nice comfortable bed for a few days. It had been too long for him. His fault—there had been willing women in Southampton. And since then. But not like this one.

He sat and watched the girl for a moment. He toyed with the idea of seduction. She looked luscious.

Her hair was an odd color when dry, with thick strands of varying shades of gold alternating with darker tints of brown, as if she had been in the sun a great deal. But her complexion proved that she could not have lingered in the sun; it was pale and creamy, without a single blemish, except perhaps, for one or two freckles dusting the end of her straight little nose. She had high cheekbones and a full, sultry mouth; her eyes were wide, thick-lashed, unusually blue, a deep color that made him think of summer bluebells.

Jamie sighed. She was beautiful. Really beautiful.

"Yes," he heard himself say, "I am traveling in that direction. Why?"

"Would it be possible for me to travel along with you?"

It was impossible to refuse. He smiled. "Of course."

Summer hesitated, then added in a soft, urgent voice, "I'm in something of a hurry, sir."

"Are you?" His dark gaze riveted on her mouth, and he wondered if her lips tasted as luscious as they looked. "Why are you in a hurry, lass?"

Jamie's gaze snapped back to her eyes when she said, "I must meet a ship before it sails."

"A ship?" His brow lowered slightly. "What ship?"

"The *Sea Dancer*. You see, I came over from America on her, and if I can just reach London before she sails again, I will be able to return home."

Her words were fast, running into one another so that he had a little difficulty in following them, but somehow, it was what she *didn't* say that interested him most.

Leaning forward, he clasped his hands on the top of the table. "How will you buy passage if you have no money?"

Summer hesitated a shade too long before saying, "The captain is a . . . friend."

"Ah. A *friend*." He thought he understood. Of course she would have a protector. Any female who traveled with an unreliable maid and a small cloth bag holding only a few items of clothing could not be as well-bred as he'd first thought. A pity. Or was it? If she was not some convent-bred miss from a fine family, it certainly left the door open to seduction.

Summer recognized from his expression what he thought and opened her mouth to explain. Then she shut it again. Why not let him think that she and Garth were lovers? It might save her from what she saw in his eyes if he thought she was already spoken for. And she could certainly carry off her part as a lovesick woman.

She met his gaze steadily. "I'm not exactly naive, sir. I know what I'm about in life, if you understand."

That single black brow rose, and he nodded silently, seeming to digest this bit of information as she had wished him to do.

"What did you say your name was, lass?" he asked after a moment.

She hesitated. Her surname was volatile. Apparently, the French were truly hated in England, and she dared not be honest. Not that she could fully trust this rogue anyway. However, *Smith* did not come easily with him looking at her so keenly. She sighed.

"Summer."

"Summer?" He smiled. "Just Summer?"

Her chin lifted slightly. "Just Summer."

Rubbing his thumb across his jaw, he met her defiant gaze with a growing smile. "It fits you. You have sunshine hair and bluebell eyes. Aye, Summer is a good name for you, lass."

"I'm pleased you like it," she said stiffly. "It's an old family name." Her mother's maiden name, as a matter of fact, had been Summers. Her throat ached when she thought of her mother, and she looked away from his intent gaze.

"Ah. I thought maybe you were born in July."

"No." He was still gazing at her with a lazy smile, and she felt suddenly restless and uneasy. "So, when may we leave?" she asked sharply.

Leaning back in his chair, he tilted it on the two rear legs and gazed at her thoughtfully for a long moment.

"Soon, *Just Summer*. If you don't mind taking a stagecoach." He watched her and saw the dismay in her face. He didn't blame her. He didn't much like the idea himself, but his horse had drawn up lame, and this little village didn't have anything decent to buy. Public coaches were always crowded and frequently dangerous. If one had enough money to ride inside, it wasn't too bad; clinging atop a public coach was sheer torture.

"I understand," Summer said with a sigh. "Are you certain that you have enough money to pay for both of us? I have a necklace that we could sell, perhaps, if you don't. . . ."

Startled by her assumption of his inability to pay, he started to correct her, then paused. It had been a few years since he'd had to live off his wits; it might amuse him to do so for a while now. Especially since it would put him in the position of gallant cavalier to a young lady in distress. It wouldn't hurt the seduction he planned at all. In fact, he found he liked the idea quite well.

"Don't barter your necklace yet," he said. "I think I have enough to pay our way to London."

Summer nodded with relief. Her necklace was precious to her. While she had changed into dry clothes, she had taken the precaution of hiding it in the toe of a stocking in her satchel, not wanting anyone to see it and covet it.

"Good. When we reach London, I will see to it that you are repaid for your kindness," Summer said earnestly, and saw an amused light flare in her benefactor's eyes.

"Will you, lass?"

She seemed surprised. "Of course."

A smile flickered at the corners of his mouth, and his voice was deliberately husky. "I won't charge highly for my services, lass. Just a simple kiss will be payment enough."

"A simple kiss?" Summer echoed, sensing that with this man who fairly radiated male vitality and virility, there would be no such thing. She bludgeoned her quickening pulse into submission before saying coolly, "I find your suggestion vulgar and shocking, sir!"

"But not as vulgar and shocking as being left to the mercies of yon innkeeper," he said with a laugh, nodding his head toward the portly, balding man glowering at them across the room. "Come, lass—it will be such a small thing to do for a man willing to put himself out to escort you safely to London, don't you think?"

Summer thought it over for several moments, then knew she had little choice. "Very well," she said with the air of a martyr, "I accept your terms. One kiss, and no more, and you will take me to the port of London."

"You may not want to stop at a single kiss," he said with another laugh. "Have you thought of that?"

"Not at all." She glared at him for a moment, then gave a soft sigh. "I'm ready," she said, and leaned across the table. She closed her eyes and put up her face for his kiss, tensing against it. In spite of herself, her pursed lips tingled with anticipation as she waited for him to kiss her.

Jamie stared at her with rich amusement, and his voice was shaky with laughter. "I've no intention of kissing you here in the middle of the common room with the innkeeper and half his staff watching us. I'll collect my payment when I'm ready."

Summer's eyes snapped open, and she felt very foolish. Her high cheekbones reddened, and her mobile lips tightened into a line. She'd not thought of that. But perhaps he had the better idea at that, especially when she noted the faintly malicious, watchful eyes peering at them from across the room.

She nodded stiffly, and the quick glance she gave him was eloquent. "Agreed, sir."

Jamie watched her with veiled eyes, knowing what must be going through her mind. She was right. He did want her. His body ached with the wanting; he shifted uncomfortably. It should be a fair enough trade. She wanted to go to London; he wanted to bury himself inside her.

Their gazes locked. He watched with detached interest the slight widening of the girl's eyes, the way her dark pupils dilated, then contracted in the smoky shaft of pale sunlight filtering through the window. She really had the most remarkable eyes, gazing out at the world from beneath a thick fringe of long, curling lashes that looked as if they had been lightly dusted with gold. . . . Embarrassed by the train of his thought, Jamie's voice was brusque when he said, "The stage should arrive any time, lass, and if we're not ready, they won't wait."

She rose from the chair and shook out the cloak he'd draped over a chair for her. Then, struck by a thought, she looked at him. "By the by—what is your name?"

His dark brow quirked in amusement. "Ah, so you've grown curious about me, have you? James Douglas Cameron, at your service," he said with a sweeping bow. "But all my friends call me Jamie."

"Thank you, *Mr. Cameron.*"

Jamie laughed, and his eyes danced. "I love a challenge, lass. It makes victory all the sweeter."

Summer shifted uneasily beneath the hand he put on her shoulder to help her with her cloak. She hoped he would not prove troublesome.

Summer poised on the end of the dock and searched the misty, shadowy shapes in the harbor for the shrouded sails of the *Sea Dancer.* Her slender body vibrated with anxiety as she tried to peer through shreds of gray fog that lay over the city, hoping against hope that she would find Garth still there. If he wasn't, her hopes were for naught. Even if she wrote her uncle to beg for passage home, she would have to stay somewhere until he replied, and she had no money.

The choppy, dun-colored water of the Thames offered no solution to her problem, no sign of the ship she'd hoped to find. Her gaze shifted, ranging over the wet and dry docks that stretched as far as she could see, warships mingling with chunky merchantmen in a tangled field of bare masts and shrouded sails. Hammers beat steadily, saws rasped, bells jangled, blocks and tackles creaked and groaned in a surging, throbbing rhythm that drowned out her last hope.

Weathered skeletons of ships being built could be seen upriver, and long rows of warehouses with low, narrow roofs and ropewalks were stitched against the sullen gray sky. Chimneys poured soot into the air, and a fine mist dampened her hair and face.

The hem of her cloak flapped in the wind, sounding like the crack of a whip, and Summer moved at last. She turned with the slow, dazed look of a person sleepwalking and saw Jamie gazing at her.

"We weren't in time," she choked out.

"I'm sorry, lass," he said, and sounded as if he meant it. He wasn't certain if he did. After all, if he'd really wanted to hurry, he could have taken the mail coach instead of passage on a slow-moving stage that lumbered over the roads in a leisurely fashion. But he hadn't. Now the late afternoon sun was only a hazy glow behind the fog.

He gave a mental shrug.

Maybe there was no sight of her lover's ship amid the packed harbor of schooners, whalers, tea clippers, and hundreds of smaller vessels, but it couldn't be gone. Jamie was well aware that no cargo ship could unload and reload in the short space of time Summer had claimed they'd been in London. No, her protector had obviously just moved berths, or was waiting his turn in the harbor. But why tell her that now? She might insist upon finding him, and that would ruin his chances of passing the night with a woman he wanted.

"I'm sorry," he repeated, and this time she looked up at him with a faint smile.

"Thank you for bringing me here," she whispered. "I ... I don't know what to do now, with him already gone." The last was wrenched from her in a helpless tone that made him swear softly beneath his breath.

Damn. Why did she have to look at him like that? He looked at Summer's oval face, her bewitching eyes, and the crown of hair that looked sun-streaked as it curled around her delicate features at the touch of the wind, and began to feel sharp pangs of remorse at his callous desire for a woman in distress. He shrugged with resignation. His conscience wouldn't let him perpetuate a lie.

"Maybe he's not gone, lass. We can check with one of the shipping officers tomorrow."

"What do you mean? Is there a chance the *Sea Dancer* is still here?" There was a surge of hope in her eyes that made his hands open and close with frustration.

"Aye. But it's late. You'll have to wait until tomorrow to find out where it's berthed."

He paused and saw the conflicting emotions pass over her face. It was obvious she had no place to go. She could not fake the genuine distress in her eyes.

"Have you no one in London you can turn to? Friends of your family, perhaps?" he asked gently. "Or business acquaintances?"

The latter suggestion was his tactful attempt to prod her memory for former protectors, or even friends of men who had kept her. If she'd just left— or been left—by her current lover, such men could be useful. He'd seen more than one woman go from being mistress of one man to being mistress of one of

his business acquaintances. It usually worked out well
for all concerned.

Summer shook her head at his suggestion, then
gave a start. "Wait!..." She halted. No, if she attempted to explain her identity to the London office
of St. Clair Shipping, how would she explain her unchaperoned presence in London? She had no illusions that a staid London businessman would believe
her to be the heiress to the shipping lines if she
showed up looking like a bedraggled street urchin.
There *had* to be another way to get home.

She tried not to think about what would happen
when she returned to New Orleans. There would be
no explanation that would satisfy Barton Shriver, and
she knew it. She was doomed to marry that odious
Freeman Tutwiler.

I crave the wench in my bed. . . .

"Wait?" Jamie prompted, and her miserable blue
eyes swung to him reluctantly.

"Never mind," she murmured. "It wouldn't work."

Jamie perched negligently on a wet stone bollard,
one leg dangling, his lean brown hands resting on his
knee. "So what are your plans, lass?"

She gave a slow shake of her head. "I don't know,"
she whispered again, feeling the hot prick of tears behind her lids and trying to blink them away. "What is
there for a woman to do in London?"

Jamie couldn't help it. He laughed aloud, then
wished that he hadn't. Her head flung up, and her
eyes were wide and blue and hazy with unshed tears,
her full lips quivering with reproach.

"Och, lass," he said quickly, rising from the bollard
to approach her, "I dinna mean tae hurt yer feelings."

Her hot, swimming eyes raked his tall frame. He
wore a cutaway jacket of superfine that had seen better days, and his fawn-colored pants fit into the tops
of well-worn boots. His shirt was of fine linen, but was
badly wrinkled, and his cravat was tied carelessly and
unstarched. A dress sword hung at his side but looked

well used. She could only conclude from his attire and the cheap fares on the top of the coach from Pyrford—a nightmare of terror for her—that he had very little more money than she had. It was gravely insulting that he would dare amuse himself at her expense.

"It doesn't appear to me, sir, that you are in any position to look down on me," she said in a sort of snarl that gained her his rapt attention. "Especially as you are little more than a rogue, living off your wits!"

An amused expression flickered briefly on his face, and Jamie did not deny it.

"Aye, lassie, so what if I am? Do you see me wailing on the end of a pier? No. I can take care of myself right enough and not depend on some man with a full purse to dole out a few coins here and there."

Incensed, she faced him dry-eyed, with hands on her hips and her voice scathing. "Perhaps if I wanted to steal from helpless women, I could speak with such confidence myself!"

Jamie's eyes narrowed ominously. "I dinna steal yer bloody purse," he growled softly, and Summer mistook his roughly spoken denial for guilt.

She was too upset to pay attention to the dangerous flare in his eyes. Anger and disappointment spurred her into a frenzy, and she lashed out like a frustrated child.

"That's your story! I saw you staring at me in the inn, and you watched me go up the stairs to my room! It would have been easy enough for you to—"

Her angry words ended in a muffled shriek.

She hadn't seen him move, but his hands were around her arms in a steely grip, his face only inches from hers.

"Don't ever accuse me of something, lass, unless you've seen it with your own eyes. And even then, you'd best think twice about it."

He didn't raise his voice. It was filled with such quiet menace, however, that Summer's lips clamped tightly over her clacking tongue, and she nodded. Jamie set her back carefully, then took a step away. His gaze burned into her. Summer stood quietly and waited.

"I'll see to your food and lodging for the next few nights," he said after a moment, "until you find the ship or a way home."

"I have no way to pay you," Summer whispered around the lump in her throat.

Jamie gazed at her in thoughtful silence; he finally lifted his one dark brow in a slightly mocking gesture. "I think, lass, that we will find a way for you to pay me for my trouble. Do you understand my meaning?"

Thinking of the kiss he had been promised but not yet collected, Summer flushed and nodded. In her confusion and distress, it did not occur to her that this tall, dark man with the look of a savage and the manners of a gentleman meant much more than a simple kiss.

"I understand," she murmured, and Jamie gave a satisfied nod.

His smile was softer, less harsh than the mocking twist of his lips earlier, and he put a gentle hand on the small of her back to guide her away from the pier. Summer felt his eyes on her and looked up. Her breath caught in her throat at his steady gaze and the dark fires burning there. She felt a moment's uneasiness and wondered if perhaps she had agreed to something that was far more dangerous than she'd first suspected.

Chapter 4

Sedan chairs wobbled past, heavily laden beer wagons strained across the stones in loud rumbles, and ornate coaches with shiny crests and liveried footmen clinging to the boots careened importantly from the narrow, filthy streets of the port toward the more respectable parts of the city.

The gray mists had dissipated, and the late afternoon sun hung low in the sky, a hazy red ball of fire.

Jamie slanted Summer an appraising glance. He had offered to carry her satchel for her more than once, and she had stubbornly refused to relinquish it. His brow knit with irritation. Did she have the national treasure in there? A pistol? Or did she still think he had stolen her stupid purse?

"It was your maid, you know."

Summer looked up at him. "Excuse me?"

"Your maid. She's the one who was responsible for the theft of your purse."

Summer would have liked to deny that, just for the sake of proving his arrogance wrong, but she couldn't. Her lips pursed. "Why do you think that?"

"Because I saw her talking to two men in the inn. They looked a rum sort, shabby, fairly devious."

Annoyed with both of them—him for being right,

herself for being blind and stupid—Summer snapped, "Why didn't you tell that to the innkeeper?"

He was amused by her question. "Would it have made any difference? All he wanted was his money. And it was *your* maid."

She thought for a moment. Carriages rolled past, and she stepped quickly aside as huge wheels rolled through a deep puddle, spraying mud everywhere.

"She let them in my room, didn't she." It was not a question, but a statement.

"I'm pretty sure of it, lass."

"How could he have done that to me?"

Jamie glanced at her. "He?"

She gave an impatient wave of her hand. "You don't know him. He gave me money for my passage home and hired the wretched, faithless creature who stole it from me!" Her small hands clenched into fists around the bone handle of her cloth satchel. "How could he!"

Not certain who the unfortunate *he* was but fairly sure it had to be the ship's captain and her erstwhile lover, Jamie prudently reserved comment. He knew that even a cast-off lover and the most fiendish man in the universe would be defended if any but his wronged amour spoke ill of him.

"Stay close to me, lass," he said as their walk took them further into the city, but his warning was unnecessary. She shivered and tucked her hand into the bend of his arm, reassured by the hard bulge of muscle she could feel beneath his coat sleeve.

Never had Summer imagined such squalor. A loud cacophony arose, filling her ears with noise. Beneath her feet, the loose stones of the street were slimy with foul-smelling matter. Ancient, sagging buildings formed dark passages less than five feet wide and filled with refuse and decaying garbage. In these gloomy alleys, young urchins garbed in shreds of rags pursued the hope of a penny or ha'penny, crying shrilly at the tops of their lungs, their cries only mingling with the louder noises.

"Sad, isn't it?" Jamie said when Summer cast a sympathetic glance at a scraggly-haired girl of about five. "There are packs of them living in the stews and alleys. They've been known to strip the unwary of clothes and money in less than thirty seconds, like barracudas. It's the only way they can survive."

Looking at the bands of children with old eyes and scabby faces, Summer could believe it. There was nothing of the child in any of them, only a driving instinct for survival. Her heart ached for them, and she shuddered with distress.

Thankfully, after traversing dangerous, dark passages that twisted and turned through evil-smelling streets where the cry of "Stand clear!" meant pedestrians should hug the nearest wall immediately or risk being splattered with the contents of a chamber pot flung from an upstairs window, they emerged into sunnier, wider streets where Summer could draw in a decent breath of air. Commerce was brisk.

Here, the cries of the beggars were drowned out by cries from vendors. "Ho, buy my China oranges!" "Ho! Hot chestnuts here." "New eels and mussels here!" "Milk-o! Buy my milk-o. . . ." Voices vied with one another to catch the ear and eye of possible purchasers.

Sedan chairs swayed alongside smart carriages and high-stepping horses, and dogs yapped underfoot. There were a few dandies lounging about, young bucks come to find excitement, but for the most part, the populace here was composed of vendors, shopkeepers, and middle-class citizens.

There was an air of shabby gentility to these streets, where sunlight slanted fitfully from behind high gabled roofs, and smoke puffed into the air from hundreds of black chimneys. A froth of flowers occasionally flowed from a basket or cast-off cooking pot, a touch of civility in an uncivilized world.

Summer slanted Jamie an irritated glance when he began to whistle cheerily. "Must you?"

"You don't like my choice of tunes, lass?"

"It seems incongruous to be cheerful here."

"Why? Haven't you ever seen a flower in a rock pile? I daresay that flower wouldn't care that it was surrounded by chunks of stone. Beauty stands alone."

"How poetical." She shifted her satchel to her other hand and ignored his offer to carry it for her. It was bad enough that she was in his debt; she had no intention of being a trusting fool again. "What, by any stretch of the imagination, makes you think that's beautiful?" she asked when he began whistling again. "And what is it?"

" 'Lady Castlereagh's Air.' It's a Scottish tune. Do you like it?"

"It's fair."

"Only fair? I suppose you prefer American tunes, lass?"

She felt slightly churlish pricking him when he had taken her welfare to heart, but there was something so insolent and arrogant about him, something so *confident*, that she couldn't resist.

"Do you know 'Hail Columbia!'?"

"How about 'Gypsy Lady'?"

"That isn't American," she began, but when he started to sing, she stared at him in horror. "Stop it! Oh, what are you doing!"

Bowing from the waist with an exaggerated sweep of one arm, Jamie gathered amused stares from passing pedestrians as he sang loudly.

"*. . . he's gone with a gypsy la-a-dy. La te do, la te do da day, la te do la te day, he whistled and he sang til the green woods rang, and he won the heart of the la-a-dy . . .*"

When Summer tried to back away from him, her cheeks a high, hot color, Jamie grabbed her by the wrists. His lean fingers tightened, and his brow rose impudently when she resisted.

"Stop it, you madman!" she hissed at him, jerking

at his strong grip. Even her eyes felt hot, and she tried to ignore the people who had stopped to listen. "Have you gone mad?"

But Jamie ignored her with a blithe insouciance that made her writhe inside. How could he make such a spectacle of himself?—of her?

Someone began to play a mouth organ, and instead of stopping Jamie, it only made him sing more loudly.

"Oh, saddle to me my jet black steed, the brown one is not speedy, oh, saddle to me my jet black steed, to seek and find my lady. . . ."

"Stop!" she moaned in a futile plea for anonymity, but he held her fast, his black eyes dancing as the crowd grew larger. A few well-dressed souls were kind enough to toss coins at them, and they clinked on the paving stones. Small ragamuffins darted forward to snatch at them.

Summer held her satchel close against her body, still straining away from Jamie. A coin hit her on the shoulder, and she gave a furious jerk of her head.

"You're causing a scene!" she spat. By this time, the crowd had begun to nudge too close, and the glance she cast around her was vaguely frightened. Some of her fear must have finally penetrated Jamie's smug complacency, because he caught a glittering coin in one fist and stopped singing for a moment.

Turning to his audience, he executed a graceful bow of thanks, pulling Summer closer to his side when she would have fled.

"Many thanks for these gestures of your appreciation," he said into the smiling faces that pressed close. "It's more than enough for two poor souls lost in such a grand city. . . ." He flexed his arm to bring Summer back against his side as she tried to twist away.

"You melodramatic idiot!" she snarled. To her, the few coins were not worth the embarrassment.

Jamie's lips curled with amusement, and he seemed to enjoy her discomfiture. Another coin clinked on the stones, and he bent gracefully and scooped it from the ground to toss it to the tattered old man still playing his mouth organ. Grinning, the old man caught it in a grimy fist and whirled away into the crowd.

"Shall I continue, lass?" Jamie asked. "We could earn a goodly sum if you would join in with me."

"Lunatic!"

He held up one hand and showed her the dull gleam of coins. "There's at least a tanner here, lass. If I sing a little longer, I could earn us a half-crown or more. . . ."

"I don't care!" Her throat was tight with humiliation, and she could see the gleeful, slightly malicious faces that were obviously enjoying her predicament. Were people so starved for entertainment that they would consider this enjoyable?

Apparently so. One girl, bolder than the rest, edged so close that Summer could smell her unwashed body.

"'Ere, guv'nor," the bawd said saucily, "ditch th' carpin' baggage, an' cum wi' me. I'll sing wi' ye right enuf!" She laughed at the expression on Summer's face, and added lewdly, "An' I'll ha' ye singin' a dif'rent tune in a trice, I will, ye 'andsome devil!"

Jamie grinned. "As tempted as I am, sweet lass, I'm afraid that I can't accept your kind offer. . . ." He winced as a hard foot trod on his instep, and shuffled his feet from under Summer's harsh tread. "As you can see, I'm already spoken for by a jealous mistress—ow!" He nimbly avoided her second kick in the shins and moved to curve an arm around Summer's waist, half lifting her from the street.

"Aye, an' ye'd best find ye a suit o' armor a'fore ye bed her ag'in!" someone called.

Laughter followed them as Jamie half dragged, half escorted Summer down the street, and he could feel her fury in her resistance.

"Gi'e over, lass," he grumbled. "Ye're bruisin' me."

"I'd like to . . . to choke you!"

"What was so bad about that?" he demanded. He paused in the gloomy shadows at the mouth of an alley and set her down sharply. "It was only a bit of fun, and you act as if I've committed some crime."

Summer couldn't speak for a moment. A bit of fun? When they had no money and no place to sleep, and all of London waited voraciously? It just didn't register with her. She had not had *fun* in years; she couldn't remember what *fun* was supposed to feel like. There was only endless waiting in her life, waiting for time to pass, for something—maybe someone—to rescue her from tedious existence. But in her wildest dreams, she'd never considered singing in the stews of London as entertainment.

She didn't have to explain; Jamie saw, suddenly, in the eloquent lack of understanding in her face, that she had no idea what he was talking about. For a moment, he felt a pang of sympathy for this lovely girl. What must her life be like not to have enjoyment in it?

"Ah, lass," he said on the wings of a sigh, "I'm sorry if I distressed you." He put a finger beneath her small chin to tilt her face up to his. His touch was warm and meant to be comforting. A faint smile curved his finely cut mouth. "Maybe someone should educate you in laughter."

Summer brushed away his hand. She nodded because her throat was too tight to speak. Her fury eased slowly. The ringing of her pulses eased even more slowly when he touched her. This man was dangerous; he was more dangerous than a highwayman or common thief. This man could steal more than mere possessions, and she knew it.

Jamie let his hand fall back to his side, and he lifted his head to gaze down the street. The sun was sinking quickly now, rimming the sooty rooftops with a rosy glow.

"It's almost dark. I think we need to find shelter for the night, lass," he said to her, and smiled slightly at the accepting shrug of her shoulders. "Agreeable now, are you? If you'd been so agreeable a dab earlier, we might have enough money to stay at Ibbetson's hotel, if not the Clarendon."

"I believe you value your singing voice much above its worth," Summer said tartly, and he grinned.

"Ah, you've got your fine humor back, I see. Well, never mind. We've enough blunt to get us a room for the night."

"*Two* rooms, I hope." Summer met his startled gaze with a narrowed stare. "I prefer sleeping alone."

"Do you, lass?" He smiled. "When it comes to sleeping, I find that preferable myself. But we're not talking about sleeping, are we?"

Her gaze wavered uncertainly. "Aren't we?"

"Aye, lass, maybe we are," he said cheerfully. His dark eyes twinkled with mischief. "Unless you're lucky."

"I'm usually not." Summer smiled with relief and hefted her satchel to her other hand to get a better grip.

"Let's hurry," she added. "I don't like the thought of being out on the streets after dark."

"I've a mind to eat first," Jamie said. "There's a wee bit of time before it gets dark. Are you hungry?"

"Starved."

"How did I know you'd say that?" He tucked her free hand in the crook of his arm and elbow, and walked her from the alleyway down the street, skirting overflowing gutters.

As shadows deepened shops closed, and only vendors were still hawking their wares. Jamie stopped and bought a hot mutton pie, some gingerbread, and spiced wine.

"Keep your eye on your satchel, lass," he warned Summer when she set it down to take the bread, and she immediately snatched it up again. She saw the furtive shadows moving in the alleys, slinking along the closed storefronts and into the streets.

"Are we safe?" she asked anxiously.

"As safe as my sword and arm can keep us," he replied with a laugh. "Don't worry, lass. I think I can manage most of these ruffians." He turned to count out coins to the vendor for their meal.

Summer looked at some of the scruffy characters filling the streets: the pawnbrokers offering to advance a few shillings on stolen clothing, the chimney sweeps with their pitiful climbing boys in tow, and the inevitable sailors bargaining with weary-eyed prostitutes. This was the closest she'd ever been allowed to such decadence. A shiver racked her slender body. She'd never felt so afraid before. If she'd been in New Orleans, she'd have known where to go and where not to go. But here—! Even with Jamie as protection, the unfamiliar city seemed evil, seething with sin and depravity and death.

Jamie turned around and saw the expression on her face, and read it fairly well. He glanced at the frightening turmoil of the streets.

"I won't leave you. Not until you find your friend's ship tomorrow."

"Do you think I will?" She stepped closer to him. A faint frown creased her brows. "I don't know what I'll do if I don't find him."

To his surprise, Jamie felt a sudden surge of protection for her. It not only surprised him, it left him feeling slightly uneasy. He'd not felt that way about any woman, save his mother and sisters, not since he'd been a green lad awash in the first silly pangs of love. And he recalled too well what a fool he'd made of himself then.

Gruffly, he said, "You'll find your bonny lad. Then you will be safe enough."

Summer nodded, and Jamie pulled her along with him as he strode down the unlit streets. He knew of an inn not too far away, shabby but decent. For some reason, he began to be impatient for the night to commence, to feel the girl beneath him and forget about any romantic, ridiculous notions of protecting her. Was he a bloody knight, for God's sake? No, he was a man, with a man's needs, not some mythical character who ran around England saving damsels in distress. And he hoped this cat-eyed girl with more beauty than common sense realized that. Theirs was a bargain of convenience and no more. He'd brought her this far. He owed her nothing.

"Keep up, lass," he growled at her more harshly than he meant to. "We're almost there."

Whale-oil lamps spattered light erratically in the murky gloom, and it was with no small relief that Summer finally let herself be led into the shadowy doorway of an inn. Her satchel banged against her knees, and though it was light enough with her pitifully few possessions, it had grown cumbersome to carry. Her arm ached, and she shifted the cloth bag to her other hand as Jamie spoke with the innkeeper.

The innkeeper eyed them both for a moment, his iron-gray eyebrows moving up and down with suspicion. "I'll 'ave ye know tha' this is a decent inn, me fine buck-o, an' wi' no goin's-on."

Summer's chin lifted, and her eyes flashed with hot sparks of embarrassment at his steady regard. When she opened her mouth to tell him in no uncertain terms what she thought of that remark, Jamie gripped her arm so tightly that she gasped instead.

"Of course, sir," he said politely. "My wife and I just need lodging for the evening." His fingers tightened firmly on Summer's wrist when she tried to pull away. "You understand, sir, that I can pay in advance."

"Aye?" The innkeeper looked at Jamie more kindly. "In advance, ye say? I 'ave jus' th' room fer ye an yer missus, sir, tha' I do."

Summer was forced to swallow her anger until they were in the room with its single bed and the innkeeper had gone. Then she shook her arm free of Jamie's grasp and glared at him.

"You should have said I was your sister!" Her voice shook with anger. "Now, all we have is a single bed!"

"Unless you want to find yourself sleeping on a bed of rags in a gin shop where no one cares if you're married to the person next to you or not," Jamie said with a cool glance at her, "you'll appreciate the fact that I saved you some embarrassment as well as discomfort. Even shabby inns have their standards, you know."

Summer gulped her hasty words and struggled to keep from yielding to dismay. "You're right. I understand, I guess." A heavy silence fell as he absorbed her apology. Then he shrugged.

"You understand?" His eyes surveyed her slowly. "I wonder if I do. You change about as swiftly as a weathervane. First you blow this way, then that, until you go in circles."

Jamie unbuckled his sword belt and coiled it in a single loop and laid it on a flimsy table near the door. Summer did not glance at the wide bed in one corner. It seemed a bit too dangerous at the moment. She stood stiff and erect in the center of the room, keeping a wary eye on him.

If he noted her uneasy rigidity, he didn't mention it. Instead, he bent to retrieve a short, lethal-looking dagger from the top of his right boot and laid it next to his sword. Then he shrugged out of his jacket and tossed it carelessly over the single chair in the room, a straight-backed cane chair that had seen much better days. His hands moved to his waistcoat and unbuttoned it.

Summer swallowed a lump in her throat. "What are you doing?"

He glanced up at her. "Making myself comfortable. Why?"

She swallowed nervously. "I just wondered."

Her knees began to crumple, and she wished he hadn't put one foot up on the chair, because she badly needed to sit down but had no intention of approaching the bed. It loomed large and sinister in the corner. There was the thud of his boots hitting the floor, and Jamie stood in his stockinged feet.

Summer's fingers grew tighter around the bone handle of her satchel, and she had the wild thought that she might end up standing this way all night. It seemed likely. What on earth was he doing now?

Closing her eyes, she felt a wave of tension grip her muscles. He was unbuttoning his shirt and looked as if he had every intention of undressing completely.

"Please," she said in a strangled tone, "preserve some semblance of modesty!"

"I think you've enough for both of us, lass."

"Please!"

There was a muffled oath before he growled, "Aye! And why not?"

She peeped from beneath her lashes and saw with a gush of relief that he'd stopped at unbuttoning his shirt. A slice of dark skin flashed briefly as he moved back to the table, and she had an impression of hard, taut muscles and a light pelt of black hair that dipped below the waistband of his pants. Her throat tightened alarmingly, and she made an instinctive move away from him.

He was too overpoweringly male, too frightening, and she wondered if she wouldn't stand a better chance on the streets.

"Mr. Cameron," she said in a faint croak when he moved toward her, "I think there's been some mistake."

"*Mister* Cameron?" Jamie shook his head. "Aye, lass. I have the same thought." He gently pried her fingers loose from the handle of her satchel and set it carefully on the floor. He was frowning. "Why are you still wearing your cloak?"

She dared a glance toward the dark grate. "It's cold."

"Cold? Faith, lass, it's May!"

"It's cold," she insisted stubbornly, and gripped her

cloak around her as if to prove her point. She tried to look at his face, but his bare chest was distracting. She saw with a spurt of fascination that his skin was smooth and brown, much darker than Garth's. Did he stay in the sun too? She knew literally nothing about him but his name and the fact that he was bold and cocky.

And that he wanted her.

Summer jerked her gaze up to his face and saw his amusement. Instead of reassuring her, it infuriated her. She took refuge in her anger, keeping it as a barrier between her and this dark, enigmatic man who triggered a response in her in spite of her resistance.

"It seems to me," she snapped, "that if we have enough money for wine, we have enough for a few pieces of coal!"

Jamie followed her glance to the unopened bottle of wine he'd placed on the table. It was coated with dust and hardly expensive, but he understood with the male logic of previous experience how skittish a female could be with a new lover and kept his temper.

"Aye, lass, we do. But if we drink enough wine, we'll not need the coal." He glanced meaningfully toward the bed. "And I see blankets on the bed that would keep us warm."

She took a step away, and he stifled a sigh. She looked so damned frightened, as if he was about to ravish her and toss her out the window to the mob. What did she think he'd do to her? Hadn't he cared for her well enough these past twelve hours or more? She couldn't be so ingenuous that she didn't know what came next. Any woman who'd spent several weeks aboard a ship with her lover would certainly know how to go about pleasing a man.

Pausing uncertainly and not quite understanding his silence or his sigh, Summer couldn't help casting another glance at the bed. A faded, patched counterpane was tossed over it, and several pillows lay limply at the head. She edged away from Jamie and half turned.

"I'll take the bed," she announced.

Jamie straightened and met her gaze. His eyes had the most absurdly long lashes she'd ever seen on a man, and Summer took an instinctive step backward. By this time, her dancing steps had taken her almost across the room to the bed. If she lowered her hand, she could brush the tips of her fingers over the frayed stitches of the patched coverlet smoothed over the mattress.

Slanting a glance at the bed from beneath his lowered lashes, Jamie's mouth curled in amusement. His gaze skipped back to her face, and she flushed at the mockery in his eyes.

"Aye, lass, I'd the notion that you would like the bed. It never occurred to me to doubt it." He walked toward her, his stockinged feet padding quietly across the floor and making her think of the boneless stride of a lithe cat.

Summer didn't move, was frozen in place; if she moved forward, she risked contact with him; if she moved in any other direction, she would have to go over the bed. That action engendered certain nuances she wanted desperately to avoid.

A faint frown dipped Jamie's single brow over his eyes as he saw her immobile terror, and he wondered for a brief instant if he'd been mistaken. There was much more to her state of nervousness than simple unfamiliarity. Did she think him that much of a savage, perhaps?

"Here, lass," he said shortly, and reached out to untie the strings to her cloak. "Let's see what we can do about getting you warmer...."

Caught between the devil and his den, Summer turned in a blind move that took her into his arms. They closed around her in a light clasp, and she surged against him like a trapped ferret. With the bed behind her and Jamie in front of her, she was neatly snared.

But then her luck turned. She twisted and stepped from beneath his arms, leaving him holding her cloak in his hands. He tossed it carelessly toward the chair and missed. It slid in a dark blue heap to the floor and lay there, but Summer didn't spare it a glance.

She stood near the window now, quivering with an excess of emotion that made Jamie pause.

"What gives, lass?" He raked an impatient hand through his hair and fixed her with a steady, dark gaze. "I'm no' in th' mood tae play games," he added in a thick, muttering brogue. "Naow are ye comin' tae bed wi' me, or no'?"

Summer understood most of what he said, his meaning if not the specific words. She stiffened.

"*No.*"

His face grew dark, and his eyes narrowed. "No? Just no?"

"I believe that's easy enough to understand." She was regaining her composure now. Talking to him was much more comfortable if he was several feet away.

"Then you don't intend to keep the bargain you made, lass?" His soft, silky tone didn't fool her. She recognized the steely undercurrent and saw the fine white lines that bracketed his mouth.

"Bargain?" She shook her head, and pale tendrils of hair whipped her cheek. " 'Twas only for a kiss, no more."

"Nay, lass." His gaze was hard and direct, and he would not release her eyes. "The bargain was for much more, and you know it."

Unable to escape that compelling gaze or the lashing contempt in his voice, Summer lifted her hands palms up in a gesture of helpless inquiry. "I didn't know it. I swear. You only said—"

"I only said that I would trade one for the other, and you agreed. But don't worry. I've never had to beg for a woman, and I don't intend to begin now."

Pivoting on his stockinged foot, Jamie began buttoning his shirt as he stalked to the chair where his boots lay. He sat down and began tugging them on while Summer watched with growing dismay.

She couldn't lose him. Not now. There was no one in London who would help her if he left her. She'd be alone in a city that she'd already seen was ruthless and uncaring. She'd perish.

"Mr. Cameron," she said around the sudden lump in her throat, "I didn't mean it." Bitter bile rose in her mouth and she swallowed it, knowing that she was about to make the most demeaning sacrifice she'd ever made. What else could she do? Survival seemed to involve few principles, just a hard, driving instinct to live.

He'd paused and looked up at her, and a cynical little smile kicked up the corners of his mouth.

"Didn't mean what, lass? Yes or no? Or do you intend to go back and forth between the two till Hogmanay?"

She stared at him blankly. "Till when?"

He gave an impatient shake of his head and stood up to stomp his feet into his boots. "Never mind. It doesn't matter. You can have the bed. And the room. And even the damned bottle of wine. I should have known better."

Desperate, she lunged several steps forward, twisting her hands in front of her. "You're not going to leave me!"

"Why not? You can go back down to the port tomorrow and find your precious lover, and he can take care of you." He gave his right foot a vicious stamp, and it finally slid into the heel of the boot. "It was a daft notion anyway, lass. It's always simpler to tumble a wench who doesn't act as if she's a cut above a man."

Stung, Summer said, "That's not true! I mean about me thinking I'm above you." She flushed at his sardonic gaze, and clarified, "Well, not now. Maybe I thought that at first, but that was before I knew you."

"Lass, you don't know me now." Jamie shoved his arms into his waistcoat and didn't bother to button it before he shrugged into his jacket.

Summer approached him in a hesitant, desperate little glide that made him swear softly beneath his breath, and she put her hand on his sleeve.

"For pity's sake, James Cameron, don't leave me to the hard mercy of this city," she choked out in a whisper.

He damned her more loudly this time, but knew when he looked down into her small feline face that he would stay. Fickle little bitch. Why did she have to appeal to him like that?

Shoving one fist inside the other, he looked down at her and heaved a sigh. "Do you think you could spare me your true name for my troubles?" When Summer hesitated, he laughed softly. "Not even that, eh? Yet I'm to keep you and protect you, and when we find this wonderful lover who abandoned you, I suppose you expect me to stand there with my hand out for his reward?" His voice hardened. "He's more likely to draw steel on me for my pains, lass, in case you don't know it! Do you think a man who'd let you go so unattended in a strange country will welcome you back? Don't look for it!"

Flinching at the truth she recognized in his words, Summer let her hand fall away from his sleeve. "You're right," she said tonelessly. "I'm a fool to think otherwise of him."

He snorted. "Folly seems to be contagious lately."

Summer heard the slight softening in his voice and dared hope he might relent. Suddenly, she longed to see the mischief dancing in his black eyes again and hear his deep teasing voice coax her from a temper.

Daring a peep at him from beneath the curving veil of her lashes, Summer had a startling thought: This man fit the requirements of a knight in shining armor much better than Garth Kinnison had ever done.

Chapter 5

Dawn came slowly, creeping like a thief into the shabby room in a mantle of gray light. Both of the occupants were wide awake.

"I'd certainly like to know what you've got in that damn bloody satchel that you think is so important," Jamie said testily. He slashed Summer a glare from beneath his lashes. "You act like you're carrying around sacred relics."

Summer's reply was cool and dignified, shaming him for his ill-temper.

"Some of my things *are* sacred—to me."

He looked away from her, staring out the window of the shabby inn at the growing daylight. His fingers drummed on the windowsill, and he tried to get comfortable in the cane chair and failed. He'd spent the entire night on the floor—on the floor!—wrapped in a thin blanket with an even thinner pillow under his head, and he had a right to be in a bad humor. His back ached from the hard scrubbing of oak against his shoulder blades all night long, and he had another ache that couldn't be eased so easily.

It was a sweet mystery to him why he still thought he wanted her. She wouldn't even tell him her last name. Hell, he didn't even know if she'd given him her real first name. What kind of silly name was *Summer*, for God's sake?

And now she sat rigidly on the edge of the bed with the suffering look of a bleeding martyr on her face, when all he could think about was pushing her backward on the mattress and shoving himself inside her until neither one of them could move. He blew out a long breath and stood up.

"I suppose you rested well?" he drawled sarcastically. "*I* certainly didn't."

Summer shifted quickly and gave him a wary look. She clenched her hands tightly in her lap. "Do you think I couldn't hear you swearing and twisting in your blanket all night? You kept me awake almost till dawn, and now you act as if I should commend you for your fortitude." Grudgingly, she added, "At least you stayed, and I do owe you a debt of gratitude for that."

"Keep your bloody gratitude!"

She winced, and he felt her watching him as he struggled into his boots. He shoved his feet into them and stomped on the creaking boards of the floor, swearing softly under his breath.

Summer watched steadily. "What can I do—besides *that*—to change you back?"

He flashed her a tight glance. "Back to what?"

"To a human being instead of a surly bear."

His smile was nasty. "Do you know any incantations?"

"A few." She met his gaze coolly. "My maid—at home—is from Santo Domingo. She used to teach me spells because it amused her."

Slinging his jacket from the chair, he retorted, "She should have taught you how to make a full purse from an empty one, lass."

"If we have no more money, I can pawn my necklace," she offered. She jumped slightly at his snarl.

"What do we need money for?" He gave his right foot another shove against the floor, and his heel slid down to the sole. "Damn Hoby. Why can't the man make a boot that keeps its fit for longer than—" He stopped and thought a moment. "A year? A year." He sighed. Well, maybe the famed bootmaker did well enough. It'd been a year or more since he had purchased these boots, and he'd worn them near every day. And gone a'swimming in them of late.

Lifting his head, he fixed Summer with a baleful eye and repeated, "Why do we need money?"

"I'm hungry."

There it was, plain and simple. The selfish little brat was hungry. Did she think he lived to serve her? She reminded him appallingly of his sisters, who were the most spoiled little beasts he'd ever known to exist. They thought all he had to do in life was accommodate them; that he had done so, frequently, didn't bear remembering at this moment.

Jamie wrenched down hard on his ill temper. If he was going to be honest, he had to admit that it was galling to his pride to be rejected. Especially after striking a bargain with her. Of course, acting like a rejected suitor didn't help.

"So, you're hungry." He tried to smile. "I think I've enough blunt to cover that particular problem."

She hesitated. "Does blunt mean the same thing as money?"

His head jerked up again, and there was a brief flash of humor in his dark eyes. "Aye. What'd you think it meant?"

"I wasn't certain. That's why I asked."

Buckling on his sword, Jamie had the thought that this girl had no idea of how to take care of herself. She was alarmingly naive when it came to survival. He couldn't help but wonder how she had managed to retain that slight air of innocence, considering her occupation.

When he'd stuck his *sgian dubh* into the top of his boot, he squared his shoulders and regarded Summer for a moment.

"I know a place where we can buy hot, fresh bread right out of the oven for a penny, and they'll give us fresh milk to go with it," he said. He was rewarded by a look of glad relief in her eyes. "For tuppence you can get sweet country butter to spread on it."

Summer stood up and smoothed her skirt. "And for three pence?" she asked with only a slight tremor in her voice.

"You can kiss the milkmaid," he replied promptly.

She smiled. "Let's save a penny."

He gave her a crooked smile in return. "Maybe you would like to take her place, lass?" He said it jestingly, but there was a faintly guarded look in his eyes as he waited to see what she would do.

"Only a kiss?" She hesitated. "Is this the branch of peace?"

"Maybe."

Swirling her cloak around her shoulders with a flourish, she moved across the room to stand close to him. She smiled and murmured, "I intend to honor my debt."

Jamie started to refuse; he'd only meant it in jest, he told himself, but then he knew with a bitter irony that her refusal of him the night before had stung his pride. Maybe a kiss was a poor substitute for losing himself in her soft body, but it was a small salvaging of his pride.

Standing on tiptoe, Summer wound her slender arms around his neck and pressed close, her lips brushing so lightly over his that it was almost a whisper of touch. His arms closed around her instinctively, and though she gave a quick recoil, she yielded after a moment.

Moving his mouth slowly over her half-parted lips, he tasted the smooth satin of her with gentle pressure. Then, still gently, he pressed his tongue inside her resisting mouth. Just the touch of his tongue against hers made a hot flame shoot through him, and his grip around her tightened. A half-groan welled in the back of his throat. He was weak. This was ridiculous. She was offering her lips to him as if it meant every-thing, when it truth, it meant nothing. He'd tasted lips a'plenty; why should these be different?

His hands splayed across her back, and he silently damned her cloak as he felt mostly material instead of her firm hips beneath his palms. He wanted to feel her next to him without anything between them, ex-cept perhaps a heated flush of passion. That would be more than enough to end this ridiculous farce, to ease his stupid pride.

Kissing her harder now, his tongue plundering her moist, steamy mouth in heated strokes that made him shudder with need, he thought he heard her moan. His hand tangled in her hair, and he pulled her head farther back, tracing his lips over the sweet arch of her throat to the delicately curved line of her collar-bones. He lavished a few kisses on the fluttering pulse cupped in an ivory hollow, then found her mouth again.

Dragging in a deep breath, he felt her sag against him and realized that she was shaking. It surprised him. Was this just another woman's trick, perhaps? Hadn't she already played enough of those on him, luring him into this situation when she had no inten-tion of keeping her promise?

He drew his head back and looked down at her. Her eyes were closed. Her lips were slightly swollen from his kisses and trembling, and her breath came in soft little pants, as if she had been running. Long, silky lashes shadowed cheeks that were flushed with heat, and as he held her against his body he could feel the hammering of her heart against his chest.

"Summer," he muttered thickly, and lowered his head to kiss her again.

She couldn't turn away. She couldn't move. All she could do was *feel*, and it seemed as if everything below her neck—no, eyebrows—was on fire with some strange kind of burning that made her palms moist and her thighs ache. No, it wasn't her thighs that were aching. It was *there*, that shadowy place that had no name in her astringent vocabulary. Indeed, for the first fifteen years of her life she had ignored its very existence. She couldn't now. Now it throbbed and ached, and sweated with some nameless reaction that this man had ignited in her, and she didn't know what she was supposed to do.

Hanging in his arms, listening to the thunder of his heartbeat and his ragged breathing, Summer seethed with indecision. Her head lolled back helplessly when he kissed her throat, her lips, the curve of her jaw . . . her breasts. He pushed aside the edges of her cloak; then he drew down her lace-edged bodice and held the quivering, rose-tipped globes in his palms, touching them lightly with his hands, then his mouth, flicking the scalding whip of his tongue across them and making her shudder convulsively. She didn't even realize when she began to whimper.

Shuddering, Summer felt the rigid pulse of his body nudging her soft belly, hard and insistent and frightening, but she couldn't move. She couldn't have pushed him away if her very life had depended on it. A white-hot heat enveloped her in a fuzzy haze that made her want to do nothing but cling to Jamie, to let him hold her and kiss her and make her body react in ways it never had before. She was going mad, she thought hazily, stark, staring mad. She must be. There was no other reason for her quiescent surrender.

She moaned softly.

Hearing that faint, tortured sound, Jamie knew she was his if he wanted her. All he had to do was lift her into his arms and cross the room to the bed, and he could do what he'd wanted to do since he'd seen her come into that dreary little inn in Pyrford. He could take off all her clothes and kiss every inch of her that interested him; he could spread her slender thighs and put himself inside her and stay there until all the oceans dried up if he wanted to. And he considered it strongly.

But then, summoning up the last vestige of dignity she possessed, Summer managed to mumble through dry, parched lips, "I think I must be deranged. . . ."

That was enough to save her for the moment. Jamie lifted his head, his eyes heavy with passion, and felt her quivery assertion all the way to his toes. An inexplicable thrum of laughter rattled in his throat, and he swallowed it.

"Do you?" His fingers nudged up her chin, and he tapped her lightly on the cheek until she opened her eyes. They were hazy beneath the fan of her gilt-sprinkled lashes, and he smiled. "Why do you think that you're deranged?"

"Because . . ." Her voice, soft and lugubrious, drifted for a moment, then she dredged up the energy to finish, "I can't think. I can only . . . feel."

"That's not so bad."

"It is when you're feeling in places you didn't know you had," she replied glumly, and closed her eyes again. She leaned into him, and he could feel her legs quivering against his thighs. It certainly didn't do anything to lessen his reaction to her.

Her naive honesty kept him from doing what his body was screaming at him to do and take her; he began to wonder if it was the right time for it. Then he began to wonder why he hesitated.

"I don't usually behave like this, you know," she said into his chest, and he felt her warm breath puff against his skin even through the linen shirt he wore.

"You don't?" He kissed her forehead. "How do you usually behave when a man kisses you, lass?" He felt her languid shrug.

"I don't know. You're the first."

His hands grew still against her. "The first man to kiss you?"

"No, the first man to make me behave this way."

He could understand that; she'd said in her oblique

way that she drifted from man to man for protection,
and he'd observed that females who used sex as a form
of barter rarely enjoyed it. It was a business, and they
cultivated passionate reactions in a firm, professional
way that left him cold. He'd never favored purchased
women. Until now.

And now, because she somehow reminded him of
his favorite sister, with her rather touching courage
and hot flashes of temper, he would not take her unless she asked him. How Cat would enjoy it if she
knew!

Holding her tightly against him, he shifted her to
one side and waited for his erection to ease. It was
tight and painful in these damned snug-fitting pants
he wore, and a bloody nuisance at times. A man could
rarely keep his more private desires private. What
fashion denizen had decided it was stylish to blatantly
display a man's physical attributes anyway? he wondered irritably. Some fiendish woman was responsible, he was certain.

Summer hung limply in his embrace, and he eased
her over to the bed and set her on it gently. She was
flushed, and her expression was suffused with desire
and confusion. A damnable combination. Jamie was
half-bemused, half-wary. He realized with a sudden
twist of irony that he was in as bad a state as she was.
What a farce! Why had he ever yielded to the curiosity
to find out what had happened to her yesterday? He
should have left her bobbing like a cork in the river
and gone on his way. He'd not find himself in such a
damnable situation now if he had.

He knelt beside the bed and waited for her breathing to steady. And his.

"Well," he said when he saw the high color recede
from her face, "are you still hungry?"

Summer had to swallow twice before she could answer. "I think so."

He stood up and let his hand drift through the
tumble of her silky curls, idly watching them curl

around his fingers. Dragging the backs of his fingers across her high cheek, he marveled at the satin texture of her skin, then let his hand drop to his side.

"We'd best fetch our bread and milk before it spoils," he murmured. "It's dangerous to buy fresh milk after eight in the morning on a warm day."

Summer nodded and readjusted her cloak, which hung around her neck by the slender strings. Everything was changed now. Their relationship had taken a subtle twist in a completely different direction, and it was because of a kiss. Or several kisses. Whichever, it amazed her how powerful such a simple act could be, and how far-reaching the consequences.

Desire thrummed between them now, and it wasn't just his that stirred her senses. Because of his kiss, she felt a strange sense of need; or maybe she was only just now able to acknowledge it. Whatever it was, she looked at Jamie with new eyes—and with anticipation.

"Smithfield," Jamie said, waving a hand toward an area rife with cattle and sheep. "And that's the church of St. Bartholomew the Great over there."

Summer's gaze drifted from the canals where flat-boats were poled along under a heavy weight of live cattle, and to the stone arches of St. Bartholomew. They were still a great distance away, but she could see perfectly from the crest of a paved hill.

"We don't have to go down there to get fresh milk, do we?" she asked doubtfully, and he grinned.

"No, I think we can find it a bit closer." He pointed to a girl swaying between two heavy cans of milk suspended from a yoke of sorts over her shoulders. "A milkmaid."

While he purchased a loaf of hot bread from a barrow, haggling good-naturedly with the vendor over the price and a pannikin of free milk, Summer watched him.

She was having trouble sorting out a jumble of

half-formed thoughts and impressions and the thinking of years of habit. Jamie had changed things in the space of a few minutes' time, and she didn't know quite how it had happened to her.

At the age of ten, she had first met Garth Kinnison. He had been only twenty then, fresh-faced, golden, and filled with the arrogance of youth, and she had liked him. At the age of thirteen, she had fallen in love with him; at the age of sixteen, she had idolized him and thought of him during long nights when her body was performing all kinds of strange tricks on her; and at twenty, she had stood on the end of a quay in London and made an absolute fool of herself over him. It had been a long, steady devotion and had weathered his good-natured regard of her as a child—until that devastating moment when he had bluntly rejected her.

But she had never, *never* felt for Garth Kinnison what she had felt for James Cameron just an hour before. It was shocking. And it was frightening. How could a complete stranger turn her world upside down like that? And the dolt didn't even seem to realize what he'd done to her with his casual seduction.

Now look at her.

She wanted to bury her face in her palms and weep with shame; she wished Chantal were with her.

The Caribbean maid was wise in the ways of love and almost every other human emotion; she'd once offered to explain the mystery to Summer, but Madame St. Clair had not thought it time.

"You're too young, poppet," her mother had said with a laugh. "When you're older, it will all be explained to you."

But by the time Summer had grown old enough, her *maman* was dead. Chantal had explained calmly and succinctly that the yearnings of body and soul were frequently at odds. Now she had discovered that Chantal was right; there was a wide gulf between the passion of the spirit and the awakened urges of the body.

This was so different from anything in her experience. She knew what Jamie wanted; he wanted her body. His desire was obvious and untrammeled by scruples. She might be innocent, but she was not stupid. When he looked at her with male need in those dark, glistening eyes beneath extraordinarily long lashes, it was easy to read what he wanted.

What did *she* want?

"Here, lass," Jamie said, coming to her with a hot, crusty loaf of bread and a foamy mug of milk. He held them out as if they were the crown jewels, and Summer gave him a smile when she took them.

"Thank you," she murmured. It would be suicide to look at his eyes, those dark, laughing eyes that made her soul turn inside out and her heart drop to her toes.

"Butter?"

Her head jerked up. "Excuse me?"

"Do you want some butter for your bread?" Jamie wagged his head toward the barrow of bread and the aproned vendor. "Fresh country butter from Yorkshire is ninepence a pound."

"Oh. No. No butter."

His brow rose. "We've the blunt for it, lass. Unless you crave several pounds...."

Summer gave a start. His casual comment brought to mind the nightmare of Freeman Tutwiler. *I crave the wench in my bed....* Her fingers dug into the bread she held, and she saw that Jamie was looking at her closely.

Managing a smile, she shook her head. "Just bread. And my milk."

Somehow, her appetite had vanished. She could barely swallow the bread for the odd lump in her throat, but she ate enough of it to satisfy Jamie. Then she dusted the crumbs off her cloak and drank her mug of milk.

Jamie had wandered a few feet away and was looking at a row of cheeses spread upon a cloth. A soft wind blew, and Summer could smell the evidence of cattle in the fields below. She wrinkled her nose. London was an odd mixture of urban and country. Gazing out at the peaceful fields she could see stretching beyond the city, rolling in gentle swells like the ocean, it was hard to imagine the seething mass of humanity huddled in the East End.

It was hard to imagine the rest of her life being spent as those poor wretches, but that might very well happen if she did not find the *Sea Dancer* before it disgorged its cargo and sailed. Even New Orleans would be better than being adrift in London. She would handle Tutwiler and her uncle as best she could. Those, at least, were familiar evils.

"Are the shipping offices open now?" she asked Jamie when he returned from his perusal of the cheeses, and he nodded.

"Aye, lass." His gaze flicked over her. She wouldn't look at him. His lips thinned into a slight smile, and he gave a careless nod of his head. "At the risk of offending you, may I suggest that we ride to the docks in a chair? I think it prudent to arrive as if we are persons of some consequence instead of mere ... thieves."

Startled, she asked, "Why would I be offended?"

"Everything I do seems to offend you. Or distress you."

She looked away from him. "Not *every*thing ..."

"Dare I hope for your approval?" His voice was mocking, and she slanted him an irritated glance from beneath her lashes.

"You, Mr. Cameron, would dare anything!"

That seemed to please him, and he was in a much better mood when he hired a chair for them to go to the estuary and look for the ship she sought.

•   •   •

When the chair—which Summer discovered she detested—swayed to a stop and settled on the paving stones, she leapt out without waiting for assistance. It had been close inside, even with one of the drapes pulled back so she could see out, and she'd been appalled at how many risks the men carrying the chair took with her safety. Now she understood why Jamie had cautiously presented the idea of the chair to her. He knew, of course, that it was a mad, dangerous mode of travel.

He took her elbow, and if he noticed her tense silence, he didn't mention it. London's sluggish, muddy estuary was packed with ocean-going ships: clumsy, wide-bottomed East Indiamen vied with tea clippers, whalers, galliots, and schooners, as well as a vast assortment of other vessels, all searching for space to unload cargo.

"The delays here are appalling," Jamie observed. "The system of legal quays has grown inadequate for the massive amount of goods that are processed here."

Summer recalled Garth saying something about legal quays and plunder, and frowned. "Is there a serious loss of merchandise because of this?"

"Thousands of pounds, I'd say. The city just opened up the new docks and is planning more. It will help, even though it may not be enough. With Napoleon running mad all over Europe, commerce is brisk."

"Napoleon?" Summer gave a nervous start at the famous name. It brought to mind her uncle and the treachery he planned. She licked her lips nervously and wondered what had happened while she was at sea, and if her uncle had been involved. "Why do you say he's running mad?"

He seemed amused and shrugged. "Because it's true. You don't agree?" There was a barbed edge to his question that put her on her guard, and she tried to recall anything Jamie might have said about the first consul of France. She couldn't recall a single comment, not even an opinion about the French. She looked at him cautiously and tried for a diplomatic remark.

"I suppose Napoleon *has* gotten out of hand...."

"An understatement." His voice was rough. "Summer, I just spent ten years in the military, and a great many of them were spent fighting the French. Three of my cousins were killed while I watched; I couldn't do a damn thing to help them. And then my best friend was taken prisoner, and when he got home—" his voice cracked slightly, "he was only a shell of what he had been. They tortured him for what they thought he knew. Or fun. Look, I may not be a great authority, but I can recognize a power-mad despot when I see the results of his campaigns."

Summer couldn't look at him. She was afraid he might see her past in her eyes, might find Barton Shriver's treason reflected on her face. Concentrating on where she was walking—anything not to have to see condemnation in his eyes—she nodded blindly.

"Yes, I'm sure you're right."

He snorted. "I am right. And I detest the French."

Summer avoided a large mud puddle in the street and lifted the hem of her cloak. Her breath strangled in her throat. She was twice-cursed as far as he would regard it. A French surname—though having spent her early childhood years in the Carolinas made her feel more American than French—and niece to a man in league with Napoleon. She drew in a shaky breath.

"You hate a country of people because of one man?"

"Sometimes." He shrugged and put a hand on her arm to guide her around a broken crate of what looked to have once been egg trays. A strong, sickening smell made Summer put her hand up to her nose. "I think I'm just weary of war," he said when they'd passed the rotten eggs. "I used to dream of the French at night, with their swords and flowery curses, all com-

ing at me at once. Thank God, it's over. For me, anyway."

"But you said you detested the French." She
slanted him a quick glance. "Do you think that's fair?"

"Summer." There was an odd tautness in his voice.
"Are you by any chance French?"

"No." She was telling the truth. She was an American. But she was afraid she would be very Gallic to
this man. He might not consider her American mother
and half-American father a saving grace. She would
certainly have to continue keeping a guard on her
tongue and not let a French phrase slip out as she
had with the innkeeper in Pyrford.

Managing a shrug, Summer said lightly, "I just feel
sorry for a man who has so many enemies, deserving
or not." Her voice sharpened. "And you must remember—it's England that is at war with France, not
America."

"I remember. But that could change any day."

"I doubt it. Even Napoleon would not dare attack
America," she said much more convincingly than she
felt. If her uncle had his way, it wouldn't be long before Napoleon did just that. Dear God! She could feel
Jamie looking at her oddly and wondered what he was
thinking. He shrugged.

"Maybe not. I wouldn't worry about it, though. You
look upset at the idea," he said softly, and her chin
tilted.

"Do I?"

"It seems that way."

"Appearances can be deceiving, I suppose."

Jamie grinned. "Aye, lass, that they can." He tucked
his arm around her shoulders and pulled her next to
him. "Won't you miss me when you're gone with your
bonny ship's captain?"

"Not for a moment." Her lie didn't sound con-
vincing even to her. He seemed to know it. She
pressed her lips tightly together. "Where is this shipping office?"

"Right there, lass." Jamie pointed to a long building with a low-pitched roof. "I'll wait out here." He met her startled gaze steadily. Then he sat down on a stone bollard that was obviously just for decoration and put his hands on his knees. "Take your time."

Shrugging, she hitched her satchel from one hand to the other and walked toward the shipping offices.

Jamie shifted restlessly, wondering what was keeping her so long. How long could it take for those damned clerks to look in their ledgers and find the name of her lover's ship? And what was he doing bringing her to him? He felt like one of the Covent Garden procuresses seen of a night with their brightly garbed doves in tow. And it was doubly amusing, considering he wanted her and hadn't taken her. He still didn't know why not. She'd certainly been ready for him.

Damn. It wasn't as if she was an innocent; why hadn't he done what his body had so urgently wanted him to do? He would certainly be in a better mood now. But no. He had let her absurd naiveté duck under his guard and soften him. It was silly, really. Wouldn't his father laugh himself hoarse if he knew?

Bruce Cameron considered his fourth son a complete, hopeless rake, and there was very little that Jamie had done to change his opinion. It wasn't that he hadn't tried as a youth, because he had. It was only after he'd stopped trying that he'd accomplished anything in his life.

Jamie shifted and squinted against the press of the sun in his eyes. Another hour without rain. How unusual.

"Mister Cameron?"

He jerked. He hadn't seen her come out of the shipping offices. Straightening, he saw at once that her visit had been futile. For some reason, he felt a fierce surge of relief, then smothered it.

"How did it go, lass?"

Her voice was strained. "They informed me that the *Sea Dancer* sailed for the coast of France early this morning."

Jamie was surprised. "It did? How did it manage to get rid of its cargo so quickly?"

"It seems," she said, in a bitter little voice, "that Captain Kinnison preferred selling to the French to waiting until his cargo spoiled while he was anchored in the harbor. At least Garth didn't lie to me about spoiling cargo."

The last was torn from her in a wretched little voice that sounded painfully vulnerable, and Jamie stiffened against the impulse to take her into his arms and try to smooth away her hurt. Apparently, her lover really didn't want her back. *Garth Kinnison?*

"I see."

She glared at him. "No, you *don't* see! You don't see anything but what you want to see...." She broke off, then said miserably, "I'm sorry. That was uncalled for."

"It's all right, lass." He swallowed his sympathy. He didn't think she'd appreciate it anyway, and he was beginning to feel like his youngest sister, Margaret Ellen, who took in stray animals and drove their father to distraction with her efforts. What would Bruce Cameron say about a stray American?

Lifting both her hands palms up, Summer met his calm gaze with a rueful smile. "It seems that I must sell my necklace, after all. Would you be so kind as to direct me to a moneylender?"

"It's not worth enough to buy you passage home, lass."

She stared at him uncertainly. "How would you know?"

"I've seen it." He shrugged at her wide-eyed stare. "I looked through your satchel this morning when you went to the convenience. Your necklace would only get you halfway across the Atlantic. Then you'd be shark bait."

Her mouth tightened, and she gripped the handles of her satchel until her knuckles whitened. "I don't believe you!"

"It's true. You have two pairs of stockings—one with your necklace in the toe—a water-stained dress, two muslin chemises, an extra petticoat, and another pair of shoes. With cheap silver buckles." He shrugged. "Not very nice of me, I know, but you got my curiosity up. I began to think you might have contraband in there."

"You . . . you *brigand! You rapacious toad!* Filth and unmentionable bandit!"

Jamie eyed her narrowly. "Are you quite through, lass?"

"Ohhh!" She seemed at a loss for words, and her small hands clenched into fists. He believed that if she had had a weapon, she would have used it on him. He sighed.

"I didn't take anything from you. I merely exercised, ummm, caution and judicious observation."

"You snooped!"

"Snooped?" He nodded thoughtfully. "Aye, I suppose I did that. Forgive me. T'was only my concern for you that prompted it."

Summer looked away from him. Her mouth was stretched in a taut, miserable slash, and her tilted eyes were shuttered against him. He felt suddenly sorry that he'd snooped and even more sorry that he'd confessed to it.

"Come on, lass," he said to her. "Let's go."

Her lower lip quivered suspiciously. "Where? Where do I have to go? With you? With a man who's a snoop and a . . . a pirate? I don't think there's much of a future in that for me!"

Her scorn stung, and Jamie's mouth tightened. He eyed her hotly, and she took a wary step away from him. *Damn her.* Did he look that wicked a fellow? He must. She could certainly make him feel that way. He grabbed her wrist when she edged away and dragged her up against his hard body. His eyes burned into her face.

"I'm tempted tae just walk awa' frae ye, lass," he said in a thick brogue that betrayed his agitation. "If ye dinna like bein' wi' sich a hard mon, then ye should gang awa' wi' a mon wha' suits ye better!"

"Oh, speak English instead of that garble!" She hunched her shoulders, but her chin was tilted defiantly at him and his temper began to inexplicably cool.

"Don't insult my Scottish accent, lass."

"Is that what that is? I thought you had the heaves."

His brow shot up. "You're not very tactful, are you? It could become dangerous."

"I suppose you think I should cower in a corner because you're angry with me?" She shook back the loose strands of gold-and-brown-streaked hair from her face. "I'm used to men trying to intimidate me, Mister Cameron. I learned several years ago that I could cower or choose survival."

"And so you chose to alienate the only man who has been foolish enough to help you?" His mocking voice made her flush.

"I know you think I'm terrible, and maybe you're right," she said in that quick rush of words that she used when she was agitated, "but I don't think I can bear being abandoned again. Not unless it's my idea."

Surprised by this brutal honesty, Jamie found that his anger had completely disappeared. He hesitated. Should he offer to pay for her passage home? There was still the matter of what he wanted from her; what she'd offered to him only a few hours earlier with her lips and eyes.

He looked past her for a moment and thought of all that he had to do. He didn't have time for this. He had business responsibilities he might as well take care of since he was in London. His family would be wondering why he hadn't arrived yet.

Jamie remembered the feel of her soft mouth under his, and swallowed hard. *No contest.*

"Come on, lass. I'll take care of you until we find a way for you to go home."

Summer went with him as silently and meekly as a child who had just been rescued from a disaster of her own making; he didn't try to fool himself into believing that her docility would last.

Chapter 6

"I thought you had no money," Summer said with a slight frown as Jamie led her up a tight, narrow stairway of the inn where he had taken them a room. It was dimly lit and smelled of cooked cabbage, a stench that seemed to permeate even the dark wood paneling. Stairs creaked ominously underfoot, and there were vague scuffling noises in the shadows. The dingy ceilings were dark with smoke stains.

"I've a few crowns left," replied Jamie, pausing in front of a scarred door and frowning at it before reaching out to shove it open. Unoiled hinges creaked loudly.

Summer stepped close behind him, her face reflecting dismay at the tiny room. A sagging bed huddled in one corner under a window, and a rickety table held a cracked bowl and pitcher. The grate was dark and empty.

"Well," she said after a brief moment, her voice brisk and light, "this is better than sleeping in the alley."

Jamie's mouth curled in a smile. "Aye, lass, that it is," he agreed with only a trace of sarcasm. He swung the door shut and turned to watch her. She set her satchel on the bed and tested the mattress, her small face screwing into a frown that she quickly tried to hide. It was obvious that Mistress Summer was more used to fat feather beds than thin mattresses stuffed with corn husks. Had her lover been good to her before tiring of her?

His black brow quirked in a sardonic slant. Garth Kinnison, she'd said. Her fine lover who had abandoned her so ruthlessly.

Rubbing his thumb across his jaw, Jamie narrowed his eyes. Summer perched on the edge of the bed with her legs crossed at the ankles, graceful, her movements as fluid and practiced as the steps of a dancer; the small shake of her head to toss back gold-weaved strands of hair looked as calculated as the way she threaded her fingers together and made a steeple of them beneath her chin. Eyes of a deep, stabbing blue beneath curving black lashes gazed out the window at the shift of light and shadow on brick buildings across the street. Her posture was as vibrant as a painting by Caravaggio.

She was feminine, hurt, alone; much too vulnerable for him to take advantage. But he couldn't help the surge of pure lust that filled him when he looked at her.

Jamie unbuckled the light dress sword from around his waist. He unsheathed it and pretended to inspect the slender blade for nicks and scratches while he surveyed Summer. She didn't glance in his direction, but kept her gaze on the open window.

He gave a practice swing with the rapier, a controlled move that brought it in a glittering arc through the air. A rivulet of silvery light sparked from the lethal edge as it made a soft, singing sound that captured Summer's attention at last.

Pointing the tip of the thin blade toward the uneven boards of the floor, Jamie met her gaze and uplifted brow with a smile. "So, lass," he said in a deliberately idle tone that was meant to impart no special importance to his query, "what is your real name?"

She gave a start. "What do you mean? Summer is my real name."

"The only one you have?" His smile was a mere parody of patience, and he knew it.

He could see the doubt in her eyes, the hesitancy in her slowly tightening posture. She didn't want to tell him her name; she didn't trust him enough. It would have been obvious to a stone statue.

She turned her head and looked back out the window. Her gaze was fixed on a chimney swift clinging to the bricks on the outside wall, and she seemed to be struggling with herself. Then she looked back at him with a cool stare that mocked his curiosity.

"Smith. Summer Smith."

"Oh, aye. Smith." He made a vicious swipe with the fine rapier and saw her jump. "An unusual name, Smith. Are you by chance related to the Smiths of Northumbria? Sydney? No? Then perhaps you are—"

"I'm an American," she cut in coolly. "I have no English relatives."

"I believe we've already established that fact, lass. I just had the daft thought you might want to be honest with me for a change."

"I've been honest with you." Her gaze was bright with anger, and her small chin tilted at him stubbornly. "I've answered your questions truthfully."

"It's what you *don't* say that intrigues me most." Jamie met her hot blue gaze with a cool speculation. "And now that it seems as if we will be companions a bit longer, I'd the ridiculous notion you might want to end the farce."

The anger in her face altered slowly to uncertainty, and he gave his rapier another swash through the air before sheathing it again.

"Farce? I don't know what you mean, unless, of course, you are referring to this morning."

He felt the burn of anger. "Aye, that was a farce,

all right." He tossed the rapier to the surface of the small table with a clatter. "Perhaps we should deal more directly with one another, my fine lady."

Turning back to her, he stood with legs slightly spread and braced as if for battle, and the light breeze that wafted through the open window teased his ebony hair. He could almost feel her wary tension, and it didn't lighten his mood any.

"I want you," he said bluntly, and saw with a savage burst of pleasure the way her eyes widened, the pupils absorbing light in a rush. "I want to put myself inside you and stay there until you take a ship back to America. Is that too much to ask?"

"Apparently not for you." She stood up, and her hands shook slightly as she smoothed a deeply ingrained wrinkle from her skirt.

Jamie watched her throat work with silky ripples of muscle, and her voice was slightly quivery. She lifted her shoulders in a brief movement that lacked her previous grace; it was clumsy and nervous.

"All right," she said after a moment. "If that's what you want." She hesitated when he didn't say anything. "I'll bed you."

Jamie stared at her. Frankness worked more quickly than subtle seduction, after all. It certainly seemed to in this case. Had he known it was that easy, he would not have spent the previous night gathering oak splinters in his backside.

"Is that what you want, lass?" he couldn't help asking. Her reply reminded him that he frequently asked too many questions.

"No, but it does seem fair. After all, I owe you a heavy debt that I cannot repay now." She paused and sucked in a deep breath. "I do ask that you will help me find a way to secure passage home, in return for bedding you."

The mercenary little minx. Her putting it on the level of a business transaction certainly destroyed the mood.

He raked a hand through his hair and threw her a bitter glance. "And if I told you I had no money?"

He wanted to see what she'd say; he wanted her to *want* him. Was that too much to ask of her? Why not bed him for the simple reason that he was not an ill-favored fellow, and that she liked him? But he knew he would not say those things.

Summer looked away from him again and seemed to be studying the dark brown little swift that clung to the side of the wall outside. It darted away in flight suddenly, and she turned her face back to his narrowed gaze.

"I'll bed you anyway," she said. "Even if you cannot help me pay for my passage home."

Before that could go to his head however, she added in a determined voice, "I told you earlier that I know how much I owe you for your rescue of me."

"Yes," he said bluntly, "you do." *Damn her.* That cold professional purpose again. He couldn't understand how other men would want such chill commerce involved in what should be an episode of searing heat and driving passion. Sex would lose most of its erotic flavor if mired in such prosaic terms, it seemed. It certainly did now.

But he had asked her, and she had agreed. The only thing that seemed left to do was to embark on the finish to this odd vignette in his life and then forget it. And her. He'd put her on a damned ship back to America and go on to Scotland as he should already have done.

Shifting nervously from one foot to the other, Summer looked as if she were about to leap out the window after the chimney swift when Jamie took a step toward her. He paused and forced a grim smile.

"Not now, lass. Payment can be deferred until later. I think that we should inject a little ... romance into it, don't you?"

"Romance?" She looked at him as if he had two heads. "If you wish."

"I wish," he ground out from between his teeth, and wished that he'd never begun this ridiculous, humiliating charade. It was galling that she didn't seem to desire him in the least; it was acutely humbling that a woman of her experience would not even want him for a price. Or for gratitude. Not that he wanted her to want him for those reasons. He'd never been in the habit of thinking of reasons for wanting a woman or her wanting him. Now, since having had the extreme misfortune of meeting this tawny-haired chit with an alluring face and even more alluring body, he found himself in the disagreeable position of inventing reasons for bedding her.

The obvious one should be enough. Just thinking about it aroused him, and he was certain she would notice it if she only dared glance at him.

"What do you have in mind?" Summer asked after a moment of suffocating silence. "I mean"—she colored hotly—"how do you intend to invite romance when we have no money, and we are here?" She indicated the room with a wave of her hand.

He saw her point immediately. A dusty bottle of wine would hardly satisfy any female's idea of romance; not here in this room that reeked of cabbage and stale sweat. He hesitated, then gave a shrug.

"Have you ever been to Vauxhall Gardens? No, you could not have been," he answered his own question. "You said this was your first trip to London."

"And my last."

"Just so," he said politely. "Then you should see the Gardens. They're beautiful at night, and there is a replica of a miller's wheel that turns round and splashes water in a pretty display of bright lights— very impressive."

Summer sucked her bottom lip into her mouth in a move that was vaguely erotic, though she didn't seem to know it. "I don't have anything to wear to an elegant exhibition." She indicated her wrinkled gown with a twist of her hand. "This is hardly suitable."

"I think I can manage to rectify that." A spurt of wry amusement slanted his mouth in a smile. "Females do know how to beg quite prettily," he murmured.

She stiffened angrily. "I am *not* begging!"

"Fine. Suggesting, then." He gave an eloquent shrug. "Call it what you like. It sums up to the fact that we could both use some decent clothes."

Her foot tapped against the floor irritably. "And I suppose you've a fortune stashed away in your coat pocket?"

"No." His thick lashes veiled his eyes. "But I can get some quickly enough."

"Really?" She crossed her arms over her chest in a convulsive embrace and raked him with a scornful glance. "I find that difficult to believe after our pleasant journey up from Pyrford, when we were forced to ride atop the coach, and the wind and that insane coachman's whip almost peeled the skin from our faces!"

Stung, he glared at her. "It cost more than we had to ride inside, remember? And maybe I liked the thought of a little adventure. Or maybe I just wanted to see if you had any backbone." He was thoroughly insulted by her derisive tone, and her obvious disbelief in his abilities to provide for her.

"Adventure?" She laughed scornfully. "You just didn't have the money to pay for better. Not even your fine street singing would have earned the extra three crowns to ride in comfort, so what makes you think you can earn enough to buy us any clothes?"

"I don't think it," he growled, "I know it."

Picking up his sword again, he buckled it on, grimacing at the wary expression that flickered over her face. She looked at him nervously.

"What are you going to do?"

"Come along, my sweet, and you'll see."

"No. I have no desire to be embarrassed again by your silly caterwauling on public streets."

He glared at her. "What do you want me to do—
steal it for you? I suppose you think I'm Robin Hood?"

"Not hardly!" She gave an indignant sniff. "Robin
Hood was a gallant knight who knew how to treat a
lady. And how to provide for the poor. All you have
is a rusty sword." Her smile was nasty. "And an over-
abundance of larceny."

Jamie's temper flexed against iron restraint, and
he fought the urge to shake her hard. He should be
used to the way women did battle; hadn't his sisters
used the very same tactics time and again? His hand
closed around her wrist.

"I'll show you how to get money—*come on!*"

Summer resisted but quickly found herself bun-
dled down the cabbage-reeking stairway and out into
the streets. When Jamie pressed close, he felt her
shudder of apprehension. His stomach tightened with
irritation. She obviously thought he was prepared to
do murder for money.

He slanted her a fierce glance. Well, maybe he
would do something dangerous, he thought recklessly,
to prove to her that he could. And would. It would be
rather like fighting dragons for her—or tilting at
windmills—but it held a certain appeal to him in his
present frame of mind.

Maybe Miss Summer Whatever-her-name-was
needed to have proof of his prowess. Dammit, he
would show her that he had no trouble in providing
whatever they needed by his wit and his strength.
Then, perhaps, she would look at him with different
eyes.

Half dragging her cloak, Summer trotted to keep
up with Jamie's long-legged strides. He was in a temper; she had seen the flash of fury in his eyes when
she'd mocked him, but what did he expect? Now she
began to wish she hadn't been quite so snappish. He

was apparently about to do something quite foolish to prove her wrong.

Jamie walked swiftly, winding through the crowded streets and pulling Summer with him. He led her to the mouth of a shadowy alley between two leaning buildings.

"What are you doing?" she began, but he quickly motioned her to silence.

"Just stand and watch, milady."

There was something in his tone and his taut stance that alerted her to danger. Her scalp prickled, and she curled her fingers into the damp brick of the building.

"I will never forgive you if you do something rash," she began in a hiss, but his hand flashed out to curl tightly around her wrist. He quieted her with a look from beneath his brow, and she sputtered into silence.

He was a madman. An utterly deranged lunatic who would get them both into prison. Or at the end of a hangman's noose. She knew it. There was something too predatory about the way he stood at the mouth of the alley watching people pass within a few feet of them. What did he mean to do? Hit some unfortunate soul on the head and take his purse?

She felt the muscles in Jamie's hip and thigh tense, and her heart slammed against her ribs as he took several steps forward. Now he stood just beyond the opening to the alley. His stance radiated danger; his legs were spread, and he balanced lightly on his feet. He'd drawn his sword, and it filled his right fist. The long, thin blade glittered in the hazy shaft of light that penetrated the lowering gloom of tall buildings and narrow, twisting alleys.

Summer smothered the whimper in the back of her throat. She was no idiot. If Jamie was caught, she was just as guilty as he was, no matter that she'd hung back and not helped in whatever madness he had planned.

The alley stank of refuse and decay, and behind

her in the tottering pile of trash and garbage, a rat
squealed. It was answered by a snarl and rolling growl,
and Summer dug her fingers into the brick wall and
edged forward. Rats. She'd always hated the red-eyed,
vicious little vermin, and now she was standing ankle-
deep in the ooze and slime of an alley in St. Giles
rookery and listening to them battle over some forgotten scrap of rubbish.

Then there was no more time to worry about the
rats or anything else; instead, she saw the shadow of
prison or execution loom over her when Jamie lunged
forward.

She didn't hear what he said, only saw the flash of
his blade and the quick response from his victim. Her
throat clenched in a spasm of fear; what if he was
killed? What would become of her? Dear Lord, she'd
allowed herself to be drawn into another nightmare.

Jamie's victim looked quite capable of inflicting as
much injury as the villain. He was tall, whip-thin, and
handled his sword as expertly as his assailant. Summer winced at the clash of blades, the metallic ringing
slicing through the air with deadly intent. The stranger
met the cool thrusts of Jamie's blade with an efficient
parrying that was evidence of skill even to Summer's
novice gaze. She flinched again when Jamie darted
beneath a lethal lunge in a sinuous twist of his long
body.

He presented a much larger target; he was taller
than the man he'd attacked, and his shoulders were
broader. Why hadn't the idiot chosen a small man
who looked clumsy, if he had to be so foolish?

Her hands clasped together fitfully, opening and
closing on the folds of her skirt in a compulsive movement that she didn't notice. Her bare arm grazed the
damp brick of the alley and left a long scratch on her
forearm, but she did not notice that, either.

To Summer's untrained eyes, the fierce duel
looked to be closely matched and lethal. She literally
wrung her hands with fear for Jamie before she began

to notice how easily he moved about the other man, how deftly he evaded his thrusts, while he delivered blows that drove his opponent steadily back against the wall. She caught her breath as the two men drew closer to her; sweat streamed down the stranger's face, dripping into his eyes and wetting his neckcloth. He stumbled once, an almost fatal error, and Jamie laughed softly.

Summer looked at Jamie. In the hazy light and with his one black brow drawn down over eyes as dark as midnight, he made her think of fabled villains: Jean Laffite, noted pirate and rakish buccaneer, and maybe Sir Henry Morgan, an English pirate from a distant century. Jamie looked perfectly capable at that moment of dispatching his victim as easily as any self-respecting villain would have done.

Her throat clutched. She slid a gaze toward the street. Could she make it without being seen? Or distracting Jamie? The urge to flee was almost overpowering, and she poised on her toes indecisively.

Then she saw Jamie's sword tip slide up and under his opponent's guard to catch his sword beneath the hilt and send it flying. It clattered to the stones, and the two men stood looking at each other and breathing hard.

Jamie spoke first.

"Fairly fought, sir. And now I'll have your purse."

His victim swore long and viciously but reached for his purse. He tossed it to Jamie with a snarl.

"The Charlies will be on you before you get down the street, you blackguard!"

Laughing, Jamie caught the purse in his free hand. A wicked grin squared his mouth. "Those sluggards? I don't think so. Have you seen a one of them come to investigate the noise? Nay, sir, and you won't. The watchmen are too scared to come into this section of town, but not you fine bucks who search for ways to ease your ennui."

Summer saw from the man's face that he would

have liked to kill Jamie, and she clung weakly to the brick wall and tried to keep from being noticed.

"Damn you!" the man grated from between his teeth. His cravat was limp and untied, and there was a long rent in the superfine material of his coat, but he was unharmed and very unhappy. "Whoreson! Scurvy bastard!"

"Tut tut, sir. Such language. You insult me." He smiled at the splutter of incoherent oaths that followed. "And now, if you please, I would like to know the name of the man who gave me such poor sport this evening."

The tip of Jamie's sword wavered between them, and when the man pressed his lips together and glared at Jamie, it moved forward to nudge the thick folds of his neckcloth.

"Your name, please," Jamie repeated softly, and Summer wanted to scream at him to just take the stupid money and run before he was caught. Daylight would be gone soon, and there were no lamps in this section of town to cleave the murky gloom of night should they be caught here.

After a pulse beat and the slightly increased pressure of the blade against his neckcloth, the defeated buck muttered in a tight voice, "Kenworth."

Jamie's brow rose, and he immediately slackened the sword's pressure on the man's throat. "Not Lord Kenworth of Arlington Street, Mayfair, perchance?"

A furious glitter and spare nod was his answer, and Jamie laughed. " 'Pon rep, Geordie, what do you in the stews of St. Giles?" Silence and a narrowed gaze was his answer, and he took a step away from Kenworth into the deeper shadows. "Shouldn't you be in Covet Garden surveying the nuns of some bloated abbess?" Amused mockery threaded his voice, and Kenworth flushed.

"You'll pay for this, you whoreson!"

"If I do," Jamie said with a mock bow, "it will be with your money, sir. My felicitations to you. And just so that you do not pursue me too closely, for a moment...." The tip of his sword flicked out so swiftly it was a blur, and when Jamie stepped back again, Kenworth's snug-fitting breeches were in sagging tatters that revealed much more than he would want to parade down crowded streets.

Summer could barely move when Jamie darted into the shadows where she stood and took her by one hand, half-dragging her with him toward the far end of the alley. She recalled the rats, and resisted.

"No! Not that way—"

He gave her a sharp tug, and his voice was harsh. "Do you want to run straight into the arms of the Charlies, my sweet? I don't. Don't be stubborn now. Your moment will come later."

She didn't ask him what he meant but stumbled blindly after him. Shuddering as they dodged piles of decaying food where beggars picked edible scraps with furtive gestures, she had only a vague impression of snoring drunks lying in filthy gutters, small children tugging at the skirts of their drunken, slatternly mothers, and rib-thin shadows with huge, burning eyes staring at her from the darkness.

"Don't look anywhere but ahead," Jamie warned her. "Or I might end up fighting again."

She believed him. And when they finally emerged into the daylight and she sucked in a deep breath of air that she had earlier considered tainted, she felt suddenly free.

Jerking away from him, she met his gaze when he stopped and looked down at her. "Some Robin Hood you are!"

A faint smile crooked his mouth. "I take it, lass, that you are unhappy about my method of obtaining enough money to purchase you a fine new gown?"

"I consider you a dangerous maniac!"

"No more maniacal than a female who proposes to gambol about London alone, I would say," he returned coolly.

She bit her lip sharply to keep from blurting out the harsh words on the tip of her tongue. After all, he *was* her only protection in a city too wicked and depraved for any lone woman to survive.

"I see that you have decided prudence is a wise course." He gave a nod of satisfaction. "Very commendable. And now, milady, we shall purchase your apparel for this evening. It must be as special as its wearer."

In a tight, furious voice she choked out, "I cannot wear clothes purchased with stolen money."

His palm cupped her chin, and she could almost feel the rattle of amusement in his touch. "But you will. It's part of the bargain you made with the devil."

Summer had the despairing thought that he had certainly named their agreement aptly. She had sold her body to a man who appeared to be a collector. But was that very different from offering herself to Garth? She'd done that, though he hadn't wanted it. And that, too, had left her feeling used and bruised.

"I wonder," she said, looking up into his handsome face, "if you will find the bargain worth your time in the end."

"I trust very much that I will, my sweet, or I would not have made it."

"No, I don't suppose you would allow yourself to be cheated," she murmured with a faint smile. "You strike me as a man who demands full payment of a debt."

"Aye, lass," he said softly. "But I also repay my debts in full. It might serve you well to put me in *your* debt."

She looked away from that compelling midnight gaze. "I don't know how you expect me to accomplish anything like that," she muttered.

He laughed. "Lass, women have always found ways to put a man so deep in their debt he can never shake free."

She thought about that later and remembered something Chantal had once said to her.

"A mon, *caree*, him don' a'ways think with him head like the womon mus' when it come to love. No-no, at such a time mos' ev'ry mon be too busy thinkin' with parts of him body that wa'nt meant for it. Think you that it could be a useful thin' to know, hmmm?"

Summer sighed. It certainly was. Maybe if Jamie was in her debt, she wouldn't feel so vulnerable. The only trouble was, she knew that where he was concerned, she had very little control over her reactions.

Chapter 7

"How do I look in my stolen finery?" Summer pirouetted gracefully, and the hem of her skirts flowed around her ankles. She felt Jamie looking at her from across their room at the inn, and a hot, burning flush began low in the pit of her stomach. She shouldn't have teased him. His velvety dark gaze brushed over her so intently that she almost felt it.

"More lovely than I thought possible, lass." His smile mocked her sarcasm. "Even in stolen finery."

She looked away from him. "This isn't right."

"Even for Robin Hood? We stole from the rich to give to the poor, remember? And we gave most of it to those hungry urchins for food. Kenworth should be pleased to have his money go to such a good cause." Jamie laughed. "He won't be pleased, but he should be. I'll pay him back, if you like."

"With what? He had a *lot* of money in that purse."

"Not as much as he's lost in a single hand of macao, I'd wager," Jamie muttered. He straightened. "Forget Kenworth and his bloody purse. Do I look like a rogue or a man of the world?"

"A rogue, of course. But a well-dressed one. All right, you strutting peacock, you don't look bad at all," she said quickly when he took a step toward her.

Jamie grinned. "No, I don't, do I?"

"And so modest too!"

"All life's virtues rolled into one man, my sweet."
He gave a flick of his wrist, and linen cuffs fell over
his lean brown hands in a spill of white lace. More
ruffles frothed from the deep vee of his quilted waistcoat embroidered with gold threads, and his snowy
cravat was tied with careless perfection around his
neck. The dark navy coat of superfine fit superbly
across his broad shoulders, and his tight fawn pantaloons ended in the tops of high, gleaming black boots.

Such a combination of clothes would have been
quite presentable on almost any man; on James Cameron, it was devastating. Sable hair brushed his forehead in neatly trimmed locks and flowed over his ears
and high collar in the back; he'd shaved, leaving only
inch-wide strips of whiskers in front of his ears and
scraping away the rough stubble that had darkened
his jaw. Now he looked more civilized; until she
glanced into his eyes and saw the devilish lights glowing like dark star-fire.

Summer's throat tightened in spite of herself, but
she had no intention of playing his game. Not by his
rules. It was bad enough that she'd agreed to sell herself, but the thought of having to compliment her pur-
chaser was too galling to swallow.

"So, madam?" he said when she remained silent
and still. "Do I pass your inspection?"

"It's quite obvious to me that someone has spoiled
and petted you shamelessly."

"Is that any way to talk to a man who bought you
finery like this?" he teased. "Come, lass—I'd have a
compliment or two to warm my heart."

"I have no intention of adding or detracting from
your already ruinous vanity," Summer retorted. She
smoothed the skirts of her new gown with an awkward
gesture when he just smiled. She looked out the window at the fading light of day and tried to ignore him,
but he wouldn't let her.

He reached out and took one hand, then the other, lifting her arms wide. "I don't mind adding to your already overweening vanity a bit, lass. You're beautiful. Not that you weren't before, but there's something about wearing a new gown that adds a certain spark to a woman."

"How observant you are!" She knew her voice was tart and didn't care. Hadn't he done enough? He'd risked not only his life today, but hers. And all for a few pounds and some new finery that would be shabby and worn within a few months.

"I should be observant," Jamie said, and she squirmed at the drift of his eyes over her low, square-cut bodice that had no saving grace of lace to hide the swell of her breasts. Somehow, the sheer fichu that had come with the stark white muslin gown had become lost. Or thrown away.

Jamie's gaze lifted to her face. "And I know better than *not* to notice new feminine finery—and the lovely form it graces. I've no desire to listen to complaints of injured feelings the rest of the night because I didn't make just the right compliments."

Forgetting that she had just pinned her hair up into silky ringlets atop her crown, she tossed her head back and stared up at him.

"What makes you so knowledgeable about females, may I ask? Or do I have to?"

Shrugging, he said in a light, laughing voice, "I have five sisters. I should know everything there is about the predilections and complaints of females from infancy to adolescence."

"Five sisters?" She shook her head disbelievingly. "You must be the only son. Which, of course, explains why you are so spoiled." She was doomed to disappointment with that theory.

He grinned. "Hardly. I'm the fourth of six sons."

"*Dear Lord!* Your poor parents!"

"They've borne up well." Jamie released one of her arms and gave her a small twirl. Her long skirt belled out, and Summer felt a whisper of air tickle her knees. White silk stockings so sheer as to be almost nonexistent skimmed her legs; the new kid slippers matched the simple white gown that was caught just beneath her breasts with a blue satin ribbon.

When she looked at Jamie's face, she saw the flare of light in his eyes and searched frantically for the thread of their conversation. Sisters. Brothers—ah! Parents.

"So, your parents are still alive, then?"

"Yes." Jamie looked out the window. "The sun will set soon. I'd like you to see the Gardens before it grows too dark."

Feeling slightly disappointed by his avoidance of more personal conversation, Summer stood still while he draped a light shawl over her shoulders. His hands brushed her arms in a soft caress, and she shivered.

"Ready, lass?" He held out his arm, and after an almost imperceptible hesitation, she laid her fingers on his sleeve and allowed him to escort her out the door and down the stairs as if she were a queen.

Vauxhall Gardens was a delight. It had first opened in 1661, when it could be reached only by means of boat; the lush gardens had survived in popularity primarily because of an ever-changing variety of amusements—and the prime lure of vaguely illicit paths through mazes of thick bushes that provided shadowed alcoves. The latter, of course, titillated young lovers' imaginations . . . and a great deal more.

Jamie had always found the Gardens lovely, but lacking in fascination for him. If he wanted to flirt in the moonlight, he could always do so with much more privacy than the crowded walks the Gardens provided. But somehow he had sensed that Summer would be enchanted, and so he had suggested it as his concession to romance.

Romance. What a foolish notion. It had very little

to do with what he had planned, but it had been obvious to him that Summer would cling to her professional pose until he lost interest if he didn't do something about it.

The trick with the duel in the stinking alleys of St. Giles had been pure temper. He was half-ashamed of himself for yielding to anger and the smothering desire to see Miss Summer's arrogant composure crack. How had she been so damn sure he couldn't provide for her? And then to compare him so unfavorably to Robin Hood—no, she had deserved a comeuppance, even if he had got carried away.

Now he had to send Lord Kenworth back a full purse in the morning. It was only fair. He'd just stood there in the alley and waited for the first man with a sword and a half-good arm to pass by. Kenworth—fribble though he might be—did not deserve to lose his purse for the sake of impressing a woman, no matter how lovely.

Jamie had the glum thought his father had been right; the elder Cameron had frequently predicted ruin for his most rebellious son and snorted that he'd probably hang as a highwayman one day, just for the sheer devil of it.

Well, the devil had got into him, all right, and he had risked all to see wide bluebell eyes fill with scared admiration. It had almost worked. Almost.

Summer had been scared, but Jamie'd seen bloody little evidence that he'd impressed her with his swordplay or his daring. And he couldn't say he blamed her. It'd been a damn fool trick, and he didn't know what had made him do it.

Well, it was over now, and they were at the Gardens. Summer was clinging to his arm and gazing around with shining eyes, and later he would take her back to the shabby little inn and do what he'd been wanting to do for two days.

"Where's the music coming from?" Summer's fingers nudged his arm. "I hear it, but I don't see it."

"The Grove. It's down the Grand Walk, where it bisects with the South and Cross Walk, and forms a large area with trees. Musicians play in the orchestra pavilion there. Hook plays a lot, and sometimes Haydn." He shrugged. "On some nights there are masquerades, when everyone comes in mask and costume."

"And you find it all quite boring." Her voice quivered with irritation. "I can tell by your tone of voice, and you think you are being very kind and condescending to bring me here."

"Kind, yes. Not condescending." He looked down at her upturned face and smiled. "You can be alarmingly blunt at times, my sweet."

"Can I? I thought that was what you preferred." Her hand tightened slightly on his arm. "After your speech earlier today, and the charade that has already been played between us, I thought frankness would be a welcome change."

His brow snapped down, and he closed one hand around her arm just above the elbow.

A less-crowded walk stretched in a parallel line to the graveled walk they were on, and Jamie steered her in that direction. Music crashed in the background, a stirring piece that sounded more like a call to arms than anything remotely romantic. Laughter mixed with the babble of loud conversation around them and faded some as they drifted farther away from the crowd. Jamie put his hand in the small of Summer's back and gently turned her to face him when they reached an archway that featured a realistic painting of Mediterranean ruins.

"Frankness would be a splendid change," he said. "Let's see if we can manage it without coming to blows."

Smoky shades of doubt clouded her eyes, and in the dusk lit by hundreds of hanging lamps, Jamie saw confusion shimmer on her face just like the multicolored glow of lantern light.

"Are we referring to anything in particular?" she asked in a wary voice.

Smothering his impulse to laugh—she would only think it was at her and not the absurdity of the situation—Jamie lifted his brow. "Several things in particular."

"I've lost the inclination, I'm afraid." She smiled at him brightly. "Sorry."

He tucked his fingers under her chin. This was not going at all well. How did he ask her about herself without looking as though it mattered? And why didn't she offer him the information? She already knew more about him than he did her, and he was damned if he knew why. It certainly wasn't because he hadn't asked a hundred times.

"Tell me about Captain Kinnison," he said, and let his hand fall away from her face.

"Garth?" She seemed startled. "How do you know his name?"

"You mentioned it earlier. At the shipping office." He smiled. "An obvious oversight on your part, I see. 'Twas because you were upset, I suppose."

"Yes," she muttered. "I was."

"Do you love him?"

She gave a start. "My, we *are* aiming for frankness tonight, aren't we! Why didn't you tell me that the price of admission to Vauxhall Gardens was three shillings, ten truths? It's too much to pay."

"Bitter little thing, aren't you?"

"It's hard not to be lately." This last was said with a thick sigh that made his mouth tighten.

"Don't you ever look on the bright side of things, my sweet? After all, you found a protector, and I've offered to help get you home. It's more than most lasses find when they're stranded in London, I'll warrant."

Her bright head shook slightly. "I suppose I do sound rather greedy, don't I? It's just that I had all these high ideals at one time, and it seems as if life has taken them all away and left me little in return." A faint smile curved her lips, and he wondered if she'd let him taste the promise of them before she shifted away from him.

Summer reached out and stripped a slender branch of its leaves. The stacked leaves formed the shape of a flower in her fingers, green and shiny; she squeezed them between her thumb and forefinger, and the illusion exploded in a shower of small petals over the walk.

"Well," she said, dusting her hands together, "I seem to spend all my time complaining lately."

"I've noticed that," he said dryly. "Is it a family affliction?"

She couldn't help a little laugh that was almost a sob. "It must be. My father used to say that we were all doomsayers! Except for my brother, and he was so young I don't suppose he ever thought about much beyond ingesting his name in alphabet tiles."

"Not much laughter in your life then, lass?" Jamie propped a boot on the seat of a stone bench and looked at her.

"Enough. Sometimes, when I think back, it seems that we were always laughing—and sometimes, I think only of the times we didn't." She shrugged. "It's been a long time since there was much room for it in my life."

"Is that where Kinnison fits in?"

She eyed him warily, and he could see the consternation in the clean, pure lines of her face. Her lips quivered slightly. He started to change the subject, then decided not to. He wasn't that generous. By God, she *owed* him some answers.

Letting out her breath in an explosive little sigh, she shook back the gilt strands of hair that had strayed into her eyes. "I suppose. Except that I've loved him since I was ten. Or maybe only thirteen. He seemed too unattainable at first."

"That's a long time for a love affair." His lips flattened into a smile when she glanced at him sharply.

"Really! I meant, of course, platonic devotion!"

"I would think so. Ten is rather precocious, even for an American."

Summer dug the toe of her shoe into the gravel of the walk in an industrious effort to form small hills, and watched her handiwork with rapt attention. Then she lowered the flat of her foot and smoothed it out with a crunch.

"I thought Garth cared more about me than he did. It was my mistake." The deep blue of her eyes was smoky with a pain he could empathize with, but he said nothing. She looked up and beyond him, fixing her gaze in the distance. "At first, you see, he viewed me as a rather skinny, clumsy little girl with tangled hair and freckles. Then, as I grew up a little, he withdrew from me. Sort of an acknowledgment of the changes taking place in my body, I suppose."

A faint smile tugged at the corners of her mouth. Her slender fingers toyed with the dangling ribbons that caught her dress beneath her breasts.

"That does happen, I'm afraid," Jamie said when it seemed as if she expected some sort of response. "I had a fervent case of raging love for the wife of one of my father's friends when I was eleven. She thought me cute and adorable until I reached fifteen and six feet in height. Then it was not so cute anymore, and my father took me aside and told me that if I didn't stop tagging after her, I'd find myself facing the business end of her husband's sword. It was a crushing blow."

"It's very difficult for me to imagine you being crushed by a refusal," Summer said with a lift of her delicate brows. "I would think you would just do what you wanted and whisk her away."

Jamie had no intention of telling her that when he had reached twenty, he had consummated his infatuation with the then-widowed Lady Elgin. Somehow, it didn't seem pertinent to the moment.

"Is that what you did?" he asked Summer. "Run away with your handsome captain?"

She hesitated before saying, "In a way. It was sort of an accident."

Jamie could just imagine the sort of accident she meant. He'd had experience with young women who managed to find themselves in his bed, and not a one of those episodes had ever brought him anything but trouble. Strong-minded females set on capturing a man's interest could stir up a hornet's nest no male could ever imagine. He almost felt sorry for this Garth Kinnison.

Until he looked at Summer's miserable face and thought of her being stranded in a foreign land with no more ado than the shedding of an ill-fitting coat. A hefty purse, the careless arrangement of passage home, then forgotten. At least he had always ended his affairs with finesse when possible and had never just sent a lass on her way with a pat on the bottom and cheery farewell.

He looked at her tight expression and put his hand over hers. "You're shredding your sash." Her fingers grew still. "So, here you are, and you're still in love with the bonny lad who left you behind."

Summer sucked in her breath sharply. She didn't deny it or confirm it. Her smile was bitter when she said, "I've been disillusioned."

"Ah. Disillusion. A devastating slap in the face, isn't it?"

"I daresay you've never experienced it," Summer shot at him with a quick flash of her eyes. "You're too cocky and arrogant to have been annihilated by that particular emotion!"

"Am I?" He shook his head. "Appearances can be so deceiving, lass. I found myself to be quite disillusioned the first time I faced a complete stranger who wanted nothing more than to slice me to ribbons simply because I happened to be wearing a different uniform. War had always been romanticized, you see, and where I was reared, it was common to go reiving of a night. There were always a few skirmishes to get the blood boiling, but with men who were my neighbors. Sort of a friendly warfare." He shrugged. "There was nothing friendly about fighting the French."

"I know it was horrible, but that's a different kind of disillusionment."

"Is it?" He pushed slightly at the seat of the stone bench with his foot, and it rocked beneath his boot. "Not so different, lass. Disillusionment may come in different forms, but all of them make a person feel rotten."

Summer gripped the edges of the Kashmir shawl draped over her shoulders and drew it more closely around her. It was a bright saffron, providing a vivid contrast to her stark white muslin dress.

"So," she said lightly, "now you know what you wanted to know. I'm a cast-off female, jilted and deserted, and at your mercy. And you promised me romance and entertainment this evening, not a prolonged discussion of disappointments in love."

"Aye, lass, you're right." Jamie straightened. Then he leaned forward and brushed his lips lightly over Summer's in a startling kiss. His eyes burned into her when he drew back. Her lips were still half-parted with surprise, and the long wings of her lashes had lifted to afford him a glimpse of something warm in her eyes.

"I'm not the kind of man to leave a lass stranded," he said softly. "You can trust me."

"I think," Summer said slowly, "that it's myself I cannot trust, sir."

It was a very promising start for the evening, Jamie thought with heightened anticipation. Very promising.

The graveled pathways were even more crowded when they left the secluded offshoot. Dusk hovered ever lower, and the Chinese lanterns glowed like colorful fireflies.

Summer shivered as shadows grew deeper and the sun no longer warmed the air. With the breeze drifting off the water, it was cooler here than in the city, and she was glad she had worn the yellow shawl. She pulled it more closely around her and tried not to think about later.

"Punch, lass?" Jamie asked, and she nodded. Anything to warm her, give her courage to face what lay ahead. Or was she only fooling herself? Somehow, she knew that James Cameron would not force her if she did not want to keep the bargain she'd made. Maybe it was pride that kept her resolved.

Or maybe it's because he started a fire that can't be ignored....

Jamie returned with the cup of arrack punch and pressed it into her hands. Tipping the small cup, she drank deeply. It was potent, more potent than she'd realized it would be. She choked slightly, and with an amused lift of his brow that made her want to pinch him, Jamie gave her a helpful slap between her shoulder blades that nearly dislodged her ribs.

"Better now?" he asked solicitously.

She shrugged from under his hand. "I think I'll live."

"A comforting knowledge, I vow."

"Do you enjoy deviling me?" Summer asked abruptly. "Or do you just have a fiendish sense of humor?"

Dancing lights sparked in the lustrous black depths of his eyes, and he was grinning when he asked in an innocent tone that wouldn't have fooled a flea, "Do you think I would take pleasure in the misfortunes of others, lass? I'm wounded that you think so little of me."

"The devil you are!" Summer felt her frustration at her circumstances well higher. She wanted to return his easy quips with the same light air he possessed, but she couldn't. Her emotions were in too much of a turmoil to let anything resembling weakness seep in under her guard.

"You're right," Jamie said, and she gave an annoyed shake of her head when he added lightly, "I revel in the black rites. I dabble with demons. I like seeing you glare at me." He took her hand in his. "Come on, lass. The world won't come to an end if you enjoy yourself."

She jerked her hand away. "Maybe not your world. I have come too close to it in mine." Her throat ached with what she didn't say, what she couldn't say. A man like this one would not understand. He'd never been buffeted about by the winds of change; he still had his siblings and parents. What could he know of loss? Of an uncle who would sell his country like Esau's birthright? And his niece as well?

I crave the wench in my bed.

God, those words would haunt her forever. And then, when she had sought comfort and security with the only source available, she'd been turned away with callous efficiency.

"Summer."

Looking up, she realized she'd loosened her grip on her cup of punch, and it had spilled onto the grass.

Jamie took it from her loose clasp. "Maybe you'd prefer some spiced wine," he said, and when she nodded, he added, "It's not as strong. There are supper boxes in the Grove, if you would like to eat."

"What is a supper box?"

"A small alcove with a table, chairs, and exorbitantly priced food. It has privacy curtains, whimsical paintings in oil, and stains on the carpets." He lifted a brow. "Some of the origins of which are rather sordid, I fear."

"You make the supper boxes sound delightful."

"Don't I?" He curled his fingers around her wrist in a grip that did not suggest he'd let her go. "Come along, Lady Summer. I intend to show you how to play of a fine spring evening. It will be good for you."

"I dare suggest that your notion of what is good for me is at variance with mine," Summer said, but did not try to pull away from him.

It was just as well. When they strolled down the Grand Walk, it had grown much more crowded. Wild young bloods roamed the byways, searching for fair game. These nattily dressed young men thought nothing of blatantly and embarrassingly ogling any female who took their fancy and did so to their own amusement.

Summer was more annoyed than amused to find herself the object of such attention and refused to acknowledge any of the attempts to catch her eye.

"Aren't you going to do anything?" she demanded when one particularly aggressive young man was actually bold enough to blow her a kiss.

"Why should I?" Jamie looked at her with an indulgent expression. "As long as these coxcombs keep their distance, they can admire you all they want. Besides, they're only foxed and probably trying to annoy both of us."

"Well, it's halfway working. *I'm* annoyed." She stifled a surge of resentment when he laughed.

"You're just cranky. You'll feel better after you've eaten."

But when they had eaten baked ham sliced as thin as parchment and an assortment of biscuits, cheesecakes, and fresh fruit, she was still out of sorts. It could have been because Jamie had insisted upon hand-feeding her the ripe strawberries until the sticky juice ran down her chin in runnels of red. She wiped at it with a napkin.

"You look as if you're wearing paint," he said with a laugh, and did not seem to mind at all when she glared at him.

"I would be if I had any."

"No! Are you one of those females who smears that

horrid concoction of mercury and lead over her face?"
He shook his head. "You'll die young, my sweet. The
stuff's deadly poison."

She looked at him a little uncertainly. "I use a little
rice powder, carmine, and on occasion, a Turkish
tincture around my eyes."

"A waste of time. You hardly need any of those
cheap artifices."

"Aren't you the gallant, now."

Clasping her hand in his, Jamie ignored her attempt to pull it away. His lips thinned slightly with
his smile as he held her jerking hand, and his sable
eyes danced with wicked delight when she snapped a
curse at him.

"Such language, my lady. Shall I throw open the
drapes so that you may shout it to the world?"

She stared at him coldly. "I don't really care. You
might as well. This box smells of stale perfume and
unwashed Englishmen."

"Maybe you should shout that to the world."

"Maybe I should!"

Leaning back in the cushioned chair, Jamie flicked
back the edge of a stained curtain and a rush of fresh
air filled the stuffy box. It was on the bottom tier, and
anyone passing by could easily see the occupants.

Summer flashed Jamie a glowering look. He smiled
at her. "If you're not having a nice evening, we can
always return to the inn," he said in a silky tone that
made her stiffen.

Her throat tightened, and she stared past Jamie to
the crowd of elegantly garbed guests of the Gardens.
Glittering lanterns swayed in the trees and along the
paths, and the music still throbbed, though she could
barely hear it above the noise of the crowd.

She knew quite well what Jamie meant; she was
well aware of the subdued sensuality in him, the
hooded glances and soft caress, the slight touch of his
hand on her cheek at times. He made her think of a

patient tiger. It unnerved her. It terrified her. It intrigued her. She swallowed and looked back at him.

He seemed to be waiting with polite attention, but she saw the brief leaping flare in his black eyes that told her he was only waiting for the evening to pass. He'd been the perfect gentleman, teased her gallantly, bought her whatever her heart desired; but he was waiting until they returned to the inn for his pleasure to begin.

"I'd like to see the Cascade," she said after a moment, and knew he was probably amused by her reply. Procrastination was not usually successful, and she knew that well enough, but she just couldn't bring herself to go back yet. Not yet.

If he was amused, he didn't show it. "At your pleasure, my sweet," he said languidly, and leaned back in his chair to gaze out at the crowd with a bored stare. "It does not begin until nine o'clock. When you've had enough of the Grove, I can show you the other interests in the Gardens," he offered after a moment, and Summer accepted this gladly.

"I'd like that. And I think I've had enough of the Grove now."

He pushed away from the linen-draped table and stood up, holding out his hand for her. When she put her fingers into his palm, she felt a small jolt grate along her arm at the touch.

"I'm not what you may think me," Jamie said with a kind of baffled look when she jerked away from him. The sensual glint in his eyes had been replaced by puzzled curiosity. It was obvious he didn't know what to make of her skittish reactions to him; that was fine. She didn't either.

"Lord, sir, I should hope not!" she managed to say with just the right touch of flippancy. It worked. He laughed.

"Maybe I should have said that I am what you think me. Women seem to prefer rogues."

"That would explain your popularity then." Summer let her eyes meet his long enough to feel it all the way to her toes.

"Look at me like that again, lass," Jamie said in a rich purr that made her breath grow tight in her chest, "and I will forget about Vauxhall and kiss you until you swoon."

"I never swoon," she said promptly.

"Shall we give it a try?" He took a step closer to her, and Summer danced lightly away.

"Later, perhaps. In the meantime, sir, I believe you promised me laughter and romance. Shall we seek it?"

For the first time that evening, she felt in control. It was vastly comforting. She had no intention of letting him know the havoc he wrought with her senses. He was too conceited by half already. She stuffed her irritation with life and with this impetuous rogue into the back of her mind and strolled the Gardens with him.

They ambled along the Hermit's walk, where a tangled growth of trees and bushes bounded one side and sloping downs the other. Silvery moonlight mixed with the lantern glow in a pretty collage of erratic light, but it was dim and shadowed in places. Faint squeals of laughter drifted on the air.

"Lovers' Walk," Jamie said. "It's dark there, with paths so close it's hard to walk but easy to embrace."

"Hence the name," she said dryly, and he nodded. In the wash of moonlight his hair looked as polished as a mirror, reflecting splinters of silvery gleams like trapped fireflies. She was tempted to touch it.

"Shall we test the rumors of passion found between the hedges?" Jamie murmured. He caught her hand and brought it up to his mouth. His lips grazed her skin and made it vibrate with reaction.

"Just rumors?" she managed to say calmly. "No anxious mamas crying foul after a night at the Gardens?"

"More than a few, my sweet, more than a few."

Summer leaned into him when he urged her closer;

she spread her hand against his chest and felt his heart beat with strong, steady thuds. He smelled of fresh air and soap, and that personal masculine fragrance that was uniquely his. It was arousing.

When he tilted back her head with his finger hooking just beneath her chin, she was waiting for his kiss. It was inevitable. She'd been waiting for it since the last time he'd held her this way and hadn't known it until now.

He didn't kiss her mouth at first. Instead, he brushed his lips over the line of her brow, then skimmed the high curve of her cheek. His fingers worked the quivering column of her throat with smooth, circular strokes, playing lightly over her skin. When his head bent, silhouetted against the swaying collage of lights behind him, Summer closed her eyes and surrendered to his kiss.

Parting her lips with his tongue, Jamie flicked it in enticing teases against the velvety inside of her bottom lip, sliding it in and out with steamy strokes that made her want to open to him. Then he breathed in, taking her tongue inside his mouth, pulsing in increasing rhythm.

It was arousing, making her ache inside, urging her closer to him, and she put her arms around his lean waist to hold him. Her head spun. Jamie was the only stability in a reeling world. Nothing seemed the same when he held her like this. Nothing. Not even herself. Especially herself. She didn't *know* herself anymore. The old Summer would not have done this.

But this new Summer, this empty, hollow Summer who could not feel anything but tangibles, had given her trust to this tall, dark rogue who swung from madness to savagery with remarkable agility.

One moment he was fairly sane; he spoke lucidly, made decent promises. The next moment, he was a satanic thief in a St. Giles alley, using his sword with startling ferocity. And she had agreed to sleep with him. She was as mad as he.

Jamie's breath was coming quickly, and his arms went around her to pull her closer into him, curling her body into the hard angle of his with a groan. He lifted his head and looked down at her when she shuddered against him.

"We canna stay here, lass," he said in that thick burr he seemed to use mainly in moments of stress. "Not like this."

"No," she agreed in a husky whisper, "not like this."

"I think it's time we left."

She nodded, not trusting herself to speak.

His voice was faintly wry when he said, "You'll have to give me a moment to recover before I go into the light."

Summer didn't understand at first, then remembered the hard ridge of his body against her stomach and knew it must concern that; she flushed. She was fiercely glad that he couldn't see her that well in the dim light.

When they emerged from the shadows of the walk to the path that crossed it and led to the Grand Walk that ran parallel the length of the Gardens, Jamie held her close to him. A bell rang, and they were caught in a press of people surging down the avenue to see the Cascade. Summer had a vivid impression of laughing faces and fashionable gowns of muslin and silk as they were swept along for several yards.

"Enough of this," Jamie growled under his breath, and caught her by one arm to pull her to the side. "We'll wait it out here." An elm spread its branches over them, and he leaned against the rough bark of the trunk and observed the rush of the ton in a pell-mell dash to view the scene of a contrived waterfall.

"They remind me of guinea hens, don't they you?" Summer murmured thoughtfully as the fashionable paraded past with loud laughter and chatter.

"Guinea hens?"

"You know, the fowl that chatter and gabble constantly, until one wants to strangle them just to have peace again. We had some once." She shook her head. "A disaster. They gathered at the back stoop and surrounded anyone unfortunate enough to go that way, all gabbling shrilly the entire time."

Jamie had followed her gaze; he grinned. "They do have a startling resemblance to guineas at that, my sweet. Shall I be so unkind as to inform the ton of your opinion of them?"

"I can't imagine they would be interested in my opinion of anyone or anything English," Summer remarked with a sigh. "I'm afraid that England is not very impressed with me."

His hand moved to touch her lightly on the back. "That is fairly understandable considering the manner in which I first met you, but I believe that if you were to stay a while, that might change."

Summer slanted him a quick glance of surprise. "I could never stay."

"Why not?" Jamie shrugged. "Your Captain Kinnison is gone, and you have no home to go to."

Stunned, Summer didn't know quite what to say. Did he mean stay with him? Cautiously, she said, "I never said I have no home. I merely said that I was an orphan. There's a vast difference."

"Not that vast. Unless you have other plans."

"Well, yes. I mean, I can't stay here. I want to go home."

His hand moved up to the nape of her neck, then fell away. He muttered something under his breath, and when Summer asked him to repeat it, he said impatiently, "I should have thought of this, but I see a gentleman I know. He's coming toward us, and I'll be forced to speak to him. Even when I say something odd, try not to react."

"Odd?" Summer followed his gaze and saw a tall, thin young man with chestnut hair approaching. "What do you mean by odd?"

"You'll see quite shortly, if I'm not mistaken." Ja-

mie swore softly again, and his hand shifted to curl
around her arm. "It will be to your advantage to fol-
low my lead, lass."

While she was wondering just what he meant by
that, the smiling acquaintance reached them. She had
a brief impression of a brightly colored waistcoat glittering with a gold fob and a lifted quizzing glass on a
silk ribbon.

"I say, Westcott, where have you been hiding such
loveliness?" the man asked. He raked Summer with
the quizzing glass, smiling broadly when she stiffened.

"Where you couldn't find her, of course, Epson."
Jamie gave an elegant shrug when the man turned to
him. "She's family. A sister."

Summer started. Sister? Had he gone mad? How
would he explain the fact that his hand had been very
comfortably resting on his sister's neck in an unmis-
takably intimate fashion? And who was Westcott?

"Your sister?" Epson was repeating in a faintly malicious drawl. "How quaint, Westcott. I didn't realize
you were so . . . close . . . to your family."

"I am. But not that close, Epson." There was a
vaguely amused warning cloaked in his casual reply
that even Summer recognized. His hand moved to
stroke the back of her neck in a leisurely caress, and
she stiffened.

Now she was certain he'd gone mad; she could see
from the disconcerted expression on Epson's face that
he apparently thought so too. A hot flush rose in her
cheeks. Was she supposed to suffer his caress or knock
it away and pretend some sort of sisterly rebuke? But
how would any sister react to her brother's public fon-
dling? *Damn him!* How did he intend to crawl out of
this without branding himself a shocking libertine?
And her even worse?

Shifting so that his hand slid over to cup her shoulder in a loose clasp, Jamie brought Summer the tiniest
bit closer to him. "This is my brother's wife, Epson,"
he said, with open amusement quivering in his voice.

"As she is in London and he is *not*, I have decided to play the gallant."

This Espon could understand, and he grinned. "Ah. Quite the thing. Does your brother—which one, may I ask?—know about your *tendre* for his pretty wife?"

Summer felt Jamie's careless shrug and tried to keep from blurting out any number of vile imprecations. If she had had any intentions at all of staying in London, this event would certainly have ended them.

"I'm not certain which brother she belongs to—" Jamie paused and looked down at Summer with a slight frown, pulling his one dark brow down over his eyes. "Do you recall which one, my sweet? Ah, no matter. I daresay he'll remember, and that's all that counts."

Quivering with fury, Summer clenched and opened her hands several times beneath the flowing edge of her shawl. She wanted to sink into the graveled path and never be seen again. She wanted to inform this Epson person that she was not Jamie's sister-in-law, nor was she his mistress. Most of all, she wanted to give James Cameron a vicious pinch.

"You are a cold devil, Westcott," Epson was saying, "but then, you always have been. Will we be seeing you at Brooks's any time soon? There's the certain matter of a loss I'd like to recoup."

"I'm certain I'll find time. Perhaps next week."

"Are you in residence? I hadn't heard," Epson began, and was interrupted by another gentleman every bit as elegantly dressed, with manners equally as elegant.

"Hullo, Epson," the newcomer drawled, repeating Epson's act with the quizzing glass and making Summer glare at him. " 'Pon rep, you're in good company." He made a small half-bow that looked vaguely ridiculous considering he was drunk and portly. "My apologies, madam, for being out of sorts," he said, then flicked a glance toward Jamie. "Westcott. Thought you were in Egypt somewhere."

"Obviously not, Hobbs."

Summer felt Jamie's hand take her arm, and through her haze of fury, she heard the belated introductions.

"Lady Summer, may I present Lord Epson, Mr. Hobbs, both gentlemen to be avoided at all costs."

His tone was light and frivolous, meant for a drawing room or parlor. This was social conversation, meaningless and trivial, and Summer had certainly heard enough of it to recognize it. She inclined her head and swept a half-curtsy to the men as she had been taught to do when she was a small child.

"How do you do, gentlemen," she said softly, and hoped that her voice did not betray her fury and dismay. She felt Jamie's gaze on her and knew that he was probably aware of the thundering emotion raging in her body.

"Your servant, madam," Lord Epson said. He tilted his head to one side. "I don't believe I heard which of Lord Westcott's brothers you are wed to...?"

Jamie cut in smoothly. "I didn't specify, Epson. And of course, it would be too bad of you to pry."

"Of course." Epson grinned, and Hobbs lifted his glass.

"Wed to your brother, Westcott? How droll! You Scots do have excellent taste in women, I must say, and Lady Summer is a prime article. Oops. Spoke out of turn. 'Scuse me, my lady. It's the punch, I'm afraid."

"That's quite all right, Mr. Hobbs," Summer said coolly. "I found the punch to be a bit overbearing myself." She let a faint rueful smile curl her lips. "My dear brother-in-law had to practically hold me up a few moments ago. I think my spell of dizziness has passed, however, and I would like to go home now." She turned to look up at Jamie. "Please, dear brother? I'm feeling strong enough to leave."

"By all means," Jamie said instantly. "Regrets, gentlemen."

"You're a wretch, Westcott," Epson said with a laugh, "to give me such a tale! Can't say I like it above half."

"You'll recover, I'm certain of it." Jamie tucked Summer's hand into the angle of his bent arm and gave the two men a polite nod before moving away.

Summer could feel their gazes behind her, and when they were out of hearing, snarled, "I hope you're happy! Why on earth did you say such terrible things? And why are you using a false name?"

His arm flexed, gripping her hand more tightly in the angle. "I wasn't certain how much Epson had seen. When it was obvious he had seen more than he should, you became my sister-*in-law*. That simple."

"And damning!"

He shrugged. "That too."

"What are you going to do about it?"

"Not a thing. It's already obvious to me that Epson has realized I would not actually proclaim a possibly dangerous—maybe illegal—union with my brother's wife in public. And then he will think that you are merely some lovely, unattainable Venus with a peculiar reaction to arrack punch."

"Why did you lie to me about your name?"

"I didn't."

"Why do they know you as Westcott?"

He blew out his breath in an explosive little sigh. "It is my title, not my name."

"Title!" Summer reeled at this unexpected news. "What do you mean by that?" Her voice shook slightly, and she jerked to a stop beneath a colonnaded arch to look up at him. "Aren't you—" She couldn't go on, and he gave her a faint smile.

"Penniless? Nay, lass. Nor am I a runaway soldier. I am merely ... retired. With a pension in gratitude for saving the duke of York from his own clumsiness on the battlefield. In this case, my grateful king was generous enough to bestow upon me a title and estates that had been reverted to the crown. Nothing grand, I assure you, but grander than the fourth son of a Scottish earl could expect."

It took a moment to absorb this information, and Summer was only vaguely aware of the press of people around her and Jamie's intent gaze. She looked up at him. His midnight eyes were fixed on her face warily, and she knew he thought she would be angry. He was right. What a fool he had made of her!

"Damn you!" she hissed at last, and he immediately put his hand on her wrist in a steely grip.

"Yes, damn me all you like, but not in public. If you will exercise a little self-control, I will give you every opportunity to regale me with your latest opinion of my character flaws." His fingers tightened even more, and he drew her slowly toward him when she tried to pull away.

"Sweet lady," he drawled in an unmistakable warning, "I do not intend for you to rail at me here."

Summer didn't offer a protest or a word when he walked her from the Gardens and hailed a hired hack. And she did not say a word when he gave a completely different address from the shabby inn. When he gave her an assurance that he would send someone for their few possessions, she lifted her shoulders in a mute shrug. It didn't matter at the moment.

Chapter 8

Wrenching open the door of the hired hack, Jamie leapt out, then turned to put out his hand for Summer. She hung back.

"Where are we?"

"Sixty-six Bruton Street, Mayfair." His hand closed around her wrist. "I'm tired of shabby inns and sleeping on the floor, and I had the quaint notion that you may balk at sharing the bed tonight."

She looked at him uncertainly, then her gaze shifted to the house. Moonlight washed over mellow brick walls and gleaming white porticoes that stretched along the front. Palladian windows bore tiny quarrels that reflected the glow of streetlamps in thick, leaded glass. A broad lawn looked as if it was in need of a gardener, and flower beds sprouted clumps of weeds among struggling blossoms.

"Is this your house?" she asked, returning her gaze to Jamie.

He drew her from the hack. "Come inside and find out. It's much more effective than lounging about out here in the dark and wondering."

Thrusting a few coins into the coachman's outstretched palm, Jamie cupped a hand under her elbow and escorted her up the flagstone path. No lamp was lit. The windows were dark, and Summer made a nervous motion with her hands.

"What's the penalty for stealing a house?"

"Ah, lass, you have no faith in me." His hand spread over her back, and he moved her gently forward. "Is it because I'm not what you thought me? Is a blatant rogue more trustworthy than a depraved viscount?"

She gave an irritated tug at her shawl. "Is that what you are? A viscount?"

"By pure chance, my lady." He gave a strong pull on the bell and turned to gaze down at her with a smile, resting one broad shoulder against the doorframe.

Summer could see the chipped, peeling paint on the door now that she was close. "The house is not in good repair," she said.

"No," he agreed. "It's not. I believe it stood empty for some years before the king found someone to foist it off upon. Just my luck."

She shifted on the stoop, and he pulled the bell again. It could be heard faintly from the outside, a shrill jangle to summon a servant.

"Is there anyone here?" she asked. "Why don't you have a key?"

He made an impatient motion with his hand. "I don't need a key. Tidwell is always here. Or someone. It's just that I wasn't expected for a month yet."

"I see."

His mouth curled in a smile. "Do you, lass?" Cupping her chin in his palm, he leaned forward to brush his lips across hers. She didn't resist, but she didn't participate. He drew back and sighed.

Summer looked up at him and opened her mouth to speak, but at that moment the door swung open to admit them. A tall, balding man with a dignified air stood in the opening, and his brows rose slightly.

"Lord Westcott! You were not expected, sir!"

"I know, Tidwell. It's all right." Jamie pulled Summer with him into the entrance hall, and she sidled past the steward with a nervous twitch of her skirts.

Though dimly lit, the entrance hall was impressive. A high ceiling soared overhead in a blaze of gilt and painted murals; an unlit chandelier with quivering crystal globes was suspended from the midst of the shadowed glory, and it tinkled softly. Statues, some life-size, were scattered along the walls, and twin staircases at the end of the hall swept toward the second floor. A thick Aubusson carpet woven in a single roll stretched from door to far wall. The quiet, tasteful decor radiated an aura of wealth and social position.

Summer slanted a narrowed glance at Jamie, who returned it coolly. Her lips flattened into a grim smile.

"I see that I underestimated you, sir. Perhaps it was because of your propensity for robbing innocent men at the point of your sword."

"That would be a factor, I imagine." Jamie flicked a glance toward Tidwell's impassive countenance. "As the lady is a bit ... overwrought, perhaps she should be shown to a chamber now, Tidwell."

"Very good, sir." Tidwell turned toward Summer and waited politely.

But she was not to be cheated of speaking her mind and resisted Jamie's suggestion. Her gold-streaked head tilted back with a trace of arrogance in the movement.

"I was right, you know." He watched her warily, his devil's brow slightly lifted as if curious. Summer's voice was tinged with bitter irony. "You are a rogue of the first water. I shouldn't wonder if you don't hang someday."

"That has been mentioned before," Jamie said tightly, "by others who know me much better than you do. I daresay you might all be correct in that assumption. However, I've no intention of discussing it here and now."

"Why is it that I have the idea you won't ever find the right time to discuss it?" Summer asked quietly, and turned to Tidwell. "I'd like a room with a view, please," she said to the nonplussed steward, who glanced at Jamie.

Upon seeing his master's slight shrug, Tidwell bent his head slightly. "Of course, madam. Please accompany me."

Jamie watched Summer glide gracefully behind Tidwell and had the sour thought that she had somehow turned the tables on him again. It had not escaped his notice that she had not divulged any personal information about herself to him beyond the fact she was orphaned and alone; nor had it gone unnoticed that she left out some of the most pertinent details about her life. That she would feel insulted that he had not told her of his more fortunate circumstances seemed rather trivial in that light.

Striding across the entrance hall to a door opening off the right, Jamie entered a shadowed room and fumbled for a lamp. He couldn't find even a candle in the gloom and went back into the hall. Fortunately, a sleepy-eyed footman, who had been roused from his bed, came out from the pantry, and he bore a slim taper in a brass holder.

After the lamps had been lit in his study, Jamie threw his long frame into a high-backed cushioned chair in a boneless sprawl. He was tired. And he was disgusted. And if he were to be completely honest with himself, he felt rather foolish. He should have told Summer the truth right off, but he'd wanted a bit of sport. And then he had found himself mired in an increasingly complicated situation that required diplomacy and tact to secure his ends.

It didn't help to know that he'd been an idiot. Every time he allowed himself to become involved with a woman who wasn't forthright in her manner, he ended by making an ass of himself. It was as certain as sunrise. *Damn.*

Slinging himself up from the chair, Jamie stalked to a small walnut table and wrenched the stopper out of a cut-crystal bottle. He splashed brandy into a snifter and sipped at it as he wandered the comfortable room with easy, stuffed furniture and landscape paintings by Jacob van Ruisdael and Thomas Gainsborough. He liked the house. He'd been here only once before, and that was in the past year; he'd looked forward to coming back and refurbishing the house. It needed it.

There were moments when he felt undeserving of the high honor and reward he'd received for his rescue of the duke of York, but when he recalled how narrowly he'd escaped death himself, he supposed it wasn't *totally* undeserved. The duke was a hefty man, and Jamie had to practically throw him atop his own horse after seeing him go down in battle.

It had been one of those dangerous, unexpected moments in the chaos of warfare, with men shouting and horses screaming, and the thunder of artillery around him. Blades had flashed through acrid smoke, and the smell of blood and death had seeped into his bones. He'd been shouting out orders when he'd seen with astonishment the duke riding madly through the fray.

It had sent a shock down to his toes, and he'd tried to make his way to him through the press of battle, only to arrive split seconds after the duke went down. After that first horrible moment, when he'd thought him killed, he'd seen that he was only stunned. It had taken much effort to heft the bulky Frederick atop his own horse and send him safely behind the lines.

The monarch's gratitude had been prompt, for Frederick was King George's favorite.

Now here Jamie was, housed in a grand town house, with a title and country estates to boot, as well as a generous pension. It was, Jamie thought wryly, what his father had deemed sonsy.

Unfortunately, his luck did not seem to be holding where females were concerned—one particular female, at any rate. He took another sip of brandy and turned as Tidwell paused in the open doorway.

"Are things quiet, Tidwell?"

"Yes, my lord, your guest is comfortably situated for the night. I have seen to the appointments of the blue chamber for you, sir."

"And the lady?"

"Has been ensconced in the green bedchamber. Overlooking the courtyard."

When Tidwell had bowed himself from the room, Jamie went to stand at the long windows. He looked out into the shabby garden, watching moonlight embellish the grass and untidy beds of plants. A sundial graced one corner, and a stone bench wrapped round with ivy squatted close by it. In the hazy light, it looked lovely and romantic, a spot for lovers to walk.

He smiled mirthlessly. What did he know of romance? He knew more about physical love than he did that elusive quality, though no woman yet had complained. It had been, in fact, the scorn of his first love that had shown him how ridiculous it was to chase after romantical notions. She had not been at all impressed with chivalry or quixotic love and had let him know it. It had been a scalding lesson in humiliation.

And his abortive attempt this evening to inject romance into his seduction of Summer had proven once again how easy it was to be a fool.

Curling his fingers around the slender stem of his snifter, Jamie swallowed the last bit of his brandy and put the glass aside. Romance didn't have to enter into sex at all. It was much better left in books and poetry.

He took the stairs to the second floor two at a time. It took him several minutes to find the green room that looked over the courtyard. He wasn't familiar with the house and found the room only by chance. He heard Summer moving about as he passed the door, then turned back.

Pausing outside the door, he put a hand on the latch and hesitated. Suddenly, he felt like a green youth again, an unlicked cub with his first woman. This was ridiculous. He'd been with his first female at the age of twelve, and he certainly knew what came next. So why did he feel so awkward and uncertain?

His hands knotted and unknotted, and his stomach gave a sharp twist. Then he tapped lightly on the door and swung it open.

Summer knew it was Jamie. She'd been expecting him. A curl of apprehension tightened, then eased inside her, and she turned to face him.

He stood still in the doorway, one arm upraised to prop against the frame, his other hand still on the door latch. He wasn't wearing his coat or waistcoat. His white shirt was open at the neck and vivid against the shadows behind him, and he looked confident and very male lounging in the doorway.

"Come in," she invited because there seemed to be little choice in the matter. He was already there, and it was his house. She'd made a bargain with the devil, and he'd come to collect his soul....

Moving with languid grace, he stepped inside and shut the door behind him. It closed with a slight click that sounded much too loud.

A fire burned in the grate; lamps had been lit and fresh sheets spread on the four-poster bed against the far wall. Tidwell was extremely efficient, and his staff well-trained.

Summer waited near the fireplace; a veined marble hearth reflected the flames in glowing, erratic patterns. A painted fire screen with long-plumaged birds depicted in a tropical tree stood to one side, and she reached out to trace a fingertip over the design.

She could feel Jamie's gaze, saw from one corner of her eye his fluid pace across the room toward her. A knot formed in her throat. She studied the pretty pattern of colorful birds on the fire screen as if it were the most fascinating thing she'd ever seen.

He still hadn't said anything. Did he mean to talk to her? To continue their argument? She'd thought about it and decided that it didn't matter. Honor demanded that she live up to her given word, and she would; there was no need for recriminations or discussion. It didn't really matter if he was a villain or a viscount. Not to her. Not when it was all said and done.

After tonight, he would secure her passage home, and she would never see him again. She knew enough about the world to know that, though she'd been fool enough to think for a time that a simple kiss would be all he required. How idiotic she had been! How naive!

She'd told him she knew what she was about, and he'd taken her at her word. Now he expected her to be experienced, and she had never even kissed a man as she had kissed this James Cameron, or Lord Westcott, or whoever he was. His kisses were a scalding revelation in how much she did *not* know.

Her head lifted, and she dredged up the remaining remnants of her pride when he came to stand by the fire and lean against the mantel.

"I ask that you be patient with me, sir. I'm afraid that I rather overstated my ... accomplishments."

A faintly amused smile thinned his lips. "Did you? I wondered."

She looked at the floor, at the curved lines of a small table topped with marble, at a graceful cushioned chair, and back to the fire screen. She looked everywhere but at Jamie. She knew too well the power of those midnight eyes of dark jet beneath absurdly long lashes.

Her bent head was washed by the soft pulse of firelight and meager candle-glow. In spite of it, she felt an iciness to the very marrow of her bones and had the distracted thought that she had not been this cold since being in England. It left her shivering, and she cupped her elbows in her palms and held her arms tightly across her chest to still the tremors.

"Summer."

She looked up and met the devastating force of his gaze and released the breath from her lungs in a soft, sighing, "Yes?"

"Would you like to take a walk in the garden?"

Whatever she'd been expecting to hear, it wasn't that. Her eyes focused on him, on the slightly wary expression in his eyes and the flat compression of his lips. And she was equally surprised to hear herself murmur, "Yes, I'd like that very much."

Jamie escorted her down the wide, curved staircase and through a series of corridors until they reached a shadowed room with french doors. He rattled the latch, then swung it open, and turned back to take her hand.

"Watch this step. It's crumbled in places," he said as he helped her down. They walked out onto a moon-washed terrace of stone tiles. Another set of steps led to a small patch of garden with a sundial and stone statues, urns, and benches. A dry fountain was at the hub of a wheel of flower beds. A gentle fragrance lightly spiced the air, and night birds could be heard rustling in bushes and trees, lilting songs drifting into the dark sky.

"Even untended, it's a beautiful spot," Summer said after a moment. "I can almost visualize how lovely it will be when it's had some hard work." Jamie's arm slid around her waist, and she caught her breath at the touch but did not try to move away. Slightly nervous at his proximity and the situation, she tried to think of something to fill the silence.

"At home we have a small courtyard and garden. It used to be very beautiful. Ma—my mother"—she caught herself before the French *Maman* slipped out—"and I would work there sometimes, because she said it was the best place to look for peace." Her throat worked, and she waited a moment before continuing.

She could feel Jamie's gaze on her, knew he was wondering if she was about to cry.

Turning in the curve of his arm so that his hand now rested on her hip, she looked up into his shadowed face.

"You needn't worry about me crying. I rarely do that anymore. I may begin to, and even grow some tears, but they never fall." She shrugged. "I think I weep more from minor annoyances than I do the true tragedies in my life, anyway."

He stepped sideways, so that he'd moved away from her, and let his hand fall to his side.

"I wasn't worried about your tears. I've seen enough of them from my sisters to tell the difference between minor and major tragedy." When he smiled, moonlight deepened the slight grooves on each side of his mouth. "You may find this hard to believe, but as a boy I used to tease my sisters a great deal. I learned how to stop just before they cried from anger or frustration."

"Because you hated to see them cry?"

"No, because my father would give me a thrashing if I made them cry." He grinned at her sharp exclamation. "You thought I was going to admit to some grand and noble sentiment, didn't you?"

"I confess that I did." She shook her head. "I should have known better."

"Yes," he said, slipping his arm back around her waist and walking her across the terrace to the steps, "you should have."

Small stones in the grass beyond the terrace led to the sundial; the bench close-by was thickly woven with ivy and jasmine, but someone had cleared enough of it so that the seat was free of leaves and vines. It seemed to beckon in the still, quiet peace of the garden.

Jamie raked the edge of his hand across the bench to ensure it was swept clean, then seated Summer with a gallant bow and a smile. She eyed him closely. He was being nice. Too nice. Why? Why this elaborate charade? They both knew why he'd come to her room. Had he changed his mind?

It was unsettling, and the anticipation was making her nervous. Yet, in spite of all the questions and fears she had, she realized that a part of her was enjoying his attention. That secret feminine part of her liked masculine homage, reveled in it. It overshadowed the resistance she'd been building up against him by easing her fears. She knew what he was doing, and yet she needed for him to do it.

Strange, that in only two days she'd managed to forget Garth Kinnison completely. For ten years he had been foremost in her waking thoughts, and now this arrogant rogue had come along and usurped him. It was baffling; it was frightening.

Summer glanced quickly at Jamie sprawled easily beside her. He was looking at her with a lazy smile, his eyes half veiled by long, spiky lashes. If she hadn't known better, she would have thought he was ignoring her.

"Tell me about New Orleans," Jamie said when the silence deepened, and the night birds' sweet songs had faded into indistinct mutters. "I've never been there."

She lifted her shoulders and tilted back her head. "It is just like a lot of other cities, I suppose. Like London, it has a busy traffic of ocean-going vessels that come up the Mississippi River from the Gulf. So, we have a varied collection of people from all parts of the world there."

"I know the statistics. Tell me what you like about it."

A dreamy smile curved her mouth, and she put her hands on her knees and swung her feet like a child, feeling the greenery tickle the backs of her calves.

"In the springtime, before the weather gets too warm and sticky, I like to go with Chantal to the market. We go early in the morning, and the air is crisp and cool and filled with interesting smells. The coffee

at the Café du Monde is strong and hot, and the beignets are flaky and covered with powdered sugar.
Sometimes in the Place d'Armes there is music. And
at the market itself there is every kind of merchandise
you'd want to buy. My mother always scolded me for
going with only Chantal along, but Papa never minded.
He said that no one would dare bother the—"

She jerked to a halt, horrified at what she'd almost
said. *The daughter of Jonathan St. Clair.* Dear God.
Though it shouldn't have made as much difference
now as it once had, she still didn't want him to know
who she was. Not now. Especially not now. She would
be leaving. It wouldn't matter to anyone but her who
she was. And besides, he'd said he hated the French.
Her name would be a dead giveaway, and he would
cut her, just as Garth had cut her.

"Bother the?" Jamie prompted. "Bother the what?"

She wet her lips with the tip of her tongue and
flashed him a shaky smile. He was looking at her much
too closely.

"Bother the likes of us. Sorry. I lost the thread of
the conversation."

"That sounds a little lame, my sweet," Jamie commented. His lazy smile didn't quite reach his eyes. "Are
you certain you weren't going to confess something
very revealing? Some deep, dark secret?"

She hoped he couldn't see her flushed cheeks in
the cool slice of moonlight. "Sorry to disappoint you.
I suppose it would sound much better if I confessed
to being a dangerous criminal or something, but I've
lived a very dull life."

"Not from what I've seen of it in the past two days,"
he drawled. "Some women go their entire lives without being stranded alone in London, little though you
may credit it. I daresay it would be the most exciting
thing that happened to some of them."

"I sincerely hope that I never have such excitement in my life again," Summer said so earnestly that
he laughed. To cover her embarrassment and near-

blunder, she said in a rush of words, "Now that I've told you about me, tell me about you. Why did you bring me to London when you had no intention of coming here yourself?"

"Because you needed to come." He seemed amused. "Are you complaining about it now?"

"No. I just wondered. You said you weren't expected here for a month yet." She paused. "Were you on your way to visit your family?"

His bootheels scraped across the grass with a swishing sound as he shifted position on the bench. He raked a hand through his hair and blew out his breath in a sigh.

"Yes, I guess I was. I've been putting it off. I'm not sure why, except that my father will ask all sorts of questions I don't want to answer, and my mother will shove eligible females at me, and my brothers will want to arm-wrestle, and my sisters will want me to do things for them that I don't want to do." He paused and slid her a rueful smile. "Until this moment, I hadn't realized how much I did *not* want to go." A shrug lifted his shoulders. "When I left the army, I didn't want to go home, I didn't want to come here. I needed some time for myself, some time to grow a little more civilized again. War releases a lot inside a man, and I didn't feel like facing anyone yet. Especially them."

"Don't you love your family?" Her voice was a shade tight, and she smothered the sudden fierce longing for her own family.

"Of course. It's just that they're a bit overwhelming at times. And they all know what's best for me." He closed his eyes for a moment, and recited obvious platitudes.

" 'You're not doing with your life what should be done.' 'Settle down.' 'Don't settle down.' 'Stay in the army.' 'Don't stay in the army.' "

He opened his eyes and looked at her. "See? The only thing they all agree on is that I should do anything but what I'm doing. Or at least, that was their attitude before last year."

"And last year," she said flatly, thinking of his title and estates, "you changed their minds."

"Not really." He grimaced. "I just stumbled into luck that turned out to be profitable. My father wrote a letter of congratulations but stated that I had done nothing that any other man couldn't have done. He's very hard to please, but at least he isn't pressuring me to go into the clergy now."

"The clergy?" Summer tried to imagine the piratical Jamie as a clergyman and couldn't manage it. "Why on earth did he ever think you might fit into the clergy?"

"Because a younger Cameron son has always gone into the clergy, and he hoped it would tame me a bit."

"My, you must have made quite a reputation for yourself with your family."

"Apparently," he agreed. "I don't know why. Just because I once caught the tapestries in the hall afire and almost brought down the house, they've all considered me rather dangerous since then. A totally unfair assumption. It was my brother's fault. Dallas hid in a suit of armor after we quarreled, and I was trying to smoke him out."

Summer laughed softly. She tried to imagine a youthful Jamie with his slashing brow and wickedly dancing eyes and found it fairly easy. He must have looked a great deal as he had when he'd stood on a London street corner and sang ballads just to embarrass her.

"Do you know that's the first time I've heard you laugh?" Jamie murmured. "You should do it more often."

With a smile still pressing her lips, Summer shook her head. "There's little to laugh at in my life, usually. I'm afraid I don't have the range of amusements that you seem to have."

"That could change."

"I don't see how." She took a deep breath and looked up to meet his gaze. "It seems rather hopeless at times."

"Nothing's hopeless, lass. Hard, maybe. Elusive at times. Not hopeless." He frowned slightly. "This Kinnison who brought you here—do you still want to find him?"

She wanted to throw herself against his chest and tell him that she didn't care about Garth anymore, that maybe she never had, not like she did Jamie. Garth's handsome, golden face had been replaced by hot sable eyes that could suck her soul from her body.

But she didn't.

"No. There's no point in it now. He's gone and won't be back for me." Her eyes shifted to the dry fountain in the center of a wheel of flower beds. "I suppose that Garth did what he thought best at the time. It wasn't malicious, just ... unfortunate."

"Aye, for you anyway." He raked a hand through his hair again and slid her a quick glance that made her heart skip a beat. Then his mouth quirked in a potent smile. "Of course, if he hadn't deserted you, we would never have met."

"Yes," she agreed with a funny little catch in her throat, "that's true. I'm still trying to decide if that's good fortune or ill."

"Let me know when you've reached a conclusion, lass."

He took her hand between his palms, and she jerked at his touch. It jarred her as deeply as the electric touch of a static generator she'd once tried at a fair, sending ripples of shock up her arm.

"Easy, lass," he said with a lifted brow. "I'm not trying to hurt you, only hold you."

"Those two are remarkably close in effect." She slipped her hand from his without looking at his face. She knew he'd been studying her closely, and she couldn't bear what she would see in his face.

It did her no good.

He put a hand beneath her chin and tilted her face up to let the moon bathe her features in light. "I won't hurt you. I just want to love you."

Her heart lurched, but she knew he didn't mean the only definition of love she wanted to hear. No, he had something much more physical in mind, much more wrenching.

When he brought his face closer to hers, she closed her eyes and waited. His lips brushed lightly over her mouth in a silky pass, and his fingers encouraged her face up a bit more to give him freer access. It was exquisite torture, and Summer felt her face grow hot. She was shivering now, her body racked with tremors that almost shook the stone bench. Jamie drew away.

"Open your eyes," he said, and she peered at him from beneath her lashes. "Why are you so frightened? Do you think I would hurt you?"

"I'm not frightened. I'm nervous. I can't help it. You make me feel this way, and I don't know why." Her voice grew tight with frustration. "I wish I wouldn't react like this too, so you needn't think there's something I can do about it."

"All right, lass, all right." He drew her into his embrace and rested his jaw atop her head. She could hear his heart thudding, and his breath drag in and out of his lungs. One hand lightly caressed her back, moving in small circles at first, his fingers massaging the space between her shoulder blades.

Summer's face was pressed against his chest, against the bare skin where his shirt gaped open, and she felt the tiny, soft hairs tickle her cheek. He smelled faintly of soap and brandy, a diabolical combination as far as she was concerned. It filled her nose, making her light-headed. Or perhaps it was his touch that was making her feel giddy.

A bird warbled and was answered by another. Somewhere in the distance, a bell chimed the hours. Small night noises that sounded familiar yet foreign grew louder as she remained nestled in the angle of his chest and thigh, and slowly she began to relax.

His hand moved from her back up to her neck, fingertips slowly massaging, lifting the weight of her hair from her neck to stroke there. She bent her head forward and closed her eyes. His other hand caressed her shoulder, and he dug his fingers into the tense muscles of her neck, then worked back down the slope of her spine.

Summer arched against his hands. He continued massaging in smooth, rhythmic motions, thumbs and fingers pressing in delicious circles that made her body begin to feel boneless and liquid. Leaning against him, letting his fragrance fill her lungs and his hands work magic, she slowly became aware of an aching emptiness inside her. She needed this man, this beguiling rogue who exasperated and amused her, made her want to run away and made her want to stay.

It was insane. Even more insane was the fact that she was beginning to writhe with a nameless yearning that urged her closer and closer to him.

His hands spread in her hair, his thumbs stroking up the underside of her chin and his fingers rotating along her scalp, silky skeins of hair coming loose from the pins and falling over his cuffs.

Summer felt rather than heard his voice, a deep, rich purr that went all the way to her toes.

"Feeling better, my sweet?"

"I'm not sure. . . ."

"This isn't relaxing?"

"I can't tell. I can't feel anything below my eyebrows, I think."

In a voice thick with laughter, he said, "When it wears off, let me know. I've a remedy for it."

"I've a feeling you do," she murmured.

Her head lolled to one side, and she slanted him an assessing glance. He was still smiling, his lips tucked at the corners and grooves etched on the sides. Her heart clutched. He was so handsome. A dark knight. A man who had rescued her, saved her from certain disaster; hadn't she prayed for a knight in shining armor that day in New Orleans when she'd hidden in Garth's closet?

James Cameron might not be exactly what she'd had in mind when she'd murmured that prayer, but he had certainly taken up the gauntlet for her. If only . . .

If only he would want her for more than just a night. She wanted love; she needed to be loved. Not for her money or who she was, but for herself. With Jamie, she had that chance. He'd not known—still didn't know—about her money; not that he needed it anyway. If she confessed to him that she was Summer St. Clair, half-French and niece to treacherous Barton Shriver, she might not get that chance. Did she dare confide in him now? After all, he only wanted her to ease that masculine hunger so evident in his midnight eyes. He didn't think beyond the night, beyond the bedroom.

But she did. She longed for sunshine days and starlit nights, for love to wrap around her like a cocoon. She knew what it was to have the security of unquestioning love, and she wanted it again.

Her doubts and hopes vanished in a burst of reality as Jamie stood up, drawing her with him, his hands still on her possessively. He kissed her, lingeringly, his mouth easing over her lips to her cheek, then her ear. His breath was warm and made her shiver, and he pulled her hard against his front.

There was a raw urgency and power vibrating in him that left her half-frightened, half-impatient. She couldn't move for the force of it.

In a voice husky with need, he said against her ear, "I need you, lass. I want to bury myself inside you; I want to feel you around me, and hear you say you need me too."

God. Why did his husky voice in her ear make her

stomach lurch like that? And her heart leap and fill her throat so that she could hardly breathe?

She *should* be telling him that she would have to break her word, that she couldn't let him make love to her; she *should* be saying that she'd never been with a man before, and in view of those circumstances, he should understand why she must refuse him; she *should* be pulling away from him and telling him quite firmly that she had to leave England before she lost her heart and what was left of her sanity to his sweet tempting.

But she said none of those things.

Instead, Jamie led her from the garden bench back up the steps, into the house, and upstairs to her bed-chamber. And he shut the door behind them and swept her into his arms and strode across the room with her to the wide, drapery-hung bed.

Before she could offer a single protest, Summer was lying on the mattress and he was over her, his mouth smothering anything she might have said. And Summer knew at that moment that she was lost, body and soul.

Chapter 9

Low lamps flickered across the room, not quite reaching the shadowed alcove of the bed. Every place Jamie's hand touched, she burned. He lay over her, his weight pressing her into the mattress, shifting some of it to his elbows as he propped up to gaze down at her face. He drew his fingers along the line of her throat and down.

She shivered; she was on fire, yet could not stop the tremors racking her body. When his palm came to rest on the curve of her breast, she closed her eyes. Just that light, feathery caress made her entire body ache, made her thighs clamp together to still the throbbing in that nameless place. She didn't understand it. How could he so easily do this to her?

Still fully clothed, her muslin skirts rucking up over her knees, she was vaguely aware that he was tugging gently at the ribbons beneath her bodice, untying them and drawing them aside. It loosened her gown. She wore only a shift beneath it, a wispy garment that was a shade lighter than the muslin dress; her white silk hose were tied at the knee, and her pumps had somehow come off. When she twisted beneath him, her gown rode even higher, and her thighs gleamed palely in the gloom.

"God," she heard Jamie mutter as if from a great

distance, his hand skimming up her thigh. His fingers tangled in the flimsy material of her gown, and he jerked free with an impatient twist.

Lying half atop her, he put his weight on one elbow and bent his head to kiss her. Still kissing her, his mouth moving softly, gently on hers, he peeled away the bodice of her gown to free her breasts. Summer felt the assault of cool air and wondered why steam didn't rise from her body; she was burning, blazing with a heat that coiled inside and out.

The satin sheets were slick and cool beneath her fevered skin as she turned blindly, adding a lush sensuality to the shadows and firelight; the world was composed of hazy light and hazier emotions. Jamie's every movement was a torment of sensation, and he seemed to know it.

Dragging his fingers over her skin, he teased the rigid peaks of her breasts into tight buds that tilted toward his mouth for his kiss. He obliged by flicking his tongue in a scorching, wet caress that made her breath lodge in the back of her throat.

She breathed in short, panting gasps, and her hands dug into the cool linen of his shirt, knotting it beneath fingers that curled and uncurled in rhythmic motions. Silky strands of his sable hair drifted over the arched line of her throat as he lavished attention on one breast, then the other, and she could hear someone making small, moaning noises.

With a shock she realized that it was she who was making those sounds. Urgent little moans drifted in the steamy space between their bodies.

"Please," she managed to whisper, not knowing quite what she wanted but only that there had to be *some*thing to end this torment, "please . . ."

"Easy, lass, easy." Jamie shifted to pull her gown from her in a single stroke of his arm, his mouth still pressing kisses along the line of her throat to her ear. He caught her hands in one of his when she made an involuntary motion to keep it, gently disengaging her fingers from the thin muslin. The silk stockings peeled away even more quickly, and the wisp of sheer slip followed.

Before Summer could react to the sudden absence of her garments, Jamie slid his body up and over hers. He was still clothed, and she could feel the cold press of his tiny pearl shirt buttons against her skin. They should have melted against the heat of her; it was terrible, this fiery blaze that consumed her, made her open for him eagerly.

Gasping at the slick, cool feel of satin sheets beneath her hips, realizing that his hands were touching her where she'd never been touched before, Summer moved against him in a last, brief protest, a concession to belated instincts of self-protection. Spreading her hands against his chest, she pushed.

"Nay, lass," Jamie growled in her ear, his brogue growing noticeably stronger, " 'tis too late for sich as tha'. Ye're wi' me naow, lass, an' I'll no' be stayed."

She might have protested at his arrogant assumption that he could do as he willed with her even if she offered an objection; but his mouth was over hers too quickly, drawing her breath into him, absorbing her fear and replacing it with heated longing.

Kissing her fiercely, he shifted slightly, and she could feel his hands fumbling with buttons and clothes. Then he lifted away, was gone only a moment; and when he came back and put one knee on the mattress beside her shivering body, she realized he was as naked as she. She looked away quickly, before curiosity and something warm and curling inside drew her gaze back to his powerful frame.

Firelight washed over him, gilding his body with golden lights, emphasizing the leonine musculature of his trunk, arms, and thighs. He was well-made. She lowered her lashes, glancing away, then was drawn back by a pulsing curiosity older than time. A fine down that covered his chest dipped to his groin; he

was fully aroused. The stark realization of male virility
struck her almost physically.

A fine trembling seized her then. This was it: the
moment many virgins feared and waited for at the
same time. She'd heard often enough that dire consequences befell young women who were foolish
enough to yield this far without benefit of matrimony,
and though she knew vaguely that this must be true,
a part of her still refused to believe it could be as bad
as all that. Common sense dictated the knowledge that
if it were, it would be done far less often and with
more discrimination.

When she jerked her gaze from that shadowy area
to his face, she saw amusement mixed with desire.

"D'ye no' like wha' ye ken, lass?" he murmured,
lowering his body to slide over her in a potent rub of
flesh.

She couldn't answer; she couldn't speak at all. Her
throat was closed with some response that she'd never
experienced before, and she could only gaze into the
dark midnight of his sultry eyes and nod. He smiled.

Scraping his long, lean body slowly over hers in a
burn of heated sensation, Jamie nudged her thighs
apart and slid between her legs. His head bent quickly
to capture her lips in a kiss, and his hands caught her
wrists in a light clasp and drew her arms away from
where she'd crossed them over her breasts.

"Nay, lass," he breathed against her parted lips,
"dinna try tae hide sich beauty frae me."

A shudder passed through her, but she couldn't
distinguish fear from need. She didn't know what she
wanted; all she knew at that moment was that she
ached where he was touching lightly with his hands,
drawing his fingers up her screamingly sensitive inner
thighs to the pale nest of curls that hid her from him.

Dragging his hand slowly through the silken tuft,
he brushed his fingers over her in a caress that made
her leap against his hand. His mouth muffled her cry,
and he rotated his palm in a motion so erotically sweet

and overpowering that Summer's entire body felt ablaze. The ache between her legs swiftly altered to a gathering rush of moisture and clutching muscles that bewildered her, and she lifted her lashes to look into his dark, burning gaze. She was panting with reaction, shivering and burning and drifting in a haze of conflicting sensations.

While he kissed her chin, then nuzzled that satiny spot beneath one ear, Summer said with a sort of moan, "This is all so ... so incredible. . . ."

A low laugh filled the delicate whorls of her ear, and she felt Jamie's warm breath stir the damp tendrils of hair that curled over her neck. "Aye, lass," he agreed. "I've th' same notion."

Summer had the distinct impression they were speaking of different things, but then it didn't matter anymore.

Bending lower, Jamie kissed her nipples, the smooth, firm flesh under her breast, then trailed hot kisses over the ridged curve of her ribs and to the flat, taut mound of her belly. She gasped when his tongue flicked at her navel; her hips arched, and she tangled her fingers in his hair to tug sharply.

"All right, lass," Jamie murmured against the quivering skin of her stomach, "I'll end th' waiting for both of us."

He lifted himself, spreading his hands on the mattress on each side of her head, and she had a brief glimpse of his intense expression: dark, liquid eyes, mouth thinned into a slash, brow straight.

She lifted her arms and put them around his neck to draw him back down. His lips grazed her cheek, found her mouth, clung.

Then he was moving upward, his knees gently shoving her thighs farther apart, his body slowly wedging into the vee. Summer felt him pulsing against her: hot, velvety-soft and hard at the same time. She tried not to twist away, tried not to avoid the burning pressure of his erection, but when the searing scrape shifted to a sharp pain, she couldn't help her body's quick jerk or a small, soft cry.

Pausing, Jamie lifted his head to look into her face; he was frowning. His body was tense, his erection throbbing against her. She couldn't quite look at him, uncertain what had happened, only aware of the ache between her thighs and the sudden, fierce glitter in Jamie's eyes.

"Wha' is this! Are ye no' wha' ye said ye were, lass?"

She knew what he must mean; her lower lip caught between her teeth, and she veiled her eyes with her lashes. Wincing, she heard him curse harshly, then he was rolling away from her, and her arms fell to her sides.

For some reason, she felt vaguely humiliated. Somehow, being a virgin was suddenly as bad as *not* being one.

Jamie lay facedown on the mattress beside her; his long golden body was pressed deeply into the satin sheets, and she could feel his muscles tighten. His hands were curled into fists, his forearms cradling his head. He seemed to be struggling for control, and several minutes passed before he spoke.

From the depths of the mattress she heard him growl, "Is this some kind of daft game you're playing?"

She couldn't answer for a moment; his withdrawal had been too abrupt. She felt abandoned, shamed, and still ached with a fierce emptiness.

With a little catch in her voice, she said, "I'm not playing a game. I thought this was what you wanted, what we agreed to."

His dark head lifted, and he said through his clenched teeth, "You never told me you were a maiden, lass. You said you and Kinnison were lovers."

Her throat worked. "I loved him. He never loved me. He never even kissed me, not like you have. I didn't want you to know ... know that he might not care enough about me to come back for me."

Gripping the satin sheets so tightly they were wadded into knots, Jamie glared at her. She could see anger and uncertainty in his gaze and reached out to touch him on the shoulder.

"I still will ... I mean, I want you to ... to finish."

His heavy-lashed eyes widened slightly, and his mouth curled into a grim smile. "Not nearly as bad I want it, I vow. But I've never yet taken an untried maid. I've too many sisters not to mislike a man taking what he shouldn't without the benefit of a marriage license." His lips were flat with a grimace. "Somehow, once it's gone, tha's no' th' same thing...."

He blew out his breath in an explosive force of air, then put his head down on his crossed arms. Summer could hear faint, muttering oaths, and shifted uneasily. She felt suddenly exposed, and reached out to draw the edge of the sheet over her body. Tremors racked her, and she felt the scalding heat of Jamie's hip and thigh pressed against hers and wondered what it would have been like for him to finish that shattering act.

Several minutes ticked past as they lay there, naked and barely touching. Then Summer felt Jamie move, turned her head to see him roll over on his back. He bent the leg nearest her, pressing his foot into the mattress, hiding his groin from view.

When his head tilted to look at her, there was a faint glimmer of humor in his eyes, and she felt a wave of relief wash over her.

"I appreciate your offer," he drawled, reaching out to glide a knuckle over the sheet-covered mound of her breast, "but I don't intend to allow you to overpay me."

She swallowed, and a hot flush stained her cheeks. "I wasn't—I mean, it wasn't just to honor a debt."

"I know. I think I can tell genuine response from a charade, lass." He dug his thumbs into his closed eyes and rubbed, then put his clasped hands behind his head and stared up at the jade velvet swagged over the bed. His voice was glum. "It would be quite a bit more convenient if you had been with a man before, but I won't be the one to bleed you."

Summer should have been astounded, grateful, delirious with delight, ecstatic. She was none of those things. Just why did this rogue have such complicated, convenient morals? There was an aching, bewildering emptiness inside her that gnawed at her soul, and she didn't know how to ease it. But she did know that this was one more rejection, and she didn't intend to suffer it silently.

"A fine time to get moral on me, James Cameron," she said in a bitter voice that drew his astonished gaze. "Do you think I appreciate your taking me so far and then leaving me like an unwanted bride at the marriage altar? I don't!"

"Lass—"

"And I don't care a fig for your silly reasons for all that you've done since dragging me out of that river!" She snatched at the satin sheet, pulling it up to her chin. "You have humiliated me. Please leave me alone."

Curling his lean body to a sitting position, Jamie stared at her. Their gazes clashed, then he gave a shake of his dark head.

"Och, I dinna ken wha' logic lodges in a lass's brain," he muttered in a harsh tone. He flicked her a brief glance as he left the bed, and his jaw was hard and set. "Ye're a daft burd, an' I'll be glad tae send ye home."

"Speak English," she snapped. She didn't know how she was supposed to feel in a situation like this, had never imagined such a thing happening to her. She wasn't at all certain who was more confused, but at this point, it hardly mattered.

"I'll be glad to see the last of you," Jamie said with a snap to his voice that matched hers. He moved around the end of the bed and picked up his clothes, then flashed her a tight smile. "I'll pay for your passage home first thing in the morning."

"Fine!"

Jamie didn't bother to dress, but left with his clothes slung over his arm, arrogant and furious as he slammed out the door. Summer felt the hot press of tears behind her eyelids, but blinked them back. Her throat was tight. What did she care if he was angry? Why should he be? Why should she be? She briefly closed her eyes.

She was going home. She'd never see that laughing-eyed Scotsman again, and she didn't know if she was glad or not.

Chapter 10

Weak sunlight slanted through the quarrels of the windows in the breakfast room, throwing diamond-shaped patterns on the carpet and table. An intricately worked white lace runner was spread from one end of the table to the other, and a plain candelabrum with three branches sprouted from the center.

Footmen moved from table to pantry and back, bringing dishes filled with everything from kippers to kidney pie. Summer gazed down at her plate, pushing at her food with a three-tined fork.

Jamie watched her from the other end of the table, a distance of perhaps ten feet. He felt a rush of irritation. Couldn't she at least feel *some* gratitude that he had not taken her? Instead, she acted as if he had done the opposite and raped her in screaming protest. He shook his head. He'd never understand the female mind. It defied logic.

When Tidwell approached with a neatly folded edition of the *Times* on a silver tray, Jamie leapt at the diversion. He shook it out and held it up in front of him, pretending to read and drink his coffee. Let her think he wasn't at all affected by what had happened.

It galled him that he was. Why should any woman pretend a lack of virtue? It was baffling, and he wished his mother weren't so far away so he could ask her. Fiona Cameron was a woman who would speak her mind, and he doubted she'd ever played these ridiculous charades that had plagued him for the past forty-eight hours.

"Mister Cameron."

Summer's voice was soft and cool, with that alluring drawl that had intrigued him from the first. He lowered the edge of the paper to look at her.

"Have you any notion when a ship for America might sail?"

Damn her. She looked delicate and lovely, with that glorious hair that was not quite blond and not quite brown curling in adorable little wisps around her face.

Even with the memory of the previous night shading his every thought, she made him want her.

"None." He rattled the paper as if impatient. "I have obviously not had the opportunity to inquire. Would you like for me to abandon my breakfast for it?"

She flushed, a fragile pink that made her eyes look an even brighter blue. "No. That's quite all right."

"Then perhaps you won't mind if I send someone to make the inquiries for me?" He lifted his brow when her chin jerked up. "That's one of the advantages of having capable servants, you see."

"Yes," she snapped, "so it is!"

"Still angry, lass?" He smiled. "A pity. Didn't you sleep well?" He hoped, viciously, that she had tossed and turned all night long, as he had done. It had been one of the longest nights in recent memory, even longer than the night he'd spent with his backside scraping the floorboards of an inn while Summer slept in the bed.

"I slept perfectly well, thank you."

Summer's face gave nothing away, and he had the thought that she had probably slept soundly. It figured. He still had an ache that made even his head hurt, and she looked cool and composed.

Jerking to his feet, he tossed the unfolded newspaper to the table. "I'm glad to hear it. I trust you won't mind a small delay before I see to your passage home. I hadn't planned on being in London this soon, but since I'm here, I have business matters that I can take care of. If you need anything while I'm gone, Tidwell will see to it."

Her face blazed with high color, but she gave him a nod and said quietly, "Thank you—my lord."

The last was an afterthought, an obvious attempt to widen the gulf between them. He managed an amused smile.

"Who's been teaching you the proper form of address, may I ask?"

"Tidwell sent a maid, Letty, to me. She was kind enough to instruct me in how one should address an important man like yourself."

There was an edge of malice to her words, and he took it silently. No point in dignifying her inference. And they both knew she thought him a charlatan anyway, luckily managing to win a title and estates that he didn't deserve and could not hope to fulfill nobly.

With a silky smile, he asked, "And how should I inform the servants to address you, madam? There must be some sort of title we can impart upon you."

She rested her chin in the cup of one palm and smiled. "Miss Smith will be quite adequate, thank you."

"I daresay." He flicked a glance toward a footman who came in from the pantry with hot coffee, then looked back at Summer. "Make yourself at home, *Miss Smith*. As I will be busy for a time, I leave you to your own ends."

When the door to the breakfast room shut behind him, he had the irritated thought that if he was fortunate, he would not have to see her again until the day she left England behind. It was too wearing on his body to endure the sort of tension she inflicted upon him.

Summer had the same thought. She sat silently,

looking down at her plate and feeling the curious gazes flicked toward her by the footmen. Damn them. She didn't care what they thought. She didn't care what Jamie thought.

What a liar she was.

A sigh slipped from her, and she attacked her kippers—horrible, salted little fish—with a vengeance. She felt better almost immediately. Looking up, she intercepted a glance from a footman and flushed slightly.

"Will you please hand me the newspaper?" she asked to ease her discomfort and banish the knowing lights in his eyes.

"Certainly, madam." The *Times* was placed into her hands, and she smoothed out the wrinkles Jamie had inflicted on it.

She'd only asked for the paper to keep from feeling so foolish, but as she turned it over, her eyes skimmed over a familiar name. Her heart dropped to her toes. Her fingers tightened in the news sheets with a loud rustle. Under a bold heading, her name leapt out at her:

AMERICAN HEIRESS ABDUCTED—REWARD

Miss Summer St. Clair, late of New Orleans, was taken from her home by person or persons unknown. Heir to the St. Clair shipping concern and fortune, and niece of Barton Shriver, who is president of the St. Clair lines, Miss St. Clair is said to be of uncommon beauty, with dark blond hair and blue eyes. . . .

There was more, but she couldn't read it. Apparently Messrs. Fontaine and D'Aubigny, her father's solicitors, were prepared to pay handsomely for her return unharmed. It did not mention Tutwiler, she'd noticed, and she was glad.

A sudden, sinking feeling gripped her. If Jamie

read this, he would know the truth. Not even the dullest wit could miss it. She had to tell him. She couldn't risk his finding it out this way, even if she *was* leaving.

Chewing on her fist, she stared blankly at the slant of sun coming in the window. It would have to be done with care and tact, of course. And at just the right moment.

A month later, Summer was still in London, and still at 66 Bruton Street. It seemed that there were few New Orleans–bound passenger vessels with room for a lady aboard; since the war had escalated again, travel had become dangerous and crowded. Most vessels were being used for warfare, not passengers.

Moreover, her true identity was still unknown to Jamie. With a streak of cowardice she hadn't known she had, Summer had avoided telling him the truth. It was amazing, and indeed shaming, to discover that she had so little true courage, but it didn't ever seem to be the right time or place. And even more amazing, he had not read that damning paragraph.

She'd scoured the papers every day for a week afterward, and it never appeared again. Perhaps it wouldn't.

In the meantime, the weeks passed quietly; she saw Jamie rarely, and then he was a polite stranger who sometimes gave her faintly puzzled glances. It was obvious why. He must be wondering how he had ever been coerced into keeping such a petulant creature in his house.

On occasion, she would hear him come in very late—or very early, depending upon one's point of view. Most of the time she was asleep, however—dreaming about a man with a wicked grin and dancing black eyes.

All he had to do was to stop to talk to her on occasion, give her a smile, bow politely over her hand, and her heart fluttered like a trapped bird. *Infantile behavior!* She'd already been through an infatuation with Garth Kinnison; was she mad to have fallen into another one?

Of course. It would have been obvious to a stone gargoyle that she was quite, quite mad.

Her insanity did not extend to refusing Jamie's offer of a hefty purse, however. A loan, he said when she hesitated, his voice sarcastic and his one black brow lifting with sardonic amusement. Though she had gritted her teeth and taken it, she'd felt a flash of resentment at his attitude. One would think it was *he* who'd been wronged.

Taking Letty, Summer had gone into the city in Jamie's coach. They left the coach at the Two Swans and ventured out. The little maid seemed to know where to shop, and by the end of the morning, they stood by a stone bollard on the corner of Exchange Alley with arms full of bandboxes and paper-wrapped packages.

The bollard, which had been erected by the city to lessen the danger to pedestrians on the paving stones of being run down by coaches and curricles flashing past, provided Summer with a place upon which to lean while she removed a pebble from her shoe. They were new pumps and a bit loose.

Letty balanced the packages, grumbling a bit at the amount of them, and shifted from one foot to the other as Summer untied the laces holding on her new pumps. Stockings and shifts, cosmetics and combs and brushes and hairpins, filled quite a few bundles.

"I'll help you," Summer said as she swiftly tied the laces back around her ankle, affording a glimpse of white stockings and shapely calves to passersby. Straightening, she reached out to take a few of the packages from Letty.

It happened so quickly, she could never recall later exactly what had occurred. She was grabbed from behind, an arm around her waist and one around her neck, and hauled backward. There was only time for a shrill scream, and she had a brief impression of Letty standing with her mouth open, packages filling her arms.

Struggling, choking as the arm increased pressure, she heard a rough voice snarl at her, "Shut up, y'little bitch!"

Instead of terrifying her, this sent her into a frenzy. She bucked and kicked and clawed at the arm around her neck until black spots danced in front of her eyes. She was vaguely aware of Letty launching herself at the attacker, screaming shrilly in her Cockney voice, and the man cursing both of them.

Then, as suddenly as the assailant had appeared, he was gone, releasing Summer with a thump and a shove. Dazed, she saw the reason in a rather portly gentleman with knee breeches and a silk hat, his dress sword drawn and a most indignant expression on his fleshy face.

"The damn bloody cutpurse!" he shouted, shaking his sword at the fleeing man before he turned his attention to Summer. "Are you hurt, m'dear?"

Letty helped her up, and Summer smoothed her skirts with shaking hands. Her hair was tumbled around her shoulders, and her face was scratched; she could barely speak for the bruises on her throat.

"I think I'm all right," she managed to croak.

"Shall I send my man with you? You look quite shaken."

" 'Ere," Letty began irately, "w'y don' ye see us ta our inn, sir? 'Er laidyship is a fright, an' if sumpin' were ta 'appen ta 'er, 'is lordship 'ud 'ave my 'ead, 'e wud!"

Startled, the gentleman quickly recovered. "Of course. I thank you for reminding me of my manners," he said with a courtly bow. He offered his arm to Summer. Shall we, m'dear? I've a notion to squire a beautiful woman about."

By the time they reached the Two Swans, Summer had begun to recover from her fright. She found her knight-errant to be a rather charming man, witty and jolly, and shrewd. His name was Mr. Fox, and she introduced herself—with a slight flush—as Miss Smith.

His eyes twinkled at that, but he absorbed the information gravely. "I'm very pleased to make your acquaintance, Miss Smith. Of Mayfair, you say? I don't seem to recall any Smiths, but then, my memory isn't as good as it once was."

He was delighted to learn that she was American and asked a great many questions. "I've managed to put myself in quite a scrape a few times espousing the Americans," he said with satisfaction, and Summer got the distinct impression that he didn't mind it at all. "Of course, that is all done for me now."

When they reached the inn and the coach was drawn up for her, Mr. Fox gazed at it for a moment. His mouth tilted in a faint smile, and he turned to Summer. "M'dear, would it be an inconvenience if I were to call upon you at some future date?"

Summer had no illusions that he wished to embark upon a flirtation; there was something else in his shrewd gaze, something puzzling and vaguely distressing.

"I'm not at all certain that would be the thing, sir," she said after a moment. "My ... brother ..." *Lord, what a dreadful liar she was!*

"Ah, I understand."

She thought for a horrible moment that he truly did understand, and when he opened the coach door for her, she knew it for a fact.

"Give my regards to Lord Westcott, Miss Smith. I have met him a time or two. A handsome Scot, if a bit fearsome."

There was a brief, appalled silence, then she met his gaze and saw that it wasn't malicious, only curious and searching.

"Yes," she said, "I shall do that."

"Good day to you, madam."

Summer had no idea whom she'd met until Jamie was informed of the incident. He was coldly furious.

"Do you have *any* idea who that was? Any at all?" he bit off. "Mr. Charles Fox, former opposition leader of the Whigs and bosom friend to the prince."

Stunned, Summer sat quietly kneading her skirt in her hands. Her throat hurt, and he was behaving as if she had somehow invited the disaster.

"So? What do you expect me to do?"

"Do?" His expression was savage. "I expect you to remain here. Send a servant to make your purchases from now on. Unless you like being assaulted, that is. Ah. I see from your sulky expression that you don't like that. Too bad. Look, my little *demivierge*, unless you want to be courted as one of the fair Cyprians of this city, you'd best remain here and relatively hidden until a ship to New Orleans can be—"

Surging to her feet, she glared at him. *"Demivierge!* Do you think I don't know what that means? You damn strutting cockerel! 'Twas your lusty urges that brought me to that end! That and your stupid behavior at Vauxhall. Now anyone would believe that I'm your mistress, not your sister. Or your sister-in-law!"

"Summer—"

"Damn you!" Hot tears stung her eyes. To be called a half-virgin, a sexually active innocent stopping just short of the actual act, was, to her, the greatest of insults. She saw Jamie flush, but his jaw tightened with obstinate pride when she snarled, "Lecher!" at him.

"Probably. But at least I'm honest about it." He left then, but not before warning her not to leave the house again. She heard a distant door slam and his bellow for a horse, then it was quiet in the drawing room.

A fire flickered on the grate. Candles glowed in serene ellipses of light. Summer sat stiff and still in one of the new chairs with lyre-backs and curved legs.

He was right, she knew, and the incident had frightened her, but she still smarted from his callous disregard of what she'd suffered. What was there to do now but wait?

And waiting was one of the things she did not do well. One of the many, she had discovered in her short life. She did not sing, did not play a stringed instrument, did not keep her clothes tidy or her bureau drawers. She obviously did not organize her life well, either. And now she was to wait.

So, she waited, caught between yesterday and tomorrow, with no present to give her ballast. And she fretted, with nothing to do but wander from the library to the garden and back.

It was Tidwell who suggested she dabble at gardening, and Summer found it her only release for growing frustration with days empty of entertainment. And Jamie.

Gardening, as her mother had said, provided a certain peace. Summer took pleasure in delving into the black earth of the beds, pressing small, fragile plants into the still-cool dirt, smelling the rich humus, then reaping the sweet satisfaction of watching the blossoms lift limp heads to the sun.

The day Lord Epson came to call, she was in the garden wearing an old dress, with a straw bonnet atop her head and a small spade in one hand.

Tidwell announced him from the low steps of the terrace, and when she turned, Summer saw with dismay Epson's elegant frame mince down the walkway toward her. She stood uneasily brushing the dirt from her skirts, fully aware of his highly amused gaze resting on her.

"Lady Summer," he said, his hesitation over her title obvious, "I must say, you remind me of a woodland creature! Does Westcott insist upon you toiling in his garden?"

His obvious distress eased Summer's discomfort. Smiling at him, she tossed aside her small trowel and peeled off the gloves she wore.

"Actually, my lord, he doesn't even know I'm out

here. If he did, I'm afraid my pleasurable days in the garden would end."

She flicked a glance at Tidwell. "Please bring us some refreshment." When he had gone into the house, she allowed Lord Epson to escort her to the bench she'd sat on with Jamie that first night. Ivy still twined around the stones. Summer seated herself gingerly, as if the sturdy stone seat would disintegrate beneath her.

"I vow," said Epson, slanting a dubious glance at the ivy and jasmine curled around the stone bench, "you are even more lovely portraying a woodland nymph than I recalled from the Gardens."

"Is that so?" Summer smiled, fiddling with the ends of the ribbons tying her straw hat on her head. "Is that what you came to say today? Or did you come to visit Westcott?"

She'd dealt with men of Epson's ilk before. She knew the look about him, the air of innocence to disguise the underlying ennui and mischief. A faint smile curved her mouth as she watched Epson's face.

" 'Pon rep, Lady Summer, you are a devilishly outspoken lady," he said uncomfortably. "And I didn't come to visit Westcott. I came to see you."

"Ah." She tied and untied the blue satin ribbons under her chin. "I'm honored, sir."

"Are you?" Smiling, he shoved a hand through his fair hair. "I admit to hoping you would greet me with a certain amount of pleasure."

Summer flicked his elegant attire with a jaundiced eye. Lord Epson appeared to be a coxcomb, a dandy, with his yellow and purple waistcoat, fobs, quizzing glass, the snuffbox he picked from his pocket, and the monogrammed lace handkerchief he used when he gave a delicate sneeze. He certainly seemed rather tame to her, especially after a man like the Scotsman.

Drumming her heels nervously against the weeds beneath the stone bench, Summer said, "Guests are always welcome, my lord. I regret that the viscount will not be back for a while yet, but—"

Epson waved a negligent hand. "I saw Westcott a short time ago. He was deep in the throes of a game of macao. Or was it whist? No matter. Looked to be foxed to me. Might be a while before he returns. Something about a lovely lady in Covent Garden anxiously awaiting him . . ."

His pale eyes sharply surveyed her heightened color. "I will be frank, my lady. I wanted to talk to you alone."

Summer shifted uncomfortably and shredded the ends of her sash. "I cannot imagine why," she began, then glanced up and saw the shrewd glitter in Epson's eyes. Of course. He had not been fooled for an instant by their masquerade that night at Vauxhall Gardens. And he was intrigued. She smiled. "On second thought, perhaps I can imagine. You wish to know my relation to Lord Westcott, am I correct?"

"An extremely perceptive young woman." Epson gave her his most charming smile. "I seem to have heard something most recently, let me see—would it have been about a young lady set upon by bandits in her room at an inn? Yes, and there was a gentleman there who came to the rescue, I believe. Perhaps you—"

"What do you want?" Summer eyed him coolly. "I perceive that all this information you have so carefully gathered is to further some end, my lord. Do you care to enlighten me?"

"I do admire a woman who doesn't quibble." Epson lifted his quizzing glass and raked her thoroughly. Much too thoroughly as far as Summer was concerned. "My wants are quite simple, my lady." He smiled broadly. "I fancy you."

Summer frowned. "I believe that your visit is ended, my lord," she said, standing abruptly, and Epson only smiled more widely. He swung his quizzing glass by its satin ribbon, round and round the end of one finger.

"Sweet lady, I meant no offense. I harbor only the

greatest admiration in my breast." He put one hand over his heart, and Summer gazed at him warily.

"I repeat, my lord—what do you want?"

"Some truths." He put out a hand to touch her cheek, and she recoiled from him. "I cannot help but wonder why you remain here."

"If you had done more thorough research," Summer said in a tart voice, "you would have discovered that the reason I am here is because your English ports are crowded, and I cannot secure passage on a ship home."

"Ah." Epson's brow lifted slightly, a pale imitation of Jamie's gesture as far as she was concerned. "I regret to inform you that someone has been leading you astray. There are any number of spaces available on ships sailing from Southampton." He coughed politely, flicked open an enameled snuffbox and took out a pinch, then gave a delicate sneeze into his lace-trimmed handkerchief before he continued, "Perhaps your presence here is desired more than you know."

Summer said nothing. She gazed at him with what she hoped was polite attention, while she tried to hide the turmoil his words caused. Would Jamie have deliberately lied to her? Why? It certainly couldn't be because he wanted her to stay, not in light of the fact that he had taken great pains to ignore her the past month.

"Ah," Lord Epson said in a soothing tone, "I see that I have given you food for thought." He gazed at his snuffbox for a moment as if seeing it for the first time. "Have you ever partaken of snuff, milady? No? Pity."

"I repeat," Summer said icily, "why have you come?"

"And I repeat, milady—I fancy you." He slid a hand down her arm to catch her wrist. "It should be obvious to you by now that Westcott does not intend to assist you as he must have promised, and it seems that he has grown tired of your charms." A faint smile tilted his mouth. "I am not so easily bored by beautiful women as our noble Scot seems to be. And I will not make empty promises. I will cherish you above all women!"

Summer drew her hand from his light clasp. His palms were as smooth as a woman's, and that made her slightly scornful.

"Truly, my lord, I think you have misread me. I am not what you appear to believe. Nor do I need another protector in my life." She waved an arm to indicate the house. "As you can see, I am sheltered reasonably well, and if Lord Westcott seeks carnal pleasures elsewhere, that is his business." Her eyes met his startled gaze coolly. "I am not so foolish as to fall in love; nor am I foolish enough to think you cherish me, either. You merely want what most men want—a warm, willing female of acceptable form and face. I am not interested in your offer, sir."

Epson had recovered his composure. "I find myself devastated, madam," he said with a curling smile. "Should you reconsider at any time, I will be at your service. And who knows? P'raps you will find me a more considerate lover than Westcott."

"There shall never be an opportunity to disprove that, I am afraid," Summer said coolly, and saw the brief flash of anger in Epson's eyes.

"To your regret, my dear lady." He paused, then said with malicious relish, "You know, Westcott is a man said to have a quick temper and lasting memory. There are three things I happen to know he cannot abide—a cheat at cards, a liar, and anything French. Perhaps you should keep that in mind and not dismiss me so completely."

Her throat worked. "I will do that, my lord."

"Forget it at your own peril, sweet Lady Summer," Epson said softly.

Summer couldn't quite recall what she said in parting to Epson. She thought him an odious toad, but his careless information made her heart burn. And somehow, most painful of all, was the thought of Jamie with another woman. He would, of course, seek out other women. He was a virile man, and he'd not be without feminine companionship for long. Why hadn't she considered that? And why did it make her want to weep into her gardening gloves?

Sucking in a deep breath of fresh air and English earth, Summer realized she would have to leave before much more time went by. She was in dire danger of losing her heart to a handsome Highland rogue who certainly didn't seem to want it. . . .

When Jamie returned to Bruton Street late that afternoon, he found Summer in the garden. Her face had smears of dirt on it, and she was attacking a weed-choked flower bed as if it had risen up in revolt.

Faintly startled, he stood for a moment and watched her hack at the weeds with what he thought was uncalled-for ferocity. Her small gardening trowel was caked with black earth, and the shears she wielded so savagely were sticky with lopped-off stems. She appeared to have been pruning as well.

A faint frown dipped his brow as he watched her. It was obvious that she was filled with barely leashed frustration, and he couldn't say that he blamed her. He'd fret too if he were caged, no matter how gilded the bars. Plague take it, why was this so complicated?

His interview with Mr. Fox had not been satisfactory at all and left him feeling vaguely uneasy. Of course, that worthy knew much more than Jamie would have liked for him to know about his life, but that couldn't be helped. Fox made it his business to know. And he thought that the attack on *Miss Smith* had not been idle chance or the work of a cutpurse. After all, there had been no attempt to take her purse, just to take her. Jamie couldn't help but wonder why but knew better than to ask Summer. He'd get no answer for his pains, only aggravation.

So why was he here now, watching her ravage a flower bed with a trowel? It defied logic. Perhaps he just liked the way she held her tongue between small white teeth as if that would keep it from wagging. He smiled. He knew better. She fenced well with that formidable weapon, this little American with the feline face and glossy tumble of sun-and-shadow hair.

He leaned against a column of the gazebo and watched her.

She finally noticed him and sat back on her heels. There was no sign of welcome in the fiery blue gaze that scanned his casual attire—boots, pants, and white shirt open at the neck—and he smothered a sigh. He hadn't really expected a welcome, but he'd thought perhaps she might greet him with some semblance of civility. He'd certainly given her enough time to forgive him for his last verbal blunder. Forgiveness. So much for that ridiculous notion.

He traversed the paving stones to the flower bed with a show of confidence.

"Digging for treasure, ma'am?" he asked in what he thought was a light, teasing tone.

She brushed back a dangling strand of hair from her eyes, smearing more dirt over her cheek and forehead. "And if I am?"

Definite hostility. What had he done to annoy her now?

Jamie kicked at a loose paving stone with his boot. He felt a wave of irritation. She made him feel like a callow youth. His dark brow lowered.

"Why aren't you wearing one of the new gowns I paid for?"

"To dig in the garden?" She lifted her shoulders in a shrug. " 'Twould seem rather ungrateful."

She stressed *ungrateful*, and Jamie's mouth tightened. "Aye, I suppose it would," he said more roughly than he'd intended. "And you do insist upon being grateful, don't you, lass?"

Stabbing the gardening trowel into the ground,

Summer rose to her feet and faced him. She reminded him of a trapped ferret for a moment; her body almost trembled with suppressed emotion.

"In my position, there is very little else for me to do but be grateful—and *wait*! You, of course, may gallivant about town gambling, drinking and ... and wenching. And if I sound a bit out of sorts, perhaps it's because I don't appreciate being lied to!"

He eyed her cautiously. "Lied to? About what?"

Her throat worked for a moment, and her small chin quivered slightly. "About the availability of passage on a vessel bound for New Orleans. I have been given to understand that such passage is—and has been—available for some time."

"Really? And who, may I ask, so kindly divulged such intelligence to you?"

She shifted uncertainly, scuffing the toes of her pumps through the weeds. "Lord Epson."

"Ah. I see. And when did that gallant see fit to drop by?"

Not quite meeting his gaze, Summer stared past him to a point unknown. Her blue eyes still radiated frustrated anger. "Earlier today." Her gaze shifted, challenging him. "I sent a man to the docks to check on it for me, but he has not yet returned. Was Epson correct?"

"What would a denial avail me?" He met her scorching gaze with cool eyes. "You seem to believe whoever happens to say something you want to hear."

She glared at him. "Do you think I want to hear that you have lied to me? That there is available passage and you won't part with the necessary coins to purchase it for me?"

"Is that what you think?" He felt a wave of fury wash over him, roughening his speech to a thick brogue. "Ye think I am sae stingy a carl tha' I wa'd no' gi'e ye th' paltry coins tae lea'e?"

Meeting his fierce gaze, Summer put her hands on her hips. "I infer from your garbled speech that you are angry and probably because I'm right. What other reason would there be?"

"Is't no' because ye're a sweet-tongued lass," he growled at her, and struggled for control of his temper. It was amazing how quickly she could goad him into fury. If he hadn't known better, he'd have thought she didn't mean to do it. A suspicious brightness in her eyes made him look at her more closely, and he shook his head. "Lass, you may go with Tidwell the next time he visits the shipping offices, if you like. I've a man at the St. Clair lines who is to inform me the moment there is something suitable."

He put out a quick hand when she stumbled back and away from him. "Are you going to argue about that?" he asked when she shook his hand from her arm. "Faith, ye're the most fidgety female I've ever met!"

"I'm not arguing about it," she said. "I'm just angry because you told me nothing. Now I've sent someone to check on it, and—oh, never mind! You act as if I've some kind of disease and you don't dare stand around me too long or you might catch it." Her head tilted, and she shook back the hair from her eyes, almost losing the straw hat she wore. There was hurt pride in her tone when she said softly, "I offered you the most precious gift I had and you spurned it, then you make me feel as if I've done you some horrible wrong. And now your friends visit and obviously regard me as a harlot, and I'm to suffer it quietly. Maybe you didn't lie, but shouldn't I be allowed some anger?"

Wincing, Jamie was quiet. He wanted to call Epson out, and he wanted to erase the hurt from Summer's eyes. It was a moment before he said, "I didn't mean to cause you pain, lass. Or to insult you. I will deal with Epson, trust me on that."

His fists clenched and unclenched at his sides, and he dug the toe of his highly polished boot into the dirt of the flower bed. "As for the other—I did not intend insult. It was much harder for me to refuse than it would have been to take what you offered. I only wanted to spare you the mistake of doing what could never be undone." He shrugged. "I could have chosen my words more carefully, but it was, you understand, a very awkward, *uncomfortable* moment for me too."

"You seem to have recovered rather well."

Jamie's gaze snapped to hers, and he opened his mouth to give her a furious retort, then paused when he saw the crystal gather of tears in the corners of her eyes.

"Lass! Tears?"

"Not for you, James Cameron," she said with a wrenching gasp, "not for you! They're for me. No one ever asks me what I want, or what I think, or even *if* I think! You smug men just go blithely along making decisions that affect me without a fragment of concern as to whether I agree or disagree, or anything else! I hate all of you!"

A strangled sound locked in her throat, and she turned blindly away. Jamie leapt forward and turned her in his arms to face him. She tried to pull away, curling her small hands into fists and beating his chest when he held her.

"Dinna fash yerself, lass," he murmured, letting her beat rhythmic strokes on his chest, his fingers curled lightly but firmly around her upper arms. Her wild flailing gradually stilled, then she leaned into him, pressing her face against his shirt. His arms went around her.

It was disconcerting to have her breasts pushing into him, the light, delicate fragrance of her hair and femininity in his nostrils, and he damned his immediate, inopportune arousal. Even the scent of dirt and some sort of odorous weed did not dim his need for this girl. He put her back from him after a moment.

She wasn't crying. There were faint tracks where her tears had been wiped away, making mud of the dirt on her face, but she looked at him with eyes only slightly misted.

"Pardon me," she said politely. "I seem to have lost control for a moment. And I've soiled your shirt."

"That's quite all right." He took her hand, holding it when she tried to pull away, and led her to the garden bench. She shied from it, and he was firm. "Sit down, Summer. I want to talk to you."

She sat down and looked at her hands. "I was afraid you might."

"Why won't you tell me your real name? Is it that well known, perhaps? Are you hiding from someone?"

She seemed to be struggling with herself, and Jamie waited more patiently than he felt. This situation was inexplicable. What on earth could she be hiding that would make someone want to harm her?

"Summer?"

She looked up at him, sucked in a deep breath, and said quietly, "I cannot tell you."

His brow snapped down. "You don't trust me. You think I might do you harm, is that it?" He laughed harshly. "Thank you for your confidence in me, lass."

She put a hand on his arm. "No. It's not that. You just might think my reasons are unimportant."

"Ah. Much better. Now, instead of being a vile villain, I am a thick-skinned oaf who can't possibly understand the more gentle emotions that might compel a woman to hide the fact that she has spent over a month in the unchaperoned company of a man. I see. Do you think I would shout your name aloud if I knew it? Do you think I would parade you in front of the magistrates, for God's sake?"

"No!" Her hands twisted together, winding into the thin material of her skirt and wadding it into knots. "Don't you understand anything? Lord Epson knows that you rescued me from that stupid innkeeper and that you have taken me into your protection! He naturally assumes that we are lovers; no amount of denial would convince him otherwise. And your Mr. Fox—

though he seems much more discreet—is well aware that I'm not part of your family. So, if I do not leave England quickly and anonymously, my family will soon know exactly where I've been and with whom!"

She was panting slightly, out of breath, her eyes wide and smoky. Jamie felt a hot curl of betrayal.

"You said you were an orphan."

"I am! I've just an uncle. And he could make life very unpleasant for me. Even more than he already has."

"I see."

She shook her head so vigorously the straw hat tilted awry. "No, you don't. All you can see is personal injury that I won't confide in you. There's no point in discussing this further."

He stood up. "Aye, lass. I agree. There's no point in telling the truth when a lie will serve as well."

An exasperated sigh blew a pale strand of hair that had drifted into her face. "I haven't lied. I just haven't told you everything."

"And you think that's fair?"

"Obviously, I do."

Jamie's mouth tightened, and he stared down at her pale face and heavy-lashed eyes for a long moment. *Damn her.*

"I seem to recall a great deal of righteous indignation when I forgot to mention I was not penniless." He gave her a slight smile when she flushed. "But now, because the shoe is on the other foot, I hear evasion justified. You are a fickle, treacherous female, Lady Summer."

Her chin lifted defiantly, and she met his gaze without blinking. "Thank you."

"I suppose I must admire such an ability to contradict oneself without showing a trace of remorse, but somehow I find it difficult."

"How unfortunate for you."

"And for you. . . ." His hands flashed out, and he grasped her wrists and pulled her to her feet and hard against him. He was angry. Why did she push him so hard? He'd tried to be fair, tried to do what was right, and she scorned him every step of the way.

God's blood, just touching her made his body react. He allowed her to move away from him a few steps, keeping his grip on her wrists. She was pushing him to the brink of his self-control, and he didn't seem to be able to get a grip on himself.

His lips flattened into a grim smile when he saw her gaze drop, then her eyes widen at the hard bulge in his tight pants; he made his voice insulting.

"Don't make the mistake of thinking that just because my body responds to you, I do. I don't want you."

A very female smile curved her lips. "Really?"

He swore softly under his breath. *The vixen!* She was enjoying his discomfort, reveling in the power she had over him. His voice was harsh. "Really."

Summer arched a brow. "If you will recall, my lord, I was freely offered to you at one time. You spurned me. I did not think it at all gallant—or manly of you." Her smile widened, and her voice was a soft purr. "But maybe I was mistaken in thinking that you were more manly than you are. . . ."

His jaw worked. He was so aroused, he was aching, and she watched him with eyes as blue and cold as sapphires, enjoying his struggle. Maybe she taunted him because she felt safe that he would not act on his desire. Jamie began to feel his noble principles fade in the press of lust and wondered harshly if she knew what she was doing to him. *Damn all virgins and their teasing.*

"May I suggest that you are treading on thin ice, my lady?" he ground out, his eyes narrowing when her tongue flicked out to moisten her lips. "Damnit, Summer! . . ."

She laughed, softly, her eyes sparkling with malice, and he jerked her close.

"My sweet, since you seem to be offended that I

did not take what you freely offered, I've reconsid-ered," he said in a tight voice, temper flaring so hot in his eyes that he could see its reflection in her face. "I will take your precious maidenhead, as you seem to be in a hurry to give it away. And then I will put you on a ship to America if I have to dump you in a jolly boat and row you across the Atlantic myself."

A small gasp escaped her when Jamie lifted her into his arms and stalked toward the house, but he paid no more attention to that than he did to the avid stares of the servants when he passed them on the staircase. Summer struggled; she lost her straw hat and one of her shoes. Her skirts worked up around her knees, revealing slender calves and smears of dirt on her white silk hose.

Jamie shoved open the door to his bedchamber with a boot and kicked it shut behind him, then crossed to the bed and dumped her on its wide sur-face. He followed her, dropping his body across hers.

"Oh no," he said, capturing her arms and holding her wrists in one tight fist, "I don't intend to be so generous as to allow you to beat on me again. I'll take only your sweet kisses now, lass."

"You'll have to take them, because I won't give them freely!" Her body bucked under his weight. She glared up at him.

His mouth crooked in a smile. He could feel the rapid beat of her heart, the slamming of blood through her veins.

"I think," he said softly, "that I can prove you wrong on that score, my sweet."

Chapter 11

Summer felt compelled to offer resistance despite having goaded him into reaction. Part of her had known, even while she was pricking him, that he would not swallow her insults. The other portion of her brain—the demented portion—had urged her on.

She wanted him to make love to her, to finish what he'd begun a month before and not leave her aching at night in her lonely bed. If she was to go back to Louisiana and risk a loveless, hateful marriage, then she would at least taste sexual pleasures beforehand. Freeman Tutwiler would not get a chaste bride.

And James Cameron would not take her easily; he would pay for his refusal of her before she yielded to him. Pride demanded it.

He rose to his knees on the bed and held her hips wedged tightly between his muscled thighs; slowly, methodically, he removed her clothing, stripping away her gown and shift and stockings and tossing them to the floor, swearing softly when she hindered him.

Late afternoon sunshine trapped her squirming body in a relentless glare, and Jamie touched her intimately. His hand moved from her face, down her throat, to the high swell of her breasts and lingered. Summer felt a hot, choking press of air in her throat at his lazy caress, felt the burn of his gaze as sharply as she felt the searing touch of his hand and the warmth of the sun.

An internal fire blazed higher, and she throbbed with expectation. She knew what would come next; the last time had prepared her. She waited for it, ached for it, but would not ask for it. Nor would she help him, not when he was so arrogant.

Still holding her wrists in one hand as if she might escape him, Jamie fumbled with his buttons, and Summer saw that he meant to take her without undressing. Somehow, instead of dampening her need, this inflamed it. He was hot and ready for her, and he spread her thighs with one hand, his fingers moving cleverly to the silky curls there to make her ready for him.

She gasped, arching against his hand, biting her lower lip to keep from crying out. Jamie bent and kissed her mouth, his tongue forcing her lips apart as if to prepare her for the final thrust of his body. She couldn't help it; she kissed him back, fervently, desperately, touching his tongue with hers in lightning thrusts. She took him inside her mouth and held him, and when she felt his body move lower and his erection nudge her, she opened for him.

He pushed in a strong, relentless motion, the invasion burning her, making her buck beneath him. A sob caught in the back of her throat, and when he was in that first tiny bit, she swallowed the silent protest. Maybe it was over. Maybe this was the worst of it. She relaxed slightly.

Her breath was absorbed by him, and the small cry and sudden stiffening of her body when he pressed into her in a swift, merciful thrust was quickly accepted.

Lifting his head, he said against her lips, "Easy, lass. Only this first time, only this first time . . ."

He felt so heavy inside her, filling her completely, a raw, burning scrape of him against her most private, tender parts that was slightly painful and extremely exhilarating at the same time. Summer heard her own whimper and tried to keep it back. All the blood in her entire body seemed to have rushed to that one spot, and she ached with exquisitely sensitive shudders.

Jamie was breathing hard, one hand planted on the bed beside her head, the other still curled around her wrists and pushing them into the pillows. She'd thought him imbedded into her as far as he could go, but then he pressed further, stretching her, making her legs jerk convulsively until they were around his hips, her feet grazing his thighs.

"God," he muttered, and lifted his head to gaze down into her eyes. "Summer, are ye a'right, lass?"

There was such a concerned expression in his dark eyes, mixing with the sensual glitter, she felt a sudden surge of love so overpowering she wanted to weep with it. Her voice was choked.

"Yes, I'm fine."

She wanted to tell him to go ahead, that whatever he did would be all right, but she couldn't bring herself to say those words. Maybe he heard them anyway, because he began to move finally, with slow, delicious thrusts that took him all the way in, then partially out, rubbing along the screamingly sensitive parts of her body in a tantalizing rhythm.

Twisting beneath him, she tried to meet his thrusts, her feet digging into the mattress as she pushed upward. She could feel her body convulse around him, and he gave a soft, wordless groan. He pounded into her faster and faster, kissing her eyebrows, her closed eyelids, the tip of her nose, and then finding her mouth.

Summer felt the gathering rush of intensity pool in the pit of her stomach, and she tingled all over. His mouth left hers, and he released her wrists; she put her arms around him, sliding her hands down his back, feeling the cool linen of his shirt beneath her frantic fingers.

She could feel something bewildering happening to her; her body raced toward some nameless goal, and her brain struggled to keep pace. Dimly, as if it were coming from a great distance away, she heard her voice calling his name.

"Jamie . . . Jamie, please . . ."

The searing thrust and drag of him inside her increased in tempo, and he shoved forward with a groan. His shirt had come open somehow, and the linen and pearl buttons rubbed against her in places; his taut-muscled chest rasped across the sensitive peaks of her breasts, heightening the tension.

"Reach for it, lass," he muttered thickly when she rose against him in a clutching embrace. He caught her hips in both his hands and pulled her up, shoving into her so fiercely that she couldn't muffle the loud, anguished cry that left her.

It was half sob, half explosion of relief, and she heard his moan of pleasure mingle with hers. His body went rigid as he exploded inside her, his powerful frame shuddering with the force of it. Then he sagged against her, slowly resting his weight on his elbows and putting his head into the curve of her shoulder and neck.

"Lord, Summer, ye're a sweet lass," he said softly. His breath tickled her ear, stirring the damp tendrils of pale hair that had come loose and were caught beneath her. She was trapped by them and couldn't move to turn and look at him. She stared up at the ice-blue swag of brocade above his bed and surrendered to the sweep of satisfaction that left her weak and drowsy. Her eyelids grew heavy, and she was vaguely aware of Jamie shrugging out of his clothes and coming back to lie beside her.

Dusk deepened the shadows in the room. Sunlight was a muted, tarnished square of gold that slowly narrowed into a thin shaft filled with swimming dust motes. The house was quiet; few sounds could be heard. Time hung in drowsy, lazy suspension.

The huge canopied bed was shadowed and dark; Jamie held Summer next to him, her spine curved into the angle of his chest and thighs. He could feel her soft, velvety buttocks against his groin and pressed his face into the slope of her shoulder, inhaling her fragrance, letting the pale, silky wisps of her hair tickle his nose.

Jamie shifted slightly, and heard Summer's soft moan of sleepy protest. He smiled against the bare satin of her neck. She felt good in his arms, soft and warm and cozy. He'd almost forgotten how good it was to hold a woman that way, secure in the aftermath of sex.

He'd pulled the coverlet up over them. It only half covered Summer, leaving one milky-white breast exposed. He reached out to gently cup it in his palm, weighing it, his thumb dragging across the nipple and making it tighten. She didn't wake but only stirred restlessly.

Easing his palm down the luxuriant length of her side to her thighs, he tucked his fingers between her clasped legs, parting them slowly. Blood still smeared the ivory flesh, ample evidence of her innocence.

Lying back on the pillow, Jamie felt a surge of regret. He shouldn't have taken her, no matter the provocation. She had been innocent, and he had ruined her. *Damn.* It would have been much more to his liking if she had been the ride-under of that sea captain, as she had first claimed; then he could have taken her with no compunction. Yet, even that idea set ill with him now. For some reason, he felt a fierce surge of protection concerning this girl. Another *Damn* racketed around in his brain.

Grunting sourly, he slung his legs from the bed and crossed the room. When he returned, he sat on Summer's side of the bed, his weight dipping the mattress. She shifted slightly, moaning a faint protest. He dipped his hand into the washbasin he held and lifted out a dripping-wet cloth. It was cold, of course, and when he scrubbed it over her thighs, she woke with a gasp and a jerk.

"Oh! What are you—?"

"Cleaning you up, my sweet." Jamie watched her through the veil of his lashes, saw her flush when she realized the reason for it. She lay back down and closed her eyes, crossing her arm over her face and lying rigidly while he bathed her.

It was an enjoyable task for him—of course, he was not the recipient of a cold bath. Gooseflesh pricked her smooth skin. A light shudder contracted her muscles, and he noticed with great interest that her nipples were tightly beaded. He flicked his forefinger across a peak, and she opened her eyes.

She said nothing, but her mouth was thinned into a line that denoted irritation. He gave her his most charming smile and said, "Sorry."

By the time Jamie had finished washing Summer, dragging the cloth over her thighs, her stomach, her breasts, he was fully aroused. As he was as naked as she, it was instantly apparent. Summer flushed and looked away, then looked back.

Sitting up, she said with only a slight quiver in her voice, "May I . . . touch you?"

He sucked in a quick breath and nodded. "Aye, lass. If you like."

Slowly, as if afraid it might bite, she dipped her hand toward his groin, her fingertips lightly grazing him. He bit back a groan and tried to concentrate on the last rays of sunshine lying in patches on the carpet and radiating a hazy glow. Then her hand, warm and soft, touched him again, cradling him in her palm, her fingers stroking. He felt the blood surging in his groin in a slapping pulse.

Half-embarrassed, he sat in awkward silence while Summer examined him. It was sweet agony. The muscles in his belly contracted in an involuntary motion, and his breath came in short, heated drags of air.

He tried for humor. "Now that you've tamed the dragon," he said lightly, "shall I show you how to put him through his paces?"

Her eyes moved reluctantly to his face. "I'd never once imagined that a man was made like this," she said in a matter-of-fact voice that eased his discomfort slightly. "I always wondered. You know. Sometimes when you held me next to you there was only softness, and sometimes, there was this hard ridge. It makes sense now. I thought one of us had an affliction."

Laughter caught in his throat, and when her brows lifted slightly as if offended, he couldn't help it. He laughed aloud. "Och, lassie," he said when she withdrew from him, "dinna be mad a' me. 'Twas jus' tha' ye looked so satisfied a' solvin' th' mystery...."

"I suppose I am," she said after a moment, a slow smile curling her mouth. "You can't imagine what it's like to be told nothing, and then just to be thrown into a situation. Why do you suppose that men are always well-informed about such matters, and women aren't?"

Not having the least desire to get into that kind of discussion with her, Jamie said practically, "Because most parents want it that way. It's the same with my sisters."

Rising from the bed and the stinging influence of her touch, Jamie put away the washbasin and cloth, then came back with a candle. He lit the lamp at the side of the bed. Painted figures on the glass globe seemed to dance of their own accord, throwing patterns on the wall and bed hangings.

"Jamie?"

It was the first time he could recall her actually using his name so familiarly, and he turned to look at her.

"Aye, lass?"

She pleated the edges of the sheet between her

fingers, watching intently as if it were of vital importance to fold the bedclothes. Jamie sat silently, waiting until she was ready to talk.

"I don't want to go home," she said finally, her voice a low whisper of sound. "Not now. Not for a while." Her head came up and she fixed him with a stare. "May I stay with you—no questions asked? No commitments?"

Jamie didn't know what to say. He shifted uneasily and caught the quick chagrin in her eyes.

"You're asking for something you don't want," he said in a rough voice.

She sat stiffly, drawing up her knees under the sheet and curling her arms around them. "I see."

"Nay, lass, I dinna think ye do." He drew in a deep breath to ease the shock of her request. Moving closer to her on the bed, he cupped her chin in his palm and lifted her face to stare at her with a worried frown. He dragged his thumb across her lower lip in a gentle caress. "You can stay, but I'm not certain it's the right thing. . . ."

"You didn't seem to worry about that a few minutes ago!"

Drawing in a deep breath, he muttered, "No, and I know better than that too."

His hand dropped away from her face; he saw the shock in her eyes, in her white-lipped expression of pain, and damned himself. He was a rogue; she'd named him right. He had taken what he should not have, when he knew better. What was it about this one girl that made him lose all reason?

During this past month he had done his best to stay away from her, playing cards until dawn, drinking port when he hated the stuff, listening to highborn, bored noblemen trade quips and names of tailors as if there were nothing more important to do. It had left him restless and filled with distaste. He'd grown as bored as the men he held in contempt, and thought of Summer.

She didn't bore him. She irritated him, amused him, intrigued him, puzzled him—but she didn't bore him. And he hadn't even bedded her until now. It was a startling revelation. No woman had retained his exclusive interest this long before, not even the most agile in bed.

Why?

It hit him then, with the shock of a broadsword, and he tensed; he grew still and stared past her, his eyes fixed on rosewood cupids and hearts and vines carved into the posts of the bed. What an apt design for this bed.

His gaze shifted back to her after a moment; he took one of her hands in his and shook his head slowly.

"No. You can't stay without the truth. And not without commitments. It would never work."

She nodded as if she'd expected him to refuse. "Yes. I understand. I didn't expect you to want . . . to allow me to stay."

A faint smile curved his mouth. "I didn't say you could not stay, sweeting. I just said not without commitments."

Warily tilting her head, she regarded him silently for a moment. "What are you talking about? What kind of commitment do you mean?"

"Summer, I know you probably won't understand, and God knows I don't think I do either, but after this"—he indicated the bed and the faint smears of blood on satin sheets—"I can't let you stay without doing the right thing by you. I took you, so I should make reparation."

Instead of the look of pleased surprise he'd half expected, she jerked her hand from his and scooted back on the bed. Her eyes blazed with rage and something else.

"Damn you! Do you think I'll let you make that kind of decision about my life? And for that reason? No! It's *my* life, and *my* tarnished reputation, and *I* want to be the one to say yea or nay." Silky wisps of hair whipped across her flushed cheek, and she shook with agitation.

"You nodcock, you didn't *take* me—I gave myself to you. I would have fought you like a wildcat if I hadn't wanted you to have what you think you stole . . . Oh. I see that I've insulted you." Her mouth tightened. "That's too bad. Though I'm well aware that men like to be the instigators of any manner of crimes perpetrated upon a female, this time, you will just have to accept the fact that I was perfectly willing to be ravished."

"I'm glad to hear it."

"Are you? Odd. You don't *look* particularly glad about it. Your male pride, no doubt."

That stung. "Aye," he growled, "no doubt."

"Poor Lord Westcott," she mocked, dragging a hand over her eyes and glaring at him, "you aren't nearly as bad—or as good—as you thought."

"Bloody hell! You sound smug enough about it!" he bit off, and shoved up from the bed, glaring down at her.

Hugging her knees, she lifted her chin. "I am smug. I have not only managed to relieve myself of my virginity, I have effectively ruined my uncle's plans for me."

His dark brow lowered. A cold knot formed in his belly at her triumphant, hazy stare. Somehow, there was a bit too much satisfaction in her voice and expression.

"What plans do you mean, lass?"

After a slight hesitation, she said, half-defiantly, "He had arranged a marriage for me. To someone I detested."

Jamie just looked at her. A marriage. She was affianced to some man, and he had just taken her maidenhead. Oh, what an iniquitous little soul she had.

"I don't suppose," he said politely, "that you could have thought to mention this an hour ago?"

"I saw no need for it."

"I see." He smiled. He thought he was behaving with exceptional calm under the circumstances, but apparently his smile didn't convey that. She scooted away from him until her naked spine was pressed so hard into the headboard, it should have left an imprint.

"Perhaps, Miss *Smith*, you might have considered that your uncle and your fiancé might protest at my having been importune enough to take what you offered? It's been known to cause duels in certain circles."

"Has it. How fascinating." She ran the tip of her tongue over her lips. "That shouldn't affect you. They're safely in America, and we're here."

"I see. Has it occurred to you," he began in the same calm, pleasant tone, "that ships arrive in London daily?"

"Not enough time."

"There has been," he growled, his fury boiling over, "if they left right after discovering you gone!"

She paled. It was obvious she hadn't thought of that. She recovered quickly, saying briskly, "That doesn't matter now. I'm certain my uncle will not do that. He'll send someone else."

"Ah, so now I don't know just who is going to be looking for me with a sword or pistol, correct?"

Shifting uneasily, she muttered, "I hardly think—"

"I concur wholeheartedly with that!" he said so fiercely that she quailed. "You hardly think at all! Damnit, Summer, you foolish little chit, you've probably created a furor!"

Her throat worked rapidly, and her lips trembled, but her words were fairly steady. "What ... what do we do?"

"Oh," he said cuttingly, "so now I'm to have a say in this? I appreciate your confidence."

She had the grace to look contrite, but it certainly didn't help.

Shaking his head, Jamie put on his pants and buttoned them. Barefoot, he padded across the floor to a table and pulled the cork on a decanter. Then he sprawled in a chair and sipped potent Scotch whisky.

Summer remained quiet, dressing in silence, her movements pale shadows in the soft light. She looked at him from time to time, searchingly, as if he held her life in his hands. Actually, it was the other way around.

He sighed heavily. What a coil. It was a good thing he'd already decided he wanted her. He'd be in a devil of a fix if he hadn't. He looked up at her; she was trying not to look at him, and he felt a certain amount of satisfaction about that. She *should* feel guilty.

"Summer." He saw her quick start and almost smiled. If it had been under different circumstances, he would have teased her. He set his empty glass on the small table at his elbow and rose from the chair. "Do you still love this Captain Kinnison?"

"You've asked me that before."

"Aye, and I got a silly answer for my pains. Do you?"

"No."

He nodded. "All right. Now I'll have the truth from you, lass."

"The truth?"

"Your name. Your uncle's name. Your intended husband's name."

Her face paled, and her hands clenched into the material of her gown. "Why?"

"Why do you think? Do you really want me shot by a stranger? Unkind of you. I should at least know the names of men who'll be wanting to kill me when they find you."

Summer's gaze narrowed. "I don't think they know where to look for me. All they'd know is how I got here."

"If Epson can discover your little secret, I've no doubt any man with half a brain can do the same."

Jamie crossed to her and took her hand. "The truth, lass."

"No." She actually gulped when he swore terribly. "I can't," she said. "And it doesn't matter who they are."

"Like it didn't matter that you forgot to mention the poor fool who's your fiancé?"

Jerking away, she flared, "You don't know what you're talking about! You don't know what kind of man he is, nor do you seem to care! Stupid, egotistical males, banding together like tragic lemmings, even when wrong!"

Scorn etched her voice; she wouldn't let him touch her, but skipped away from his outstretched hand. "Oh, no, I shan't tell you a thing!"

"This is not some kind of game you can play because of feminine pique," Jamie said coldly. He felt the hot lash of temper and held tightly to his self-control. "There will be no raps on the wrist with a folded fan or shrill scolds. A coil like this one can cause bloodshed."

"Are you afraid?"

He took a step toward her, then stopped. He should be familiar with this tactic; God knew, his sisters had used it enough.

"Only of devious females," he said lightly, and went to pour another glass of whisky. It burned down his throat and into his stomach and still didn't drown his fury.

He had to think. He certainly couldn't think with her in the room, staring at him warily, half-defiant, half-afraid.

"I think we should continue this discussion tomorrow, sweeting." He smiled into his whisky when she looked at him with her blue eyes filled with suspicion. "After we've had a good night's sleep."

It was quite obviously not what she'd expected to hear.

"Oh." She stood there uncertainly. When he reminded her that she was in his bedchamber, she flushed. "Yes. I—I'll see you in the morning."

It was only after she'd gone, shutting the door behind her with a decided snap, that he allowed himself to release the build-up of anger. Snarling, he threw his glass across the room and watched it shatter against the marble hearth. A childish display of temper, and it afforded little relief, he thought with disgust.

It was quiet in the breakfast room. Only a faint clink of silver dishes and trays broke the silence as footmen glided from pantry to table and back. Summer could feel the tension. It crackled with a life of its own, as she dared a glance toward Jamie.

Gray daylight slanting through the long window behind him gilded the back of his head, leaving his face shadowed. She could see the dark slash of his brow as he looked down at his plate, and she felt a pang of remorse. Her throat closed, and she bent her head.

Summer felt an odd quirk in her chest. She'd got over her first flush of anger at him for being so pompous; but she still did not intend to tell him who her uncle was, or who she was. James Cameron would recoil in horror from her if he knew that her uncle was Barton Shriver, who'd made himself well known in political circles as a conniving, treacherous little sneak rumored to keep a foot in each opposing interest.

And if the French won in Europe as Napoleon planned, they would march triumphantly into New Orleans again. A year after the purchase, all the French troops and officers still lingered in the city, and her uncle was deep in league with high French officials.

How would James Cameron react to the news that he'd harbored a girl with the taint of France about her? Epson's words haunted her.... *he cannot abide, a cheat at cards, a liar, and anything French. . . .* And she was guilty of two of those three things.

She should never have yielded to temptation and asked him to keep her. It had been weak and foolish and, in the prosaic light of day, useless. No, she had to leave. There was no other end to this situation.

Her heavy-lashed eyes lifted in a sweeping glance, and she saw Jamie's gaze riveted on her. Her heart thumped with alarm.

"I have to leave London," he said in a flat, emotionless voice that made her throat ache. "I've put it off as long as I can." He held up a small rectangle of paper that she saw was an envelope. "My family seems to miss me so much that I'm threatened with a visit from them if I don't go."

"And that would be bad?"

He tossed the envelope to the table beside his plate. "It would be unbearable. I'd never get them to leave, and my sisters would run me mad wanting me to take them places and show them the sights." Dragging in a deep breath, he said, "No, I've no desire to see them descend upon me here. I can avoid it by going there, then leaving when I like."

Keeping her voice cool and polite, Summer said, "You are telling me that since you must leave, I need to make other arrangements, I take it."

A mirthless smile curved his hard mouth. "Nay, lass. That is not what I'm saying at all."

"Forgive me—" She paused, frowning at him. "I don't know what you mean."

His dark brow rose in a mocking gesture, and she squirmed uneasily in her chair, feeling a sudden cold knot form in her chest.

"I mean, lass, that you should make yourself ready for a journey to Scotland."

Summer's fork clattered to her plate. "You've gone mad! Scotland? To your family? Why, that would be a slap in the face, to take . . . take . . ."

"My mistress?" He laughed hollowly. "Aye, that it

would be. And I don't think my father would swallow it well at all. No, I'm not taking a mistress with me," he said, and his eyes were focused intently on her face. "But my wife would be well accepted."

Blood drained from her face, and she couldn't speak. Now she knew: he had truly gone mad. She tried to ignore the sudden leap of her heart; it would be folly to entertain such a notion for one moment, and she knew it. It was obvious he didn't love her. But, because she was a romantic fool, she had to ask.

"Why would you marry me?"

"Why?" His laugh was faintly ironic. "Odd that you should ask. Are you expecting a passionate declaration on bended knee, perhaps? Ah, I see by your blush that you were. And I'm unkind enough to be disobliging." His voice lowered slightly, shifting from the harsh crack that left her feeling flayed and exposed. "Damnit, you could have thought enough of me to tell me the truth."

"Yes." She looked up to meet his angry gaze. "I could have. But I didn't." A small salvaging of pride, but very unfair. And untrue besides; it wasn't him that she'd not believed in, it was herself. Her lies. Her subterfuge. The humiliation of having to confess to it.

Jamie sat back in his chair, clenching and unclenching his hand on the table. Summer stared at it. It was a big hand, capable, strong. Lean fingers. Tanned skin. He could do a lot with that hand. It could be harsh, and it could be gentle. She'd felt both.

But she wanted love from him; nothing else would compel her to marry him willingly. She looked up at him again.

"This is not a logical solution," she said. "You don't even love me."

"How well do you love your fiancé?"

Her brows drew into a fierce little scowl, and she could feel her face tighten. "That's not the same thing!"

"I disagree."

"You don't know anything!" She laughed angrily. "Lord, why do I bother? You're going to do what you like anyway, so just drag me to Scotland." Her jaw thrust out. "But I *won't* marry you!"

Shoving away from the table, Jamie rose to his feet. "I find most feminine logic completely incomprehensible, I'm afraid. It's unfair of you to expect me to understand why you ask to stay with me one moment, then reject an offer of marriage the next."

Summer, too, had risen to her feet, and she was staring at him with her hands curled into fists of frustration. He was furiously angry beneath his calm; she could see the hot lights in his eyes that betrayed his temper. Well, she was not in the best of moods herself, and for him to make wild statements was a bit too much for her.

"I'm leaving," she said evenly, and saw his black brow shoot up. "I will not stay under the roof of a madman for one moment longer than I have to do."

"And where will you go?" came the silky inquiry. "To Epson, perhaps? He would be delighted. And he has such a novel way of ridding himself of old mistresses too. You might want to check into that, by the way, before you rush in where you might find regrets."

"You're despicable." A thrum of anger made her voice shake slightly.

"Oh, aye, lass. An honorable marriage proposal is a damn dastardly burden to put upon a young woman who has just been relieved of her maidenhead."

Summer gazed at him warily, hearing the barely controlled fury in his voice. Perhaps she should be a bit more cautious; he looked almost dangerous, glaring at her with searing lights in his eyes, his mouth a taut slash in his face.

"Maybe not despicable," she relented, taking a step away from the table, "but at least ridiculous."

When he moved toward her, his boneless, lazy

stride a study in menace, she yielded to the spurt of fear that hit her and bolted.

Jamie caught her just inside the marbled entrance hall, a hard hand flashing out to close over her arm and whirl her around. "Let go of me," she demanded, but he only put both hands on her.

Half lifting her from the black-and-white tiled floor, he gave her a hard shake, much as he would have shaken a rebellious puppy. Surprisingly, there was no Scots brogue in his voice, and his words were slow and achingly clear.

"I said you were going to marry me, girl, and you will. Whether you or I like it, we are both caught in a trap that might have been avoided with a little honesty at the outset."

Wincing, she tried to protest, but his hard hands and the rough shake he'd given her left her breathless. A sob caught in her throat. If he noticed it, he paid no attention. Her hair hung in her eyes from the shaking, and she could barely see him, but that was probably a blessing.

"I'll get a special license, and we'll be married, and when your uncle and betrothed show up, there won't be a lot to be said." His voice was flat. "And before we're wed, you had best see fit to give me their names."

Dangling so that her toes barely brushed the floor, she was vaguely aware that someone had stepped into the foyer, but drumming anger, fear, and wounded pride made her reckless.

"I will fight you with my last breath, James Cameron!" She kicked her feet, striking him on his shins, and heard him swear at her. "I will not be treated this way! I will not ... marry ... you!"

The last was said a bit breathlessly, as he had shoved her away from him to protect his knee-high boots from being scarred.

"Aye, ye will, lass," he growled furiously. "Or I'll bed ye in ev'ry inn up an' down th' length of England, sae help me, I will! We'll see how yer pride'll stomach tha'!"

Even with his thick burr, she understood him. He set her on the floor, and she flung back her head to stare up at him with brimming eyes. He was breathing hard, and his face was set in cold lines; a grim twist came to his mouth as he looked up and past her.

Noting something in his gaze, Summer turned slowly and saw two tall men standing just inside the front door. They grinned when they saw they'd been noticed, and one of them strode forward with long, easy strides.

"Och, ye're a doughty lover, ye are, Jamie! An' i'st a wonder th' wee puir lassie is'na fallin' all o'er ye wi' delight a' yer romantical ways."

The lilting brogue convinced Summer this tall man with a shock of fair hair and brilliant blue eyes must be a countryman, if not a kinsman, of Jamie's. Her gaze flicked over them. They all had the same cast to their features, strong, rugged faces and single straight brows, though the coloring in all three men was different. Her suspicion was confirmed when Jamie gave a sour grunt.

"Dallas. What are you doing here? I just got Mother's letter this morning."

"Came tae fetch ye, Jamie lad," Dallas said cheerfully. His gaze swept over Summer's flushed face and rebellious eyes. "There's tae be a wedding, I take it?"

"No," Summer said before Jamie could speak, "there most certainly will not!"

"Aye," Jamie growled, his gaze burning into her, "there will be."

Staring up at him, seeing over his shoulder the wide grins on his brothers' faces, Summer had a sudden, sinking feeling that she had lost control of her destiny yet again.

Chapter 12

Tidwell held open the front door, and Summer paused in the opening. She could feel Jamie behind her and didn't turn around.

"I suppose you know that this is ridiculous." Her chin was tilted defiantly. "And illegal."

"I'll grant you ridiculous," Jamie said in a cool tone, "but 'tis not illegal." When she turned to look at him in surprise, she saw the tightly curling smile that failed to reach his dark, heavy-lashed eyes. "Not where we're going."

Summer's head jerked back around, and she gripped the edges of her cloak tightly. A thrum of apprehension whirred in her chest as she stepped out onto the portico.

A gleaming black coach with ornate fittings had rolled to a halt in front of the house, and a coachman wound the leather ribbons around his gloved fist and waited. Hooves scrabbled on the paving stones, and the jangle of metal bits and harness sounded loud in the gray, foggy morning.

Jamie spread a hand on her back and pushed her forward with a slight urging that indicated his impatience—and obstinacy. Her footsteps scraped over the walkway, pebbles grinding underfoot. Dallas and Ian were already waiting for them by the coach, holding three horses saddled and ready.

The two Scotsmen looked as tall and forbidding as Jamie. Dallas was big and blond, Ian was whip thin, with hair a shade lighter than Jamie's and riveting blue eyes. So different, yet so similar.

She flicked a glance toward the horses and realized with a spurt of anger that Jamie intended to ride outside with his brothers. He didn't even have the courage to ride with her! Damn him, and damn the entire Cameron family, she thought viciously, jerking to a halt by the coach.

Shooting a dark look toward the Camerons, she saw that Ian had the grace to look faintly chagrined, while Dallas looked only amused. Jamie, of course, looked grim and very unapproachable. She turned on him in a whirl of muslin and dark blue cloak.

"Why are you doing this? You cannot want it any more than I do."

"It doesn't matter what either of us want." Jamie blew out his breath in an irritated sigh. He flicked a narrow glance toward his brothers.

Dallas and Ian took several tactful steps away from the coach; they seemed suddenly fascinated by the brass fitting on the harness of the coach horses. Summer didn't glance in their direction, though she was acutely aware of their presence.

"If you would just send me back to New Orleans," Summer began, and Jamie put a hand on her wrist.

"Summer. Enough. We've talked until there's nothing left to say."

Flinging her head back, she flashed him an angry smile. "Perhaps there's nothing left for *you* to say, but I have an entire repertoire of comments I can make."

"I'm certain you do, lass." His hand tightened briefly, and the dark brow lowered. "I wouldna suggest it, though."

"I'm sure you wouldn't! Rattle-brained ox!" She jerked her hand free and whirled away from him.

When she might have pushed past him, he leaned forward in a swift, graceful movement, placing the palm of his hand against the coach and barring her way.

"Don't make a scene," he said softly. "It will only end with you as the loser."

Achingly aware that he was right, that she would end up looking like a childish fool, Summer stood rigidly still.

From the corner of her eye she saw Letty approach warily and climb into the coach with an uneasy glance toward them. So. She was at least to have her maid.

"Summer." Jamie was reminding her that she was wasting his time. Her mouth tightened.

"I'll never forgive you for this," she said around the cold knot in her throat. She felt his shrug, then he was pulling her back and lifting her into the coach. He set her on the velvet squabs and stuffed the trailing hems of her gown and cloak inside with her.

"That's up to you, lass." He leaned into the open door and looked up at her as she glared at him. He grinned suddenly, a wide, potent grin that jolted through her. The shock of it made her breath catch, and she barely heard him say, "But I think you will change your mind about it after a babe or two."

Whatever Summer might have replied to that was, mercifully, drowned out by the noise of the slamming coach door and restless clatter of horses' hooves on stone. She sat in stony silence as the coach lurched forward. Letty had obviously decided the better part of valor was silence and did not offer a single comment as her mistress seethed.

Glaring out the window, Summer barely saw the elegant houses in Mayfair as they passed. She was furious that her wishes had once again been ignored. Why must men equate women with children? A patient smile, indulgent pat on the arm—"Yes, yes, my dear, I realize that I have ruined your life, but it was better I than you"—and the poor woman was left to make what she could of the shambles. Why had she thought James Cameron might be different?

An arrogant, stubborn, pigheaded Scot was Jamie. Just as bad as Barton Shriver in his way; at least Jamie had some kind of scruples, however.

Summer tried not to think about what might have been had she met Jamie at a ball in New Orleans, or a cotillion. There would have been music and laughter, and he would have smiled that rakish smile that made her heart drop to her toes and her blood heat, and she would have put her hands in his and danced with him until the sun rose the next morning.

But of course that was sheer fantasy. Reality was the stark truth she hid from him; it made her mouth dry and her palms damp. And she had lied. She had lied like a fiend because he wouldn't leave her alone, but kept badgering her to tell him the names of her uncle and her fiancé. Hurt pride and anger would not allow her to tell him the truth; now she wondered if she shouldn't have been honest.

Summer stared out the window of the coach as it moved briskly through London. She barely saw the beautiful parks, the splendid architecture, the spires of St. Paul's, or any of the other sights she'd only glimpsed before. She didn't care about them.

Why should she be so unnerved? she wondered crossly. He wasn't the kind of man to resort to physical violence with her; she knew that. What would Jamie do if she told him the truth? The worst he could do was look at her without any laughter at all in those mocking black eyes. Yes. That was the worst. No, it wasn't. He might walk away from her and never look back.

It hit her then, that her cowardice had a name: Love.

"I'd say yer bride's not willing, Jamie lad." Ian slid his older brother a frowning glance. "How do you expect to coax her to agree to a marriage?"

Jamie's jaw knotted, and he flung Ian a harsh look

that spoke volumes. It had begun to rain, a soft, misting rain that made traveling a damp affair, and the idea had occurred to him more than once that Summer might protest to the very end.

Rubbing his chin with a broad hand, Dallas offered, "If ye like, I kin ta'e a strap tae her till she yields, lad."

"Thank you," Jamie bit off savagely. "I'll keep that in mind."

Dallas grinned. "If she's a stubborn lass, ye ken use th' thumbscrew."

"Are you enjoying yourself, Dallas?"

The blond head nodded with pleasure. "Immensely. I never thought to see ye wed, much less to a lass who canna bear the sight o' ye!" He chuckled. "I dinna know there was a lass wha' wouldna fall right in yer lap wi' a sigh of pleasure."

Jamie flicked him a wry glance. "Neither did I."

Nothing was said for several minutes. The coach moved briskly ahead of them, digging deeper ruts into the roads now that they'd left London behind and had progressed into the gentle swells of the Midlands.

Ian nudged his mount closer to Jamie's horse and got a flashing frown for his pains. It didn't deter him. "She's a bonny lass, Jamie."

"Aye."

"I canna help but wonder if there's more behind your need to marry her than just to avoid her relatives."

"So you said last night."

Another silence fell, and Ian and Dallas exchanged shrugging glances. The evening before had been spent in long discussions over good Scotch whisky, and nothing had been decided but that there would be a wedding.

Dallas pulled his cape more closely around his broad shoulders and dug his chin into his chest. Rain wet his face and clung to his eyelashes. "I agree tha' if ye don't wed th' lass, there'll be trouble. But ye must hae known tha' at th' first."

"Aye."

"Damnit, Jamie! Will ye no' talk to us? We're yer kin, an' what affects ye, affects us."

Turning, Jamie looked at Dallas. "Not always."

"This time, likely."

Jamie acknowledged the truth in that. Dallas had a way of getting right to the point at times. "Aye, if her uncle catches up to us, there'll be trouble for all. But I'm not sure if he's the one we should be worrying about," Jamie added.

"Wha' does that mean?"

"That someone tried to abduct her off a city street in broad daylight, and Fox is investigating."

"Fox!"

Jamie grimaced. "Aye. He happened to be the gallant who rescued her, and he saw the man. He's convinced it wasn't a simple cutpurse."

"So," Dallas said slowly, "ye mean tha' th' lass might be in some kind of trouble?"

"I can't think of another reason she wouldn't tell me the truth. After all, I already know about her uncle and her fiancé. Unless those are lies too." He tried to say it lightly, but Dallas and Ian gave him sharp looks. Shrugging his shoulders under the greatcoat, he added, "She's no' very truthful. And when she lies, her eyes blink too fast."

Dallas grinned. "At least ye've got warning!"

Grunting, Jamie flashed him a sour glance. "That's no' very consoling."

"An' ye're bound tae wed her, truth, lies, and all."

"Aye." His voice was grim. "I'll wed her. And when we're wedded and bedded, I'll get the bloody truth from her if I have to shake it loose!"

Chuckling, Dallas said, "Ye sound a wee bit too certain of tha' for a mon wha wae havin' sich troubles wi' th' lass today! Aré ye sure she'll e'en hae ye in her bed?"

Slashing a glaring scowl at his brother, Jamie muttered tightly, "She's no' a maid any longer. She'll have me."

Ian laughed, drawing another glare. "I think, brother, that you overestimate your strength. Or your charms."

Spurring his horse ahead of his brothers, Jamie ignored their amusement at his expense. *Bloody hell.* Ian was probably right. In her present mood, Summer certainly didn't seem especially friendly. If he'd known a simple marriage proposal would bring this out in her . . . he'd have done it anyway. He had to have her. Not just in bed. That wasn't fair to her. She wasn't the kind of woman who could live with that way of life. No, he wanted her, and he wanted her the right way.

Wouldn't his father be astounded? Jamie put his spurs to horse and let it run, relishing the cold wind and the whip of rain in his face. Damn her.

Why did he care?

Faith, but it was a mystery why! She bedeviled him. She was a stubborn, mistrustful little wretch, and yet he did nothing but think of her. It rankled that she did not confide in him; it was infuriating that she refused to tell him the barest details about her life. And to have kept secret the fact that she was a maid had been the worst of all. His fists clenched around the knotted reins, and he swore softly.

She had erected a barrier between them and would not let him pass. But he would, by God, he would.

Shuddering, Summer had the thought that Scotland was a wild, untamed country; much wilder than even the stretch of wilderness beyond Louisiana to the west. With high rocky crags that still bore mantles of snow and deep, rushing streams that the Camerons called burns, the Highlands looked primitive and desolate.

And she was there with only a timid maid and three men who seemed infinitely more predatory in this country than she would have guessed.

She'd watched uneasily as Jamie seemed to change; once England was behind them, and even Edinburgh, he'd become less civilized and more dangerous. The stark, breathtaking beauty of the land lent these Camerons an energy that had not been as apparent in the refined house in London. It was puzzling and vaguely frightening; it made her think of leashed tigers suddenly set free to leap and snarl with joy at their liberation.

Wearily, Summer allowed herself to be escorted from the coach and into another inn just before dusk. It was raining again. As usual.

Spreading a hand against her back, Jamie urged Summer toward a peat fire burning on a wide stone hearth, while slender, dark-haired Letty scurried behind them. The maid went to warm her hands by the fire, and Summer stood stiff and still, staring out a rain-misted window.

"Wait here, lass. I'll make arrangements," he said, and she nodded without looking at him. He'd become distant in the ten days of travel, and she'd frequently caught him gazing at her with a brooding stare that had been unnerving to say the least.

Well, it was his decision to marry her! It certainly hadn't been hers.

Summer refused to examine her motives for continued protest. She'd thought about it so much, her brain should have turned to mush. Maybe it had. That would certainly explain why she had meekly allowed him to make every decision concerning her welfare in the past ten days.

She flicked a glance toward the three brothers. Maybe she had an excuse. No woman could have withstood these determined Camerons for very long, nor man either.

Dallas reminded her of Jamie; he was constantly teasing and laughing, frequently infuriating Jamie, always enraging her. Ian, however, seemed sweeter natured, less inclined to tease but just as laughing.

Blond Dallas looked as she'd always imagined a Scotsman, big and fair and brawny. Jamie and Ian, Dallas had told her with a thread of teasing laughter, were known as Black Scots.

"Throwbacks, lass," he'd said, slicing his scowling brothers a glance. "I'm no' embarrassed by 'em, mind ye, but I thought ye micht wae like tae know why they're no' as han'some as they should be...."

His teasing comments had brought immediate objection from Ian, and the lively discussion that followed had ended in a wrestling match. Summer had been appalled at first, but Jamie had simply shrugged as if it was of no matter. He was right to ignore them, for they repeated the scene in a hundred different, irritating ways during the trip.

Now, watching them range about the small inn like lithe, restless lions, she wasn't certain if those brigands in her bedchamber had done her a good turn or ill by stealing her purse and leaving her adrift. Whichever, meeting James Cameron had certainly changed her life.

"Lass?" Summer's head jerked up, and she saw through bleary eyes that he was holding out his hand. "They've a room for you and your maid."

Summer rose from the bench where she'd sunk without realizing it, and nodded. Jamie walked her up the narrow stairs, and she saw that the room he'd taken for her was large and clean. A high four-poster squatted opposite windows with the shutters thrown open, and the faint scent of rain, smoke, and peat filled the air. A new fire burned in the grate, reflecting off the brass firedogs.

She could feel Jamie's hand at her waist, almost resting on her hip; she burned where he touched her, and she tried to ignore it.

Stepping from under his hand, she ambled across the room to the window and stared out. The hills seemed to fold in on themselves in stretches of green and outcroppings of gray rock. Soaring trees showed

black against the fading light. Streamers of smoke
from a hidden crofter's cottage drifted into the air,
floating on wind currents like mist. And in the distance, sounding faintly shrill and eerie, a curl of music rose and swayed on the wind.

Summer gave a start. "What is that noise?"

"Bagpipes." Jamie came to stand behind her at the
window, a faint smile curving his mouth. "Angus
MacFarlane, if I'm to guess. He plays in defiance of
king and weather."

"They're outlawed?"

"Nay, but they were after Culloden, and Angus
played on for thirty-six years. It's been legal since the
Proscription was rescinded in '82." The faint smile
tucked the corners of his eyes. "I wore the kilt, lass, while
in the British Army. I was part of His Majesty's Scottish
regiment and sported the kilt, sporran, and bonnet. We
were easily recognizable on the battlefield." He touched
her lightly on the cheek. "But 'tis no' my past I'm wantin'
to tell you now, but our future."

She waited warily, sensing something different in
his mood. This was the first time he'd sought her out
in private since they'd left London. Rain spit through
the shutters in a fine mist, and she stepped away from
the window, keeping her gaze focused on Jamie.

She felt suddenly shy; awkward. There were odd
lights in his eyes when he looked at her, and he looked
as ill at ease as she felt. Her hands knotted and unknotted. The urge to escape was born, grew, became
overpowering. Where was Letty?

Jamie caught her hand and, as if reading her mind,
said, "Ian has taken a fancy to your Letty; she's been
delayed. I have a mind to say something—"

"I'll not have my maid terrified by your brother!"
A wave of indignation was the perfect excuse to avoid
whatever it was in his eyes.

Jamie's brow flew up. "I dinna say he wae going
tae rape her, lass!"

Summer took a skittering little step away from him.

To her horror, she felt the prick of tears, as well as the surge of anger in her, and was as bewildered as she was driven.

"You damn Scots think that all you have to do is want something and it's yours! Well, that's not so!" She dragged in a deep, aching breath of damp air and peat smoke. "I'm not yours for the taking, or to be ordered around, and I've told you this before. Nor is my maid to be passed around so lightly, as if—"

"Lass." He reached her in two long strides. His hands curled around her wrists to hold her in a light clasp. "In case you haven't noticed—which it seems you haven't—your Letty is quite taken with Ian. And as for taking you, I seem to recall your wanting me to do just that." His cool eyes met her angry, hot gaze. "I'm not complaining, mind. 'Twas what was on my mind, for certain. And I think I'm paying right well for it now."

Jerking free, Summer felt the aching press of tears increase and struggled against them. What was the matter with her?

"When will you get it through your head that I don't want to wed you?" she snarled at him. "And if *you* consider it as a punishment, how do you think I feel?"

He seemed taken aback. He held out a hand, but driven by temper and some nameless, painful emotion, she slapped it aside. He let his arm fall to his side, and his face was hard and expressionless.

"It doesna matter how you feel. We'll reach Cameron Hall tomorrow. I expect you to behave as my betrothed should."

"Do you mean weeping and wailing and gnashing of teeth? I presume that is how any poor woman betrothed to you would react!"

Stung, Jamie growled, "Don't embarrass both of us, or you may regret it."

"I make no promises, James Cameron," she said

softly, fiercely glad to see the fury in his eyes. "You'll
just have to wait and see what I'll do."

Jamie stared at her for a moment, then he swore
softly under his breath and left her. She heard the
sound of his boots echoing in the maze of hallways
and wondered why she felt so dreadful. He deserved
it. Maybe she deserved part of the blame for the situation, but at least she hadn't forced him into anything. He had acted of his own free will, but she was
not being given that opportunity.

And tomorrow, she was to meet the rest of the
Camerons.

She began to dread arriving at Cameron Hall. It
would be overflowing with brawling Scots like Jamie,
arrogant and vital and intimidating. She would be
swept along on whatever tide they wished. She
couldn't hold out against Jamie alone, much less
against his family too.

And she couldn't hold out against the rising tide
of her own need and emotions, though she knew she
must. It was futile to continue resistance, but a compelling need to be loved for herself drove her to it. If
Jamie would only say that he loved her, she would wed
him without another word.

A faint, bitter smile curled her mouth. Summer
moved to stand at the open window again and heard
the mournful wail of the pipes lilting over the crags
and glens. It reflected the misery in her soul, somehow; the strange, haunting music seemed to sob of
lost love and hope.

Cameron Hall, Summer discovered, was a simple
name for an elegant, sprawling castle of polished red
stone. A river swept around the walls in a glittering
scythe, banked by gardens ablaze with tender flowers.
Fruit trees flourished, and bushes spread flowering
limbs along the ground in a windy dance. A sweet,
gentle fragrance spiced the air with tempting scents,

promising a heavy harvest. Four towers rose above the
tips of alder and elm trees, and the castle was Gothic
in construction. Rain obscured rolling hills and high
crags surrounding it; it looked to be a medieval for-
tress nestled in a jeweled glen.

"Oh, my God," she breathed, and flashed Letty a
stunned glance. The little maid looked as owl-eyed as
she felt.

The coach rumbled across a stone bridge and under a rusty-looking portcullis, then drew to a halt in
the inner courtyard. Jamie and his brothers had ridden ahead and were dismounting and cursing the rain.
Only a few retainers rushed out to greet them, gladly,
grabbing reins and smiling happily.

Summer had a quick impression of walls draped
in ivy, a stone fountain, and muted pink and gray
flagstones before she saw Jamie approaching the
coach. She swallowed sudden apprehension, and her
fingers dug into the folds of her cloak. How would
these people receive her?

Panic throbbed like a live, trapped creature inside
her, and she tried to steady her hands from trembling.
Now more than ever, she could not marry James Cameron. His family weren't simple farmers or comfortable merchants; these people lived in a *castle*, for God's
sake, and were not likely to welcome their son's choice
of wife—especially upon discovering the motive behind it. No, this was doomed from the beginning.

"Easy, lass," Jamie said when he opened the door
to the coach and she almost bolted from it. He seemed
to sense her trepidation and pulled her close. He
smelled of smoke and horse and rain, and Summer
shivered. Her chin lifted in a gesture of nervous pride.
She would face them with dignity.

If Jamie was still angry with her for her harsh
words from the night before, he'd forgotten. Or taken
pity on her. Now he shepherded her forward, past the
curious eyes of the retainers and the amused regard
of his brothers. The rain made it easy for them to

hurry under the arches and through the door being held open.

"Lord Jamie," a beaming man greeted him, and flicked Summer only a brief glance.

"Dugald." Jamie paused just inside the door, his arm still possessively around Summer's waist.

"Ye're no' here in time fer yer faither's feast day," the gray-haired man said with a shake of his head and a grin, "but I warrant tha' ye'll ma'e up fer it." His gaze slid over Summer again, polite and assessing.

"I warrant so," Jamie agreed.

Summer could see beyond Jamie to the wide hall with doors opening from it. Tapestries hung on the walls, and a suit of battered, soot-stained armor stood guard just past a door. She was suddenly reminded of Jamie and Dallas as boys, and smiled as she recalled the story of the fire in the suit of armor.

The smile was still lingering on her mouth when a tall, imposing woman approached with quick strides. Summer's first impression was that she was very young, but when the woman drew near, she could see faint slivers of gray at her temples and flecking her deep chestnut hair. Fine eyes beneath soaring brows were a lustrous brown, and her face was patrician, barely lined.

"Jamie," the woman Summer knew must be his mother said, stretching out her hands, and her son turned. He moved forward easily, embracing her with affection. Turning with his arm still draped over her shoulders, he laughed when she said sharply, "I had to send Dallas and Ian for you after all this time! Have you forgotten how to get home?"

"No. I was just delayed."

His mother's gaze shifted to Summer, who stood erect and silent, uncertain of her welcome.

"So I see. Introduce me to the lass, Jamie, or have you abandoned all your manners?"

Faintly surprised that she had little of the Scots burr that frequently thickened her sons' words, Summer murmured a reply to the introduction. *Countess of Glendale?* She must have looked confused.

Speaking quickly, Jamie's mother said, "But you must come and meet the rest of the family, my dear—Summer, is it? And don't let names and titles distress you. We're very informal here, as you will soon see."

Informality was an understatement when it came to the raucous group of siblings that inhabited Cameron Hall. As soon as they discovered Jamie was home, he had a swarm of sisters clustered around him, laughing and teasing, sulking when he teased back. Redheaded, blond, brunette, they adored their brother, it was easy to see.

And they all slid curious, measuring glances toward Summer when she was introduced. Her chin lifted slightly. If she was to be assessed, she would at least assess in turn.

Apparently, her steady gaze met with approval. Faces eased into smiles, and their greetings were friendly. So much for the first test, Summer thought irritably. Why did she feel it was important for these people to like her?

The great hall, where they were gathered, must have been very cold and forbidding at one time, but comfortable sofas, chairs, huge carpets, and wainscoting made it appear very welcoming. The high, vaulted ceiling was supported by massive timbers, and huge circles of lit tapers shed globes of light. A massive fireplace at one end that looked large enough to roast a whole ox burned with a thick log, and an odd mixture of paintings and deer antlers hung on the walls. The feminine touch of flowers in vases should have looked out of place but somehow didn't.

Jamie led Summer to a cushioned sofa near the fire, and murmuring something about finding his father, left her. She felt a quiver of apprehension but quickly found herself an object of attention. Somewhat helplessly, she yielded to their efforts to make her comfortable. And to find out more about her. It was apparent, that they were all very curious about her.

"Are you really an American?" a young girl with bright eyes of blue and hair like cornsilk asked, flouncing down beside Summer with an expression of friendly curiosity. "I thought you would have dark hair, with feathers in it."

Stifling a laugh, Summer said, "Those are Indians. I come from a city in Louisiana. We live in houses, as in the cities here." She smiled. "And the only feathers I wear are in stylish hats."

"Oh." The girl seemed to digest this, then said in the same friendly fashion, "My name is Margaret Ellen. You may call me Meg. May I call you Summer?"

"Yes, of course . . ."

Summer was laughing, telling Jamie's younger brother Robert about the alligators coming into town during the rainy season and terrorizing a fat constable into climbing atop an old cannon, when she looked up and happened to see Jamie. He was watching her with an odd smile on his face, his dark head tilted to one side.

He lounged against a far wall, a cup in one hand, his hair falling over his forehead, and his eyes thoughtful. Her words stuck in her throat.

"Go on," the insistent voice at her side urged, "you were saying about the alligators?"

"Uhh, yes—" Summer dragged her attention back to the young man at her side. Robert was about her age, maybe a few years younger, and he had the same fair hair as many of his siblings. Dark eyes much like Jamie's stared back at her. "Alligators. Yes, they live in the swamps, which we call bayous, and sometimes they eat small animals and even children."

Shivering with delight, one of the girls leaned forward. "Do they eat grown children?"

"On occasion." Summer couldn't help a smile when the girl grinned gleefully and said she wanted to put one in the courtyard fountain.

"To keep Robert and Elizabeth from being mean to me!" she added with a bubble of laughter.

"Keely," her mother warned, and smiled at Summer. "You have quite enchanted them with your generous conversation, my lady. But I believe that my son wishes to speak with you before we get ready for our evening meal."

Summer's glance met Jamie's again. She didn't know if she should be relieved or apprehensive. Not that it really mattered. None of her feelings had seemed to make the least difference to anyone concerned. Certainly not Jamie.

"This way," Jamie said when Summer joined him, and she flicked him a closer glance. There was no laughter in his eyes, only a dark, closed expression that made her wonder if he was angry with her. Not that she cared about that.

After leading her to a large, airy room with light paneling and soft draperies at the tall, mullioned windows across one wall, Jamie shut the door softly behind them. Summer turned in a whirl.

"Have you had a pleasant afternoon?" he forestalled her by asking. He walked to a small table and snapped open a decanter. "Whisky, my lady?" he murmured, "or do you prefer something lighter?"

She ignored the offer. "What did you want to talk to me about?" He gave her a brooding glance over the rim of his glass.

"You seem to have captivated my sisters. And my younger brother Robert too." The strange glance again, as if he wanted something from her.

"Is that what you wanted to say?" Summer lifted a brow high. "I don't see the need for this privacy then."

"Damnit, Summer, gi'e over!"

"And why are you and your brothers the only ones who speak such a garbled tongue?" She moved to a table and let her fingers trace over fruits and vegetables carved in the manner of Grinling Gibbons. Jamie was staring at her from under his straight black brow, and she flung her head up to meet his gaze.

"I don't know," he said flatly. "Maybe because we spend a lot of time out in the Highlands. It comes and goes with me."

"I've noticed."

He leaned against a massive desk, his hand in front of him and fingers curled around the glass. "Have you, my sweet? I'm flattered. I thought you'd stopped noticing me at all."

She dug viciously with one finger at the carved fruit basket on the edge of the table. "I could hardly do that with you forcing yourself on me like you do!"

"Do I?" At her quick narrowed glance he said, "Force myself on you, I mean. Odd. I can't seem to recall one instance since London."

"Wasn't that enough?"

"I also seem to recall you forcing back, but we've been over this innumerable times." He sipped at his whisky. "Is that what you intend to claim, Summer? That I've forced myself on you?" When she didn't answer, he shrugged. "I suppose it would absolve you of any blame."

Stung, she snapped, "That's not what I meant! I'm talking about the ... the ..."

"Wedding," he supplied helpfully. "If that is the word you're searching for."

She put her face in her palms and drew in a deep breath to steady her voice. "Jamie, you need to forget that notion. It won't cure anything."

"I've talked to my father," he said as if she hadn't spoken, "and though he had quite a bit to say that I'd rather not share with you, he mentioned that we can be wed in the kirk in two days."

"Two days!"

"Aye." His gaze was wary. "It will be legal. Since the Marriage Act does not include Scotland in its restrictions, there's no need for guardian consent or waiting."

"Ah, now I see why you came here," she said bitterly. "I thought it was just some urge to drag me several hundred miles for a lark. You seem prone to lunatic actions."

"And this is one of them. I know. You've mentioned that before too."

She felt trapped and panicky. It was happening without her permission. She was being swept along again on tides she could not control.

And he still hadn't mentioned love.

Stiffening her spine, Summer walked to the long windows and looked out over the courtyard. It was well tended. Neat paths led through rose gardens, and beyond the castle on the swelling, rolling hills, she had seen bell heather, red clover, buttercups, and bluebells scattered here and there in the meadows. The Tay Valley, someone had said—Mary, she thought, a lovely, composed girl who'd not been wed long and who had a direct smile and gentle look about her. It seemed at odds with this wild, unruly Cameron clan.

She turned back to look at Jamie, the gray light behind her, gilding her hair and leaving her face in shadow.

"I'm not unaware of the honor you do me by asking," she began, half frowning at the triteness of her little speech, "but you must know that our union will bring only misery to both of us."

"How would I know that, lass?" He seemed genuinely surprised, but a little angry. "I know you think you've got some deep dark secret that will make monarchies crumble and the heavens fall, but I am more inclined to believe it's one of those woman things that keeps you so on edge."

"Woman things?" She bit her lip to keep from saying what was on the tip of her tongue. Her fingers curled into her skirts. *"Woman things!"*

Obviously seeing his error, Jamie strode to her and took her roughly in his arms, ignoring her protest and effort to shove him away. He gave an angry laugh when she hissed at him to leave her alone.

"I should have done that from the first! But I didn't, and now I'm willing to make amends, and you're too stubborn and shortsighted to see what anyone else can see with only one eye. . . ."

"Which is?" she snapped, glaring up at him. "The fact that I've been asked to wed a lunatic? Yes, I suppose that is readily noticed. I shan't wonder if we don't end our days chained together in a yard and baying at the moon. And your fingers are too tight, if you don't mind." He released her arms and took a step back. His mouth tightened, and he gave a slight shake of his head.

"Which is, that whatever your bloody secret is, it does not matter. You can deal with it much easier if you have a husband at your side." He frowned at her strangled gasp. "It can't be just that your uncle arranged a marriage for you. There's more, but you won't tell me. I'm tired of waiting, Summer. I want your true name. I don't want any more lies."

Shoving her fist to her mouth, Summer stared at him with wild eyes. What would he say when he heard her name? He was looking at her so intently now, his black brow snapped down over his eyes in a devil's scowl, his mouth a harsh slash in his face. No, he would never understand why she had lied to him about anything; or why she couldn't let him know she hadn't trusted him not to be a fortune hunter like the others. An affront to his pride, she'd noticed, was not taken lightly at all.

She was damned if she did, and damned if she didn't.

Chapter 13

The wedding was over in a matter of minutes. Afterward, wearing a huge signet ring that felt strange and heavy on her hand, Summer sat stiffly in the great hall, which had been hastily decorated. Guests and family celebrated with a great deal of noise at the long tables set up, and music drifted down from a balcony. Tartans were everywhere. Men wore the kilt, sporrans, stockings, and bonnets, and women wore embroidered white blouses and silk tartan skirts. Silk arisaids, or feminine versions of the plaid, were slung over backs and pinned with glittering brooches.

Summer shifted in her chair. Didn't anyone seem to think it odd that they had wed so quickly or that the bride was unwilling? Apparently not. Lady Glendale had casually mentioned that Highlanders had once raided the Lowlands for their brides, slinging them over their horses and bringing them home.

With a proud glint in her eyes, she'd said, "My own mother was a borderer from Clan Douglas. My father, The Mackay, rode from Glen More to steal her for his bride. It caused a small war, but he kept her."

Apparently, Summer decided with dismay, unwilling brides were a source of pride. She suppressed a shiver at the barbarity just below the smooth surface of these people in their silks and velvets. There were moments she found it utterly fantastic that she was among them and that Jamie—teasing, laughing Jamie—had been born here.

Her fingers tightened around the stem of the gold goblet in her hand, and she recalled with a frown that Jamie could be every bit as barbaric and ruthless as his ancestors. Or so it seemed to her.

There had been no room for refusal in his insistence that she sign legal documents, and she had done so; she had not signed her real name. In the end, it hadn't mattered. He had wed her anyway. No love spoken, no tenderness between them. Just a marriage she wasn't certain was legal. Dear God, what had she done?

Looking up, Summer caught the gaze of Bruce Cameron, earl of Glendale. He was a formidable man and frightening. Even his wife and children referred to him as The Cameron. He vaguely terrified her.

It was evident where Jamie had inherited his straight black brow and flashes of menace, but she found it hard to see any humor in the earl's face. He was a handsome man, tall and broad, with no trace of age or bulk on him. Golden hair and pale eyes made him look approachable, from a distance, but strong, set features offered no temptation for idle chatter.

Shuddering, she recalled their mercifully brief conversation and the unflinching gaze that had pierced her. He had asked, once, if she cared to divulge her true surname, then looked at his son when she'd stubbornly shaken her head.

"If you wed her," the earl had said with a grunt, "you'll have a merry time of it, I ken."

Jamie shrugged. "You and Mother have survived 'merry times.'"

"Aye, that we have." There was a trace of satisfaction in the rough, growling voice. "And she's led me a de'il of a dance now and then."

" 'Tis what inspired me to wed," Jamie said with a

grin. "I was lonely for the music of a hot-tempered shrew."

"You arrogant cod's head!" Summer flashed, and saw the amusement in Cameron eyes. Only Jamie's quick hand on her shoulder had kept her from rising from her chair, and she'd sat stiffly and furiously silent while father and son talked.

For all that her presence mattered to either man, she might as well have been in Persia. They talked around her, discussing the legal entanglements as if she were not there at all. Fuming, Summer had finally summoned enough courage to speak.

"This is all very well and good, but have either of you gentlemen concerned yourself with the fact that I do not wish to be married?"

"Nay," the earl said gruffly. "You dinna have a choice, lass. Didna Jamie tell you how it would be?"

"Oh, yes, he told me how *he* wanted it." Her chin lifted slightly. "No one has asked—or listened to— what *I* want."

Leaning forward, his huge size intimidating, the earl had said softly, "And if you're carrying a bairn, lass? What of that? You'd make it a bastard?"

It must have been obvious from her stunned expression that she had not considered the risk of pregnancy. Summer had subsided into silence; it took a few moments of consideration before she'd decided, reluctantly, that the possibility existed. Her courses had come the week before Jamie had bedded her and not since.

Still, a sense of caution forbade her to divulge her real name, and when Jamie asked—his eyes icy and his tone harsh—"What is your family name?" she'd gulped and picked one out of the air. "Johnson."

His hand tightened on her shoulder. "Nay, lass. 'Tis not." He reached to lift the necklace she wore, the tiny gold chain her father had bought her, with the damning initials of entwined *S*'s. "I despise a liar," he said in a biting, savage tone. Lean fingers dug into her chin to hold her head still, and she couldn't help a slight flinch. "I'll hae yer name, naow, wi' nae more o' yer damn lies!"

"Sinclair," she gasped, and his hand dropped away.

It was close to the truth, she'd thought, an Anglicized version of St. Clair. Hopefully, not close enough to betray her.

His brows had snapped down; he'd looked thoughtful for a moment but had accepted it, muttering that it was a good Scottish name for a lass from America.

She'd flinched at her lie but not spoken. Nor had she met the earl's narrowed gaze.

And so now she sat, wed to Jamie, with no words of love between them, only responsibility.

She pleated the folds of her wedding dress between her fingers in a nervous gesture. Fiona, Jamie's mother, had managed to put seamstresses to work in short order, and the blouse was of white silk, with silver gilt embroidering the neck and sleeves and shot through the material. The skirt was silk tartan, and she had a plaid thrown over her shoulder and pinned with an exquisite brooch Fiona said had been her mother's. The plaid was long, streaming down her back and almost dragging on the floor, and now it draped gracefully over the edge of her chair, pooling in a silken puddle. Her unbound hair—another Cameron tradition—curled in soft wisps around her face, falling to her waist.

His dark eyes widening when he saw her in the shadowy stone kirk with arched windows and ornate altar, Jamie had said huskily, "Faith, ye're lovely, lass!"

There had been no teasing or mockery in his gaze, only genuine appreciation. She'd wondered, briefly, what he would have done if she'd told him how beautiful a man he was in the kilt, cocky bonnet with its crest and feather, and bottle-green velvet jacket with lace jabot and cuffs. Laughed, probably. And agreed. Damn him.

She looked at Jamie now. He sprawled indolently at her side, his big hand toying with a golden goblet, a wary expression on his handsome face. Summer felt a pang of regret. She'd been so angry, so taut with emotion, that she had not spared him a civil word the entire day.

Jamie. Did he know what he did to her with his dark eyes and teasing smile? Probably. He must have won many a girl's heart before leaping into her life as he had. Yet, *she* was married to him. Her heart lurched.

He was a big, hardheaded rogue with more arrogance than any one man should possess, but, oh Lord! how happy she would be if only things were different, if only her deceit and lies didn't stand between them.

Jerking her eyes away from him, she focused on the dancing couples in the middle of the hall. Music from the balcony was lively and quick, with oboes, flutes, drums, and violins. A bagpipe keened in lilting skirls.

Summer cleared her throat. "That's a pretty tune," she said to Jamie. Her hands clutched nervously on the table. "What is it?"

His midnight eyes shifted from the dancers to his wife. " 'Young Highland Rover.' " One hand still cupped the goblet in lean brown fingers, but it felt as if he'd actually touched her. "Shall I have the musicians play 'Lady Castlereagh's Air' for you?"

Recalling that day on the streets in St. Giles, Summer smiled and shook her head. "No. I think not."

"A smile, lass?" He leaned toward her, and she could feel his gaze. "Tha's the first I've seen today— nay, in a week or more."

Her eyes met his, and she sucked in a sharp breath. A blaze kindled in black depths, hot and wanting, making her skin burn and her heart leap.

Jamie put up a hand, cradling her chin in his palm, his fingers lying lightly along her jaw. "Funny, sad little lass. Is wedding me so hard for you? Am I such a dowie man tha' ye would hate me so?"

"I don't hate you."

"No?" His mouth curved in a faint smile. "Our guests must think differently. I've had two old dames ask if I took ye from yer mam too early."

Slightly indignant, she asked, "And what did you say?"

"The truth." He grinned. "That I stole you away and you hae fought me like a she-cat."

"That's not quite the way it is," she began, then saw the teasing lights in his eyes. *This* Jamie she knew. This laughing-eyed man with the devil's brow and glitter in eyes like midnight was familiar to her. She drew in a breath of relief. "I tolerate you," she said after a moment. "I don't hate you."

"Ah. A distinction, however fine, is always welcome." The disturbing hand dropped away from her face, and she felt suddenly bereft.

To cover her confusion, she reached quickly for wine. The tall goblet was heavy, made of gold and encrusted with jewels. She dragged it up, holding it with both hands, and deep red wine sloshed over the rim.

"Let me," came a husky murmur, and Jamie reached out to put his hand around hers, steadying the goblet. He tilted it for her, and Summer took a deep drink. She didn't want him to take his hand away, though his touch was sending tiny jolts up her arm and all the way down her spine.

When he set the goblet down, his hand still around hers, he bent forward to brush the wine from her lips with his mouth. Summer closed her eyes. She trembled from head to toe with a fine shivering at the light, warm brush of his lips against hers. His tongue slid over the wine-damp curve of her lip in a slick motion, then inside, and touched her.

A gasp hung in her throat. It was so intimate a kiss, so arousing, that she was suddenly aware of where they were. Apparently, Jamie was too, because he drew back with a soft sigh.

"Damn tradition," he muttered, flicking a glance toward the guests crowding the room. His gaze slid back to her. "You know that we're to sit here at the head table like two prize bulls on display."

"Yes." She tried to regulate her breathing again and found a measure of success. "Your mother told me. It's the tradition to sit for a time so that the guests may drink our health in toasts. And we're to lead a dance or two."

"Aye." Jamie sat back in his chair. "Do you know how to do a reel of any kind, lass?"

She hesitated. "From what I've seen, these dances look very similar to what I'm used to. And of course, I can do the minuet and the polonaise."

"Then I guess we'll have to dance," he said glumly. "I feel I should tell you, it's no' my favorite pastime."

Another smile. "I would think you'd be very good at it."

"Aye, lass, I am. But my sisters abused me as a partner so many times, I'm ruined for anyone else." He shook his head. "Our dance lessons used to end in lively battles, I can tell you that. We went through so many dancing masters that my father threatened to sit in on our lessons with a whip."

Summer gave a soft, suffocated laugh. "And did that threat work?"

"Aye. Admirably well. But I still don't care for the dance at all."

There was soon the opportunity for her to judge Jamie's dancing for herself, and she wasn't at all surprised to see that he had not exaggerated. He danced very well; his fluid grace was startling considering his size. Summer noted his chagrined expression as he stepped forward, bowed, took her hand, and circled, then moved on down the set, and a spurt of laughter welled in her.

By the time Jamie was across from her again, she was laughing, breathless, her eyes shining and her lips parted and wide. Her arisaid was draped gracefully over one arm, and silken filaments of gilt hair swung with her movements, brushing against her slender hips as she stepped lightly to the contredanse.

Partners for a moment, they skipped down the path made by two rows of dancers. Jamie smiled lazily at her.

"You like to dance, I see."

"Yes, I do." Her lips were curved in a broad smile. "I hate to think I've wed a man who doesn't."

He turned her under his arm with a graceful twist of one hand, lace cuffs tumbling over his wrist to scrape against her arm. "I imagine we can come to terms on that, Lady Westcott."

Lady Westcott. Dear God, she hadn't thought about that. Everything else had occupied her mind so fully, the title had been forgotten. She stumbled, and he caught her; a small frown lowered his brow until she managed a smile, then she was once more gone in the steps of the dance.

When they met again, Jamie asked abruptly, "Do you wish to sit down?"

A glint of mischief flashed briefly in her eyes, and she said innocently, "No, my lord. Tradition calls for us to dance."

He loosed a soft oath, and she laughed, her blue eyes mocking him. She had only an instant's warning before he answered the unspoken challenge in her gaze.

Heedless of his partner and the other dancers in the set, when Jamie saw her laughter, he jerked to a halt and pulled Summer into his arms, bending his head to kiss her fiercely. He held her close against him in spite of her first startled struggle.

Realizing they had become the focus of attention, Summer stopped her efforts to jerk free. She hung there in his arms while the music played on and guests began to laugh. Then he loosed her, stepped back, and swept her a bow.

"Shall we take our seats, my lady?"

Flushed, embarrassed, and well aware of the indulgent glances at them, Summer could do nothing but comply.

"Why did you do that?" she flung at him when they were seated again, and he smiled.

"Because you looked so tempting, laughing at me and daring me to make a scene. I've no horror of such scenes, you may have guessed."

Recalling his ballad singing on crowded London streets, she gave a short nod. "I have noticed that."

A footman approached, bearing silver platters of roast meat and pastries, and Summer turned away from her husband. She presented him with her back as she chose several delectable oatmeal cakes and black buns rich with currants, candied peel, apple, nuts, and spices. She blatantly ignored the proffered platter of haggis.

Sprawling back in his chair, Jamie watched her. A high flush stained her cheeks, and the long sweep of gilt-sprinkled lashes hid blue eyes that were bright and vivid. His fingers drummed impatiently on the linen-covered table, and he cast occasional glances toward his parents.

Fiona and Bruce Cameron were among the dancers. The sight of his austere father dancing a lively reel had always seemed faintly incongruous to him, but he knew his mother loved it. A smile curled his mouth. Fiona and Bruce had a stormy marriage, but none could say they didn't love each other.

From the time he was in leading strings, he'd heard the occasional distant sounds of their arguments. His parents made it a rule never to fight in front of their children, but unless they'd ridden to Edinburgh to quarrel, they could not have hidden their battles. Slamming doors and flaying words were not easy to muffle.

Jamie watched as his mother slid her husband a sly glance and twitch of her skirts, and saw the earl's lazy grin. Aye, well matched they were. The Cameron, slow to anger but formidable once roused, and fiery Fiona, quick-tempered, constantly laughing, teasing her husband either into or out of rages.

In spite of the example of his parents, Jamie had never felt the same compunction to marry as his older brothers had. Now only Ian was still unwed. And Robert, of course, who was only nineteen. But Jamie was truly wed, and to a lass who was more mystery than mistress.

He wondered what she'd say if he told her he'd married her because he loved her, not because her uncle and fiancé would demand restitution. He'd tried to tell her, but the time never seemed to be right. And he doubted that she'd believe him anyway. Odd that his father had little trouble believing him, or his mother. They'd merely smiled, nodded, and accepted it. It seemed that everyone could see it but Summer.

His gaze flicked back to her. She'd tasted of all the cakes and buns she'd chosen, but eaten very little. He could feel her uneasiness, and knew she was thinking about the coming night. So was he.

Memory took him down well-traveled paths, and he could almost feel her satin thighs beneath his palms, the sweet fragrance of her skin in his nostrils. God, how many nights he'd lain awake and thought of her like that. How many mornings had he woken with an ache. . . .

His hand clenched in the tablecloth, knotting it. A brisk thump beat in his chest, and he tried to still the surge of blood pooling in his groin. It would be too readily evident beneath his kilt if he was asked to stand up, and he was damned if he was going to provide more entertainment for the fine guests his parents had invited to his wedding.

One hand found Summer's shoulder, his fingers caressing the nape of her neck, burrowing under the weight of her hair. He loved her hair, the cool silk of it flowing over his hand and the wispy texture when he crushed it in his fist. He wanted to put both hands in it and pull her head close, raking his fingers through her long tresses while he pushed her down into a mattress. Lord, he was making himself crazy, and if he didn't stop, he was going to startle the guests and shame his parents by taking Summer upstairs without waiting for the usual tradition to commence.

Damn tradition!

It seemed to take forever for a reasonable, decent time to pass. He could smell Summer's soft fragrance, and it kept him tied in knots; he watched the windows, and when the light had begun to fade, he lifted his goblet of whisky and stood up.

Summer gave a start. She'd been talking to Catriona, Jamie's married sister, and when she felt him stand, she saw the guests' attention shift to their table.

"Turn to him," Catriona whispered, and Summer obeyed.

He towered over her, and she knew, suddenly, that the moment had come to go upstairs. A wild throbbing began in her chest. She shouldn't fear the bridal bed like a virgin, yet she did. For some reason, the thought of wedded intimacy with Jamie carried far more significance that what she'd already done.

Jamie held out his hand, and Summer put hers into his broad palm. He lifted her slowly from her chair. She could feel everyone looking at them, and though the music still played, a plaintive tune that made her think of wind in the trees, it had grown very quiet.

"Take up your cup, Summer," he said softly, and she did with her free hand, feeling her knees quiver beneath the silk plaid skirt. She hoped no one saw.

Still holding her other hand in his, he turned to the assembled guests, some sitting, some standing, and said in a loud, clear voice, "I drink a toast to the health of my beautiful wife, Lady Westcott."

A round of cheers rose, and goblets lifted. With his eyes on hers, he motioned for her to drink, and Summer did as he did. As she lowered her cup, she heard Catriona say in a whisper, "Now you do the same!"

In a stronger voice than she'd imagined she had, Summer lifted her golden goblet and said, "To my husband, a bold, bonny Scotsman . . ."

Jamie grinned, then tossed down the last of his whisky. More toasts were drunk, some bawdy, some sincere, and when the laughter had died down, the musicians struck up a lively tune. As the strains of "My Love, She's but a Lassie Yet" trilled into the air, Summer felt the slight pressure of Jamie's hand on her arm.

"I believe that's the signal for your departure, my lady," Jamie said meaningfully, his eyes meeting hers in a shocking jolt.

Gathering her trailing arisaid in one hand, Summer turned blindly and gratefully discovered Lady Glendale and Catriona at hand.

"This way, my lady," one of them said—she didn't know which one—she couldn't look. She felt someone take her cold hand, draw her away from the table and through the press of people. Then they were almost running up wide stone steps, past French tapestries and family portraits, up in a sweeping curve to the second floor.

By the time they reached the chamber readied for them, they were all out of breath and laughing. Summer struggled for air; Catriona and Lady Glendale were beckoning maids in the door; Jamie's other sisters and several other women were there too. Everyone seemed to know what to do. The bedchamber was a bustle of activity, with Summer at its center.

Within a half hour, she was bathed, garbed in a sheer, flowing gown of silk that barely concealed her curves, and standing nervously by the drapery-hung bed.

"Lord!" someone whispered, and Summer agreed heartily with the sentiment. It was a shocking nightgown.

A deep vee slashed the ivory silk to the waist, held by slender silk ribbons around her; a ribbon tied it at each shoulder, and the sides were open, revealing her slim, pale legs from hip to ankle. When she moved, it drifted open, and with the light behind her, her silhouette was vividly displayed.

"Don't stand in front of a lamp," Catriona said with a bald practicality that eased the sudden tension. "Or I'll not give you a ha'pence for the gown when our Jamie's through with it."

A nervous titter rippled through the room, and when Lady Glendale looked up and saw Summer's pale face with two hot splotches of color on her cheeks, she smiled.

"Mary," she said to her daughter, "fetch a claret cup for your new sister." Summer gave a start of surprise, and Lady Glendale patted her arm. "See, lass, we're all family here. It's just your Jamie who's coming to you. And he's a gentle lad, for all that he can wear savagery at times. I've never known him to do a mean thing in his life. Not intentionally."

Summer gazed at her and blindly accepted the claret cup that Mary thrust into her hands. Lady Glendale's lovely face was creased into a smile.

"Drink it down, my lady. I hear the men coming, and we'd best put you in the bed, or Jamie may have to use his dirk to keep you. If they've left it to him."

Blanching, Summer said in a strangled croak, "They're coming in here?"

"Aye." Lady Glendale sounded matter-of-fact, and she added soothingly, "It's just a bit of fun, sweetheart. While you've been preparing for your husband, the men like to prepare your husband for you. When Dallas wed, Jamie brought him to the marriage bed drunk as a lord and naked as a new-laid egg. Naturally, Sheena was angry."

"Aye," dark-haired Sheena Cameron spoke up with a grin. "I locked the silly fool out, and he had to wander the halls mother-naked until someone was kind enough to fetch him a cloak."

Summer laughed softly. The banter and laughter in the room came lightly to these people. Even when her parents had been alive, there hadn't been this ease between them. It was unfamiliar, but strangely comforting.

"That's better," Lady Glendale said, taking the empty cup from her and shoving it back at Mary. "Now. Pop between the sheets and draw them up to your chin. I don't want a riot because one of those lusty lords takes a liking to what's not his."

No sooner had Summer slid between the sheets and pulled them up, feeling lost in the middle of the huge bed, than a loud rattle sounded at the door. Her heart thumped, and in spite of the wine she'd just drunk, her mouth felt dry.

One of Jamie's sisters was at the chamber door, pulling it open to admit the men, scolding them in a laughing voice for being so rowdy.

Several pairs of hands thrust Jamie through the door, and she saw with relief that he still wore some of his clothes. She didn't know if she would have been able to bear having him arrive unclothed. Her fingers curled into the sheets as the men spilled into the room. They filled it with noise and laughter and masculine exuberance.

Jamie—shirtless, shoeless, and with the kilt hanging dangerously but still clinging to him—was brought to the bedside. Summer shrank back into the pillows piled behind her. She recognized his brothers, his father, and a half-dozen other faces, but the rest were a blur.

"Here he is, my lady," Dallas Cameron said with a laugh as he pushed Jamie forward. "Shall we finish undressing him fer ye?"

Summer swallowed her vague embarrassment and said, "No, I think I can manage it."

A shout of laughter went up, and Jamie's grin widened. Summer was aware of Lady Glendale's wink of approval, and a burst of satisfaction swept through her. Perhaps she could fit into this family, after all.

A family.

She felt a sudden pang of sadness for those she'd lost, but it didn't pierce her as sharply as it always had before, and she wondered why. Could it be because she'd been accepted into the Cameron fold without question? She now had an entire herd of relatives, and she realized how she'd hated being alone. She didn't have to be alone anymore.

Lady Glendale had taken charge and was ushering everyone from the room. She paused in the doorway, her husband's hand on her shoulder, and looked back. Jamie stood by the bed, his bare chest rising and falling rapidly from his exertions. Black hair tumbled onto his forehead, and there was a light in his eyes that made her smile.

She closed the door softly, and Jamie and Summer were alone in the wash of candle glow and firelight.

Chapter 14

Jamie moved gracefully to lock the door, then turned to look at her, making her throat ache for the proud male beauty of him. His bare chest gleamed in the rosy fireglow, flickering light dancing over smooth, flowing muscles. When he moved closer, she held up a hand to him.

The slightly wary expression in his eyes vanished, and he came forward and took her hand. His fingers were warm, strong, holding her firmly. Slowly reaching out, Jamie drew down the sheets Summer held to her breast.

His eyes narrowed slightly, and she saw the muscles in his stomach contract as if he'd just been kicked. When his eyes lifted to hers, she saw the desire burning in them hot and strong.

Nothing had been said between them. The only sounds in the room were those of the logs in the fire and the faint, muted tunes from the musicians below . . . and their breathing.

Summer's throat contracted when he put one knee on the bed and leaned over her. He bent his head and kissed her lightly on the mouth, his lips moving softly and gently. Then he stepped back and away from the bed.

Summer's eyes widened, and she flushed slightly

as his hands went to the belt holding up his kilt; she looked away delicately but was fully aware when he'd unbuckled his belt and his kilt fell away. She tried not to look as nervous as she felt when he returned to her.

Jamie put one hand on her arm as he lay down beside her, and she started. He drew back slightly. "Relax, love," he murmured. "I'll no' hurt you."

"I know." The words came painfully from a closed throat, and she swallowed. "I know," she said again.

Putting out a finger, his face shadowed with the light behind him, he toyed with the ribbons that held her gown up on her shoulders. Then he curled his hands into the sheets and drew them completely from her, rising to his knees. His dark brow lifted.

" 'Tis glad I am that you didn't see fit to meet me at the door in this," he muttered ruefully.

A thread of laughter was woven into her voice. "Your mother thought it best I didn't."

"She's right. . . ."

"Don't you like it?"

"God, lass, you're beautiful."

Summer flushed. She wasn't comfortable with easy compliments. Or mere lust. She wanted much more from James Cameron, and she didn't know if he could give it. He gave love freely to his mother and sisters and even to his brothers—would he share his heart with her too? Was there room for her in it?

Warm fingers brushed her skin as he reached for the tiny ribbons on her shoulders, and she shivered. He pulled in a slow tug, watching the sheer silk fall from one shoulder. A soft, firm breast lay free. His palm cradled its weight, a thumb rubbing across the taut, aching crest in a languorous motion that made her burn. She could feel his smile, his night-dark eyes on her.

When his head bent and his mouth closed over the beaded peak in a hot, wet caress, Summer moaned. Her breath came quickly, and she throbbed with need.

It was almost unbearable, this sweeping tension that gripped her. With his lips still on her breast, gently drawing the tightened nipple into his mouth, Jamie sought and found the other tie at her shoulder and loosened it. The silk shimmied down to pool at her waist, held there by the last ribbon.

When she arched against the hand cupped over her other breast, he spread a damp, sizzling trail of kisses across the valley between them, then captured that breast too.

Finally, lifting his head, he tugged at the sash at her waist. It resisted, and with a muttered oath, he tore it free, wrenching the silk away from her.

Lost in a haze, Summer offered no protest at his impatience. Lord, if he would only ease this ache inside her, this searing, simmering ache that made her crave his touch and strain toward him.

"Easy, lass," he said when she tried to pull him close. His mouth found her temple, her cheek, the tip of her nose. He clawed at the wisps of silk still clinging to her legs, and finally succeeded in completely removing the gown.

He bent forward, kissed her ear, her throat, pressed his face in her hair, and breathed deeply, as if starved for air; then, spreading his hands over the high curve of her rib cage and down to circle her waist, Jamie nudged her thighs apart with his knees. He didn't enter her, though his body was shuddering for release.

Dragging in his breath in short pants, he slid his palm over the almost-flat mound of her belly, tangling his fingers in the nest of curls between her thighs. She moved restlessly, and he slipped his hand lower, parting her, his fingers sliding inside.

He quickly covered her mouth with his lips when she cried out, her body jerking with reaction at that intimate touch. She was tight, and he moved slowly, still kissing her, letting her grow accustomed to his hand. When she began to relax, her thighs parting slightly, he finally moved his body up so that he fit closely against her. Then he took his hand away, pressing against her but not pushing in.

"Jamie," she said in a breathless little moan when he didn't move his body, only kept kissing her. Her voice grew urgent. "Jamie . . ." Her hips rocked, twisting sinuously.

"Aye, lass," he said against her open, gasping mouth. He took her hand in his and drew it down, circling him with her fingers, his hand atop hers. "Like that . . . aye, lass . . ." His voice grew thick and fierce, and when he couldn't stand it anymore, he moved her hand and thrust inside, his palms pressing into the mattress on each side of her head.

He was heavy and swollen inside her, probing in quick, urgent movements that had them both rushing toward a distant pinnacle. His rhythmic thrusts and her involuntary contractions swept them faster and faster, until Summer cried out loudly, her hands digging into his shoulders, raking down his back as she arched upward.

He felt her shudder beneath him, felt her hips push at him in a hard-driving rhythm, and clenched his teeth. When Summer convulsed, her body gripping him in a series of hot pulses, he exploded with a shattering release. She sobbed aloud, and her heels drummed against his thighs as she twisted under him, wresting the final pleasure for both of them.

Jamie's breath escaped in a rush between his teeth, and he slowly lowered his body until his forehead was resting on the pillow beside her. He was too weak to move; the climax had been devastatingly intense. Now he felt drained and lifeless. It was a good thing they were safe in his parents' home; he couldn't have lifted a finger to stop the worst villain.

He felt her soft, delicate hands skip lightly down the curve of his shoulder, making small, comforting circles. He couldn't move.

But when Summer's hand curled over his neck with a peculiarly tender motion, he managed to lift his head and stare down at her. In the shifting light of candle and fireplace she looked like a rosy goddess; tawny, streaked hair tumbling in her eyes, her lashes half-lowered, slightly embarrassed, her mouth swollen and bruised from his hard kisses.

Jamie smiled and nuzzled her neck. He was faintly surprised by the soft, aching feeling inside. He wondered if she felt something similar, and if that was why she was looking up at him with a vaguely bewildered expression. It occurred to him suddenly that he might have rushed things.

Lifting his head, he stared down at her with a frown. Damnit, he'd wanted her second time to be perfect, with no pain to mar it.

His hand curled into the sheets, and he fought briefly with his pride before muttering, "Summer, lass, did you—was I too quick for you?"

"Too quick?" There was a brief pause, then her voice, small and faintly embarrassed, whispered, "No. I thought it was—nice."

"Nice?" Some of his incredulous chagrin must have shown, because she laughed softly and drew his head down to hers.

"Wonderful, then. Superb. Magnificent. Excel—"

"All right, all right," he interrupted, half-amused, half-annoyed. "I understand." He kissed her quickly and rolled to the side. "A man is certainly not allowed to develop any conceit with you, I'll say that much for you."

"Is that all?" Her fingers traced the ridges of his ribs in a feathery touch that made him squirm.

"Is what all?" He caught her hand and lifted it to his lips.

"Is that all you can say for me?"

Jamie's head turned on the pillow, and he looked at her with a lazy gaze. Deliberately, provocatively, he sucked her fingers into his mouth, watching her eyes widen. Then he kissed her palm, his mouth moving up her wrist to her forearm.

Incredibly, though he'd meant to only tease her a bit, he found his body responding. Apparently, she was aware of it. She glanced down, then back up at his face, and a smile curled her lips. One hand drifted over his belly to his groin, and she stroked him lightly. His arousal was instant and complete.

"What was it you once said about dragons, my lord?" she murmured with an impish smile.

Jamie rolled over again, pressing her beneath him, his hands curving under her hips to drag her up to meet his body. He took her quickly, almost roughly, and she gasped and squirmed and clutched at him as he rode her to a thundering release. With his face pressing into the curve of her neck and shoulder, a powerful pulsing of life flowed from Jamie into Summer.

Breathing heavily, he tucked her into the angle of his chest and thighs and lay on his side, his arm curled over her.

Logs crackled and popped in the fire, chasing away the chill even June couldn't banish from the castle in the high crags of Scotland. Summer and Jamie slept at last.

Jamie made love to her several more times that night. Waking, he would find her soft body cradled in his embrace, and his own body would respond. Holding her, kissing the back of her neck and smoothing his hands over her hips, he rocked against Summer until she woke, murmuring protests but eager for him. Pushing into her, hearing her moans, he thought of the future stretching before them, filled with nights just like this one, and he smiled against her softly parted lips.

The last time was just before dawn, when the fire had burned down to only gray, sullen embers, and the candles had long since guttered. He found her by feel, familiarizing himself with her body, the swells and hollows, the tiny mole just below her right breast, the little scar on her thigh she'd said was made as a child falling from her pony. He knew the taste, the feel, the smell of her, and gloried in it.

When the sun finally rose, they still slept, exhausted and content as it climbed into the sky. Jamie sprawled on his back, one hand flung above his head, his fingers curved in the thick mane of his jet hair. Summer woke first and saw him lying beside her, his big body relaxed in sleep.

Her eyelids felt heavy and scratchy, and she blinked several times, her lashes sweeping against her cheeks. Then she focused on him, and a faint, tender smile turned her mouth up at the corners. He'd kicked off the sheet and lay in magnificent animal splendor.

It was her first opportunity to explore his body without embarrassment, and she took advantage of it. Men had no modesty at all, but though driven by curiosity, she'd not been able to be bold enough to touch and see as much as she had wanted. Now she could, and she did so frankly.

Small, pale scars showed on the dark skin in places, and she noted with interest that he was dark all over, not just tanned by the sun. As Dallas had said, definitely a throwback. She suppressed a smile. Broad shoulders tapered into long muscles on his arms, smooth and hard, knotted even in sleep. His chest was wide and thick, rising and falling in a steady rhythm, tapering down to a lean waist delineated with ridges of flat muscle across his belly. Her gaze moved lower.

Now, in repose, his body didn't look as powerful as it had earlier. The smile flirted with her lips again, then faded. His thighs were muscled, lean, long, blanketed with the same fine down of dark hair as his chest and groin. He was, in truth, a superbly made man.

Summer shifted slightly, tentatively reached out as if to touch him, then thought better of it. She drew back and rolled to her back.

An instant later, she gasped as Jamie rolled atop her, his black eyes dancing with mischief and pleasure.

"Why didn't you touch me, lass?" he asked, ignoring her flaming face and snapping blue eyes. "We both would have enjoyed it, I vow."

"Wretch! Why didn't you tell me you were awake?"

"I dinna hear ye ask, lass." His mouth had found hers again, nourishing it with his own until her breathing was quick and ragged. Lacing his fingers in hers, he drew her arms up and over her head in a lazy motion as he nudged her thighs apart. Straightening his arms, he levered his chest away from hers, thrusting with his lower body and bringing them both to a quick climax.

They'd barely had time to recover their breath before a light knock sounded on the door. Irritated, Jamie lifted his head and glared. When the knocking persisted, he flung back the sheet with a mutter and left the bed. Not bothering with a robe or pants, he barked a demand to know who wanted him.

Then, swearing, he moved to find some pants and step into them. Summer sat up in the bed, her hair tangled and cascading over her face and shoulders.

"Who is it?"

"Cat." He buttoned his pants, looked up, saw the frown of confusion on her face, and said, "Catriona. God only knows what she wants this early."

Summer pulled the sheet up around her and tossed her hair out of her eyes.

Turning the lock and yanking open the door, Jamie blocked the opening with his half-clad body.

"Cat," he began irritably, "if this is one of those damn-fool pranks of yours, it's not the time for—"

"Jamie." Catriona ducked under his outstretched arm and into the room. Her voice was low and soft, almost furtive. "Jamie, ye've a visitor below."

He stared at her. "A visitor? Damnit, Cat, what hae ye got in yer mind to do now?"

"Listen to me, you big oaf! I know you've had no sleep and you're surly, but tha's no' my fault!" Her glance flicked to the bed, the ruined gown on the floor, then back to Jamie. A faint smile touched her lips. He lifted his head slightly.

"Aye," he said in a guarded tone, "it isn't. Who's the visitor?" He stepped instinctively between his sister and the bed that held Summer.

Catriona whispered, "An American. You'd best come quickly. The Cameron sent me up for you."

"An American this early? For God's sake, the man must have ridden all night from Perth."

Nodding, Catriona muttered, "It's no' that early, and he said he did." Her mute gaze spoke volumes.

Jamie nodded. "Aye. I'm coming." She left. He dressed quickly, avoiding Summer's questions, telling her that he'd be back shortly. Kissing her, he said against her mouth, "It's no' for you to worry about, lass. Sleep till I get back."

He was fully prepared to meet with Summer's uncle or former fiancé. He was totally unprepared to meet with Garth Kinnison.

Big, blond, handsome, Kinnison stood insolently in the great hall, gazing with amused appreciation at Elizabeth Cameron. She was flirting outrageously with him right under the nose of her father, smiling and asking pert questions that Kinnison fielded easily.

When Jamie strode into the hall, he paused. A frown snapped his brows together, and he flicked a glance toward his father.

"Jamie, lad, this man has come to talk wi' you. I told him you were a'bed, but he was most insistent." There was a lazy insolence in Bruce's tone that let Jamie know he did not think much of this man.

Turning his attention from Elizabeth to Jamie, the man asked, "James Cameron?"

"Aye." Jamie moved close, his cold gaze sharp and assessing. The American was too young to be her uncle; he must be her betrothed. "And you, sir?"

"Kinnison, Captain Garth Kinnison." Jamie's startled recoil immediately registered with Kinnison. "I see you may have heard of me."

"Aye," came the growling reply, "I've heard of you."

Kinnison tilted his head slightly, then glanced at Bruce Cameron. "Is there a more private place we can talk?" he asked with a meaningful glance at Elizabeth and one or two of the younger girls.

Jamie's hands curled into fists, and the blood was slapping through his veins in a heated rush. He wished he had his dirk, or his sword. He wished Garth Kinnison would draw steel on him and give him an excuse to shove it back.

By the time the three men reached the huge study, Jamie's temper was tightly leashed. Only a small muscle in his jaw gave him away. He went to stand with his back to the windows. It gave him the opportunity to study Kinnison in the light without being closely observed himself. Bruce Cameron waved Kinnison to a chair, then took a seat behind his desk, his presence an obvious statement.

A faint smile curled Kinnison's mouth, and he nodded an acceptance. His gaze flicked back to Jamie, standing with arms crossed and deadly fury glittering in his eyes.

Garth took the chair offered and sprawled lazily in it while he met Jamie's hostile stare. He shrugged and came directly to the point.

"I'm here for Summer St. Clair. Epson says she's with you."

"*St.* Clair?" Jamie repeated softly. Damn her. And how was he supposed to swallow this, by God? French. And she knew how he felt. *Damn her!* Not that he really cared, now, about her being French—or half-French, or whatever she was. It wasn't that but the lies and that she hadn't been able to—didn't—trust him. That cut deeply.

Jamie didn't move or show by any reaction how he

felt. "A bit tardy, aren't you?" he asked coolly. "I fished her out of a river six weeks ago, after you'd left her behind."

Kinnison spread his hands. "Yes, well, circumstances took me out of London rather quickly, I'm afraid. I didn't know she'd disappeared until I returned to find a message from her uncle and a note from the ship's captain who was supposed to take her aboard. I've been looking for her ever since."

"I'm sure you have."

Kinnison shifted restlessly, and shot Jamie a half-angry look as he said, "If it's a matter of money for your time and trouble, I can—"

"Don't be stupid." Jamie indicated the castle with a contemptuous sweep of his hand. "Do I look too destitute to buy food for one small lass?"

Kinnison had the grace to flush. "My apologies." He rose to his feet. "I've ridden a long way, and I'm tired. I promised her uncle I'd find her and return her to him, and I intend to do that. If you're entertaining any notions of keeping her, I'd like to point out that she is an American heiress, and it could cause you a lot of trouble. Her uncle is president of the St. Clair shipping concern until she comes to her majority. Barton Shriver is a very powerful and influential man." He glanced at Bruce Cameron to gauge his reaction, then back at Jamie. "It would cause a great deal of conflict between Great Britain and America if this were to go too far. I trust you realize how dangerous this could be with Britain already fighting France."

Nothing was said for a moment. Bruce Cameron finally stirred, not even glancing at his rigid son. "An' if you do take th' lass back, Kinnison? What happens then?"

Kinnison's features relaxed slightly. "Then Shriver can be very generous."

"I meant to Miss St. Clair."

"Summer?" He shrugged carelessly. "Her betrothed will take her back. Even," he added with a lifted brow, "if she is slightly used."

Jamie had remained quiet, but now he straightened slowly and met Kinnison's suddenly wary gaze. "She's not used, Kinnison," he said. "She's married. To me. And I don't want to hear her name on your lips again. Ever."

"Married?" The blond sea captain seemed stunned. "To you? It can't be legal. She's not reached her majority yet."

"It's legal in Scotland." Jamie's brow lifted. "And she signed of her own free will in front of witnesses."

A low oath escaped Kinnison. He shoved one fist into the other one and glared at Jamie. He didn't dare make any threats or insist upon taking her, of course; that would be foolhardy. "Truly wedded?" he snapped.

"Wedded and bedded." Jamie met his narrowed gaze coldly and again wished that he could issue a challenge. He could not. Not here. Not now. Not under his father's roof when Kinnison had been offered hospitality. He coolly ignored the fact that Summer had been married under a false name. He intended to rectify that as soon as Kinnison left. And then he intended to make his bride very sorry she hadn't had enough faith in him to tell him the truth.

Summer was awakened by Jamie flinging back the covers and yanking her up by the arms into a sitting position.

"Why did you do that?" she asked, glaring at him.

"You need to get up." His expression was cold, his tone flat. "Get dressed in something decent."

"I'm tired." She frowned at him. "You kept waking me up all night."

There was something wrong. His black eyes were hostile. And he looked dangerous again.

"What's the matter?"

Jamie didn't answer. He strode across the room,

flung open the doors to a dressing room, and disappeared for a moment. When he returned, he had an armful of clothes that he hurled at her.

"Put them on. And hurry."

She blinked. Her eyes felt scratchy, and she ached all over. Especially between her thighs.

"I'm sleepy," she protested again, but Jamie crossed to her and dragged her from the bed. She half fell, bumping her knees on the floor, gasping with alarm. He dragged her up and over to the washbasin, and proceeded to wash her face and body with a cold, wet rag.

Angry now, Summer struggled. She almost succeeded in twisting away, but he hauled her back by her long hair, winding it around his fist. Then he held her between his hard-muscled thighs and scrubbed her body until it was a glowing pink. Half sobbing, exhausted and bewildered, Summer made halfhearted attempts to stop him when he began to dress her. That, too, was futile.

"I don't know why you're doing this," she said when he shoved a hairbrush in her hand and told her to use it.

"That makes two of us." His voice was faintly bitter, and he flashed her a baffled glare. "I suppose I should just let you go."

The hairbrush stilled in midair. Her breath caught in a painful vise in her chest. "Let me go?" she whispered. "But why?"

"Isna' tha' what ye've wanted?" he snarled at her in a thick burr. " 'Tis all I've heard frae ye."

"No! I mean, yes, I did, but not now." She swayed as he hesitated, then turned his back on her.

His voice sounded choked but a bit softer when he said, "Come on, lass." He swung open the door and motioned for her to join him.

Moving as listlessly as a sleepwalker, Summer stepped into the hallway with him. She could feel Jamie's tense fury vibrating in him and knew it must have had something to do with the early visitor. If only she weren't so sleepy and dull-witted!

Bruce Cameron looked up when Summer was pushed into the chamber, his dispassionate gaze studying her flushed face, sleepy eyes, and slightly swollen mouth. It was obvious that Jamie had kept her awake most of the night. He smiled faintly.

Jamie half-dragged Summer to the huge desk, then spread his hand on her chest and shoved her to a chair. He looked at his father. Temper danced hotly in his eyes, but his voice was cool.

"Is he here yet?"

"Not yet."

Summer's fingers curled into the arms of her chair, and she blinked furiously for a moment. "Is who here? I have a right to know. What's going on? Why are you so fierce with me?"

Moving to stand behind her, Jamie slid his hand over her shoulder and squeezed. His grip was hard, not painful, but indicated a certain menace that made Summer shift uneasily.

"Hush, lass."

"Why?" She tried to rise, but he pushed her back down, and she failed to heed the warning. Lunging to one side, she avoided his hand and lurched to her feet, turning at the same time to glare at him. "You surly devil! I demand to know the meaning of this!"

Jamie took several steps forward, and Bruce Cameron murmured a warning. "I hear Findlay coming."

Pausing, Jamie flashed Summer a black look and went to open the study door. The minister who had married them in the stone chapel only the day before entered with a look of frowning confusion on his round face. His cloak swirled around his stout frame. He took in Jamie's dangerous expression, Summer's flushed face, and the earl's remote gaze, and hesitated.

"Another wedding, is it, my lord? Was't there somethin' wrong wi' th' first papers?"

"Aye." The Cameron stood and shoved forward a

set of legal documents. "The bride's name is wrong. It should be done correctly, so there will be no doubts or questions."

Summer felt her heart drop. Her gaze flew to Jamie's, and she saw from his dark fury that he knew she'd lied. But did he know all? And did he intend to wed her again?

Obviously. He took her arm and pulled her to the desk and thrust a pen into her hand. She chewed her bottom lip, hesitant, wondering.

"Sign. Your real name, Miss *St. Clair*," he growled in her ear, and she shuddered.

Oh, he *knew* all right. Whoever the visitor had been, he had brought the information of her true identity. Did Jamie hate her now? Or was he only angry with her for the lies? It was his pride, of course, his stubborn pride.

Her head began to throb painfully.

"Sign it," came the snarling command, and she jerked.

Staring down at the document, feeling Jamie's fury, she still hesitated. She could feel his gaze on her, dark and wary, and clouded with some emotion she didn't recognize. When she would have dropped the pen, Jamie's hand closed over hers, and he dragged it to the paper. She signed, but leaned back against him when she'd scrawled her name, closing her eyes in defeat.

The minister was troubled. He looked from Summer's pale face to Jamie's angry features, then to the earl. "Is she no' willin', my lord?"

"Ask her."

Summer opened her eyes and gazed at the worried look on Findlay's face. She should say no, but she knew she couldn't. She loved Jamie. In spite of the fact that he was glaring at her as if he wanted to strangle her.

"Yes," she said almost inaudibly when Findlay asked her, "I'm wedding of my own free will."

Only partially satisfied, but unwilling to antagonize the earl, Findlay nodded. He had them repeat the vows again, and by the time they were through, Summer was half sobbing with exhaustion and frustration.

Findlay grimaced. 'I've th' notion tha' there's more here amiss than hae been said. Th' lass is overwrought."

The earl nodded. "Aye. She's had the wedding night, but no' the legal wedding. She's a sensitive lass."

A look of understanding came over the minister's face, and he nodded. "Och. Aye, tha' wad make th' lass greet, I vow." He smiled. "Dinna fash yerself, my lady, th' vows are done now, an' ye're fast-wed to a braw callant I've known all his life. Wi' him tae luv ye, ye'll be happy."

Summer began to sob.

Surprisingly, Jamie folded her into his arms and tucked her against his chest. He held her a moment, and she could hear the solid, steady thump of his heart against her ear. Then he bent, catching her under her knees with one arm and at her back with the other, and swept her off her feet. He carried her upstairs and put her back to bed. He forced her to drink a cup of spiced wine, then smoothed the coverlet over her.

By the time he left the room, she'd fallen into a deep, dreamless sleep.

Chapter 15

"Garth? Garth came for me?" Summer stared at Jamie with surprise. "How did he know...?"

"He said Epson." Jamie shoved viciously at a log in the grate, using the toe of his boot. He moved restlessly from fire to window and back, tapping a riding whip against the top of his boots with a snapping, irritating sound.

Summer nodded. Epson. Of course. That dandy would enjoy stirring up trouble for Lord Westcott. Another wedge to drive between them. She watched as Jamie—her husband, how odd that was!—prowled the sitting room with long, restless strides.

"Will you please stop that?" Summer demanded crossly, and he pivoted away from the fire to look at her. She took an involuntary step back. There was no trace of the gentle, laughing lover in his face now. She smothered her nervous tension with an effort. "You Scots can be so infuriating!"

"And I suppose Kinnison isn't?" he mocked. "A veritable paragon of virtues, I vow."

Her chin lifted. "Most of the time," she said to prick his complacency. Apparently, it worked.

He recoiled as if she'd struck him, and his jaw grew taut.

Crossing the sitting room in three long strides, he grabbed her wrists. "No lies, lass." His voice was harsh, flat. "What do you feel for Kinnison?"

"I believe we've discussed this." She tried to pull free of him, but he held her too tightly. She'd have bruises there on the morrow, she thought with a sigh. "I've already told you how I feel about Garth."

He brought her up closer; she could feel the faint vibrations in his taut muscles. "Humor me."

Eyeing him, Summer thought that perhaps she'd better. "I do not love Garth, though I suppose I shall always think of him fondly. He was my first love—my only love until now."

"And now?"

"And now—I know that I don't love him."

His hands eased slightly on her arms. "You've got a facile tongue, sweeting," he said after a moment, and released her with a shove. The riding crop had pressed into her flesh, leaving a long welt. She rubbed at it sullenly as she kept a wary eye on him. There had been a quick, odd expression in his eyes that puzzled her; bleak, sort of, as if he'd expected something from her and not gotten it.

Nothing had gone right. The brief happiness she had snatched seemed in danger of disappearing; she was achingly aware that her lies were a major cause. Of course, she could not help what her uncle was or had done, but if she had confided in Jamie and not held to those stupid lies, he wouldn't be so angry with her now.

Stupid, stupid, stupid lies!

She watched him from beneath the curve of her lashes. He was still pacing restlessly, as if he absolutely could not stand still. Several times he paused and looked at her, a kind of baffled expression on his face that made her writhe inside. Was he wondering why she'd lied? why she had not believed in him enough to trust him?

Oh, Lord, she wondered too!

Jamie snapped the riding crop across his gloved palm in a steady beat, glancing at her while she pretended to sew a square of linen with embroidery threads. Finally, she threw it down. She couldn't even pretend with him prowling around like a caged lion.

An exultant light leapt in his eyes when she tried to step around him to the door, and when he barred her way, she gave an involuntary gasp.

"Do I scare you, lass?" he asked in a silky purr. "Faith, I hope so." The crop slashed across his palm with a loud *pop*. She eyed it nervously and licked suddenly dry lips with the tip of her tongue.

"Yes. You frighten me." Her chin tilted up at him as she struggled for calm. "Does it make you happy to know that?"

"Very." The single word was snarled at her, and she retreated back to her place by the window.

This was not going well at all. Her fingers tangled in her skirts in a convulsive clasp when he began pacing the floor again. The tension between them was unbearable; she wished it wasn't there for probably the hundredth time that morning.

Several minutes passed, then Summer stuck her chin in the air and threw caution to the winds.

"I lied to you because I didn't know you at first. And you're so cocksure at times. And spoiled. You always get things your way. Well, if you had shown the least bit of inclination to a sense of decent sympathy, I might have trusted you after a while."

Her voice trailed into silence. He stopped pacing and turned to look at her. The whip tapped steadily against the top of his jackboots.

"Sympathy, madam?" His voice was dangerously soft. "For a woman who demands honesty but will not give it? I find your logic irrational. As usual."

"I'm certain you do." She paused to swallow hard, then added, "But if I remember a'right, you're the man who found it logical to rob a neighbor of his purse in the stews of St. Giles."

"Ah. Yes. But I sent it back, didn't I?"

"Yes." Her mouth twisted with light, daring mockery. "A very *logical* thing to do."

He stiffened, and the expression on his face was so savage that for a moment she thought he was going to hit her with the riding whip he held. But then, slowly, his muscles relaxed, and with a snarled oath, he flung the whip across the room.

It sang through the air and landed atop a small table, knocking over a china egg in a collection and a painted porcelain figurine of a horse. Pieces scattered everywhere. Summer wisely decided to keep silent.

"Damn you," he said softly. "It wasn't supposed to be like this."

Summer didn't know what to say. She didn't know what he meant and didn't dare ask. Conversation didn't seem to be an option at this moment.

Jamie threw her a glance that was strangely bleak and, without another word, left the sitting room. The heavy oak door crashed closed behind him. Summer sank to a chair and put her face in her hands.

She was trembling all over. He'd been so angry; he had reminded her of herself, of how she reacted when she was hurt, but of course, he was only in a rage because she'd lied like a fiend and he'd believed her. Male pride, nothing more. She didn't have the power to hurt him, not the way he could hurt her. She was glad he'd left her; he wouldn't have the satisfaction of seeing her tears.

When Summer finally dried her eyes and gathered up her courage to go downstairs again, she found the great hall almost empty. Only Catriona and Margaret Ellen were there.

Late afternoon sunshine slanted through the high windows and into the hall. A fire burned in the grate as it always seemed to do, an occasional lively ember leaping onto the stone hearth.

Dogs, cats, and a lame rabbit gamboled about Meg's feet as she sat on the rug near the hearth trying to play cards. One of the dogs spread a paw on the pasteboard pack and sent it flying. Meg sighed and gently scolded it. The dog immediately flopped on its back and thumped its tail in repentance.

"How do you keep them from fighting?" Summer asked when the cat swatted at one of the pushier dogs.

"She doesn't," Catriona commented with a laugh. "I've seen more fur fly here than at the furrier's!"

With gathered cards in hand, Meg looked up indignantly. "They don't fight. They just ... disagree."

"Pardon me," Catriona said. She stretched lazily and put out a hand for the playing cards. "Would you like to play?" she asked Summer. "I cheat at whist and piquet equally well."

Laughing, Summer played a rubber of whist with her and found to her amusement that Catriona cheated outrageously, making no bones about it at all.

"Jamie unwittingly taught me," she said with a grin. "He thought I needed to know how to keep from being cheated."

Summer smiled. "And have you?"

"Many times! It's amazing wha' one can do with th' simple turn of a card. Let me show you."

Summer learned several card tricks, including how to deal from the bottom and produce an ace at will, and spent a most enjoyable afternoon with Catriona.

When they had stuffed themselves with oatcakes, baps, bannocks, and steaming hot tea, they relaxed on the sofas. Summer felt comfortable; she liked Catriona, with her easygoing nature and lively humor. And she knew that Catriona liked her.

Turning over onto her stomach, her head resting on a pillow, Catriona fixed Summer with an emerald gaze. "Do you love my brother?"

Faintly startled, Summer replied impulsively, "Yes! I mean, I *care* for him." Embarrassed, she looked away, then said, "He rescued me when I was in trouble. He was"—she spread her hands helplessly—"my knight in shining armor, so to speak."

Catriona laughed. "Jamie! A knight in shining armor? Faith, *that's* a picture that defies imagination! More like, he would set the armor on fire."

"Yes, I believe he told me about that." Summer couldn't help a laugh.

Catriona rolled to a more comfortable position and smiled. "I'm glad to know you love our Jamie."

"He's spoiled," Summer said tartly. "I think you've all petted him too much."

"Aye. 'Tis true, I'm afraid. Hard not to, though. He's got a way about him. . . ." A sly gleam lit her green eyes. "The lasses have always spoiled Jamie too."

Not about to get into that kind of discussion, Summer began shuffling the pack of cards idly. She wasn't surprised to hear Catriona ask, "Why didn't you want to wed him?"

"There are a lot of reasons. I don't know which one is the most important." Summer looked back at her. "I'm afraid, I suppose. Everything I've ever cared about has been taken from me. If I love again—" Halting, she looked away from Catriona's eyes, not wanting to see pity. She'd had pity before, and it left her feeling as if she were somehow deficient for not arranging her life in a more orderly fashion.

"And then there was my uncle," she said softly. "He was not exactly the most well liked person in New Orleans. Friends I had kept for years drifted away. There was a taint, you see, and it clung to me too." She shrugged. "I found that it didn't really matter after a while. One can adjust to almost anything."

"Even a cateran like our Jamie, I suppose," Catriona said. She smiled. "He's not so bad. He told me about the trick with the duel in London. You insulted him. Wounded his pride. Jamie's got more than his share of pride, I fear."

"Yes, we've almost come to blows over it a few times."

Catriona rolled onto her back and gazed up at the high, vaulted ceiling. "Just so you love him, I don't care how much you two fight." She smiled. "Rob and I fight like two tomcats in a tow sack. But I love him, and he loves me." She turned her head to look at Summer. "Kissing and making up is the best part of the fight."

"I don't think that will work with Jamie and me."

"Everything can be resolved with love," Catriona said firmly. "If there's enough of it."

There didn't seem to be anything to say to that.

Her sitting room was lonely; Summer had plenty of time to reflect. She thought about what Catriona had said, and she thought about Jamie. She'd built a wall of lies between them as protection, but they had begun to crumble. Stone by stone—lie by lie—her barrier was being dismantled. When it was gone, she would be left alone with the truth. It would be a scalding confrontation, she had a feeling.

He would find out her secret: not the original secret, about her name and her uncle. That was all open to him now. No, he would find out that she loved him, and that she couldn't bear.

Knotting her hands together, she swallowed the surge of pain summoned up by that thought. Garth Kinnison's quiet rejection of her had left her humiliated and flayed and raw and vulnerable. And she knew now that she had not even loved him. Not as she did Jamie.

Oh Lord. Jamie . . . dark, impossible knight. Jester was more like it. Until lately. He didn't laugh anymore, not since he'd uncovered her lies. She'd stolen his laughter, and she regretted her lies for that reason as much as for any other.

Turning, filled with a rising tide of impotent anger at herself and the world, she wanted to lash out at something as Jamie had done at her that morning.

She wanted to feel the grim satisfaction of destroying something tangible, something that didn't matter as much as the things she'd already destroyed. . . .

Gasping with pain and throbbing frustration, Summer closed her eyes, bringing her palm down on the small table by the door. A rattling bump snapped her eyes open, and she barely caught the final china egg from the collection before it fell to the floor. She stared down at it. It was cool, smooth, heavy. Opening her fist, she deliberately dropped it on the floor, watching as it shattered.

There. That felt much better. It felt so good, she didn't even mind sweeping it up, kneeling down and scraping the tiny splinters close to the wall for the chambermaid to clean up later.

It was official now: she'd gone mad.

She'd lost body, soul, and mind to a Highland rogue who seemed to think it his due.

Where was he?

Night fell, blanketing the crags with shadows, and Summer dismissed Letty and went to bed. She didn't feel like braving the hall again. Jamie wasn't there. He'd not come home since storming out of the sitting room this morning. No one knew where he'd gone; or they weren't telling her, at any rate.

So she ignored a cold supper in her room, put on her night rail, and went to bed. She pretended not to hear Letty as she tiptoed about, and finally she was alone. Quite alone. The big, canopied bed seemed as empty as a cavern.

Rolling over, she pulled a pillow over her head and squeezed her eyes tightly shut. She'd never fall asleep. She longed to, but it wouldn't come. She watched the logs burn lower and lower and lower and tried not to think about Lord James Cameron, Viscount Westcott.

•   •   •

It was after midnight when he returned. He'd ridden out on a stallion as wild as he felt and not come back until both of them were rid of their devils.

Damn her.

He went to the hall first and found his father there, sitting in the dim light of the dying fire.

"Everyone in bed?" Jamie asked, slicing a casual glance around the huge room.

"Aye." Bruce Cameron lifted a hand with a glass in it. "The whisky's over there."

It was an invitation to linger, and Jamie took it. He was too restless to sit, so he took his whisky and stood by the cavernous fireplace. He could feel his father's gaze on him and waited.

The earl shifted slightly. "Kinnison sent word that he returns in the morning to assure himself that Lady Westcott is here of her own free will."

Jamie took a sip of his whisky. "And?"

"And I think it a good opportunity to discuss the settlement of her estates."

Jamie gave a savage growl and ground his boot into the stone hearth. "I'd like to put my dirk between his ribs."

"Aye, and that will settle a lot."

The earl's voice was slightly mocking, and Jamie felt himself flush like a schoolboy. Damn her. She'd brought him to this—making wild, improbable, boastful statements that only made him look terribly young and terribly hurt.

"It would make me feel better," he muttered.

Making an impatient motion with his hand, Bruce Cameron rested one booted leg across the other and frowned at his son. "He's got the right of it. Wouldn't you do the same if it was a lass you'd been sent to fetch?"

Jamie's head jerked up. "I wad'na hae left her like he did."

"But that's not what this is about." The earl took a sip of whisky and got to his feet. "You're angry. You've got a right to be. But that won't solve matters.

The girl has an inheritance. It must be resolved. And Kinnison must be satisfied."

"She was in love with him," Jamie said after a moment, his voice harsh. "She followed him to England. And he left her without seeing to her protection. I hardly think he is owed a great deal."

"Nay, but her uncle surely is. And there's the matter of her betrothed. Curb your savagery for a time, Jamie. I know you can. I've watched you do it the past twenty-seven years or more."

Shaking his head, Jamie muttered, "I don't know what it is, but lately I find it almost impossible to keep from throttling that lass." A rueful smile curled his lips, and he looked up to see the amusement on his father's face. "Aye, well might you laugh. I've avoided marriage all these years, and now find myself with a fickle lass who can't tell the truth to save her skin."

The earl smiled. "Maybe she doesn't realize that those are the terms. Why don't you tell her she's in mortal danger?"

"I did." His voice was dry. "And she informed me that it was my fault, because I'm not sympathetic." He shrugged. "I found it very hard not to shake some sense into her."

"I can well imagine."

A brief silence stretched, then Jamie said, "So she is to meet with Kinnison. That should be an interesting moment for both of them. Does she know?"

"No."

Jamie swallowed the rest of his whisky and set the glass down on a table. It occurred to him as a bitter afterthought that he was still in the unenviable position of receiving parental advice. It was faintly galling. Another crime to lay on Summer St. Clair's doorstep.

No, Cameron, he corrected himself. *Lady Westcott.*

Aye, she was his wife. And he would treat her as such. She could meet with Kinnison, but he wouldn't take a bloody penny of her inheritance. He didn't care what she did with it. It was humiliating to have a wife with more money than he had, and he had no intention of being considered a fortune hunter.

He'd earned his way, and a man did not have to depend on the largesse of a wife to make his way in the world. Not a real man. Not *this* man.

In that mood, he went upstairs and into the bedchamber where Summer lay asleep in their broad bed. A low fire lit the hearth; a single candle flickered on a small table near the door, and he lifted it. He set it down on a low stool near the bed and stripped.

With the fire low and the thick stone walls keeping out any warmth from the sun during the day, the bedchamber had a decided chill. It felt good to Jamie, cool air rubbing across his bare skin.

A faint stirring from the bed captured his attention, and he moved to it. Summer lay wrapped in the bedclothes, her hair flowing over the sheets in a bright tangle. He was tempted to drag a hand through the gilt and dark mane and be damned for it. But he didn't.

He turned away, pacing the shadows restlessly, his blood cooling slowly. Just the sight of the gentle mound of her body beneath the sheets had aroused him. Damn. He was besotted, a fool; why had he had to have this one girl? It was a mystery.

And she loved another man. She said no with her lips, but yes with her actions. He shoved his fist against the fireplace mantel, scraping his knuckles.

The pain felt good; it revived him, gave him a sense of place. Pain was familiar to a man who'd been in the military for ten years.

Now here he was, fast approaching thirty years of age, and trotting like a schoolboy after a lass who teased and tempted without meaning to. Aye, he was daft, for certain. And he'd wed her because he wanted to, because he'd wanted to make her his alone, and she was the only woman he'd ever felt that way about.

Leaning one arm against the mantel shelf, he rested his forehead against his hand and gazed into the low fire. She was an American of French descent, but he didn't really care about that. It was the lies she'd told him because she didn't trust him not to hurt her that rankled. Those lies mattered more than the rest because of the reason behind them—distrust.

And what had he done today?—terrorized her.

Closing his eyes, Jamie groaned. No wonder she hadn't trusted him. She was right.

He pushed away from the mantel and strode to the bed, not taking care to be quiet as he slid in beside Summer. He wanted her to wake, to know he was there. To love him.

He wanted to erase Garth Kinnison from her mind. There would be room only for him, by God, and no one else. . . .

When she turned with a jerk, her lashes snapping up and her eyes wide, he pulled off her night rail, then rolled atop her and between her thighs. She offered no resistance, and he thrust inside her, taking her mouth, kissing her lips, her cheeks, her nose, her eyes, and her brow.

Moving with strong thrusts, he cradled her breasts in his palms, bent to kiss them a moment, then moved against her until her breathing was ragged and she clutched at him with her hands. Her legs lifted to hold his hips, and he felt the gathering rush of release that came in a burning tide to both of them.

Not moving from atop her, he relaxed his long body in the cradle of her thighs, listening to her short gasps for breath, feeling her shudders around him. Resting his weight on his elbows, he pressed his face into the curve of her neck and shoulder, and breathed deeply of her soft, warm skin and the wispy curl of her hair. It smelled faintly of apple blossoms, and he thought of the soaps made by his mother.

Summer smelled good. She tasted good. He wanted to do it again, and when he felt her shift slightly, he began to rock against her.

"Jamie! . . ."

Her startled exclamation brushed past his ear, and he brought both of them to a swift climax.

Only then did he feel like moving, and he shifted to one side, pulling her up against him. His palm stroked down the glide of her hip and thigh, his fingers kneading the supple flesh in slow strokes.

He wanted to tell her that he loved her; he wanted to say that he was sorry for hurting her; but he couldn't bring himself to say those things. Was it pride? He didn't know. Ah, God, he was a fool.

Summer's hand touched him, and he tensed. Lightly, with a gentle brush of her fingertips, she trailed her hand over his body from breastbone to navel. Breathless, he waited. Her hand dipped lower, sought and found him, and he groaned deep in his throat.

"Summer . . ."

"No," she whispered, putting her other hand up to his lips. "Don't say anything. Just . . . let me."

Let her? By all that was holy, he'd have never left in a fit of temper if he'd thought for a moment that she *would*. This was all wrong. He didn't know how to take a girl like Summer, untried, naive, innocent. He felt as if he had to learn with her, learn to be patient, what to do and what not to do, but when she was close to him, he lost all sense of reason. He could think only of what he wanted to do, of ways to please her, not realizing how fast he was pushing her.

Now it seemed as if she was an apt pupil, quite astute at picking up on brief lessons.

Another groan locked in his throat, sounding like the grumble of a tiger, and he shoved himself up into her curled hand. Exquisite sensation shot through him as she proved her expertise, and in moments he was pulling her atop him.

Startled, Summer gasped, but he ignored it as he taught her the rhythm. Straddling his lean hips, she regulated the movements, and he thought once that he was going to come completely off the bed when she deliberately teased him, poising provocatively just out of reach.

Growling, he grabbed her around the waist and brought her down hard against him, shoving into her with a fierce thrust. Then his hands moved to cup her breasts, and she gasped, rocking faster and faster, until she collapsed across him with faint, sobbing cries, her breath mingling with his.

Neither of them could move; Jamie from the exhaustion, Summer from the sheer pleasure of it.

When she could, she lifted slightly to look down into his face. His eyes were wary, and she smiled.

"Catriona was right," she said softly.

"Cat? About what?"

"About making up after a fight."

He gave a noncommittal grunt, but she could see the faint kick of the corners of his mouth in a smile. Curving her palm to the sweep of his jaw, she bent and brushed her lips across his. He crushed her to him in a thorough kiss, then pulled her away to lay her next to him.

With Jamie pressed hard against her back, his breathing slowing gradually, she nestled into him and smiled lazily. It occurred to her how quickly her attitude could change and how dependent she was on him for that change.

But it wasn't anything she wanted to think about now. That could come later, when things were good between them. When they understood each other better.

Chapter 16

Tension crackled. The great hall was almost empty, save for Kinnison, The Cameron, and Jamie. And the flow of dislike between Jamie and Kinnison should have set fires in midair.

Old Dugald, who had been with the Camerons his entire life, entered with a large tray. He moved quietly to a table, cautiously skirting Jamie and glancing at the earl.

The Cameron motioned for him to set down the tray, and when Dugald had left, he turned to Kinnison. "A drink, sir?"

Garth Kinnison nodded. "Wine."

Jamie snorted. "Only women and bairns drink wine."

Refusing to be baited, Garth shrugged. "Your strong Scotch whisky is too tempting. Wine is diluted enough for my tastes this early."

His dark brow lowered, but Jamie didn't bother with a reply. He thought, savagely, that Kinnison was as Summer had first described him, a golden god, or whatever nonsense she'd spouted. Handsome. Brawny. Cocksure of himself. And he'd had what Jamie wanted—Summer's love and devotion. It made him want to kill Garth Kinnison with his bare hands.

Bringing up one leg, Jamie propped it on a low

stool and looked directly at Kinnison. "I'll not have any of her money. She can do with it what she likes. That's not why I wed her." He met the captain's curious gaze steadily.

"There's a lot more involved than just money," Kinnison said after a moment. "There are the shipping lines, the shipyards, the houses, the shops, the—"

"And she's in charge of all those?" Jamie mocked. "I dinna know our Summer was such a businesswoman."

"No," Kinnison said coolly, "but they were left to her. Her uncle manages them."

"Then let him continue."

Garth Kinnison frowned. "It's more complicated than that. She will reach her majority in nine months. At that time, she is to receive certain trusts, sign papers—damnit man, surely you must know all of this!"

"No. I didn't. Until yesterday, I did not even know her real name." Jamie said it with such savagery that Kinnison took a step back. Turning his head away, Jamie snarled, "I have heard of the St. Clair lines, and I have heard of Barton Shriver. I want no part of either."

"I see."

"It hardly matters whether you do or not." Jamie gave him another long stare. "The property can stay in trust for our sons."

Kinnison's gaze sharpened. "Is she pregnant?"

"Time will tell."

Straightening, Jamie shoved the stool away with his booted foot. His steady gaze was dark, sardonic, measuring Garth Kinnison from head to toe. They were of like height, though the blond sea captain was bulkier and looked taller. Kinnison wore a sword at his side, a slender dress sword in a plain sheath. Jamie's palms itched to fight him, but he had not worn his sword, only a *sgian dubh* in his boot top.

"Where's Summer?" Kinnison asked when he'd

taken a sip of wine. His pale eyes shifted to Jamie. "I was told she'd be here."

"Aye, and she will be." Jamie's eyes were cold. "You seem impatient for a man who didn't mind leaving her behind without a thought."

"I did what was best at the moment." Garth glared back at Jamie. "It was ... inconvenient to take her with me."

"It was damned inconvenient to her to be left without purse or protection in a foreign land," Jamie retorted. "But at least *you* weren't bothered."

The obvious contempt in his words grated across Kinnison like a sharpened knife. He stiffened and flung a wary glance at the earl. Listening idly, the earl smiled when he saw Kinnison's quick glance.

"I can call him off when there's need," he said in a soft voice that made Kinnison flush.

"I'm not asking for help!"

"Nay, and ye're not likely to get it in this quarter. I like the lass. She could have ended up in much worse strait had Jamie not been there. A man should see a thing done himself, or have it done right. But I'm not your judge. And now she's my son's wife, and I'm head of this clan, so I'll see she's cared for." He looked at Jamie. "Not that I'll have to. A Cameron takes care of his own."

Garth Kinnison was smarting from the lash of contempt and the knowledge that both of them were right. He'd not given careful enough thought to Summer's welfare and had endangered her. He was relieved that she'd fallen into the capable hands of Lord Westcott when so much could have happened but was acutely embarrassed to have caused her predicament.

Chagrin made his voice unnecessarily rough.

"Summer is not a Cameron. And she's not Scottish. I think you're forgetting that she's an American. Your laws don't apply to her."

"Aye, but we're not in America," said Jamie, and Garth's head jerked around. "This is Scotland, mon, and she's here under our laws. They apply surely enough."

Kinnison was silent for a moment. It was obvious that he recognized the truth in that, and there was little that could be said—or done—to change it. Not as long as Summer was in Scotland.

"Where is she?" he asked again, abruptly, his face hard and set.

The Cameron pointed, and both Garth and Jamie turned to see Summer pause at the entrance to the hall. She wore a plain muslin gown, her hair caught up atop her head in a mass of ringlets and tied with a blue ribbon that matched her sash. The lightweight material flowed around slender legs in a swishing motion as she approached them, her chin flung up in a gesture of nervous defiance.

The men smiled in appreciation of her beauty. Jamie crossed to her, tall, dark, his head bent slightly to speak to her in a soft tone, and Garth saw her nod. There was a possessive touch of his hand on her arm, then Jamie turned to draw her across the hall.

When Garth looked at the Scot, he saw the challenge in his dark gaze and understood. Damnit. How could he accomplish what he'd come to do in light of this? But then, it didn't really matter how Westcott felt. What mattered was Summer, and what was good for her. She was staring at him coolly.

He smiled at her. "Summer. You look well." His gaze took in her flushed face and exotic eyes, the slight tilt of them emphasized now by a glimmer of sensuality. She'd become a woman since last he'd seen her. Garth glanced at Lord Westcott again. That lusty Scot had apparently used her well, and she'd blossomed. He gave a mental shake and remembered his mission.

"I'd speak with her alone," he said curtly to Jamie, not flinching from his hard gaze. A mocking smile lifted his lips. "She's hardly likely to confess torment to me in front of you, now is she? I'd like to satisfy myself to her care."

There was a long pause, and Garth thought for a moment that Westcott would refuse. Then he nodded and, without looking at Summer again, released her and moved several feet away.

"Step over here with me," Garth invited, and put out an arm to her. He saw the quickly drawn breath, the furtive glance toward Jamie and the earl, and then she laid her slim fingers lightly on his sleeve. His thick golden brow drew down in a frown.

"Are you frightened of him, Summer?" he asked when they had paused by a harpsichord across the hall. "Tell me the truth—has he harmed you?"

She gave a breathy little laugh, and her voice shook slightly when she said, "Not as you may mean."

Garth nodded understanding. He was aware that Summer had been a virgin and thought she referred to that.

"That hurt is unavoidable in a maid."

Her startled gaze flung up to his face. "I didn't mean *that*!" She paused, flushed fiercely, then said in a sort of gasp, "He sears my soul."

Garth frowned. He didn't understand that at all. Oh, he knew females took sex much more seriously than most men, but this sounded drastic.

"Summer—"

"No, don't say anything." She inhaled deeply. "Why did you finally come after me?"

Relieved not to have to deal with feminine emotion, he quickly moved to safer ground. "To see for myself that you haven't been harmed. And to take you back with me."

Summer gave him an angry glare. "Take me back. . . ?" She glanced in Jamie's direction and looked uncertain. "Is that what he wants? You to take me back?"

Hesitating, Garth knew suddenly that if he was to succeed in taking her with him, he'd have to lie. It was unpleasant but unavoidable.

"Maybe. He didn't say so direct, but you must know

that if you stay and Shriver complains to the British ambassador, it's likely to cause a great deal of trouble for these Highlanders. They've still not recovered from the last troubles is what I hear in the village pub. The Clearances created a lot of bitterness, and lairds like Lord Glendale have to hold tight to what they've got in order to keep it. Though I hear that Glendale has been fair and not turned out his crofters like some lairds, if he angers King George—or an enemy with the king's ear—he'll lose his estates anyway."

Garth was watching her face with shrewd regard. He had deliberately played upon her sense of justice and felt a pang of remorse for it. She'd grown pale and still and was looking at him with a thoughtful expression.

"I find it difficult," she said after a moment, "to accept that my situation would cause an international conflict. Are you certain you're not overstating your case? Has my uncle pressured you to bring me back?"

He grinned. She was shrewder than he'd thought. And she knew Shriver.

He shrugged. "Maybe. But it will cause trouble if you stay. Surely you can see that."

She flicked a glance toward her husband, and Garth saw the internal struggle mirrored on her expressive little face. "I don't want to go back. I want to stay with Jamie, if he'll still have me." Her smile was wry. "He's not very happy that I haven't been truthful. And besides, you know that my uncle intended to wed me to Tutwiler, that sweaty toad!"

A faint smile curled his mouth, and he put his hands behind his back. He was well aware of the close regard of the Camerons and had no intention of provoking that dark Scot into violence by touching Summer in any way.

"I admit that your Scot is much prettier than Tutwiler. But you're still a pawn. At least you'd be a pawn with some kind of power in New Orleans."

She seemed startled by that. And doubtful. "I don't need *power*, Garth!"

He attacked swiftly, sensing the restless impatience in Westcott at their prolonged conversation. "Wed to him, your money is his to use. There have been more rumblings between the United States and England. Do you want to finance a war that will hurt your country?"

She frowned. "I know I'm an American. But I've lived in New Orleans so long that I understand the French too. Look how many different flags have flown over the cabildo. I'm not disloyal, but—"

"But you don't care if your husband uses your money to fight your homeland. I see. You denied your French blood because he hates the French—will you do the same if he decides to hate America?"

Flushing, she snapped, "That's not fair!" Her eyes flew to his. "And you wouldn't even investigate when I told you about my uncle, and how he plans to help Napoleon, so I hardly see where you have the right to criticize me."

Kinnison shifted impatiently. "Well, if you change your mind, I'll be waiting on you at the ruined monastery in Dunkeld tomorrow at four. Meet me there. To say good-bye, if nothing else."

"No. Not tomorrow." She glanced toward the Camerons. "I don't think I can get away so soon."

"Wednesday, then. I'll still be here." Garth was fully aware that the murderous glint in Westcott's dark eyes was getting stronger by the moment. He had to end this conversation before the Scot drew a sword on him. He had no desire to prick that barely leashed temper into violence yet. Maybe later, and then he'd see if that dark Scot was as deft with a sword as he was with the ladies.

"Let . . . let me think," Summer said at last in a faint murmur. She flicked another glance toward Jamie, and Garth almost changed his mind. She looked so miserable. Why not let her have her Scot, if that was what she wanted?

But he didn't say it.

Garth nodded. "That's fine." He paused, then said, "Do you intend to talk to him about this?"

Shaking her head, Summer smiled faintly. "It would be a short conversation, if I did. He's already told me that he holds what is his, and he has decided that I'm his." Her chin lifted in a gesture of pride. "Jamie wanted me when he thought I was naught but an abandoned mistress of yours. He wanted me for myself, not for my inheritance."

Garth nodded. "There are times when money gets in the way, Summer. It can hold a man back as well as it can draw him." He frowned again, and said shortly, "I will wait until Wednesday for your answer. Think about what I've said." His words were quick, and he flashed her a wry smile as he observed, "Here comes your jealous husband."

Kinnison took two steps away from her, watching Jamie's long-legged stride eat up the distance between them. He looked none too happy, and Garth braced himself when he reached them.

Jamie put a possessive hand on Summer's shoulder, but his gaze was fixed on Kinnison. "I think you've had enough time to see tha' she's no' harmed," he said in a growling burr that betrayed his irritation.

Sweeping Jamie a mocking bow, Garth smiled. "You're a grim enemy, Lord Westcott. And a stark husband. But you've not hurt her, I'll grant you that."

"Now maybe you'll be leaving," Jamie said with a glance toward the door. Garth grinned openly, and Summer gave an indignant gasp.

"Jamie! He was only concerned for me," she protested. "And he . . . he's an old friend. A dear friend!"

Garth almost groaned aloud. "No, Summer," he said quickly, seeing the fierce flare in Westcott's eyes, "he's right. I've seen what I came to see, and it's time I go."

She was frowning, her delicate brows dipped low over her shadowed blue eyes. "There's no excuse for being rude. I apologize for my husband, Garth."

There was an instant of stunned silence from Jamie. To have his wife apologize for his behavior was the worst of insults, especially to a man he considered his enemy. If she had slapped him, his pride couldn't have been more abused.

He recovered quickly from his shock, dug his fingers into her shoulder, and swung her around, then shoved her toward his father. "I'll no' hae ye apologizing for me, by God! Get tae yer chambers!"

Realizing her error, Summer turned back, her face white. "Jamie, I didn't mean—"

"It doesna' matter wha' ye meant," he snarled, driven to fury. "Ye'd best be out of my reach, ye vicious little liar!"

Two scarlet splotches of color stained Summer's face, and she hesitated. Then her chin came up in a defiant gesture that spelled trouble, and she flashed her husband a challenging stare.

"Yes, my lord. I yield to your wishes." Her voice was cool and low, and before either man could guess her intention, she stepped to Garth and stood on her toes to press a kiss directly on his mouth.

Garth didn't move, not even when Jamie reached out and tore her away from him, his hands rough on her. He watched silently, seeing the earl approach, and his hand slid toward the hilt of his sword as he waited tensely.

But Bruce Cameron had no intention of killing Kinnison, or of allowing his son to manhandle his pretty, foolish wife in front of him.

"Lady Westcott," he said coolly, and took her arm from Jamie's fierce grasp, "I believe it is time you retired. I am certain your husband will continue this conversation with you in private."

The cool, practical words were just what Jamie needed to control his raging temper. He almost had to admire the way Summer turned and walked from the hall without running, her steps light and deliberate. Then his attention shifted back to Kinnison.

The blond captain said quickly, "I am certain she meant nothing by that, my lord. It's just that I've watched her grow up. She's almost like a sister to me."

"Aye, and if one of my sisters kissed me like she just did you—" He stopped. Garth Kinnison was watching him too warily, and it was obvious he expected to have steel drawn. Jamie took a step back and resisted the impulse to reach for the hilt of his dirk. "If you've seen wha' ye came for, Kinnison, ye'd best go quickly. A'fore I change my mind."

When Kinnison had gone, Jamie turned to look at his father. The Cameron shrugged.

"Well, ye wanted a lively wife. Now ye've got one."

Jamie's glare was quick and furious. "Lively, not damn foolish."

"Sometimes, there's no' a ha'pence worth of difference a'twixt the two," the earl said with an amused smile. "I've been wed to your mother for thirty-three years, an' am still amazed by how she mixes the two sae freely."

Jamie relaxed slightly, but when he started toward the doors of the hall, his father said, "Ye'd best let your temper cool awhile if ye care about th' lass, Jamie. I'm thinking tha' you're too angry to talk wi' her now."

He was angry—furious. But more than that, he wanted to know why she'd kissed Garth Kinnison. Yet he knew his father was right. If he went upstairs now, there would only be an argument, and that solved nothing.

Turning back, he met The Cameron's eyes. "I think I'm ready for that whisky now."

Summer paced, caught between anger and anticipation. She waited for Jamie's step in the wide corridor outside the sitting room, but it didn't come. Her hands knotted and unknotted, and she ruined her muslin skirt by twisting it into terrible tangles. But Jamie didn't come. The clock ticked cheerfully on the mantel; outside, she heard wheels on the cobbled stones of the courtyard and a faint shout.

Shadows grew shorter. Sunlight angled in the window in a sharp square filled with shimmering specks. Meg's dogs barked, a cat squalled. Everything sounded normal.

He wasn't coming. Just as well. She might have said or done the unthinkable. The image of herself falling at his feet and begging forgiveness was a shattering one and made her smile grimly. She was such a fool. Why had she kissed Garth? Oh, she knew why. To make that arrogant, swaggering cock angry. To let him know that he could not order *everything* in life just as he liked it, especially her.

Of course, she hadn't really meant to insult him by offering an apology. That had been unintentional. She'd not wanted Garth to think she was married to an ill-mannered provincial.

Now he only thought she was married to a barbarian. Oh, Lord. Things went from bad to worse. Or worst.

But did it really matter what Garth thought? Not anymore, not as it once had. Now the most important thing in her life was Jamie. And he was probably down in the hall contemplating different ways to dismember her.

Not that she didn't deserve it.

Summer wheeled and paced, raking her fingers through her hair until it fell around her face and to her shoulders in tangled wisps.

She'd hurt Jamie, when she only wanted to love him. How did she tell him that? And would he believe her if she tried? Probably not. It was like the boy who'd cried "Wolf!" one time too often; Jamie would only smile politely and say something terribly witty or terribly cutting, and she didn't think she could stand either.

She felt dead. Discarded. Destroyed. Devastated. She was empty of feeling. For the moment. Until he sauntered into the room, her life, her heart, and demanded her complete and utter attention. Then it would be chaos again, and all her fine intentions would go out the nearest window like a shot.

She'd married a man who didn't love her, and now she would pay the piper for her weakness. But it was so dear a price, so very dear a price. How could she bear it? The man who'd brought her to Scotland had evolved into a hard-eyed stranger, and she hated it. Yet she blamed herself.

Guilt, guilt, guilt. She wallowed in it, breathed it, exhaled it. And he knew it. He had to.

When Wednesday came and she went to see Garth in Dunkeld, she would tell him that she couldn't go, that she was a coward ... and that even a tiny piece of heaven would suffice her.

And she would have another reason to hate herself.

Balling her hand into a fist, Summer stood at the high window overlooking the courtyard and saw nothing. Larches rustled branches in the wind, clouds scudded across the sky, and she saw only her bleak future. She stood that way for a long time before she retreated into a shadowed corner with a scrap of needlework and tortured thoughts.

A door swung open, and she looked up, her heart skipping a beat, then saw that it was the servants' door. Letty stood briefly outlined in the opening, muttering in her Cockney accent as she dragged in a heavy basket. The clean, pleasant scent of fresh linens came with her as she manhandled the bulky wicker across the room.

"E'enin' yer laidyship," Letty mumbled, hefting the big basket in her wake. "Oi'm late. There be comp'ny below, an' Oi 'ad ta 'elp wi' summat."

"Company?"

"Aye. Lords an' laidies, or summat laik 'at."

Summer's hand curled tightly around her needle-work, barely escaping the plunge of the needle into her thumb.

"Who is it?"

"Oi dunno. More Scots, is't all Oi kin tell."

Oh, well. It was none of her affair. The entire country could show up, and she wouldn't care.

"It's all right, Letty. You may do just what is necessary, if you like."

"Thankee, ma'am."

Letty put up the linens and straightened clothes, then rearranged Summer's bandbox of cosmetics and ribbons and hairpins. Summer could not seem to keep anything straight. Chantal used to bemoan the fact that her drawers and jewel cases always looked like rats had been nesting in them.

Thinking of Chantal made her think of New Orleans, and then her uncle, and Summer got up quickly from the chair. Her needlework fell to the floor, unnoticed.

Maybe it would be best if she went back to New Orleans. She couldn't be a coward; it wasn't right. She'd be responsible for more than just her own fate if she stayed.

A lump formed in her throat.

It was still there when Catriona Cameron Robertson came to fetch her.

"It's my oldest brothers," Catriona said, tilting her fiery head to the side and gazing at Summer through steady green eyes. "Kenneth and David. They've come to visit. And meet our Jamie's wife."

Summer gave a hollow laugh. "Does he claim me, then?"

A grin flashed. "Aye, though he's right surly about it. The Cameron sent me for you, because your bonny husband is being an ass."

Unable to prevent a smile, Summer hesitated. "Must I go?"

"You'd stay up here and be thought a coward?"

That stung. "No."

"Let me help you dress." Catriona beckoned to Letty. "I want you to make our bonny Jamie step on his tongue and eat his own wrath this evening, my fine lady."

Grateful that Catriona was on her side, Summer soon found herself bathed and sitting in front of the dressing table while her maid and sister-in-law discussed how her hair should be dressed.

"Oi favor it down, yer laidyship," Letty insisted, but Catriona was adamant.

"No. Hair this thick and glorious would look best in a waterfall of curls. No, you silly goose, like this . . ."

Summer smiled faintly, sitting on a stool and watching them in her mirror. It was the closest she'd ever come to having a sister, and even though Catriona was six years older than she was, there was a bond forming.

"All right!" Catriona said at last, and lifted Summer's chin so she could see her reflection. "What do you think?"

Her hair was brushed until it gleamed, then twisted up into a fetching arrangement on her crown, with tiny wisps straggling randomly. The style made her eyes look larger and even more exotic, showed off her high cheekbones, and the slender arch of her neck.

"Why, Catriona, it's lovely!"

"Call me Cat. Everyone else does." Catriona gazed at Summer critically. "You need paint. You're too pale."

"Jamie doesn't like me to paint."

"That's too bad. He won't want his brothers saying you look washed out and at death's door, either. Of course, they will have all sorts of lewd remarks to make about the reason for your paleness, so believe me, you should paint."

When Summer looked shocked, Catriona laughed. "Oh, they would not be so rude as to say them to you,

but they hold no such scruples with each other, the
daft rogues. There would be a brawl before the night
is over, and The Cameron would be angry."

While she was talking, Catriona had pulled out the
bandbox holding Summer's scant supply of cosmetics.
She applied them with a deft hand, lightly giving color
to pale cheeks, and a bit of a shine and glow to her
lips. She peered at her closely.

"Hmm. You don't need anything on your eyes to
make them show. Your lashes look as if they've been
gilded." She took Summer by the hand, and when she
was dressed in a rich blue velvet gown and matching
slippers, Catriona brought out the necklace Jamie had
given Summer the day they married. It was heavy, with
huge sapphires flanked by diamonds, but it went
beautifully with the dress. "Now," Catriona said in a
satisfied voice, "You're ready." She drew Summer with
her down the wide stone steps to the first floor.

Summer still felt like a dowdy drab next to Catriona's striking coloring, her flaming hair and glittering green eyes. She was nervous, and her trembling
must have been evident, because Catriona took her
hand and gave her a reassuring squeeze.

Their footsteps echoed down the wide corridors
and over the stone steps. Laughter and music could
be heard, and an occasional yelp when someone ac-
cidentally trod upon a dog. Summer chewed on her
bottom lip when she stopped by the suit of armor
guarding the doorway.

They were just outside the huge, heavy doors that
led into the hall, and Catriona leaned close and whispered, "Head up! No one in my family respects a
mouse!"

At first, no one noticed their entrance. The hall
was crowded with family, guests, and servants. Dogs
roamed about underfoot, and a fire burned on the massive hearth. The high, vaulted ceiling absorbed some
of the noise, as it absorbed some of the smoke from
fire and candles. Someone was playing the bagpipes.

A loud wailing skirled into the air, and was accompanied by several voices singing the verses of "The Twa Sisters."

Trying to be unobtrusive, Summer scanned the crowd for Jamie. In this vast room of Scots, blond and dark alike, it was not an easy task. Catriona urged her forward.

Robert appeared at their side, his young face serious, pale hair lying over his forehead. He exchanged a quick glance with his sister, then took Summer's hand.

"Come wi' me, milady," he said softly.

"Ah, the little minister," Catriona teased him. "And now that our Jamie's wed, you'll have to please The Cameron and go into the clergy in his stead."

A faint smile curved his mouth, and he pushed back a strand of light hair from his eyes. "Aye, and we have need of a minister in this family!"

"You'll hear no argument in this quarter," Catriona agreed. Her gaze moved past Robert. "Where's Jamie? I've brought him his wife."

Robert shifted uneasily. "She should meet Kenneth and David first, I think."

Flinging her brother a surprised glance, Catriona opened her mouth to speak, then closed it and nodded when he added, "We have new guests. The Cameron is speaking with Lady Elgin right now."

There was a brief pause before she said, "Aye, perhaps you're right."

Summer found herself propelled across the room and was soon introduced to Jamie's oldest brothers. Kenneth was tall and austere, almost as grim as his father, in Summer's opinion. David reminded her of Jamie, with a quick grin and teasing comment; his blue eyes held reams of good humor.

It wasn't hard to talk to him, and he skillfully drew her out. She talked of New Orleans, of the market, of the Place d'Armes, and of beignets and chicory coffee. She talked of the new fashions from France, and how

the war had affected the styles, and of the fact that
Napoleon was to be crowned French emperor. She
talked of everything but Jamie.

Where was he?

Restless, nervous, wondering where he was and
dreading seeing him even while she anticipated it with
a chill of expectation, Summer tried to keep her attention on David Cameron. He was telling her about
Iona, Scotland's sacred isle and the burial place of
ancient kings, when Summer heard Dallas say in a
loud, irritated voice, "A pox on her! Why dinna she
leave Jamie alone naow tha' he's wed?"

Startled, thinking at first that Dallas meant her,
Summer turned and looked at him with a frown and
faint flush. An appalled blue gaze met hers.

"Oh, Lord, I've put my foot in it naow," Dallas
muttered as he crossed the few feet to Summer. He
took her hand and led her away from David, while
she continued to look at him with a puzzled frown.
But when he began to apologize and to explain, saying that Lady Elgin was a widow, an old friend from
long ago, and that whatever was between them was
long since over and done with, she finally began to
comprehend.

There was a painful lump in her throat, and she
nodded though she didn't know why. She heard Dallas speaking, his voice quick and anxious, his brogue
thickening with every word; she finally focused on
him.

"I cannot understand a word you are saying, Dallas," she said frankly. "Your brogue is too thick."

"Aye, tha' 'tis fa' th' moment," he admitted. "I gat
nae harns tae tell o't." He stopped, shook his head,
and shot his glaring brother a rueful glance. Robert
was angry with him; it was plain.

Dallas gave a sigh of relief when he saw Catriona.
He leaned close to his sister and said something in
her ear, then bowed over Summer's hand and es-

caped. Summer had the distinct impression of a reprieved man.

Catriona searched Summer's face for a moment. "So you heard, did you?"

"That Jamie's former love is here?" She nodded. "Yes, I heard, much to your brother's dismay."

"It's not wha' you might think," Catriona said, but when Summer was finally introduced to Lady Elgin, she began to think Cat was mistaken.

There was an undercurrent of tension, of rampant sexuality, that made Summer want to flee. Lady Elgin touched Jamie frequently, on the arm, the shoulder, the back of his hand, her glances intimate, her lips curved in an enticing smile.

"So," she said in a husky voice, her beautiful brow lifting, "this is your little bride, Jamie?"

Summer gazed at the tall, willowy brunette with dismay. She was older than Jamie, in her late thirties perhaps, but her body was still ripe and firm and her face unlined. Lady Elgin's smile did not reach her eyes when she looked at Summer.

"An unusual name," she commented when the courtesies had been observed. "I take it you were born in the summer?"

Terribly aware of Jamie, of his dark, mocking eyes on her, Summer shook her head. "No. I was born in April. It's a family name."

"How quaint," Lady Elgin said in a voice that neatly conveyed the notion that it was *not*.

Summer looked at Jamie. He was leaning back against the stones of the fireplace, his arms crossed casually over his broad chest; his dark eyes were narrowed and glittering. Levering his body away in a graceful motion, he moved to Summer and took her chin in his palm.

"Paint, my lady?" he murmured. His eyes were half-closed, his mouth curved in a lazy smile; but his fingers tightened almost imperceptibly when she tried to pull away. "No, don't pull away. Painted women fas-

cinate me. I hae no' seen one since last I visited Covent Garden...."

"Don't bait her, Jamie!" Catriona said sharply, and
he flicked his sister an amused glance.

"Protecting your cub, Cat? She needs it." He released Summer's chin, letting his fingers trail down
the arch of her throat, smiling at her shiver. "But of
course, she has a way of protecting herself too."

Summer's face was heated, and her throat tight.
She wanted to escape. She could feel the curious
glances thrown at them, the slightly malicious gaze of
Lady Elgin on her, and wanted to run. But even if
she'd been able to, her pride would have kept her
there.

"I'm sorry my face offends you, my lord," she said
with cool dignity, and relished the brief flare in his
eyes.

"It's your actions tha' offend me most, madam."

Summer refused to be intimidated. "Really? Again,
I beg your pardon."

Flicking her husband a tight little glance that did
not betray her pain, Summer allowed Catriona to lead
her away. She could feel Jamie's gaze boring into her
back, could hear his faintly amused, drawling voice
behind her. A sick feeling swept over her.

"Here." Catriona thrust a cup in her hands. "Drink
this. You might as well. Jamie's certainly been doing
his share."

"He's drunk?" Summer sounded surprised, and
Catriona managed an angry smile.

"As a lord. Ian says he's been tossing back whisky
all day."

Maybe that explained his open animosity. Catriona's next words banished that hope.

"Ian also said The Cameron has kept him downstairs to protect you."

"Protect me?"

"Aye." Catriona sat down on a bench and made
room for Summer. She looked at Summer thought-

fully, then sighed. "Our Jamie doesn't get angry like other Camerons. We all shout and bellow and are generally obnoxious when we're mad at someone. He stays calm most of the time. Oh, he may say nasty things, and glare and fuss, but he doesn't really lose his temper. The Cameron says that makes him more dangerous than the rest of us. I think he's right."

Summer shook her head. "That doesn't make any sense."

"It would if you'd ever seen his devil loose." Catriona smiled ruefully. "When he finally loses his temper, he gets quite savage. It's really frightening."

"I've seen him angry," Summer said after a moment, recalling the day before when he'd thrown his whip and snarled at her so viciously.

Catriona looked surprised. "You have? Then you don't need me to tell you that he's like a fire near a powder keg, I suppose. I hope there's not an explosion tonight."

Summer, however, after the initial hurt of being used so vilely by Jamie, hoped that he *did* lose his temper. Then he would feel as bad as she did. And, after all, she'd survived his last fit of temper, hadn't she?

Perhaps, she thought fiercely, he should be worried about *her* temper!

When Ian came to where they sat and extended a hand, asking Summer to dance a reel with him, she went gladly. She would not allow Jamie's moods to ruin her evening. She had tried to apologize to him, and he'd not wanted to listen to her. Fine. Let him stew in his own juices. Let him flirt with Lady Elgin, then growl at *her*, and say ugly things. She did not intend to be daunted.

Kenneth Cameron looked from his brother to Summer. "She is a beautiful lass," he said.

Curling his hand around his whisky glass, Jamie

gazed at Summer as she danced with Ian. She was laughing, blue eyes sparkling to rival the sapphire necklace she wore at her throat. The jewels caught the light and threw it back in glittering splinters; they were nestled against creamy flesh well displayed by the low-cut blue velvet gown, and he felt a flash of anger. *Damn her, the flaunting little vixen!*

"Aye," he acknowledged his brother's compliment roughly, "she's fair to look at."

Kenneth seemed amused by his churlish attitude. "Is tha' why ye wed her? 'Twas no' for money, I hear."

Jamie's jaw tightened. "I wed her because I wanted to."

"Not for love?" Kenneth asked lightly, and was startled by his brother's scowl.

"Nay, it's not been mentioned!"

There was an awkward pause. He could feel Kenneth's close stare. He suffered it as long as he could, then gave it back to him until his eldest brother looked away. There was already the air of command about Kenneth; he would one day be the earl. Now, however, he was a viscount, and as Jamie had his own title, he wasn't impressed.

There were only four years' difference in their ages; it wasn't far enough to command immediate respect or close enough to lend camaraderie. Not that Jamie had anything in particular against Kenneth; he just wasn't about to take instruction from him in any way.

"Your lady looks gentle," Kenneth said brusquely, and when Jamie stiffened, he added, "I wouldna like to see her hurt."

"Did The Cameron send you over here?" Jamie refilled his whisky glass from a decanter on a small table. "Because if he did, you can tell him I've no intention of strangling her. Not yet, anyway."

Irritated, Kenneth said, "Here ye are, wed only two days, and ye're already at odds. Wha' will the rest of your life be like?"

That caught Jamie's attention. He looked down the years and saw friction instead of tranquillity. Depressed, he took a large draught of whisky.

When Kenneth had taken leave of him, Jamie felt a twinge of remorse. His brother had come a long way to pay his respects to his new bride, and Jamie had treated him like a traveling minstrel.

Shifting restlessly, unable to watch Summer dance and laugh with his brothers and unable *not* to watch her, Jamie left the hall. He was too ill-tempered for celebration; the memory of Summer's kissing Garth still burned into his mind. God's blood, when he thought about it, he wanted to shake her until her teeth rattled.

Then he wanted to take her to bed and plow her till sunrise.

Sighing, he paused in a curtained alcove and leaned on the wide windowsill. Torchlight barely reached it. The moon was still low in the sky, glittering over crags and into the alcove, silvery and cold. He put his forehead on the leaded window glass and looked down into the garden. He remembered the garden on Bruton Street, and how he'd tried to romance Summer.

Ridiculous. He'd known it at the time. Of course, it had seemed to work too. But what good would romance do him now?

If he closed his eyes, he could almost feel her in his arms, taste the sweet, luscious skin spreading beneath his hands, feel her close around him. Lord, just thinking about it aroused him.

When he felt a soft hand on his shoulder, he whirled, and somehow his dirk was in his hand. He didn't recall pulling it from his boot, but Lady Elgin's shocked gasp brought it to his attention.

"Sorry. You shouldn't sneak up on a man who's spent the last ten years at war," he muttered, and slid the weapon back into his boot. He looked beyond her at the empty corridor, then back to her face. "Are you alone?"

She laughed throatily, and he remembered how he'd once thought no celestial angel could laugh more lusciously. Now he merely frowned and wondered if someone would overhear.

"Jamie." She stepped into the alcove, fitting her body next to his. "I thought you might need company."

He shifted uncomfortably and shook his head. "I'm no' lonely. And I'm married."

She laughed again, and he felt like a callow youth. "So was I once," she murmured. "Don't you remember?" Her finger touched his bottom lip in an exploring caress.

He caught her hand in his and met her gaze; the light fell across her face, and he felt a moment's appreciation for her beauty. Almost forty years old, and she looked as fresh and lovely as a girl of twenty. Aline took care of herself.

"I remember," he said after a moment, and he did. He thought of long hours in her bed while she twisted and turned and taught him more than he'd ever thought there was to learn about sex. It had been glorious while it lasted.

Insinuating her body closer, in a curling twist that caught him by surprise, she reached for him at the same time. To his chagrin, his body responded immediately. It rose to her touch in a surge, pushing painfully against the front of his pants.

He stepped away, scowling. "Aline, this is not what I want."

"So?" Her fingers moved over him. He throbbed. "It's what I want. Do you think young women are the only ones with urges?"

Remembering his parents, Jamie shook his head. "No. But that has nothing to do with me."

He caught her hand, surprising both of them. His

body pulsed beneath their joined palms, and he met her gaze with narrowed eyes.

"Nothing to do with me," he repeated softly, and saw the disbelief in her eyes. He felt her tense and glimpsed the gathering anger in her face, then saw a shadow behind her.

It was several shadows. Summer, Ian, Dallas, and Sheena had left the smoky hall and were stopped short in the wide corridor, staring at Jamie and Aline.

Jamie was instantly aware of how it must look, with her hand on his erection and his hand over hers, as if he were holding her there.

Turning slowly, Aline smiled at the shocked little group and feigned embarrassment. "Oh, you have caught us. I am so sorry. We are usually much more discreet."

Silently damning her, Jamie snatched her hand from him and pushed her away. He stalked to Summer without glancing at Lady Elgin.

But she was having none of him. With two crimson stains on her cheeks that had nothing to do with cosmetics, she turned away. He stepped in front of her, barring her way, and she swung around, changing course and fleeing into the hall again.

"Jamie," he heard Sheena say angrily before Dallas told her to be quiet.

He didn't pause in his pursuit of Summer, not even when she went to his mother, breathing in short little pants, not glancing at him as he approached.

His hand closed around her wrist when he reached them, and Fiona said tartly, "I think it best if you allow her to linger a while, Jamie."

"Do you?" he asked politely without even looking at his mother. He pulled Summer toward him. She flashed him a furious, pained glance that made him wince. But she wasn't blameless today, either. His grip tightened.

"Let go of my arm!"

"No. Come upstairs."

"With you?" She laughed scornfully. "I think not, my lord."

A muscle leapt in his clenched jaw, and Jamie was aware of his mother's close regard. He felt his pent-up fury escalate, pushing him closer to the edge. He fought it. He didn't want to terrify Summer; he didn't want to lose her. She infuriated him, shamed him, but he wanted to keep her.

"Keep your voice down," he said evenly. "Come upstairs. We don't need to let everyone know our business."

Summer wrenched free and stepped just out of his reach. He couldn't grab her without it being obvious, without having to chase her, and his pride would not allow that. He waited, watching her, ignoring his mother's efforts to calm him. He'd not hurt her, had he? He just wanted Summer upstairs. And he wanted her upstairs *now*.

Standing with his long legs slightly spread for balance, he let her dance away from him, skittish as a foal, her face flushed with anger. He watched lazily. He knew how he must look standing there, relaxed, slightly amused, even indulgent. Letting his wife curvet around him like an untrained puppy. Oh, aye, what a bloody fool he must look!

Jamie smiled pleasantly. When she got within reach, he would grab her.

"Summer."

"Stay away from me, James Cameron," she warned, her eyes filled with shadowed rage.

Jamie could see his father approach. God's blood! There were no secrets in this house. Except for Summer's. Rage prodded him, and he sucked in a deep breath.

"Summer. Come with me."

"No!" Her small hands were curled into fists. She was almost sobbing. He wanted to shake her. He wanted to kiss her. She wouldn't let him within a foot of her. His mouth tightened into a slash; his voice was cold and soft.

"At least talk to me in private."

Her head flung back, and the cluster of curls atop her crown gave a silken shimmy. "I don't want to talk to you ever again, privately or publicly." She almost choked, and inhaled deeply to steady herself. "I *hate* you."

It was childish, but effective.

He stiffened. The noise in the hall receded, and his world was narrowed down to the two of them. A white-hot slap of blood thundered through him, and his chest swelled as if it were going to explode. She would take back those words, and she would tell him that she didn't love Garth Kinnison. By God, before the night was over, she'd tell him that she loved him—only him.

Summer apparently mistook his silence for dismay. She stepped away, not toward him, but within range. He simply reached out and scooped her close, one arm at the curve of her back, bringing her up and against his chest.

Now they were the center of attention. Bruce Cameron stood beside his wife, but said nothing. The music stumbled to a halt with a lingering wheeze from the pipes.

Whether by accident or design, Summer managed to straighten quickly enough to catch Jamie beneath his jaw with the top of her head. It snapped his head back, and his grip loosened just enough for her to yank free. She gave him a hard shove and caught him off-balance, sending him stumbling backward, half falling against a sofa filled with guests. He straightened slowly, ignoring the people he'd landed on, staring after Summer as she fled the hall.

After a tense silence that seemed to stretch for agonizing minutes, Jamie turned to look at his father. He took a step toward The Cameron, then halted, turned, and strode from the hall with long, purposeful strides.

"Stop him," Fiona said in a choked voice, but Bruce shook his head.

"Nay. Let him go."

"He'll kill her!"

An amused smile curled The Cameron's mouth. "Nay, wife, I dinna think so."

A metallic clatter sounded loudly from the corridor outside the hall, rattling and scouring the air, steel clanging on stone in a dissonant, ringing echo. Someone gasped.

"Och, th' suit of armor hae been vanquished, I fear," Dallas said, and shook his head. "An' th' deil is loose naow. . . ."

Chapter 17

Trembling with pain and fury, Summer turned the key in the lock of the bedchamber door, then dragged a chair in front of it for good measure. Racking sobs caught in her throat and chest, and she tried not to think of Jamie in the alcove with Lady Elgin.

Damn him, damn him, damn him!

Why had he made her love him? Why had he married her? It would have been better for her to have not known him at all rather than suffer this tearing, wrenching pain. It was almost incapacitating.

She forced herself to move, to go to the dressing room where her clothes were kept and find and drag out her cloth satchel with the bone handles. She'd leave Scotland with no more than she came with. Except the aching emptiness where her heart had once been.

Garth would at least get her back to New Orleans. And she would try to piece together her shattered life again. A life without Jamie. She winced at the thought.

A thump at the door snapped her head around, and her stomach lurched. The latch rattled, and she stared at it. Then it stopped. There wasn't the angry, vigorous beating on the door that she had envisioned, or the threats to break it down.

After a moment of silence, she went back to her packing with a bitter sigh. He didn't even care enough to want to talk to her anymore.

Her breathing was ragged, her movements jerky. She pawed through her clothes, then carelessly stuffed shifts, stockings, and gowns into the satchel. Next she moved to the dressing table and yanked open the drawers. She rummaged briefly in the jewel case, taking only the gift from her father.

She removed the necklace from around her throat, the bride's gift Jamie had given her. It was from his mother's side of the family, the Douglases, he'd said. A heavy antique piece with glittering sapphires and diamonds, it was very bulky, and she felt she was too small to wear it well, but it was beautiful.

Shoving the jewel case back in the drawer, she slammed it shut and straightened. And met the full, burning gaze of her husband. He reached out and took the satchel from her suddenly nerveless fingers and tossed it aside.

"How—" She wet her lips. "How did you get in? I locked the door."

"Did you expect me to break it down?" he asked softly, indicating the propped chair with a nod of his head. "Poor, stupid lass." He held up a key. "It was much easier to find Dugald and get a key."

She flushed. She should have thought of that. And she should have thought of the door to the adjoining room too.

Sidling away, Summer watched him warily. She'd never seen Jamie look so fierce. His brow was low, his lashes heavy over his eyes; his mouth was flattened into a grim slash, and deep grooves etched from his nose to the corners of his lips. A slight, throbbing muscle fluttered just below the surface of his jaw.

She could almost feel the tension emanating from him. It was frightening. Her eyes lifted to his, and she paled. This was what Catriona had meant about loosing the devil.

Hot, furious lights blazed in his eyes. She could see the approaching storm and took several steps back. Jamie followed.

A tide of panic rose in her. Did he mean to actually do her harm? He certainly looked as if he would. This was even more unnerving than when he had thrown his riding crop across the room.

He stalked her. Summer abandoned all pretense of dignity and courage and fled like a hare. This quiet, intent fury was not what she'd expected. She could see the difference, oh, she could see it plainly. It made her throat ache. It made her want to turn and . . . negotiate.

Jamie didn't look in the mood to negotiate. He moved softly and quietly, showing no evidence of the strong whisky he'd been drinking, and when Summer finally backed up against the high four-poster, she saw her defeat reflected in his eyes.

Desperately, she scrambled across the bed to the other side, and he met her there. She came up against his broad chest and flung herself away. Banging into furniture with frantic disregard, she careened around the room while he pursued her with grim calm.

Finally, feeling more ridiculous than terrified, she stopped and waited. She was breathing hard, her breath coming in short gasps, and he didn't look remotely out of breath.

"Are you going to kill me?" she demanded when the silence stretched too long. His answer was prompt.

"Aye. Any preferences as to how I should go about it?"

She stared at him narrowly. "Old age is an option."

"Not quick enough." He shoved a stool out of the way with a careless kick and took a step closer to her. "And not suitably violent."

"Oh." She danced out of reach. "Let me think a minute. I'm certain I'll come up with something." Her gaze darted toward the door. He stood between her and freedom. A frown knit her brow, and she chewed on her inner cheek. This was not like the angers she'd seen in him before. Where was the shouting? The release of temper? He just watched her with that cold regard; and his midnight eyes blazed with fire.

"Your minute's up."

His smile was almost lazy, and if it hadn't been for the pinched look to his face, she might have thought him merely irritated. She sucked in a deep breath. He hadn't immediately strangled her, so perhaps there was still hope.

"I can't think of a thing," she said briefly. "You choose."

"I intended to all along."

Summer watched warily as he crossed the room toward her; his strides were long, lazy, lethal. Booted feet shoved aside whatever lay in his path. She backed away from him without realizing it.

"Ah, I *do* frighten you. Poor wee Summer. Brave enough to kiss an old love in front of me, yet too timid to accept retribution." His *R*'s rolled roughly from his tongue, and she shuddered.

"Jamie—"

"No' now, lass. Now, it's my turn to talk. You had your turn downstairs, with half the Highlands listening."

His burr had thickened, but his words were clear, and she swallowed hard.

The devil's brow was a straight, angry slash across his eyes, and as he approached her, he began unbuttoning his white linen shirt. She wondered wildly where he'd left his waistcoat.

"You said you hate me," he said softly. "So be it. I canna do anything about tha'. God knows, I've tried. If I'd thought you truly did, I would never hae wed you."

The shirt was unbuttoned, and he shrugged out of it. Mute, Summer pressed against the far wall, spreading her hands against the wainscoting, watching as he began to tug off his boots.

"But we're wed now, lass, and I don't intend to allow your hatred to interfere. I'll get sons on you, and for love, I'll go elsewhere."

Summer's chin shot up. She found her voice. "I won't be a brood mare!"

"You've no choice. You could have had love. You chose not to."

Her legs trembled, and she clung to the wainscoting. "I think I've made a mistake," she said faintly.

"Aye, lass." His voice was bitter. "So have I. But it's done. I'll no' go back on my word, and I took the marriage vows."

"You forgot them quickly enough!" she spat, stung by his obvious contempt. "Not two days, and I find you in the shadows with another woman's hand down your pants!"

His smile was mirthless. "Make of tha' wha' you will. I won't defend myself."

"Because you can't!"

Black eyes narrowed beneath the thick lashes. "Nay, lass. Because I won't."

Struggling for composure, Summer dragged in a deep breath and let it out again. Jamie wore only his pants now. His boots lay on the floor, and he bent to unfasten the buttons binding his pants at midcalf. When he straightened and began undoing the buttons at the waist, she was jerked from her daze.

It was obvious what he intended; she had no intention of allowing it. Not like this. She wanted Jamie, she wanted him to make love to her, but she would not accept it on these terms, not in anger.

Waiting until he'd shoved his pants halfway down, she darted for the door he'd used to enter, the chambermaid's entrance from the adjoining room. She heard him swear at her as she wrenched open the door and fled into the wide hall. Her heart was pounding, and she didn't pause to see what he was doing.

Fear gripped her as she raced down the corridor, her steps echoing loudly, fear and something else—regret?

You could have had love....

Could she? Or was he only tormenting her? It was too late now to worry about it.

Her feet skimmed over the carpets on the stone floor as she sped toward the wide staircase that curved in a half-circle to the floor below, and Summer saw the startled gaze of a maid as she passed her in the corridor.

A muffled squeal behind her should have alerted her, but it didn't.

When a hard hand clamped down on her shoulder, a startled scream burst from Summer, ending in a choked gasp when Jamie spun her around. She had only a brief glimpse of the maid's shocked face as he heaved her over his shoulder and carried her back up the corridor.

Summer would not give him the satisfaction of offering a struggle. Spreading her hands over his chest, she half levered herself up from the painful press of his shoulder into her stomach, feeling the utter indignity of her position.

Not a word had been said between them, and after he carried her into the sitting room and dumped her on the floor, he stared at her silently.

Summer's hair had come down from atop her head and hung in wisps in her face. She batted at it, trying to preserve what little pride she had left. It was faintly galling that he'd followed her without bothering to put on his pants. No wonder the maid had squealed.

Her throat closed.

Naked and splendid in the merciless light from fire and lamps, so furious his eyes fairly blazed, Jamie made her want to fall at his feet and ask him to love her. She looked away from him. She couldn't bear it. It hurt to love so much.

She retreated into anger before she made a complete fool of herself. Another stone to fortify the crumbling wall . . .

She made her voice scornful, scathing.

"Dressed like that, my lord—or should I say *un*-dressed—are you certain you have captured the right prey? Lady Elgin must be wondering where you are."

"Summer." His voice was a harsh grate, the *R* rolling in a growl that made her shiver. She plunged on, knowing that to hesitate would be fatal.

"Oh, pray don't be shy! You weren't too shy about letting her rub on you in public!"

"Tha's enough." He took a step closer to her, and her head flung up.

"I agree. That's enough. Do you think I'll stay after that? After you made it so obvious that you're nothing more than a rutting beast?" Her hands curled into the graceful folds of blue velvet skirt, and her chin quivered slightly before she could stop it. "I won't stay here, James Cameron. Not after that embarrassment."

His eyes narrowed. "We'll leave when I say it's time."

"We?" She tossed her head angrily. "This has nothing to do with *we*! I have no intention of leaving with you." She dragged in a deep breath, seeing his mouth flatten into a grim line and his eyes fasten on her, and said quickly, "I am going back to New Orleans. Garth will take me."

It was precisely the wrong thing to say. She'd known it, but anger and pain had driven her to prick him. Still, she wasn't quite prepared for his reaction.

The taut band of muscles in his belly convulsed as if she'd kicked him, and he was on her so quickly, she didn't have time to move, or cry out.

"By God," he ground out, holding her against him, his hands curled around her upper arms, "ye'll not leave! And if I have to chain ye here to keep ye, I will. . . ."

"Chain me!" She stared at him, at the hot lights of rage in his eyes and the harsh slash of his mouth. "You would not dare!"

"I'll dare anything that pleases me." He tightened his grip, holding her when she would have wrenched away. "You won't leave me, Summer."

"Do you think I could stay after this?" Tears hovered perilously close to falling, but pride kept them at bay. "I won't stay with a . . . a devil!"

"A devil is it?" He laughed angrily. "Aye, it's said tha' I've th' devil's own temper, lass, an' I do. I breathe fire an' brimstone, an' it's been said tha' I've got th' cloven hoofs an' tail of th' devil, but I'll be damned if ye'll put horns on me wi' Garth Kinnison!"

Her dry sob was filled with angry pain. "You don't know anything, do you? You're so damned arrogant, with your wild Scots pride and your handsome face, but you just don't listen! You hear what you want to hear; or what you don't want to hear. I don't know which." Her breath came in harsh, ragged gasps. "You can chain my body, James Cameron, but you'll never chain my heart!"

She saw from the sudden opacity of his eyes that she had succeeded in piercing him. He dragged her up to him in spite of her efforts to pull away, slowly, almost lazily, a bitter, mocking smile curling his lips.

"Fine. I don't need your heart. I'll make do with your body." His hand splayed against her hips, and he held her close against his groin, until she felt him swell against her thighs. "And I'll use you well, wife, until there won't be any shadows of Garth Kinnison in our bed. Not tonight. Not ever again."

"Fool!" she raged, digging her balled hands into his bare chest.

"Aye." His laugh was filled with bitter self-mockery. "I am tha', lass."

Sweeping her into his arms, holding her hard

against him even when she tried to free herself, he strode from the sitting room into the bedchamber and dumped her on the bed.

Summer stared at him. She wouldn't fight. He was too strong. She had no intention of giving him the satisfaction of winning. But she had no intention of participating, either.

None of which seemed to matter to Jamie. He looked at her for a long moment, his heavy-lashed gaze moving almost dispassionately over her body, then up to her flushed face. He must have seen the mutiny in her eyes, the defiant challenge, for he smiled slightly.

"If tha's th' way ye want it, lass," he muttered, and knelt on the bed.

He stripped the blue velvet gown from her, leaving it in shreds, his movements humiliatingly swift and efficient. Then he pushed her back on the mattress and dragged her thighs apart and took her. He wasn't cruel, just methodical and unfeeling, and that was even worse.

She could have accepted rage; she could have taken his worst fury; his indifference to her was appalling.

When he rolled from her body to lie beside her, she thought it was finished. That he'd taken all he wanted from her. She soon found she was mistaken.

As she rolled to her side to present her back to him, lying rigid and dry-eyed, he pulled her against him. Now, in spite of her best intentions, in spite of her moans of protest, he coaxed a scalding response from her traitorous flesh. With his mouth, his hands, his body, he made her writhe under him, gasping, shudders racking her. He pushed into her from behind, one hand on her breast, the other at the nest of pale curls between her thighs.

He took her deliberately slowly, watching her gasping shudders with narrowed, calculating eyes. It was painfully humiliating to know that he could make her feel those acute sensations and not feel them himself. She was losing. She was losing everything. Words of love trembled on her tongue so hot and urgent that she felt she would die if she didn't say them.

Pressing her face into the pillow, she muffled soft cries and damning words with cool linen and feathers. Even when the aching release came, washing over her in drowning tides, she did not say them. She couldn't. He didn't want her love, only her body.

But as the candles guttered, the fire burned out, and the moon paled, Jamie took her again and again, until she was weak, exhausted, holding him to her and whispering her love in his ear. She was too frail. She couldn't hold out against his determined assault, and it was humbling to realize it.

He lay between her thighs, pinning her down with his body, his fingers tangled in the long, silky hair at her temples. Kissing her, lightly, then with bruising force, he coaxed the embers of passion to soaring flame again.

Summer gasped and arched against him, her eyes closed, her entire body throbbing with need. He seemed to know it. When she reached for him, pulling him closer for that searing penetration, he resisted.

Her eyes flew open. He was watching her, his dark gaze hot and liquid and fierce. There was something in the depths of his eyes that mirrored her need, and she frowned.

"What do you want from me?" It was almost a groan. She was panting. "What do you want?"

"Say it again," he muttered against her mouth, slowly moving inside her with erotic strokes that made her shudder and hold him, sliding her hands over his hot, damp skin. "Tell me tha' you love me." His hands tightened in her hair, and his voice was thick with passion and some emotion she couldn't define. "Tell me, sweet Summer."

Almost sobbing with relief and release and love, she said "I love you" over and over, while he inhaled the words and gave them back to her with his body.

Chapter 18

Jamie was gone when she woke. Summer blinked blearily. A shaft of gray light pried through the drawn draperies, so it must be late. Muffled sounds from the courtyard below came up on wind currents, then faded into nothing.

She closed her eyes again and pressed her face into the pillow. She couldn't think of the night before without flushing. The things she'd said, done, felt, thought. Jamie had driven her hard, not letting her rest, drawing from her everything she had to give.

And she'd said she loved him. He knew it now.

And he hadn't said it back.

Every inch of her body ached; he had explored and touched and kissed places whose existence she had politely ignored for twenty years. He had forced her to heights she had not yet seen. And she'd said she loved him.

She rolled over on her back and stared up at the high canopy swagging above. The bed was a wreck. Sheets were in a tangle, still damp, wadded up and half off the mattress. The coverlet was on the floor somewhere; she vaguely recalled Jamie yanking it off when she'd tried to roll up in it.

Where was he?

He hadn't bothered to wake her before he'd gone,

but if he'd tried, she didn't know if he could have
succeeded. Too weary to speak, she had finally collapsed, sobbing, in his arms just before daylight. He'd
held her, rubbing his jaw against the top of her head,
and told her to sleep.

She'd obeyed instantly. And now, the sharp-edged
slice of light piercing the closed drapes told her it was
almost noon.

Faintly appalled at having slept so long, and a little
embarrassed at the idea of having to face everyone
again after last night, Summer moved slowly from the
bed. After a brief battle with herself, she sighed and
tugged on the bell rope.

She needed a bath. And something to eat. And
clothes to wear. If there were any left. Jamie had been
disposing of suitable garments with alarming rapidity.

She waited in the middle of the bed for Letty to
appear, but it took a long time. By the time the maid
got there, Summer was beginning to think she was
alone in the sprawling stone keep.

"Yer laidyship," Letty said, breathless, her eyes huge
and round. "Oi didn' mean ta take so long ta git 'ere!"

"That's all right." Summer hesitated, then couldn't
help asking, "Has my husband asked for me?"

Letty shook her head and busied herself with the hip
bath she dragged from the dressing room. Summer
stared into space. He hadn't even asked for her. What
had she expected? That he would be as swept away by
the night as she had been? Not Jamie Cameron.

Her lips twisted painfully. It had been very obvious that he was no novice in sensuality, and he probably thought her inept and naive. What had been
earthshaking and shattering to her, was probably only
mildly stimulating to him. Lord, she could be such a
fool!

She recalled with aching clarity his remote, watchful gaze as he'd swept her into almost sobbing response to his skilled caresses; it had been obvious he'd

not felt the same wild hammering inside that she felt. Not then. Not until she tried to wrest away from him, and he'd held her to his chest and growled that he'd never let her leave him.

Then he had finally given her some of himself, some of the driving passion and tender words that she'd needed so badly to hear.

But he hadn't said he loved her.

She had told him how beautiful he was and how much she loved him and begged him for release, panting against the fevered skin of his shoulder, clinging to him. He'd given her that release, but he hadn't given her his love.

She'd bared her soul, trusting him at last not to hurt her. And it had come to this final, searing surrender. She waited on him, for just the sound of his voice, the flick of a smile, his touch. Summer felt a twinge of despair.

Letty helped her bathe and then pressed the muslin gown for her to wear. When Summer was dressed, the little maid began to brush her long hair, still damp from being washed.

"Blimey, ye got pretty 'air, yer laidyship." Letty gave a sigh. "Mine's plain, an' thin. Yer 'air is so thick Oi could stuff a mat'ress wi' it an' 'ave plenny left over."

Summer managed a smile. "Do the dresses I gave you fit well?"

Pleased, Letty nodded. "Aye! A l'il long, 'cause ye're taller'n me, but they fits well. Thankee, yer laidyship."

"Of course."

Letty smiled slyly. "If yer 'usband don't quit rippin' 'em offa ye, yer won't 'ave none left to give me affer a w'ile."

"It certainly seems that way." Summer tried not to look at her reflection in the mirror, knowing her cheeks would be flushed. She could feel the warmth.

Bolder because she'd not been rebuked for her impudence, Letty said, " 'Course, 'e's gone down ta Dunkeld ta fight that blond bear, so's 'e may not feel much laik doin'—"

Summer surged to her feet. "He's done what?"

Realizing her error, Letty gulped. 'Oi doan know fer sure, yer laidyship. Ye'll 'ave ta ask summat else 'bout it ta find out."

A chill stung the early morning air; a thin mist from the river slunk in corners and clung to grass. Behind the Dunkeld inn, the distant rigid cone of Schiehallion was obscured by clouds, while its more gentle neighbor Farragon humped nearby. The slashing burns, rugged peaks, narrow gorges, waterfalls, and odd, painted stones left by a people long faded into the past had intrigued Garth. The very wildness of the Highlands impressed him. It bred wild, savage men, capable of taking and holding their own.

Like James Cameron.

He smiled slightly when he saw the Scot rein his horse to a stop in front of the stone-and-timber inn and got up and went outside. He'd been expecting him.

Leaning against the wall and crossing his arms over his chest, Garth contrived to look fairly relaxed as the Scot approached. A fine rain drizzled over them, a Scottish mist glistening on the length of the sword belted at Jamie's side. It wasn't the showy dress sword, but a very businesslike saber. Garth shifted position slightly to ensure that his own sword was easily accessible.

"I would talk to you," Jamie said when he reached the man leaning leisurely against the ivy-strewn wall, and Garth shrugged.

"I thought to see you here."

They watched each other warily, like two strange dogs, as they entered the inn. When they were seated at a long table with mugs of ale between them, Jamie asked bluntly, "Do you know Fox?" He looked up at Kinnison, hard.

Garth's expression became guarded. "I've met him."

"Did he tell you where you could find me?"

Another wary glance. "Yes."

Jamie gave a satisfied nod. He rubbed his thumb across the beard-shadow on his jaw, his eyes slightly narrowed in thought. "I thought it might be him instead of Epson. That peacock doesn't know where Scotland lies, much less my father's house." He turned his gaze on Kinnison's wary face. "I find it odd that an American such as you would know Mr. Fox well enough to pull answers from him."

Shrugging, Garth said, "He likes Americans."

"Oh, aye, well I know that. He bought the king's wrath and dislike with that affection. But 'tis no matter now." He leaned forward, idly dragging a thumb over the sweating mug of ale. "Not every man can just meet with Fox. You must have friends in high places."

Garth waved a lazy hand. "I get about."

"So do I. And until Summer, I'd never heard of you."

"You've been busy fighting, the way I understand it." Garth smiled. "Isn't that how you won your title—by pulling poor Freddie from under his horse and giving him yours?"

Not about to get into a discussion on that, Jamie said bluntly, "You've a deuced too many friends in high places to be the simple sea captain of a merchantman, Mr. Kinnison. I dinna believe that is why you are here."

"I came about Summer."

"I don't mean in Scotland. I mean England. And maybe France?"

"Ah." Kinnison smiled. "You seem to think I'm involved in intrigue, is that it?"

"Aye. 'Twould seem probable."

"What is that to you?" He spread his hands. "Not

that I am fool enough to involve myself in such things, but it arouses my curiosity that you would wonder."

"Any man would wonder. You're a sight too well informed about some things."

Pulling at his lower lip, Kinnison watched Jamie for a moment. "What do you know about Barton Shriver?" he asked finally.

Jamie shrugged. "Only that he's head of one of the largest shipping lines; and that he's known to keep one foot in each political circle. He backed the Spanish, then involved himself in negotiating the treaty giving France ownership of Louisiana. He also helped negotiate the American purchase of that land from Napoleon. It is said he has few scruples."

"Aye, that's true enough. Shriver plays both ends against the middle and will ride whatever tide is highest. He plans to sell his niece to Freeman Tutwiler as bride. It will enable him to keep control of her fortune, a deciding factor in his plans." He leaned forward and stared at Jamie closely. "Shriver is like a huge spider, spinning webs and keeping his hands in many different pots. He has to be stopped before he does irreparable damage to the peace that now exists between America and England. If he successfully manages to give Napoleon a foothold in Louisiana, there will be war."

"So Summer is little more than a pawn. Her absence must trouble Shriver a great deal."

"Oh, aye! It has set him to a fever pitch of panic. She is his key to power, through her fortune. For herself, he cares nothing."

Jamie's jaw clenched. "Did you try to abduct Summer a few weeks ago?"

Kinnison was genuinely surprised. "No. Someone did, I assume?"

"Aye. Fox saw him. He was her gallant rescuer." Jamie's mouth twisted. " 'Twas more than a simple cutpurse, I fear. Would Shriver go that far?"

"Why do you think I'm here? To steal your bride?"

Garth shook his head. "Nay, because Shriver will attempt anything to get her back. He needs her. It will make no difference to him—or Tutwiler—if she is not a virgin. It's not her body they're after."

"Is that why you're here? To take her back?"

"No. Well—yes. That was why I came. I didn't want to leave her in danger. Shriver would think nothing of holding her prisoner and using her fortune through Tutwiler. I intended to take her with me, willing or not."

Jamie sat back on the bench, drawing his legs up under him; his sword scraped against the dirt floor. "Did you."

"Not for the reason you might think."

"Ah. I find tha' comforting."

Kinnison shifted on the bench and put his elbows on the scarred table. His face was only a foot or two from the Scot's. He could see the opaque eyes, the slight flattening of his mouth, and the throb of muscle in his shadowed jaw.

"Is this a fighting matter?"

"Tha' depends on your next answer."

A faint smile curled Kinnison's mouth. "I don't have to hear the question, Scot—no, I won't take her now. I would have, if you hadn't come today. I wouldn't risk Summer to a man who didn't care enough to swallow his pride a little to see her safe."

"Ye think this is swallowing my pride to come here?"

Jamie's eyes were hot, and he glared at Kinnison.

"It's cost you dear to sit here and not draw your sword on me," Kinnison retorted. "I've watched you. You want to, but you won't. Not now."

"Aye." It was a low growl, and Garth smiled.

"It's fair to say I wouldn't mind a contest myself. But I think we've both misjudged each other."

"Aye," Jamie said grudgingly, "maybe we have."

"And now, maybe we'll see to Summer's future."

"First, I'd have an answer—do you intend to leave

her be? I dinna need you hanging around her like a pet dog."

A grin squared Kinnison's mouth. "Maybe she likes it. It certainly makes her husband pay special attention to her, I vow."

Scraping back the bench with a loud scree of wood, Jamie looked ready to draw steel, and Kinnison put up a hand.

"No, laddie. It was a jest." As Jamie's tension eased, Garth gestured to him to sit down again. He seemed amused. "You Scots are a hot-tempered lot. But in your place, I would be too, I think." He grinned at Jamie's grunt. "Let me tell you why I care so much for the girl, Westcott. I knew her father well, you see. I respected Jonathan St. Clair. He was a good man, one of those ambitious men of French descent who was smart enough to use both sides of his heritage. He was able to deal with the Creoles—notedly a clannish sort—as well as the Americans and made a great deal of money. He wasn't stingy with it, either. It was St. Clair who got me my first ship, and I've never forgotten the debt I owe him. And his daughter."

Slowly relaxing, Jamie pushed at the mug of ale on the table. It left a wet ring on the surface; he dragged a hand through it, then wiped his palm on his sleeve. He looked up at Garth Kinnison and smiled faintly.

"I can well understand a debt of honor. It explains a lot." He gave a cynical laugh. "It's kept Scots alive for centuries and killed more than a few of them too."

A brief silence spun out, stretched, tightened. Garth shifted uncomfortably.

"She doesn't love me. Not like she does you. Maybe the memory, but that's all."

Jamie's jaw hardened. "I don't need you to tell me that, by God!"

Kinnison retreated swiftly. "No, you don't."

Jamie frowned down into his mug of ale. "If you are so anxious to keep her safe, why did you send her back to New Orleans at first?"

"What else was I to do? I had to go to France, and I couldn't take her with me. Besides, I have people who were paid to watch over her. Shriver couldn't harm her as long as she stayed where she was supposed to stay." He gave a short laugh. "Of course, Summer has been known to have a mind of her own. It's a great trial at times, but I have to admire her for it."

"Aye." Jamie tilted his mug of ale and looked at it. "I think some good whisky would do us much better than this. Or is it still too early for you to drink a man's drink, American?"

A ready grin met Jamie's mocking question. "No, not too early today. We have to discuss a way to keep our rebellious Summer safe, and that will take a lot of whisky, I vow."

Summer waited impatiently. When she could stand it no more, she called for Letty and informed her briskly that they were going to Dunkeld.

"Dunkeld, yer laidyship?" The maid shifted uneasily. "Oi don' think yer husbin 'ud be laikin' that, Oi don'."

"It doesn't matter what my husband likes. I intend to go and stop something foolish. Do you still flirt with the ostler?"

A faint blush stained Letty's cheeks, but she nodded.

"Good. I want two horses. One for each of us. And don't tell me you don't ride, because you must. Be quick about it. And don't let anyone see you. I don't want to be stopped."

Faintly, Letty replied, "Yes, yer laidyship!"

Summer dressed carefully. She was seething—torn between anger at Jamie for being so idiotic as to go after Garth and fear for his safety. Garth was a formidable swordsman. She didn't know if Jamie could match him. Yes, he had outdueled the gentleman in

St. Giles rookery, but how would he fare against Garth's finely honed skills?

Stupid, conceited, arrogant, belligerent Scot!

She raged inside. Fear for Jamie outweighed even her anger, and she switched back and forth between the two emotions with frightening rapidity. By the time she was dressed to ride in a rust-colored riding skirt and tight-fitting basque, she was quivering with nervous anticipation. She had no idea what she would say when she got there and only hoped she wasn't too late.

Letty led her down a back passage, but Summer still ran into the earl at the covered arch leading from the castle to the courtyard. Her heart skipped a beat when he paused and looked at her curiously; her fingers curled into the edges of her cloak. A faint smile slanted his mouth when she flung up her head in silent defiance. He would not stop her!

A steady drizzle hissed down, and for what seemed like an eternity, the earl gazed at her with a half-lidded appraisal that seemed to see clear into her soul. Then he nodded and went inside without saying a word. Summer was too stunned to move for a moment.

Recovering, she flashed a glance at Letty's pale face, and said, "Let's go swiftly!"

Mud flung up in thick clods from beneath the horses' hooves as they followed the wet track down wooded mountains toward the village. The Bran River flowed through the Tay Valley, snaking through steep gorges and flattening out in brief glens. It boiled and fussed over black rocks, foaming beneath a stone bridge.

Summer's mount clattered over the bridge. Below, amid a wedge of high hills, lay Dunkeld. Small, neat cottages lined the street, and above it, on the sloping riverbank, was the ruined cathedral Garth had mentioned. She had a brief impression of a massive tower, an uncentered window in a gable, roofless stretches, and tumbled stone, and behind the cathedral, sharp-scented spires of larch trees.

But what attracted her immediate attention was the solitary rider approaching her on the narrow road. She reined in and waited, her hands shaking slightly.

"Cor!" breathed Letty. "We're done now, yer laidy-ship!"

"Hush! Restrain your cowardice for a moment," Summer snapped at the girl, though she felt the same thumping dread.

James Cameron looked none too happy to see her. His horse, a flashy black stallion with wide eyes and pink-flowering nostrils, pranced restlessly under him. His spurs jangled, and she could hear the muted clank of his sword against the saddle as he reined to a halt beside her.

"What are you doing here, Summer?"

His irate tone did nothing to ease her anxiety, but she decided to brazen it out. "Out riding. Why?"

He flicked a sardonic glance at her, and she kept her chin high. The steady drizzle had dampened her cloak so that it hung heavily, and her hair straggled down her neck and into her eyes.

"Aye," he said, "it's a lovely day for riding."

"I need to go into the village. I have some pur-chases to make." She urged her mount into a step, and Jamie angled in front of her.

"Nay. I think your shopping will wait till another day." His level tone hardened when she swung the dun's head around to pass him; his hand flashed out to grab her bridle and hold it. "Summer. I forbid you to go."

She glared at him. Her fingers tightened on her riding crop, and she tapped it against her short boots. Her mount shied with agitation at the popping sound.

"You forbid me to go?" she repeated softly. Rain misted her face; her lashes lowered slightly over thin-ning eyes. "Who are you to tell me I can't go into the village?"

"Your husband." His mouth tightened, and he flexed his arm, dragging her resisting mount closer. "Turn around. You are going back with me."

"No, *husband*, I am not!" Her jaw clenched. She was irrationally glad to see him alive and furious that he seemed utterly unharmed. It occurred to her to wonder how Garth had fared. "Where is Garth?" she asked abruptly.

"On his way back to London, I would guess." Jamie met her gaze without a flicker. "He didn't seem to think it wise to remain in Dunkeld."

"Damn you!" A sweep of rage rose in her. Garth had said he would wait; he had lied. He had made plans to see her to say farewell, and he'd not kept them. It wasn't that she truly cared anymore about him, not that way, but it was another rejection. Her voice quivered slightly.

"Did you wound him?"

"Ah. So you think I rode down here to challenge him to a duel in your honor?" His laugh mocked her flushed cheeks. "And if I had, milady? If I had fallen on the field of honor, would you have wept for me?"

Her horse moved restlessly under her; the rain glinted in Jamie's long lashes; she could hear Letty's swift gasps for air and her tortured silence. He was waiting for her answer. His dark head, wet with rain, cocked to one side, and his hand held firmly on the dun's bridle to hold her.

She felt a surge of pain.

He didn't love her. She was a possession and he was a Cameron, and the Camerons held what was theirs. Damn him.

She looked at him.

"I would have wept for your foolishness. Now let me pass."

His gloved hand tightened on the reins. "What? No tears for a beloved husband?"

"Beloved? You flatter yourself!"

His knees tightened around his mount, and the

horse edged so close that Jamie's booted foot was brushing against Summer's leg. "Do I? I seem to recall your pledges of love last night well enough. Didna you tell me over and over again how you love me, and showed me as well?"

A hot flush stained her cheeks, and she was agonizingly aware of Letty's avid attention. He mocked her love, her words of love. Her throat closed with pain and shame, and she wished she'd never said them. He didn't want them but as a weapon. Her chin lifted with anguished pride.

"I only said those things so you would leave me alone and let me rest. You seemed," she said with all the scorn she could inject into her voice, "to need to hear them much more than I would have dreamed. I felt sorry for you, so I said what you wanted to hear."

Jamie's eyes bored into hers, and he jerked her bridle so viciously, the dun gave a startled squeal. It leapt, and Summer had to grab the mane to keep from being unseated. A faint gasp escaped her, and when she saw that he had eased his grip on the bridle, she seized her chance.

Snatching her reins, she brought her riding crop up in a swift move to bring it down on her horse and send it forward. But Jamie grabbed her other arm to pull her out of the saddle. His move put her off balance and instead of striking her mount, Summer brought the crop down on his thigh; she heard the sharp singing slice of leather against his white-clad muscle.

He swore, savagely, kicked out with his boot to shove the horse away at the same time as his arm curved around Summer's waist. He yanked, and she was lifted from the saddle and hung from his grasp, her legs dangling against the side of his horse, her breasts pressed into his body.

Her horse bolted; she felt the whip of its tail against her, heard the pounding hooves in mud. Behind her, Summer could hear Letty sobbing and saying over and over, "I tole ye, mum, I tole ye, mum!"

Still holding her crop in one hand, Summer threw caution to the winds and cracked it against the stallion's quivering flanks. She lifted it to strike again, and the frayed tip caught in a stinging lash across Jamie's cheek.

He swore horribly, not hearing Summer's gasp of apology as he yanked her even closer. Her feet banged against the horse's belly.

Already unsettled by the lash and action, the horse half lifted from the ground, screaming. Its forelegs pawed the air, and Jamie cursed in a continuous stream of panting words as he fought it back to the ground. For a moment, Summer thought she would be loosed to fall beneath those lethal hooves, but he held her tightly.

The stallion bucked and heaved, and unbalanced by his clumsy grip on Summer, Jamie came out of the saddle. Still cursing, he landed in the mud of the road with Summer. His hand still gripped her, and after the first shock of hitting the ground, she kicked and tried to roll free, but was hampered by her wet cloak and the heavy velvet skirts.

Panting, smeared with mud and damp with rain, Summer felt him roll her over and pin her down, his hands around her wrists. He glared down at her, his black brow snapped down over eyes as black as the pits of hell. The mark of the whip marred his cheek in a bloody stripe. She shuddered and closed her eyes.

Jamie easily controlled the weighted kick of her legs beneath the cloak by sliding his body atop hers, his thighs wedging them together. The abrasive scrape of her body beneath him engendered an inevitable response, and when she felt it, her eyes flew open.

He picked the riding crop out of her hand and flung it aside, holding her wrists in one hand, resettling himself in the mud and folds of cloak. His erection prodded against thighs covered by rust-colored velvet. Summer's breath was as fast and labored as his. She could hear Letty whimpering, and watched Jamie's head lift to stare at the maid.

"Go back," he said shortly. "You know the road. I'll bring your mistress home."

"But, milord, ye ain' gonna 'urt 'er, air ye?"

Letty's pitiful wail made his mouth tighten. "No more than she deserves. Have an ostler come for her horse. It can't have gone too far."

When Letty might have offered another protest, Jamie snarled at her and she squealed, digging her heels into the ribs of her sedate mount and sending the creature jogging back up the road to the barely visible castle behind the tangled trees.

Bending his head to look down at Summer, Jamie didn't say anything for a moment. Her mouth was dry. She could feel the rapid thud of her heart, feel the nudging steel of his body between her legs. The hot, angry lights in his eyes slowly altered to a steady glow; the long lashes drifted downward in a lazy motion; his features sharpened. Then he moved his hips against her in a deliberate grind and thrust that left her in no doubt of his intention.

"No," she whispered in a defeated voice when his head lowered, "no, Jamie. Not here, in the mud and the middle of the road. . . . "

"Aye," he growled against her lips, "here! It seems fitting, somehow." His hand parted the edges of her cloak, pushed up her gown, fumbled at his buttons. Then he was sliding inside her, pounding into her with a sense of urgency that made her shudder, made her body convulse in a shattering response.

It was insane. The rain pattered down on them, and the sharp smell of gorse and wet earth filled her nostrils. She could hear the tumbled rush of the river; she inhaled deeply of Scotland and Jamie, and heard with a sense of shame her lilting cry of love as she took him into her body.

• • •

He took her back to the pretty castle on his stallion, his arm around her, mud caking both of them.
No one offered a comment when they returned; nor
did anyone look directly at them. By tacit consent,
everyone overlooked the two.

Jamie withdrew from Summer again. He didn't insist that she come downstairs to the hall to eat. He
didn't say anything other than to make polite conversation about mundane matters.

She ached with what he didn't say; what he'd never
say, it seemed. He wanted her body; he didn't want
the love she had so foolishly offered. Yet she couldn't
hold it from him. It was impossible. Everything was
impossible.

And when he told her the next morning that they
were returning to England, she wasn't surprised. She
was surprised at her reluctance to leave Scotland. And
the family she'd come to think of as her own. She'd
only been here a week, yet it seemed as if she'd made
a fast friend in Catriona.

Cat wasn't at all pleased to see them leave and said
so in no uncertain terms. They stood in the hall, the
three of them, wary protagonists beneath a vaulted
ceiling.

"Is it your stubborn pride that takes you away so
quickly, Jamie?" she demanded, her lips thinning and
her green eyes troubled.

His dark gaze regarded her coolly. "No. I have
business matters to attend to."

But Catriona wasn't satisfied with that. She glanced
at Summer's pale face. "They can't be that pressing,"
she said frankly. "You're just in a temper."

The single dark brow lifted slightly. "Cat, little you
may credit it, but I do have things to do other than
provide my family with entertainment. I have estates
I haven't even seen yet, and everything the king
granted to me needs repair. That takes time and plan-

ning." His voice grew sarcastic. "You can find a new playmate when we're gone. Who knows? Maybe you'll give your poor husband the attention he deserves. . . ."

His sarcastic drawl and mocking words infuriated his sister, and they quarreled heatedly until Summer fled the hall in tears. Cat was Jamie's favorite; yet they were fighting over her. She felt responsible, somehow, though in another way, she blamed Jamie for being so pigheaded. The arrogant ox!

Blinded by tears, she ran into Dallas in the corridor. Literally. He grabbed her arms and held her away from him, staring down at her anxiously. "Here, lass! Tears? Hae my bad-tempered brother been playin' th' de'il agin?"

Embarrassed, she nodded miserably. "It's just that he and Cat are quarreling. Because of me."

"Och! Those twa wad fight o'er th' color of th' sky, lass. Don' greet, now." He handed her his handkerchief, and looked around with a helpless glance, as if hoping help would soon arrive.

A door banged, and Dallas and Summer half-turned to see Jamie storming from the hall. He saw them and paused, turning with a jerk to go in the other direction. His dress sword caught on the suit of armor by the door, and it began to totter. Summer watched with fascination as the steel armor crumpled; Jamie leapt back out of the way.

The steel helmet hit the floor first, rolling in loud rattles, the visor flapping. Gauntlets, greaves, and cuisses flew in different directions. One of the metal gloves spun across the stones in a whir, the hinged thumb shield chattering noisily. The deafening noise brought servants and family running.

"Oh, bloody *hell*!" Jamie muttered. His chagrined gaze lifted from the hauberk on the floor to Summer's mesmerized expression. Some of the temper faded from his eyes, and the suggestion of a grin flickered on his mouth.

"Another foe vanquished, Jamie lad," Dallas said

in a voice choked with laughter. "If ye'd been wearin' yon armor yesterday, ye wad no' hae tha' cut on yer cheek today."

The humor faded from Jamie's eyes as quickly as it had appeared, and he pivoted on his bootheel and left the hall. Summer stared after him hopelessly.

Chapter 19

London again. Sooty fog, the spires of St. Paul's, a leaden sky; iron wheels and shod horses ringing loudly against the cobbled stones of the streets. Summer stared out the windows of her bedchamber without caring.

For five days on the journey, she'd been sick, racking with heaves until they were dry, then collapsing weakly. In Selkirk, Jamie had dragged a physician to their room in the inn, but he had not been overly concerned.

"Spoiled meat," had been his cheerful verdict, and he'd given her a potion that was worse than the affliction.

Letty was relieved to be back, but Summer found herself missing Scotland, maybe because she'd found a sense of family there. She still got a lump in her throat when she recalled Cat's teary farewell and the brief, warm hug from Jamie's mother.

They loved her. Why couldn't he?

He'd been distant on the journey. The first few nights when they'd stopped at cozy inns, he'd come to her bed with silent passion. No words of love, no tender words. Just an aching desire that she couldn't deny and didn't want. How did she ask for love?

Her pride would never allow it.

After those first nights, she'd grown too ill for him to touch. He'd left her alone then, but she'd felt his brooding gaze on her at odd moments. She'd been much more comfortable when he rode his horse instead of being inside the coach.

Thankfully, she'd recovered from her illness only a day or two after being back in London. Tidwell had brought her a potion his wife had made, and she felt human again.

It was just as well. Jamie hadn't noticed her in the month since they had returned. He was, as he'd said he would be, busy with his own affairs. She was left on her own again; and this time without the comfort of the garden.

Gardeners had come in while they were in Scotland and trimmed hedges and planted flowers and shrubs, and made a glorious showplace from what had been untidy and practically barren. Portions of the garden were still faintly bare, but a miracle could not be accomplished in such a short time. In the three months since she'd first come to Westcott House, there had been a great deal of changes.

Three months. It seemed like a lifetime ago.

Wandering the garden one day, restless and bored, Summer was disappointed to see that few of her efforts had been left. Those unfeeling gardeners had ripped out her little plants. Overcome with anger and distress, she sank down on a stone bench, buried her face in her palms, and wept for them, feeling slightly foolish but unable to stop. Her emotions were ragged lately, on edge and lurking just below the surface.

Naturally, Jamie found her at just such a moment. His timing, she thought gloomily, was abominable.

He came to her quickly, his boots moving across the gravel path in a flash of elegant sheen. "Summer—what is it?" He glanced around. "Has someone hurt you?"

She hiccoughed and turned away, angrily trying to

wipe away her tears on the hem of her gown. He handed her a square of linen, and she snatched it with ill grace. She had absolutely no intention of telling him that she was weeping for her murdered seedlings. He'd lock her away.

"Nothing."

Her voice sounded sullen even to her.

"You're not sick again, lass?"

"Sympathy, my lord?" Her chin quivered slightly, and she steadied it with an effort. "Pray, don't strain yourself on my behalf."

His mouth tightened, and he shook his head. "I should have known you'd be as sweet-tempered as usual." He took the damp square of linen and stuffed it into the pocket of his coat, then sat down beside her. She moved away in a sidling motion, and he spread his hands on his knees and blew out his breath with exasperation.

"You're so charming when you behave as if your beauty will drive me into raping you, my love." His dark eyes mocked her when her head jerked up and she glared at him. "I don't find myself sufficiently tempted at this time, however. Sorry to disappoint."

"Believe me, I'm *not* disappointed, you conceited dog!"

"Glad to hear it. Now that we have our usual sweetly affectionate greetings out of the way, I thought you'd like to know that we're to attend an affair at Albany House. You will meet the duke of York."

"Are we?" Her eyes narrowed. "And if I wish to stay here? These are not my acquaintances, but yours...."

"You weren't given that choice." Jamie looked away from her, staring at the bright flowers and tinkling fountain. "And you will not try to avoid being chaperoned, Summer. I understand from Tidwell that you refused to allow Porter to accompany you on a walk yesterday."

"You needn't worry about my meeting a lover or

some such silly thing!" Summer snapped, incensed that he kept such a close watch on her. "And you should be gratified to know that Tidwell was so distressed, I stayed here."

"So I heard." His eyes were hard. "I thought I'd made it quite clear that you were not to roam about unattended."

"Oh, it was clear enough." She smiled nastily, winding a lock of silky hair through her fingers. "I just chose not to allow you to arbitrarily decide every aspect of my life. You understand my desire to retain some sort of independence of my own, of course."

"My understanding is not in question here." He stuck one leg straight out in front of him and kicked idly at a clump of lavender lining the path. "I just expect you to do what I ask."

"Oh. Did you ask? Pardon me. I seem to recall only a few commands left to the servants, not requests." She pushed at a strand of hair in her eyes, angrily, her mouth a thin line. "I see that I am to have no privacy at all. Of course, my lord. I shall do whatever you say, my lord; you are my master, my—thane, did I hear your sister say one time?"

"That is a feudal term, no longer used." He seemed amused now and looked down at her angry little face. "Summer, sweetheart, don't stay so angry all the time. Can you not see—?"

"All I see is that you have changed from a man, albeit a rather spoiled one, into some sort of . . . of monster!" The wretched tears again, close to the surface. Damnit. She felt like a watering pot. "You're never here. And when you are, you're cold and mean. I don't even like you anymore."

Surging to his feet, Jamie clenched and unclenched his hands, staring down at her. "Fine. But you will go to Albany House tomorrow night, and you will wear an appropriate gown. If you don't have the correct wear, send Tidwell for it. Or Porter. Even Greaves. Do not go yourself." He paused, then said,

"I wish you could wear your hair loose." His hand lifted a lambent strand of hair, and he watched it curl around his palm. "As you did on our wedding night."

"You like it loose, my lord?" Her smile was tight; she could feel it stretching painfully, felt his frowning gaze on her. "Now, let's see, I'm to wear just the right gown, and I'm to wear my hair as *you* like it, and I'm to not go anywhere by myself—is there something I've left out? Any foods you prefer I eat or don't eat? Wine?"

"Summer—"

Surging to her feet, she met his dark, narrowed eyes with a hot gaze. "Oh, I will see that I'm dressed very well for your precious duke! Never fear."

It was a promise she kept.

Glittering lights jeweled the doors and walkways of the house, and carriages were drawn up in front. It was the renewal of the Season, the small one, and Londoners were slowly straggling back from Bath, Brighton, or other summer places. Summer sat nervously in the coach, feeling Jamie's gaze on her.

"Cold?" he asked, flipping a finger over the edge of her hooded mantle, and she drew back slightly.

"Yes. I have a chill."

"In September?" He shook his head. "Good God, winter in the Highlands will be an experience for you."

She looked at him curiously. "Are we to go back to Scotland soon?"

"Not soon." He turned his head, and the light fell over his rugged features, making Summer's heart lurch. He was so handsome, with his devil's grin and wicked brow; why did she ache for him so? He drove her to the extremes of her emotions. His cool, arrogant assumption that she would do what he commanded enraged her, made her behave foolishly. She knew he was going to be furious with her.

Her palms were wet. She shouldn't have done it.
She knew she shouldn't have. But she'd been so mad.
And when they went inside, and he saw her . . .

Their footman opened the door, and her heart
pounded in a rapid beat. Her legs shook, and she knew
Jamie could feel the quiver of her hands as he turned
to lift her out. He would not allow the footman to
help but insisted upon it himself. Was he being gallant, or had he guessed how much his touch disturbed
her?

Summer flicked a glance over Jamie. He was
garbed in black velvet, the expertly cut coat fitting his
broad shoulders like a dark shadow. He wore a white,
embroidered waistcoat and had frills of Brugge lace
at his cuffs and throat. The silk cravat had been tied
in a new style—perhaps the work of his new valet, a
man who looked too rough and uncouth to Summer
to be a house servant. Greaves made her nervous, always lurking about everywhere in the house she went.
Well. No matter.

Inhaling deeply, Summer walked up the shallow
steps of Albany House on Jamie's arm, then turned in
the doorway as the steward stood politely waiting to
announce them. In an unhurried movement, she un-
fastened the ties to her mantle and let it fall aside,
pulling off the hood. She gave it into the keeping of
a footman, then stood back.

She faced Jamie defiantly, waiting for his reaction.
She had no doubt whatsoever that he would take her
back to the coach and send her home; it was what she
expected.

For a moment, there was a look of such fury in his
eyes that she wished she'd not dared; he raked her
cropped hair, the vivid blue gown with the deep-cut
bodice and almost transparent material shaping to her
legs, then lifted that dark gaze to her face. What he
saw there must have decided him to another course.

"I think ye'll make a lasting impression on th' duke
tonight," he drawled, his thick burr the only outward

indication of his anger. "An' I hae th' feelin' tha'
a'fore th' night is out, ye'll wish ye hae listened tae
me."

Her chin lifted. "If you don't approve, I can always
go home."

"Nay, lass. Ye'll stay. Ye'll stay, and ye'll brazen it
out, lookin' like a cheap baggage, perhaps, but tha'
wae as ye chose it." His glance flicked to her hair, to
the short curls rioting atop her crown, and he shook
his head. "My real regret is your hair. But tha's done."

Somehow, her vengeance didn't taste as sweet as
she'd thought it would. She'd wanted to prick him, to
show him that she was an independent woman and
could do as she pleased; all she felt was a little childish
and very, very foolish.

He pulled her firmly into the house. She barely
heard their names called out—Viscount and Viscountess Westcott—and stared at a sea of faces as they
paused in the doorway. Violin and oboes and horns
rose in the sweet strains of an English country dance,
and the ballroom was awash in bright satins and silks.
Stark-white muslin gowns of varying weight draped
lovely women like Greek goddesses. Lace draped elegantly from wrists and foamed at masculine throats,
and there was the brilliant flash of jewels.

Summer wore the Douglas sapphires around her
throat; she'd known they would draw attention to the
shockingly low décolletage of her gown. Now she felt
exposed and wished she'd second-guessed her husband a bit better. She moved woodenly, smiling au-
tomatically, instinctively making the correct social
replies. It was a farce, and Jamie knew it.

Yet Summer fielded the idle questions tossed at
her, the speculative gazes, the looks leveled from behind gold quizzing glasses. She wished she'd not worn
the gown; for one thing, the lack of decent covering
gave her gooseflesh that she was certain was terribly
unattractive. For another thing, foppish dandies
crowded around them begging an introduction to

Westcott's bride. It was a miserable feeling to be ogled, especially when she knew she'd brought it on herself. And suffering Jamie's hot, knowing glances didn't help any.

"Stop staring at me!" she hissed at him, and his brow lifted in that impudent devil's arch.

"Isn't that why you wore that gown, my love? To be stared at? I vow, it's working. Half the men in London are panting at your heels now, and before noon tomorrow, you will have so many cards and invitations, Tidwell will be hard-pressed to carry them upstairs." His smile did not reach his eyes. "I daresay you'll have every coxcomb in the entire country sniffing at your skirts."

"Just what I need," she ground out, glaring at him with the sick knowledge that he was right. "I believe I've had enough of lust without love, thank you."

She turned her head away from him when he frowned, her throat tight with misery.

"Summer," he began, putting a hand on her arm, but when he was distracted by the arrival of a gentleman in silk knee-breeches and a flowered waistcoat, he turned away.

"Your Grace," Jamie said, rolling his *R*'s in a way that made Summer look at him curiously.

It was the duke of York, an extremely affable, round-faced man who seemed to think a great deal of Jamie. Summer listened, feeling awkward and uncertain while they laughed comfortably and the duke professed himself mad about all things Scottish.

"Those Highlanders! The best fighting regiment we have, I vow! Damn glad—beg pardon, ma'am—we have 'em on our side. Run ole Boney all the way to the Steppes, we will! He can stay in the snow and freeze his arse—beg pardon, ma'am—off. Impertinent frog's been crowned emperor now, did you hear? So, Westcott—what d'ye think of the Third Coalition?" He eyed Jamie brightly.

"I think Austria vacillates a bit. She won't last if he

wins a decisive battle. Sweden and Russia have a better chance of resistance. But it will give us the allies we need for now, and the longer the war lasts, the more difficult it will be for Napoleon to raise troops and money."

The duke considered this for a moment. "Yes, that's true. Money is his besetting worry. He's gone abroad for it. Looking in every pot, so to speak, for a handout. But you know that." His gaze flicked to Summer. "Lovely wife, Westcott. Bring her to Oatlands sometime."

"I will, Your Grace."

Summer managed a smile and a murmur, and the duke was gone, whirling off with a man he called Beau.

"You look like a bloody ghost," Jamie said softly, his voice biting, and Summer glanced up at him.

"Do I? Sorry, my lord." Her voice was listless. She felt weary suddenly. Even when Mr. Fox approached, his face creased into a smile, she found it difficult to reply to his questions. She felt Jamie's frown on her, his narrowed gaze, and tried not to look at him until Mr. Fox had moved on to someone else. Then she thrust out her chin and looked up at her husband.

His black eyes were a shock, boring into her, making her heart drop to her toes. She looked away from him, gazing at the damask-covered walls and not seeing anything at all. *Damn him.* He could so easily make her ache for him. Her heart was no longer her own. It belonged to him, and he bruised it most carelessly.

When he pressed a cup of claret into her icy fingers, he leaned close as if to whisper an endearment.

"Snap out of it, you little minx. You brought this on yourself, so you'd best hold your head up and pull this off if you ever want to be accepted in society again."

His snarled words were like a dash of cold water in her face. Her eyes flashed, and she jerked her head up to meet his gaze. He was staring at her speculatively, not with anger, and for a moment, she was puzzled. Then she reacted.

"I am quite aware of that, my lord. Do you think I care a fig for what these popinjays think?" She snapped her thumb and finger together in a popping sound. "I don't. Yet while I have no raging desire to be a part of the ton, neither do I wish to have you glare at me the rest of my life."

His hand cupped her chin, his fingers lightly curling along her jaw. "Glare at you?" he murmured. "How droll you are. I'm merely admiring your beauty and gazing with rapt admiration."

She twisted from his hand, her pulses fluttering at the touch. She hoped, quite sincerely, that he didn't notice.

"Harebrained dolt! Conceited fop!"

"Redundant, my love."

She'd just opened her mouth to heap further invective on him when she heard a soft, mocking voice at her elbow. She ground her teeth and turned.

"Well! If it isn't Westcott and his new bride. 'Pon rep, Westcott, you've prigged the little lady right out from under my nose!"

Summer eyed Lord Epson with distaste. He looked even more the macaroni than he had the last time she'd seen him, in his high-heel shoes aglitter with diamond buckles and puce satin waistcoat; an abundance of lace spilled over his lean wrists.

Stroking his upper lip with a beringed finger, Epson lifted his quizzing glass. "Ah, little flower, you have certainly blossomed under the care of this ardent Scot." He flicked a glance toward Jamie and smiled. "I heard that you spirited her off to Scotland for a quick wedding. Not fair. Was it her fortune that spurred you, my lord? Or perhaps being caught without a wedding first?"

A faint smile curled Jamie's mouth. "You've always been prone to excessive verbosity, Epson. I know a cure for it, if you'd care to accept my suggestion."

"Ah, a little bloodletting, no doubt. I'm familiar with your cures, Westcott. Saw you fight once. Quite a bloody, fearsome spectacle."

"I learned in a fearsome school." His brow rose. "You should have torn yourself away from the gaming tables long enough to join us. 'Twas educational, I vow."

An ugly expression creased Epson's aristocratic face, and Summer felt suddenly light-headed. The press of people, the claret, the constant roar of voices and laughter, and the smell of perfume and candles—she turned blindly to Jamie.

"My lord, please, I feel . . . quite ill."

He turned to her immediately. "Aye, lass. I'll find you a quiet spot."

Summer was only vaguely aware of curious glances, of Jamie's murmured conversation with someone, a soft, feminine voice. Then she was lying on a brocade sofa, with a cool cloth applied to her forehead. Jamie was beside her, and someone else in the shadows behind him. A single candle burned on a high, round table, shedding weak light.

"It could be your sickness again," Jamie said softly, and Summer gave a weak nod.

"It must be. I feel so . . . odd."

"Summer, love—did you drink all your claret?"

"Claret?"

"Aye, the cup I brought you. Did you drink it all?"

Her head rolled on the sofa. "No-o. Not that I recall. But I didn't really pay any attention." Her eyes filled with tears of frustration and embarrassment. "Jamie, I did not do this on purpose. . . ."

"Hush. I know you didn't." His hand smoothed back the hair from her forehead; he bent over her, then sat back on his heels. She felt him move away from her, heard him talking with someone before she closed her eyes again.

Did she dream it? Or did he really kiss her gently on the forehead before he left her? It was hard to tell what was real and what wasn't, and she had a vague sense of drifting in a mist.

"She'll hate me for that tomorrow," Jamie observed with a wry smile. "No' tha' she doesn't hate me already."

"Ah, connubial bliss can be so wonderful," Kinnison said with a laugh. " 'Tis no wonder I've dragged my feet on giving it a try."

A shrug met his comment. "It could be better. After this is over . . ." His voice trailed into silence.

"Epson's on edge tonight," Garth said tactfully. He slid Jamie a quick glance. "What'd you say to stir him up?"

"The truth." His mouth hardened. "I still owe him a debt for another matter."

"I've a feeling you're a man who pays his debts," Garth said after a moment, and Jamie looked up with a half-smile.

"Aye. Tha's what Summer said."

Garth laughed. "She would. She can be a feisty girl at times. Even when her uncle was his worst, she fought him. She didn't lie down meekly. She's had a lot of blows in the past few years."

"So you've told me." Jamie was quiet for a moment. He felt a surge of irritation with himself. He'd done to Summer what Shriver attempted to do, force her to his will. He was no better than the man he'd sworn to kill or see hanged. Well, it was time to get this over with. Then he'd settle things with Summer.

He looked at Garth and straightened, adjusting the hilt of the dress sword he'd buckled around his waist.

"Where is the bastard? I want to see our quarry."

"Over there." A thumb jerked toward the french doors leading onto a wide veranda.

Jamie followed the motion with his eyes. His hand moved to curl around the hilt of his sword. Then he studied the tall, thin man with the hawklike features and slash of pale hair. He wore scarlet silk and ivory lace, and his face was smooth, showing none of the treachery that existed inside. Jamie's jaw hardened. He'd been waiting for this. He wished he didn't have to be so careful.

"Westcott."

Turning, Jamie saw Charles Fox strolling toward him in a rolling gait. His pleasant, fleshy face looked fairly jovial, with black eyebrows winged over deep-set eyes and a mouth ready for a constant smile.

The short statesman said without preamble, "The man you seek is dressed in a satin coat of puce, lots of frogging, yellow knee-breeches." The grin flashed. "And in case there are several of those about—which it seems there are—he is the one with the curved scar on one cheek. Gives him a right wicked air, I think."

"He's a right wicked fellow," Jamie said. He flicked a glance at Garth Kinnison. "Did you see the man?"

Broad shoulders lifted briefly. "Not yet. But I'll find him."

Fox looked admiringly at Kinnison. "After this is over and we deal with this unworthy, I'd like to talk to you, Mr. Kinnison. At length. I've a fascination with America, you know."

"I had heard," Garth said politely. His blue gaze looked up and beyond Fox, scanning the crowded room. "You should go back with me. I leave next week."

Fox sighed. "Oh, that I would, that I would! But—life here can be tedious if one does not keep up with one's own affairs." He paused, following Kinnison's gaze. "Ah—do look by the statue of Zeus. Your man waits, all unknowing. Where have you left our bait?"

Before Jamie could speak, Garth said quickly, "Safely asleep in the blue salon. Greaves is watching her. Porter watches him."

"Good man, Greaves. I've used him myself." Fox slid Jamie an amused glance. "How goes he as a valet, Westcott?"

"Abominable. Summer thinks I've lost all sense of style."

"Well, as a valet he may lack finesse, but as a bruiser and bodyguard, he's prime."

When Fox sauntered back across the room, mingling with the guests, Jamie leaned against a marble column and surveyed the room. The statue of Zeus was on a marble pedestal, and a man in puce satin lounged beneath it with the careless air of a dandy. A curved scar marred one cheek, and his hooded eyes moved constantly around the room as if he was searching for something. Or someone.

Jamie smiled. The blood sang hotly in his veins. He was ready for it to begin. It had taken a month of preparation for this moment, and he was impatient.

Music rose in a swelling crescendo; guests laughed and dipped and swayed in the minuet, graceful, earth-bound birds in brilliant plumage; elegant marble halls and damask walls provided a gilded backdrop. Jamie saw none of it but the man he wanted to kill.

Barton Shriver. Here. In London, at last. Come to find the niece he wanted to destroy. He was suddenly, fiercely glad that the man had not trusted his henchman to do it for him. Apparently, one failure was enough.

But Jamie intended to see that Shriver failed too. There would be no return to New Orleans for Summer in his plans. Not that way. When this was over, if she wanted to go home, he'd see that she went safely, as she should. He'd not hold her when she wanted to leave.

A sharp twist in his stomach tightened, then passed. He'd thought about this for the past month, ever since leaving Scotland. He'd done his best to stay away from her. God. He was a fraud. He pretended he didn't care, when all he wanted was to tell her he loved her, to hear her say it back and mean it.

Damn. He'd tell her before she left him. At least then he would know he'd said it.

Levering his long body away from the marble column, Jamie saw Garth's quizzical glance and smiled.

"Shall the games begin?"

Garth grinned. "I was just thinking the same
thing."

Stirring restlessly, Summer sat up on the brocade
sofa. She put a hand to her head in an effort to still
the sudden swimming of her senses; the room reeled
in a whirl of light and shadow. Mostly shadow. Nothing had gone right. This had to be the worst night of
her life.

A slight groan escaped her. She could hear the
music in the ballroom and visualized glittering chan-
deliers and guests—gawking, leering guests, avidly
staring at her and wondering about the Scottish viscount's new wife. At least she'd escaped them for now.

Testing her growing stability in an uncertain
world, Summer swung her legs over the edge of the
sofa. When she put her hand up to push at a curl in
her eyes, she felt the soft, short silky wisps and winced.
She'd cut it off in a fit of temper but probably regretted it more than Jamie. Without her long hair, she felt
strangely naked, more naked than with the low-cut
gown.

The necklace around her throat hung heavily, and
she tugged at it, wishing she could remove it. It was
much too big for her and dangled almost between her
breasts.

Inhaling deeply, Summer rose to her feet; a soft
scream erupted when she saw a shadow detach itself
from the others and cross the room to her. She put
out a hand as if to shove him away, then recognized
Greaves.

"Oh. It's you," she said irritably. "You frightened
me. What are you doing here?"

"Set to watch ye sleep," he replied gruffly. His face

was square, stolid, with a low brow and small eyes. He made her nervous.

"Yes, well, as you can see, I'm quite well now. I must find my husband, and—"

"No, ma'am." Greaves looked disconcerted. "No'm, ye're ta stay here. His lordship said ye were."

"Did he now?" She felt a wave of irritation grow. "As you can see, Greaves, I'm recovered. I want to return to the ballroom. You are dismissed."

He barred her path. "No, ma'am," he said slowly, shaking his stolid head, "I can't let ye do that. Ye maun stay here."

"Don't be impertinent!" When she started to move past him, he reached for her arm, and she jerked back with a soft cry. Her heart pounded, and she felt a surge of fright. He looked so determined and suddenly so frightening that she opened her mouth to scream.

It came out as a soft gurgle of shock as Greaves suddenly crumpled to the floor at her feet. He gave a soft grunt as he fell, and she stared down at him.

When she looked up, she saw an unfamiliar man gazing at her. He brandished the small statue he held. "Took care of him for you, milady," he said with a strange grin.

Summer recognized an American accent. She frowned at him, then down at Greaves. "Thank you." She shifted uneasily. "I don't know what got into him. He's never acted so strangely before."

"Ah, it's probably because of strong drink. I've heard that gin ruins many a man."

Thinking of the lost souls she'd seen in St. Giles, Summer nodded. "Yes, that's right." She straightened. "I thank you, sir. I'm certain my husband will deal with this man now."

"May I escort you to him, milady?" the man offered at once. He set the statue down on a small table and turned to her with a smile. His gaze drifted from her face to the necklace, then back. "You shouldn't wander the halls alone. You're far too lovely and might inspire some other man to do what this one tried." He nudged the prone figure on the floor with the toe of his shoe, and Summer frowned.

Greaves hadn't seemed like a man lost in the throes of lust. But then, men were always doing surprising things.

"Yes," she said with a sigh, and put her hand on the proffered arm, "I could use an escort, I suppose."

A smile flickered on his face, and Summer tried not to stare at the curved scar on his cheek.

The hallway was dark. The lamps that had been lit must have blown out. Faint echoes shimmered in the air, while the music in the ballroom lent a background.

Just outside the door, a limp figure huddled in the shadows, and she gave a start. "Oh! What on earth . . . ?"

"Drunk, I would say," her rescuer murmured. "Come on."

Summer allowed herself to be drawn with him but cast a frowning glance back. There had been something vaguely familiar about the man. And unusual. He lay sprawled in an awkward, boneless heap. Drunk. Why did men never learn?

"Are you certain we're going the right way?" Summer asked after a moment. The music was growing fainter instead of louder.

"This way is quicker," the man said. His hand moved to close over the fingers she had curled on his sleeve. "If you will just step lively now, miss, we can get there before anyone discovers your man stretched out on the floor and you gone."

"Yes," she murmured, "I suppose that would create a stir, wouldn't it?"

He smiled. "Westcott would not stop to ask many questions, I'm afraid."

She glanced up in surprise. "You know my husband? I mean, you know who I am?"

Shoving open a heavy door that led to a covered archway and smelled musty, the man laughed. "I know who you are. You're Summer St. Clair, or, as you are now known, Lady Cameron, Viscountess Westcott, or some such drivel. Oh, yes, I know who you are, my lady."

Jerking to a stop, Summer felt her disquiet increase. "I don't think you're taking me the right way, and I don't think I like you." She pulled away from him, but he grabbed her quickly.

"No, no, not again." His hands were tight, his face cruel. The scar stood out lividly on his cheek. "We're not in broad daylight now, my lady, nor are we where someone can hear you scream." His lips curled, and he laughed at her soft gasp. "Yes, you see it now, don't you? Good."

Summer struggled, but he dragged her down the closed archway and shoved open another door with his foot. A coach waited; the door swung open, and Summer felt herself being lifted and tossed inside. She sprawled on the squabs. The man leaned in and curled his hands around her necklace.

"I'll take this for my troubles," he said softly, ignoring her gasp as his knuckles dug into her skin and the gold setting dragged cruelly where the clasp held.

"Leave it be, Biddles!"

The harsh command came from inside the coach; Summer hadn't known anyone else was there. Gasping for breath, she heard her abductor swear softly.

"It should be mine. I took all the risks."

"No," the familiar voice said, and there was the sound of rustling satin as he leaned forward. Summer tilted back her head to see as he leaned into the light, and her stomach turned. Barton Shriver smiled at her, then looked back at Biddles. "You'll be paid. Leave my niece her jewelry."

The door slammed shut, and the coach rattled away. Summer still lay half on, half off the seat.

"Get up, my dear. That's a very unladylike position."

Slowly pushing herself upright, Summer sucked in a deep breath. "What do you want with me?"

A soft laugh drifted between them. She could see in the shadows a vague outline, and when he lit the small interior lamp, she swallowed hard.

"You've caused me a great deal of inconvenience, my dear," Shriver said conversationally. "And an untold amount of money." His pale hair gleamed in the light. His mouth was as she remembered it, thin, cruel, curling mirthlessly.

Seeing him again brought all the painful memories back in a rush. She drew in a ragged breath and closed her eyes. She could see her father's face, her mother's, and even her brother's, felt the same anguish she'd felt at their death. It was too cruel to be with Shriver again. He made her skin crawl. It was too easy to recall his cruelties, his hateful treatment of her, the humiliations she'd suffered in public and private because of him.

She opened her eyes when he said, "Your betrothed awaits you not far away. He was most distressed when you left so suddenly. I had a difficult time discovering your whereabouts." He smiled. "If not for Master Perkins's good memory, I should have thought you'd fled to Baton Rouge."

"Perkins? Oh. At the office." She shrugged. "I daresay you neglected to mention your wonderful plans for me to him. Perkins is a good man and would never have betrayed me knowingly."

"Of course he would—if he wanted to keep his position. He has several children, you know, and his wife is frail."

The smile again—cold, calculating. Summer looked away. Lights flashed past as the coach rolled down the cobbled streets, and she clenched her hands together. She wanted to ask about Tutwiler but did not dare. If only Jamie would find her . . .

When the coach finally stopped, Barton put a quick hand on her wrist. "Ah-ah, my dear. I see from the look on your face that you might try something foolish. Do not. You have caused me so much trouble already, I might not be able to restrain my—shall we say, harsher tendencies."

"I'll never sign over my inheritance to you," she said flatly. "Never!"

A soft laugh purred into the air. "Of course you will, my dear. It will be easy enough once you are wed to Freeman to do whatever I like with it."

A flash of fierce satisfaction surged through her. "I'm already married!"

"Ah, I know all about your Scottish lord. I also know that a marriage is not valid if there is a preceding or current contract or any controversy over such. Not in England, at any rate. And if you don't cooperate, my sweet, I shall have your unfortunate husband hanged." His fingers tightened when she tried to pull away. "No more of this nonsense! You've given me too much trouble, and I wouldn't mind slapping some sense into you!"

Summer subsided into silence. She believed him. She also prayed desperately that Jamie would find her. Where was her knight?

Chapter 20

Swaying slightly, a belligerent Lord Epson faced Jamie. He had an ugly expression on his face. The air was thick with tension, but Jamie allowed nothing to show on his face.

"When you aren't cup-shot, Epson, you may have second thoughts about this," Jamie said with a lifted brow.

Damn Epson, the silly fool! Jamie'd lost sight of Shriver and his paid footpad too; he hoped that Kinnison had seen the situation and was keeping them in sight.

Epson stuck out his chin. "You've insulted me. I demand satisfaction."

"Happy to oblige, but not here and not now." Jamie flicked a glance at the ladies, many of whom gazed with rapt attention at them. Bloodthirsty lot, these noblewomen, Jamie thought wryly. He indicated the women with a sweep of his hand. "The ladies would swoon, Epson. Shall I have my seconds arrange to meet with yours and decide the day and time?"

"I shall have to think—Hobbs, of course, will attend to the details for me. You'd do well to worry about your fate, Westcott. You've been a thorn in my side for years, ever since you almost cleaned me out at Brooks's, and I mean to see you gone one way or t'other."

Impatient to be away from Epson and his drunken hints of offended feelings and vague disasters, Jamie said in a savage tone, "Only choose something, Epson, before I skewer you where you stand!"

A concerted gasp rose from several of the ladies, and Jamie swore softly under his breath. He didn't have time for this, for the polite posturings and ridiculous threats.

By the time he managed to extricate himself from the situation, there was no sign of Shriver at all. Or Garth.

Jamie strode to the small blue salon to check on Summer and the men he'd left to guard her. When he arrived, Porter, lying in the hallway, was just shoving himself to a sitting position. He was bleeding from a knife wound, and Jamie shoved a handkerchief over the puncture, then went into the salon.

After finding Porter stabbed, he expected to find Summer gone, and she was. Greaves lay on the floor, still and unconscious, the back of his head bleeding.

Damn Epson for the cowardly, drunken sot he was, Jamie thought dispassionately. The idiot had ruined the plans he and Kinnison had carefully laid. Nothing had gone right, not one thing. He'd send someone to help the men—he didn't have time. His foremost concern was Summer.

It was obvious Shriver had her, and he had no doubt that his paid assassin was gone too.

Jamie met Garth on the stairs to the ballroom.

"She's gone," he said tersely, and heard him swear. "I suppose you lost your man?"

Garth nodded bitterly. "He went to the convenience, and I waited around like a fool. He must have left it out another door, because I didn't see him come out."

"Any idea where they've gone?"

"A pretty good one. I hope we're in time."

Disdaining carriages, they commandeered two horses and rode through the wet streets of London at a gallop. Iron hooves struck sparks on the stones, splashed water over hapless pedestrians, as the two men urged their horses faster.

The Thames stank of rubbish and fouled water. Waves slapped against muddy banks; hazy lights bobbed on tiny craft. Stone quays were slippery in the dark, and a thick fog muffled sound. Several vessels were dark shapes, barely visible in the soupy fog.

"Which one?" Jamie muttered, and felt Garth's shift of movement as he pointed.

"I've had a man in the offices keep watch; Shriver came in on a schooner. It's been anchored in the Pool below London Bridge, but today, I was told he'd moved it here."

"How many men does he have?" Jamie smiled into the thick night. "Our numbers have dwindled drastically. Webb can't be found, nor Randolph. It's obvious to me that Shriver has excellent footpads."

"Very thorough, it seems." Jamie could sense Garth's grin in the foggy shadows. "Do you think we're enough to hold him until more of my men get here?"

Jamie drew his sword with a soft clink. "Aye."

Within minutes, the two men had slipped into a dinghy, stealing it without the least compunction, and were rowing out to Shriver's schooner.

Summer sat stiffly on a bunk. Her wrists were tied in front of her. Shriver had smiled as he'd tied them with a length of silk, then knotted one end around a post.

"No more chances with you, m'dear. Besides, your future husband doesn't look as strong as your Scot. You might be able to overpower Freeman."

"One can only hope," she said coldly, and he'd left her, shutting the cabin door behind him, not bothering to lock it. She could hear the sounds of crewmen making the ship ready to sail.

Her throat ached with fear and regret that it had come to this. That she had lost, after all these months. She closed her eyes and thought of Jamie, of his wicked, dancing eyes and mocking grin, of the way he'd teased her so much at first. The past month had erased his easy laughter, and she was at fault. She wasn't quite certain how she'd managed it, but she had.

The lies, of course, those stupid, frightened lies. Why had she ever thought lies would save anything? They had only hurt Jamie; he'd looked at her so strangely sometimes, as if not quite able to understand why she had not trusted in him. If she had, maybe he would have loved her back.

Summer lifted her tied wrists and bit savagely at the silken cords. There was still a chance; if she could get to him, she could make him see that she loved him. No more harsh words, no more stupid pretense. She'd admit, openly and honestly, that she loved him. And that she trusted him.

Silly, how she'd wished for a knight in shining armor, and when he'd arrived, she'd spurned him. What an ungrateful wretch she was. She wouldn't blame Jamie if he didn't come for her.

But, oh Lord, please let him come quickly!

A noise in the passageway pulled her head around, and she sat stiffly. Then she heard Freeman Tutwiler's raspy voice and yanked frantically at her bonds. They held fast.

The door swung open, and Tutwiler stepped into the small cabin, a satisfied smile on his broad face.

"Ah, there you are, my pet. I thought for a time that I would not see you again." He shut the door behind him and came toward her, and Summer shrank back. He smiled. "Don't be shy. No reason for it now. Know all about your wedding, and so forth. Silly of you to cut your hair like that."

"Give this up," Summer said. She was surprised her voice was so steady. "My husband will be coming for me. I don't envy you when he gets here. He'll take me away."

"Fallen in love, have you?" Tutwiler seemed genuinely surprised. He took off his hat and tossed it to a table. He wore a frock coat, knee-breeches, and stained waistcoat that did not do a thing to hide his corpulence.

"Mr. Tutwiler—"

"Freeman. We're to be wed aboard ship, did you know that? Barton has arranged it." He smiled broadly. His plump cheeks almost hid his eyes when he smiled so wide, and Summer felt a raging despair.

"I'm already married. It will be illegal. I don't know what my uncle has told you, but—"

"Simple, dear. I wed you. Your property becomes mine. He and I own everything then. You aren't really married now. Not according to the law. Standing betrothal, and all that." He frowned when she sobbed. "I won't mistreat you, you know. Beat you, or anything." His voice grew rough, and she shuddered when he looked at her so closely. "I just crave you in my bed," he added in the voice that had long haunted her dreams.

She swallowed a surge of fear, forcing it past the lump in her throat. "I refuse," she said steadily.

"Ah. Can't. No say in the matter, m'dear, none at all." He smiled again. "I won't be so bad a husband. Better than that dangerous Scot you wed. Heard about him from Barton. A bad sort of fellow."

"Freeman," she tried desperately, "I don't think you know what kind of man you're dealing with when you listen to my uncle. You're just a ... a puppet! Don't you understand that? He's using you. He's using me. He'll use anyone to get what he wants. You're mired in intrigue with him that can see you hanged!"

His eyes narrowed, and suddenly he didn't seem

quite so stupid. "Don't like talk like that. We'll be well rewarded by the emperor for our help."

"*If* he wins! Do you really want to risk your life on so big a gamble?"

His round chin thrust out belligerently. "Women don't know anything about politics. The little Corsican is a brilliant leader. Our money will help him win. That's all he needs."

"You mean *my* money!" Summer raged. She buried her face in her palms. The fool. He believed everything her uncle told him.

On the upper decks, there was the thumping sound of running feet and shouts. Her head lifted. Creaks and groans signaled the preparation for sailing. Her stomach lurched suddenly. She had to get away!

Louder thumps sounded, and Tutwiler looked up with a frown. Then he looked back at Summer. "We're sailing. I do not want to hear any more from you. You'll be my wife, as I planned. Do you hear?"

"No." She faced him boldly. "No, I won't be. I'll kill myself first."

He laughed. "Silly girl. Silly, foolish girl. Do my kisses frighten you that much?"

"No, the thought of them disgusts me!"

Recoiling, Tutwiler's face settled into ugly creases. "Disgusts you! Well, we'll see about that, m'dear!" He started toward her.

With a soft cry, Summer lunged to the length of the silk ties binding her. Tutwiler strode to her and put his hands on her arms, and she screamed. She couldn't stand the thought of him touching her, couldn't bear it if he kissed her.

He tried, eagerly pressing her to him, ignoring the slide of the silk bindings between them, his mouth open and searching. She squirmed, fought him as much as her bonds would allow, panting and twisting. He caught her hair in his hands and held her head still, and she squeezed her eyes shut to close out the sight of his face so near.

Pressing her against the post, wedging her wriggling body between him and the wood, Tutwiler managed to capture her chin in his hand and kiss her.

The struggle, and the subtle motion of the ship, hit Summer with the force of a hammer. Gagging, she stiffened, and Tutwiler barely had time to move before she began retching. Vaguely humiliated, miserable, and deathly ill, she sagged against the bunk again while he scurried for a pail of some sort.

"Damn me, but I've never made a woman sick before!" came the slightly indignant voice, and Summer shuddered. She was too ill not to accept the basin he shoved into her hands.

Tutwiler patted her awkwardly. His voice was petulant when he asked, "You're not pregnant, are you? I won't take another man's child in my basket, no, I won't."

Turning her head toward him, Summer sat stone-still. Pregnant. She tried to think. No, it wasn't likely—was it? Why not? The last time for her courses had been—before she had married Jamie. And God knew that he'd given her ample reason to become pregnant. Of course. That would explain everything lately; her emotional upheavals, the fitful bouts of nausea. She was pregnant.

Summer looked up at Tutwiler. He leaned close; she bent over as another spasm of nausea hit her. Tutwiler backed quickly away, then turned around with a gasp.

From the doorway, a voice drawled, "What a novel way of disposing of a villain, my love. I've never thought of it."

Weak with nausea, she looked up to see Jamie standing in the opening, his sword drawn, his eyes glittering. His mouth was slanted in the familiar, reckless grin that she remembered so well, and she tried to smile.

Unfortunately, she could do nothing but retch.

• • •

The following events were a blur for Summer. She was vaguely aware of Jamie holding her, of Garth Kinnison taking Barton Shriver and Freeman Tutwiler into custody. They were to be taken back to the United States to stand trial for treason, and Garth had the proof.

He came to say good-bye to Summer, kneeling down where she crouched in the safety of Jamie's arms. The fog drifted around him in ghostly shreds, adding an eerie quality to the night; the noise of the King's Scottish Guard making arrests only made it worse.

"I know I'm leaving you in safe hands this time," Garth said with a rueful laugh. "I want you to know that if I hadn't had to sail to France with the packet of letters your uncle had written to Talleyrand, I would not have been in such a hurry and done you an ill turn by deserting you."

Weakly, Summer shook her head. "Not *ill*. If you hadn't, I would never have met Jamie. I'm glad. Now." She frowned. "Letters? Why did you *deliver* them?"

"How else could they be intercepted? Don't worry. I was following Governor Claiborne's instructions. He had an excellent plan. You were a surprise, I'm afraid."

"So you said." She managed a smile and felt Jamie's arm tighten around her shoulders. When Garth started to rise, she reached out and, taking his face between her palms, kissed him lightly on the cheek. "You were my first love, Garth," she said when she released him, and he stepped back with a wary glance at Jamie. "I'm glad. But Jamie is my best—and my last."

For a moment, she thought Jamie might not understand, but then he looked at Garth and grinned. "Did you hear that, Kinnison? I'm the best. Keep that in mind. You lost."

Turning her face into Jamie's chest, Summer closed her eyes, barely feeling it when he lifted her up and carried her to a closed coach.

"Do you still think I'm spoiled?" Jamie asked. He drew a finger down the tilt of her nose, smiling ruefully at her reply.

"Of course. You haven't changed at all." Grabbing his finger, she bit it playfully. "If anything, you're worse. Arrogant, conceited wretch."

He rolled over on his back and stared up at the sky. A puff of cloud drifted overhead, and the sky was a stinging blue so bright it reminded him of her eyes. He smiled again and raised up on one elbow. Summer lay beside him, stretched out on a quilt in the garden. Late flowers blossomed in neatly trimmed beds, and the smell of jasmine still spiced the air.

Her assumption that he was conceited rankled. He looked at her for a long moment.

"Well, you must admit, I seem to be saving you from disastrous situations with alarming frequency. And I'm a fair hand with a sword."

"Did I mention conceited?"

"You did." Jamie let her nibble his finger a moment, then said, "I suppose that you are not vain at all."

"As a peacock." She smiled at his surprise. "If I weren't, I'd never keep up with you."

"What makes you think you do now?"

Laughing, she ran her hand over his straight brow, then down the angle of his cheeks to his mouth. She lifted up slightly and kissed him, and he grabbed her hungrily when she drew back.

"More," he said roughly, and kissed her until they were both breathing hard. "Lord, Summer. I feel like making love to you right here."

"That should shock Tidwell."

He grinned. "Not Letty. She's seen worse."

Summer couldn't help a small laugh, but it faded when she looked at his cheek. Her fingers touched the thin white scar on his smooth skin. "I never meant to do that."

"I think it adds a certain rakish appeal, don't you?"

"Good Lord!"

He kissed her again, quickly, to smother the self-reproach he saw quivering on her lips. Leaning over her, he spread a hand on the blanket, his face only inches above hers.

"Jamie?"

"Mm-hmm," he said, kissing her throat, working his way down.

"What about your duel with Epson?"

He kissed the swell of her breasts, pulling aside the bodice. "Epson. Oh, Epson. He ran. Sobered up and left for somewhere. Won't dare show back up. Mmm. Did you know how good you taste . . . right here? Aye, tha's th' spot . . . Summer!"

Stroking her hands over his chest, she slid them up under his shirt and into the waistband of his pants. She felt his muscles contract at her touch. He groaned, a deep-throated sound, and thrust against her searching hand. Her palm closed around him, and his breathing quickened.

When she stroked her hand up and down his body, he grabbed it. "God's blood, lass. Keep that up, and Tidwell is certain to get a shock."

Laughing, Summer pulled her hand away, glad she could affect him as he did her. He buried his face in the curve of her neck and shoulder, and she shivered at the warm slap of his breath against her skin. He struggled for control and finally lifted his head to smile lazily at her.

"One more trick like that, my lady, and I'll toss your skirts and take you in the fountain."

"That sounds dangerous," she said against his throat, "but exciting."

His hands smoothed over her. "If you weren't pregnant . . ."

Her eyes danced. "Lunatic. I think you would."

"Aye, lass. I would. Twice."

A comfortable silence spun out between them. Then Summer lifted to her elbow, and looked at Jamie for a long moment. He smiled, and his voice was slow and satisfied.

"What shall we name her?"

"The baby? I thought of Jonathan."

"Strange name for a girl."

"Not if she's a boy." Summer smiled. "I want him to be born in Scotland."

"Scotland?" Jamie smiled. "Aye, tha's a good idea. I like it."

"Are you pleased with the idea of a child this quickly? I didn't know if you'd be . . . expecting something like this to happen."

His tone was dry. "I would have been much more shocked if it hadn't. It's not like we haven't invited it, you know."

His lips were just above hers, and she tilted her face to taste them. He kissed her slowly, leisurely, letting his hand stroke down the slope of her throat to her breast, then linger. He could feel the rapid beat of her heart under his fingers, the way her blood sang through her veins at his touch.

"I love you, Summer," he murmured against her lips and felt her stiffen. She pulled away.

"What did you say?"

Momentarily wary, he looked into her shadowed eyes and wondered what he'd said wrong. It couldn't have been the last thing—maybe about the baby being a girl?

"I don't care if it's a boy or a girl," he began, but she curled her fingers into his white linen shirt and shook her head. There was a note of urgency in her words.

"No. Not that. The other."

"The other? Lord, lass, I dinna know wha' other ye want. Say wha' ye mean."

"About . . . love."

He could feel the tension vibrating in her, and it surprised him. "About love?"

Jamie sat up. He felt suddenly awkward and shy. He, Jamie Cameron, who had kissed every pretty female between Perth and Portsmouth, felt shy! There she went, making him feel like a green cub again. He scowled.

She seemed to be waiting; her eyes gazed at him with expectation. He raked a hand through his hair. He'd thought it so many times without saying it; why couldn't he say it to the one woman who made him feel it?

Drawing up his knee, he rested his arm across it and plucked at the grass for a moment. Then he drew in a deep breath and met her gaze.

"I love you, Summer."

To his chagrin, she burst into tears. When he moved awkwardly, she shook her head. "No, I'm not upset. I'm just happy."

"Ah." Those tears he didn't understand at all, but he was familiar with them. "People usually laugh when they're happy, lass," he pointed out.

She drew in a shaky breath. "Good. I expect to be doing that a lot then. You've completed my education in laughter. How did I do?"

"Completed it?" He dragged her up into his arms. "Oh, no. It's just begun."

Holding her, he pushed her back against the quilt, his mouth on hers, hot and hungry. Her response met his, and she tugged feverishly at his clothes. There was a fierce urgency that dictated their movements; the warm sun beat down on them, and the wind whisked over bare thighs, hips, breasts.

"Tidwell," Jamie reminded her, his voice hot and breathless and unconvincing. She grabbed his hair and dragged his face down to hers, kissing him so fiercely he forgot about his steward. Or anyone else.

Summer moved mindlessly beneath him, needing him, loving him so much she thought she would explode with it. He moved inside her with sweet, surging strokes; she felt him shudder as his warm breath grazed her cheek, heard him whisper that he loved her.

Clutching him to her, she arched to take him all, her body aflame with love for him. Release came swiftly, rushing over them, leaving Summer shaking and teary in his embrace. He levered to one elbow and looked down at her. A faint smile crooked his mouth, and he touched her cropped hair with his hand, lightly, lovingly.

"This is forever, Summer," he said softly, and she lifted her curved lashes to look up at him and smile.

When she opened her mouth to say something, there was a loud, metallic rattle, jerking both their heads around.

"What the—!" Jamie surged to his feet, pulling up his pants and buttoning them.

"It's only me," came a muffled voice, thick with laughter, from the interior of a suit of armor.

Summer quickly arranged her gown and sat up, staring in astonishment as the armor-clad figure walked toward them in jerky, clanky movements. When it came closer, one arm lifted to raise the visor. She began laughing.

Dallas Cameron peered out at his brother.

"Jamie, lad, I came tae tell ye how sairy I am tha' ye got mad about a little jest." His blue eyes darted to where Summer sat on the quilt, her hair in disarray, a becoming flush on her cheeks. "An' I thought as how ye micht need th' armor mair than I do—"

Laughing, Jamie reached out and gave Dallas a strong shove. With a noisy rattle, he tried to remain upright and failed. He sat down with a crash. Jamie tried to pull him up again, but there was an immediate tug-of-war between the two brothers.

Summer smiled. She had her own child growing within her. She had a family. And now she had a knight with his own suit of armor. A bit battered and soot-stained, but an actual suit of armor. Not bad, she thought. Not bad at all.

If you loved *SUMMER'S KNIGHT*,
don't miss the next exciting historical romance
from Virginia Lynn:

LYON'S LADY

On Sale this fall from Bantam FANFARE.

In 1075, while Saxons struggle against Norman over-
lords, headstrong Brenna of Marwald fights a private—and losing—battle against the king's order that
she marry the fierce Norman earl Rye de Lyon, known
as the Black Lion. As her husband, Rye would have
possession of her valuable lands, but Brenna vows to
him that he would never possess her body or loyalty—
until their wedding night when Rye's tenderness is
revealed. As treachery and warfare erupt around them,
Brenna and Rye must choose between their blossom-
ing love and the loyalties expected of them by their
people.

LYON'S LADY is a thrilling historical romance from
Virgina Lynn, whose "novels shine with lively adventures, a special brand of humor and sizzling romance."—*Romantic Times*

Passionate historical romance of the
American West from

Virginia Lynn

"[Virginia Lynn's] novels shine with lively
adventures, a special brand of humor, and
sizzling romance." --*Romantic Times*

_____28622-6 RIVER'S DREAM
$3.95/4.95 in Canada
"A five-star rating. [This] ugly duckling to graceful
swan tale is bolstered . . . by a strong story line and
well-defined characters." --*Heartland Critiques*

_____29257-9 CUTTER'S WOMAN
$4.50/5.50 in Canada
"Filled with strong characterizations and one adventure after another, this book is a joy to read."

--*Rendezvous*

Ask for these titles at your bookstore or use this page to order.
Please send me the books I have checked above. I am enclosing $ _____
(add $2.50 to cover postage and handling). Send check or money order, no
cash or C. O. D.'s please.
Mr./ Ms. _____
Address _____
City/ State/ Zip _____
Send order to: Bantam Books, Dept. FN, 414 East Golf Road, Des Plaines, IL
60016
Please allow four to six weeks for delivery.
Prices and availability subject to change without notice.

**THE SYMBOL OF GREAT WOMEN'S
FICTION FROM BANTAM**

FN33 - 3/92